THE SPECIMEN

MARTHA LEA

THE SPECIMEN

CANONGATE

Edinburgh · London

First published in Great Britain in 2013 by Canongate Books Ltd,
14 High Street, Edinburgh EH1 1TE

www.canongate.tv

1

British Library Cataloguing-in-Publication Data
A catalogue record for this book is available on
request from the British Library

ISBN 978 0 85786 714 8
EXPORT ISBN 978 0 85786 939 5

Typeset in Bembo by Palimpsest Book Production Ltd,
Falkirk, Stirlingshire

Printed and bound by CPI Group (UK) Ltd, Croydon CR0 4YY
This book is printed on FSC certified paper

Part I

Prelude

Helford Passage, Cornwall. September 8, 1866.

Never is a newspaper read more intently than when it is about to be put to some other use. Their names came in and out of focus. For a few blessed moments her mind was utterly quiet, and she waited for the shaking to subside before tucking the slip of newsprint away. She ripped the next square from the string, and the next and the next until she was done. Outside the privy she leaned on the closed door and breathed the damp morning air. There was just a hint of rotten autumn settling in but nothing very definite.

As she went back to the house she tried to remember what she had been doing on that Monday a month before. She tried to remember, because she didn't want to let her mind gallop around, gathering thoughts about how many people in the country over the past two days had already seen the information hiding up her left sleeve. People on trains and at news-stands. At breakfast. On park benches, and waiting on street corners.

She was standing now in front of the bureau in the study. For such an imposing piece of furniture, its lock was a pitifully small mechanism. With the need for an actual key now positively redundant, she took up the poker from its place by the empty grate. It was simply a matter of precision and determination. The bevelled point of the poker slipped the first time and gouged a scrape through the walnut. On the fifth attempt she was able to force the poker into the space between the locked-up lid and the body of the bureau. She levered her weight onto the poker. The crack of splintering wood and the lock giving way brought Susan to the room.

"Ma'am?"

"That's quite all right," she said. "I shan't require any assistance. Except, of course, that I shall be going to London today and will need to pack." Then she turned her attention again to the bureau and set about finding the name and address of the late Edward Osbert Scales' solicitor.

SEVEN YEARS EARLIER

Chapter I

Helford Passage, Cornwall. April 1859.

The sun lay heavy on his clothes making him tired, and he had to stop for a while and rest against the rocks. They were thrust up on the beach, it seemed to Edward Scales, like wrecked ships. Hulls keeled over, encased in barnacles. A seam of white crystal pressed between layers of dark grey was caulk jammed between planks. He didn't see the rearing layers, contorted, extreme pressure distorting and forcing the horizontal to the diagonal and vertical. Only ships. He knew that they were not, could not ever have been ships, but his mind rested on that thought because anything else was too immense to confront.

The succession of small beaches on the Helford were each enclosed by high cliffs, pocked with shallow caves. Strewn with sharp, jagged rocks, the ground in between was made up of grey, white and ochre pebbles from fist-sized lumps down to number eight shot. At low tide on the Helford the bladderwrack clung to the rocks, and draped like crowns of slick hair. Not an easy terrain to walk over. He could have come by boat, but he hadn't thought of that. And he could have stayed there, too, in the shade of this wrecked ship turned to stone, to take the boots off his aching feet. And if he had done this, he might not have bothered going further. But Edward Scales moved on between the broken ribs to the other side, and stepped into her view.

Gwen Carrick was almost ready to go back up to the house when she saw him. She recognised the profile, the gait. She'd seen this man on a couple of occasions earlier that month, but he had always been in the distance, retreating, scrambling between the rocks. Now she stood up and had a better look at him. His boots were new: stout, nailed things and uncomfortable-looking; and she noticed that his calves were wrapped with gaiters.

When Edward turned again he saw the young woman standing, shielding her eyes against the steady pulsing light on the brackish water of the Helford. And he saw that this was to get a better look at him. His hat was buckled to the side of his knapsack so he could not raise it to her. Instead, he lifted his hand in a half wave. She mirrored his action, and did not move. A good sign. As he clambered up the steep shelf of shingle on the little beach, Edward wondered what he might say to her. When he stumbled near the level part of the beach she came forward still shielding her face, bunching up her skirts with her free hand. Her strides were big, confident. He saw that her hands were tanned against her pale skirt. She had the unconstricted movement of a woman not wearing a corset, though she held herself straight inside her riding jacket. Her waist was tiny over an ample—he tried not to think of what lay under her skirts. They met with a yard of pebbles between them. She was tall enough to meet his gaze without having to tilt her chin. She was bareheaded. Edward calculated the length of her hair from the size of the neat coil piled up.

"Are you lost?" she said. She could see that his jacket, a hairy tweed, was new and probably still in its first season.

It was not what he expected. He answered her slowly, "No, I don't believe so."

"Sometimes people get lost." The Cornish swirl embedded in her vowels, curling on the edge of her consonants, was very slight.

The air was still between them, and he caught a scent of her, the curious effect of sunlight on skin and hair. She smelled of herself. Not masked by soap or perfume. It was neither sweet nor stale. She was waiting for him to speak.

"I'm sorry to disturb you, Miss Carrick."

"You have the advantage, sir; have we met before?"

"Edward Scales." He bowed very slightly.

"Should I remember you, Edward Scales?"

"It is neither here nor there."

She nodded at this, and Edward felt relieved. She said, "Do you live near by, or—" She waited for him to fill in the gap.

"I have rooms in Falmouth. I have been walking."

She raised her eyebrows. "Really? All the way? You must be exhausted."

Edward caught something in her expression which looked like amusement. Was she flirting? "The distance is not so far."

An ornament in her hair flashed in the sun. She saw him looking and she pulled out a thin stick. "My paintbrush."

Edward was unsure of how to answer; she seemed to be challenging him. He said, "I've kept you from your painting. I am getting in your way."

"You're entitled to rest after your walk," she said. "But I would like to finish my picture. If you go and stand where you were by those rocks I'll put you in."

Edward relaxed. "How long shall I stand?"

She was already gathering her skirts in her hands. "Give me a quarter of an hour," she said. "No, twenty minutes."

As she made her way back to her things she turned her head, smiling, tugging her bottom lip in with her upper left canine.

Edward saw in that gesture of hers a childish glee and a suggestion of self-containment. He couldn't help being stirred by it. Neither could he help being confused by her. But, of course, she had been making things easy for both of them by pretending not to know him. Her poise had been immaculate when she had refused to acknowledge that she already knew his name. Yet there was something in the way she had spoken. The frankness of her. Almost

as if she were a different person entirely. Edward retraced his path
down to the rocks by the tide line marked out by a thick rope of
seaweed. Taking out his pocket watch he leaned back against the
rock. It dug into his shoulder.

Gwen sketched the figure of Edward Scales into her painting. She
wanted to put him in the picture, it seemed to her an absolute
necessity, to paint him into her watercolour landscape. Not just for
the sake of its composition. It gave her a space to think without
him searching her face. Because the painting was already finished,
his figure on the paper became a dark shape, without features. Yet,
his awkward posture was recognisably his, and this pleased her.
Whilst they had stood opposite each other like that she had wanted
to evade his look, which seemed to seek some sort of confirmation
from her. He would not get it.

Sometimes people get lost. She'd said it for something to fill the
surprise of seeing him. But it hadn't been the best thing to say.
Now it was there again, going around in her head as she mixed
the darkest shade of Payne's grey. The argument was two years old,
but it was as raw as ever in her mind.

"People don't get lost here," she'd almost shouted at her sister
Euphemia. "The sea is on one side and the land is on the other.
There is a path, you walk along it."

Euphemia's expression had been blank, her voice very calm.
"Mother got lost."

"She can't have, Effie, she can't have."

And then Effie's voices had started. Mrs Fernly, their aunt, had
tolerated the voices for as long as she could. It was never said out
loud. It was never mentioned in a very direct way, but Mrs Fernly,
it was widely known, couldn't abide young creatures who made
deliberate exhibitions of themselves. But much more than that, and

more importantly, Mrs Fernly had no time under any circumstances, for the jingling bells and rattling tables or anything else in a Spiritualist's parlour, least of all the Spiritualist herself and most especially if the Spiritualist began to talk in voices in Mrs Fernly's own parlour without prior warning.

Gwen and her sister had been moved back into the empty Carrick House only three months after their mother's funeral. It was fair, thought Gwen, that it should have been decided—unilaterally, by Mrs Fernly, that it was time for Gwen and Effie to cut short their stay at the Fernly's and manage at their own house. There were after all two of them and they would have the maid, as well. Gwen had felt nothing but relief. She could put a door between herself and Effie at last. And not only at night. Gwen spent most daylight hours out of doors, away from her sister. Euphemia did not exert herself at all during the day; she stayed inside the house, to preserve her complexion. If Euphemia wanted to look at a view for a moment, she made sure that it was through a north-facing window. They embarrassed each other with their habits, but there existed between them a delicately preserved understanding.

Painting in the figure of Edward took much less time than she had asked for. When the time was up he picked up his stick and bag. His second approach was much more sure-footed. He came deliberately, slowly. When he was a few feet away, she patted the shingle beside her and he sat down.

"I'm glad we have met like this," she said. "Being outside makes you much freer. Here, I have your image immortalised on paper." She handed him her sketchbook, and watched his face as he looked at her work on his knee. "Would some Power the gift to give us to see ourselves as others see us."

He smiled. "You know Burns, then."

"Burns? No, it's just something, a saying. I didn't know it was a quote."

"It's from the end of a poem: 'O wad some Power the giftie gie us, To see oursels as others see us! It wad frae monie a blunder free us——'"

She laughed. "I like that. From many a blunder free us. What's the title of the poem? I shall have to find a copy."

Edward coughed. "It is called, 'To a Louse', and its subtitle is, 'On Seeing One on a Lady's Bonnet at Church'." He looked sideways at her. She was smiling. He said, "I hope I haven't offended you."

"You haven't. I'd like to hear the rest."

"I'm afraid I don't know it thoroughly. I wouldn't want to murder it before you had read it for yourself. You needn't search though. I'll send you a copy if you like."

"That's too kind of you."

"It would be my pleasure." Robert Burns would not have been his first choice of poet to send to a young woman, whether he had only just met her or not. He cringed inwardly at the thought of her reading Burns' more bawdy efforts.

She cut into his thoughts. "Your accent was very realistic to my untuned ear."

"I spent a lot of time in Scotland as a boy. It's not a genuine accent. Only gleaned, borrowed inexpertly from my playmates." Edward felt suddenly perilously close to the edge of the dark chasm he had so far been successful in avoiding. He studied the young woman's profile with every bit of concentration he could gather. "To which address should I send the poems?"

"I'll write it down for you." She took the sketchbook back from his knee and turned the page over. He watched her write her full name and address in soft pencil. She tore off the page and handed it over. He looked at it. She also noticed that he looked at the paintings revealed by her tearing the top page out. Studies of bright red Cardinal beetles studded the glaring white of the paper Gwen instinctively held to her chest.

"I will be pleased to send the poems to Miss Gwen Carrick. May I keep this? I shall pay the artist, naturally."

"No payment is necessary, Mr Scales, you are welcome to it. Well. Now my paints are dry and I'm finished for the afternoon. Will you come up to the house?"

Edward didn't want to do that, for all kinds of reasons. He asked her if she would like to have a picnic with him. He felt himself becoming very nervous and he worried that she would see how agitated he really was. How disconcerting. The more he worried the more he was certain that she could read his thoughts. But then the sun shone brighter on the water, and she had to shade her eyes as he produced the food, so she probably did not see his reddened face after all.

Edward brought out of his knapsack two bottles of ale, a large piece of cheese wrapped in a cloth, and a small loaf of bread. He took a small knife from his pocket, and began to carve off chunks of bread and cheese. He weighed the bottles against each other and gave Gwen the heaviest, having already begun to drink from the other. "I hope you like ale. It is quite a strong one."

"It looks like you have enough. At least I shan't worry about depriving you."

"I always take more than I think I'm going to need. Once, in Dorset, I met an old vagrant who asked me for something to eat. He looked so wretched, I gave him what I had but he insisted on sharing the beer I had given him. I only had one bottle. I spent the next month convinced I'd contracted something."

"But you didn't."

"No, I did not."

"Dorset is a long way from here."

Edward took the smooth pebble he had been carrying in his

knapsack and laid it down by his side. Gwen Carrick did not notice, she was utterly absorbed in cutting more cheese and bread with her own pocket knife. One edge of the grey stone partly revealed the ridged arc of an ammonite. Gwen held her bottle between her feet. Edward saw that she was not wearing the clumpy old boots from the time before but fine brown leather shoes with a low heel and a strap, fastened by one button across the arch of her foot. It made him think of something Charles had once told him. But he could see that the eroticism of the action was entirely unintentional.

"I couldn't help noticing, Miss Carrick, those red beetles in your sketch book. To my eye, they looked quite delightful."

"More so than the study I have just given you?"

"I wouldn't say that. They startled my eye. They interest me in a different way, that is all."

"When a young woman makes a picture of a pretty red beetle, Mr Scales, it is called 'Delightful', put into a frame and a husband is found for the artist. When a young man makes an anatomical study of a Cardinal beetle, he is expected to know that it is the Pyrochroa serraticornis, and he is bundled off to university so that he can one day add to the body of scientific knowledge on Coleoptera."

"I see."

"Do you though, Mr Scales? I don't want you to admire my skills for the wrong reasons. My work is not bait; I am looking for the truth. In all things."

"I'm sorry. I didn't intend to disparage your gift."

"Gift? My talent is not something handed down from God, Mr Scales. It is hard won."

"Of course; I can see that you are very dedicated. My words were ill chosen. I meant no offence."

"But you don't offend me, Mr Scales. If I were a man, would you apologise, or would you debate the talent of an artist as divine gift, as opposed to something instilled by regular practice?"

"I suppose I would do neither. I would have entered into a conversation about beetles without complimenting the rendition on paper."

"In which case, I can tell you that I was surprised to find this particular beetle so early in the year, they are usually out in May, June and July. And it does startle the eye, doesn't it?"

"I'm sorry to have intruded, Miss Carrick. I think I have trespassed into a world in which I have no right to be. When I listen to you I see that my own existence is very dull indeed."

"I am sure it is not."

"I can assure you it is."

"Even though you may wish to see yourself as others do, it can never be done, and so I think that you may as well not try."

"You seem, despite your talk, very content with your life, Miss Carrick."

"I am content to be alive, Mr Scales, but I do not possess the quality I think you must see in me. I am quite discontent, in myself. It has been driven into me."

He caught her gaze and held it for a moment with a question in his own, but Gwen would not elaborate further. "The last time I saw you, Miss Carrick, there was something I had intended to say to you."

"I beg your pardon? Mr Scales, have you been spying on me?"

"I—I *have* been here before."

"I must confess I have seen you before as well, Mr Scales. Don't look so alarmed. I have seen you from afar, out walking once or twice, always walking away from here. I have since then wondered who you were, where you live. I must admit I have wondered what you looked like, too. It struck me you had some kind of important intention to your walking." She wanted to say that she had thought he looked at first like a tourist who had no idea of where he was, but that after a while, she could see that he did possess some passion in his stride. That a stranger, seen from a distance, could sometimes make an impression on the mind, and could work away to become something of an obsession; she had wanted to admit this to Mr Scales. There was something about his manner that told her he would understand her meaning. The puzzle of the man had struck her from time to time, and she had wondered if an opportunity to talk to him would ever present itself.

Edward was outdone by her talk. He realised that it was useless to try and broach the subject which could not be touched or coloured by any choice of word. What he had begun was more complicated than he had imagined, and as he listened to Gwen, and saw the uncomplicated manner of her evasion, he thought he understood her more completely than anything he had ever known.

He could see now that Miss Carrick was quite young; how young he couldn't guess. He knew that he must move away, that he must leave her alone. If he felt he had made an indecent intrusion previously, this seemed just as bad. Her tact, and the straightforward approach she seemed to have over something he had been unable to rationalise, made him cringe at his own rough attempts to smooth over his indiscretions. And so he knew also that he would come back, in spite of what he had promised her before, in spite of his own conscience. He'd come back again, and he would not hesitate, in his need to speak of everything, and plainly, to the creature who wished to keep her red beetle studies a secret.

Gwen came to a halt at the south wall of the kitchen garden. A bonfire had been lit and its smoke curled over the wall. She'd smelled it on her way back up from the beach. It had none of the earth or wood tones of a garden fire. Now that she was very close, she could see flakes of black drifting in the air and coming back down, too heavy to be carried far. She walked quickly now under the wall following it around the corner until she came to the gate. No one was there to watch over the fire. It hadn't been banked down; flames leapt from the heap and parts of its bulk fell away. Its position was odd; she couldn't think why Murray would have told the lad to make a fire right under the south wall where the fruit trees were trained into their tortured forms. While she was thinking about this, another part of the fire fell off the heap and her attention shot to it. Now that she could see how the fire had been constructed she lunged towards it. Sandwiched in the middle of garden prunings were books; her father's library. She saw her old friends, Bell's *Anatomy*, Duncan's *Beetles,* Mrs Mantell's engravings of Strata and Fossils, all turning back into their base element. She spun about looking for something to help her. A large spade had been left against the north wall. Gwen ran to it, not caring to stay on the paths. She felt her chest tighten with anxiety and purpose as she hauled her skirts in her arms and made her loping strides more efficient.

She attacked the heap, letting out a yell, beating the burning books with the heavy spade, her striking unwieldy and misdirected. Pages and half-scorched volumes tumbled onto the soil and continued to smoke as she turned to retrieve everything she could manage and then hurl clods of earth at the rest of the fire, still beating and yelling in between shovelling.

"What the bloody hell?"

Gwen didn't stop when she heard Murray. He took the spade from her hands mid-swing and finished the job. "Well, you've put that one out, miss. You can have a rest."

"Murray—" She had to bend over and cough.

"I'll have to have words with the lad. I thought he was a good choice, but I was wrong." Murray nudged the remains of a burned cover with his toe.

"It wasn't his fault." Gwen gasped, retching, and grabbed at Murray's sleeve. "He wouldn't know."

"He's a ruddy, half-witted goose is what he is, miss. You may as well take that as given."

"It's done, Murray. At least I found it."

"You did. What'll you want done with it?"

Gwen picked up one of the less charred volumes. The spine curved the wrong way and the now partially browned pages spewed forward and then curled in on themselves, as if they had known themselves fey and beyond saving. The leather on the spine was brittle and had bubbled in places to form strange scabs; the gold leaf had burned away in places making the title illegible, but Gwen knew the book by heart. The irreparable damage was sickening to see. She'd spent hours in the company of Lyell's four volumes, poring over his maps and folding them carefully back into place as she'd moved through his *Principles of Geology*.

"I don't know."

Gwen surveyed the mess across the earth and saw two of the other three Lyell volumes. She picked them out and tried to brush off the dirt and still smouldering remnants of other books and garden clippings. They made an awkward stack in her arms as she walked slowly back towards the house, the stink of bonfire clinging inside her nostrils, catching the back of her throat. Instead of going in by the kitchen, she took the long way round and let herself in through the front door.

The library door was closed but not fast. Gwen kicked it with the flat of her shoe and stood in the doorway hugging the charred books to her body. She supposed she must have looked deranged. She regarded her sister; so immaculately dressed, so tightly laced, gathering books with delicate soft hands off the shelves into a wheelbarrow.

She wanted to move into the room but felt herself stuck there. Euphemia in turn stopped. Neither of them said anything for a moment. Euphemia paled. Gwen heard her mother's voice very clearly in her head then. It was not, as some said of the recently dead, as if the person whispered into her ear, or stood at her shoulder. It was more a feeling that her mother was in the middle of Gwen's brain, and that the voice she heard was simply her mother's thoughts.

"Of course, I know what he says, darling Gwen. But why should I let him know? After all, he would only do himself an injury. There are some things it is better we keep to ourselves."

Gwen straightened her back and continued to stare at Euphemia who had been about to place into the wheelbarrow another book, but now she took the smallest breath and turned around, and put the book back on the shelf. One by one she placed the other books back on the shelves and never met her sister's eye. Gwen settled into her heels, and as her sister reshelved books she simply watched and waited until the last book was back in its place. Only then did Gwen move into the room. She placed the ruined three volumes of Lyell's *Principles* on the wide empty shelf they had come from. She poured herself a glass of water from the carafe on the desk and then taking up the wheelbarrow handles trundled it out of the room.

At the door, Gwen said, "Have you any idea what I am thinking?"

"No, because it is impossible to tell what a traitor thinks or feels."

"You admit, then, that I have feelings."

"And you admit it, finally. That is what you are, you can't escape it."

Gwen went out of the house and back to the kitchen garden. As she bumped the wheelbarrow down the steps, along the paths, pushed it past unclipped bushes, her anger at herself made her clumsy. She should never have allowed Euphemia to draw her into the old argument again, but the previous evening over dinner she had been unable to contain her contempt for her sister's dogged belief that the fossils in their father's collection were all remnants of the Great Flood. She had stormed out of the dining room and fetched *Strata Identified by Organised Fossils,* by William Smith. The book had landed on the table next to Euphemia with an almighty thump and had sent an empty wine glass to the floor where it had smashed. Gwen blamed herself now for having been influenced by the wine. The glow it had given her sense of righteous certainty over Euphemia's stupidity had given Gwen's tongue free licence to vent her derision. She opened the book at the place where it was marked and pushed it under Euphemia's nose.

"Are you really too stupid to understand what the words say? Yes? I'll read them to you." Gwen recited a passage, barely needing to look at the page. The words had danced in triumph—now where were they? Euphemia had tried to burn them out of existence. But they clung to Gwen, and she to them: ". . . organic remains peculiar to each stratum . . ." She pushed away the memory of her jubilance at having committed those words to memory for her father. Of having found herself standing at his desk, trying to talk to him the way she imagined he would have allowed had she been born a boy. It didn't matter. The knowledge was not his alone to keep.

Gwen rounded the last corner and stopped the barrow next to Murray. "We have miscalled the lad, Murray. This was nothing to do with him."

Murray turned and looked into her eyes, and she returned his hard stare. His eyes flickered as she saw him understand her meaning. Together they set about pulling the books from the dirt. Some were not very badly damaged on the inside and could be saved. But Smith's volume had received special attention from Euphemia, and Gwen began to find small fragments of the pages torn by hand from their binding and ripped bit by bit beyond repair. Here was a corner bearing the partial remains of an intricate illustration of an ammonite. Every book in the bonfire had been part of Gwen's armoury, as she had come to think of it, against the blinkered and determined stupidity of people like the vicar who had the intelligence to recognise the truth but turned his eye from it, and Euphemia's gaggle of black-clad visitors who shunned the truth completely in favour of spirits and their messages from the other side. Euphemia called her a traitor. A traitor to their mother and her faith. Gwen knelt down and let the pain of her grief enter her body; she let it snake through her, probing its tongue into each dark crevice.

She told herself after some minutes that it didn't really matter that the books had been burned. They were, in theory, replaceable, and the truth of what had been contained in them, the spirit of them, still lived in her head and in the heads of others. What mattered was the vicious nature of Euphemia's spite. Gwen chided herself for bringing Euphemia's desire to take possession of the house to the fore, to eradicate every memory of their blasphemous father who had detained Reverend Sparsholt in loud debate on the steps of Helford Church on the day of their mother's funeral. "She had her time in Heaven while she was alive." Gwen remembered the passionate grief in her father's voice. "Now her flesh will rot under the soil," he said, "And that is *all*, Sparsholt. That. Is. All." And so every trace of his sinful library was to be purged from the house, in order that Euphemia could fully dedicate and fashion the place to the memory of their mother. Gwen saw now that Euphemia was also attempting to annihilate Gwen's sense of herself, and her right to belong to the place. Euphemia wanted, she could see, to deny the house and its contents any hold on Gwen.

There was one thing she had now though, which Euphemia did not have, and did not know about: her new friend, Mr Scales. Gwen recalled the fossil in his hand as they had spoken that afternoon. She went over and over their conversation. Parts of it had become lost, but most of it she could remember, and its urgency.

The intensity of the conversation had soon eradicated all the usual formality and convention. They had not made polite enquiries about each other's history; they had existed fully in the moment with no regard for the past or the future.

Gwen tidied herself up, smacking dirt and ash from her clothes while Murray pushed the barrow of books to one of the potting sheds and she followed behind. Murray left her to it, and Gwen began the ordeal of assessing the damage in detail. As she examined each part of Euphemia's essay on destruction, Gwen knew that she would never mention Euphemia's existence to Mr Scales. There would be no poisoning the air with the mention of her, of what she had done, of the way she had made Gwen feel.

Chapter II

The Spiritual meetings held at Carrick House attracted a plethora of bizarre people. Like a bundle of strange insects, Gwen thought, batting at the glass in the door, blundering around the dimmed lamps. She couldn't bear it; she hated their sweaty hands and, in their wide hopeful eyes, that grateful admiration of her sister. No spirits, though, had ever come into the drawing room to divulge their secrets, to deliver their messages or even to assuage some kind of guilt of their own or of the living. It tugged at her conscience, and the knot of disdain grew in her stomach. She watched them arrive. In bundles of four they plopped out of carriages on to the drive. This Monday evening there were three carriages, and two clients had walked up the drive on foot, flapping blackly with the setting sun at their backs. "Pity help them," she said, and drew the curtains.

Gwen's absence from the meetings was enough. Euphemia did not need to be told how much her sister despised her gift.

And what Gwen got up to in the evenings, whilst Euphemia held the Spiritual meetings, was of no concern to her. Her ladies (and some gentlemen) were attentive and appreciative of her talent. Some, like the Coyne woman, Penelope, came to Euphemia in fear of a loss not yet happened. The tremble in Penelope's lips was never quite still, always expecting the wash of her son's far-travelled drowning or some other likely misfortune to be revealed to her in those meetings. Connoisseurs, some of them, and full of stories about the charlatans of the profession, who performed nothing more than parlour tricks. Euphemia did not have a repertoire of tricks, only an inexhaustible supply of voices, which could dance across the room and whisper into her clients' ears. There were never any rappings in Euphemia's drawing-room, nor tinkling bells. She did not have a table with a wobbly leg apt to rock uncontrollably in the gloom. The only glistening things were her clients' wide and thankful eyes, and after they had gone, the coins in the discreetly placed dish. And most gratifying of all was not the counting out of the coins and the entries in the book she kept, but the fact that she had never once solicited custom. Never placed anything so vulgar as an advertisement in a paper. In fact, Euphemia considered herself more than a little apart from other clairvoyants. On the rare occasions when an introduction to another Medium looked as if it might have been in the offing, she was quick to discourage without appearing ungrateful or rude; though she did often feel incapable of hiding her feeling of condescension. Her isolation seemed to induce a certain kind of expectation amongst her clients. Her talent was unsullied by the riffraff. Like those young girls in Europe who suffered from visions of the Virgin, she was pure and she wanted to keep it that way.

It was a mixed bunch tonight; too many for the table in the drawing room. Many new faces, which always gratified her. Euphemia began with her induction talk. She didn't like the way her voice sounded in the dining room but there was nothing which could be done about it now.

"We must remember to keep in mind the fact that the spirits are sensitive," she said. "And for this reason, of course, we will only refer to ourselves by our Christian names." She paused for a second. "There will be no communication from the other side for a 'Mr Smith' but a spirit may wish to talk to 'John' or 'Harry'. And the spirits, of course, make no promises other than to speak to you if your heart is open and free of doubt."

Naturally, Euphemia was always "Miss Carrick" to these people;

how on earth would she manage to remain in control of the event otherwise. Her gaze travelled around the table and settled for a moment on a young man whose complexion, temporarily ruddy with excitement, was sickly. He licked his lips and his hands trembled as the introductions flowed around the company, the hush punctuated by the hesitant voice of each new client saying their name out loud. Euphemia smiled. They all looked at her and told her their names; the rest looked at the one speaking. It was all ticking along, but she kept the young man in the corner of her eye. As it came to his turn, she could see that she had been mistaken; he was not so very young after all. She looked into his eyes.

"Ch-Charles. I'm Charles. Hello." He looked up at the ceiling and searched in the air above their heads.

"Welcome, Charles." She noted him as difficult, perhaps an unbeliever, and moved on to the woman sitting next to him.

"Good evening, I am Penelope."

"Welcome, Penelope. So lovely to see you again."

Chapter III

Helford Passage. April 1859.

Paths meandered down each side of the cleft in the garden crowded with old rhododendrons. Palms, which had once been ships' ballast, now sprouted rich fronds of growth. Camellias flushed a pink frothiness into the wet green of spring alongside the magnolias' burst of waxy petals. Stands of bamboo, once tidy and slim, were now out of control, pushing their spiked shoots throughout the grounds. Bisecting the garden, a stream fed unkempt pools for carp where none swam; along its banks the formidable gunnera leaves pushed up from their hairy crowns. Edward saw all of this in his mind because the night sky was especially overcast. The day had begun well, with a clear horizon over the sea, but the bank of cloud now obscuring the moon and making his progress difficult had come and built up its volume as it moved over the sea towards this part of the south Cornish coast. He doubted, now that he had finally met Miss Carrick in daylight, that she would be there waiting for him for a second time in the dark chill of the summerhouse. She had made him keep a promise, and already he had broken it. He had come back again hoping to redeem himself, to explain that he couldn't have kept away in daylight, that he couldn't possibly have let the chance to see her face pass. Her manner on the beach had encouraged him. And yet he was nervous, so much more nervous than he had ever been about anything in his life. And he was exhausted. The seven miles had tripled. Early that morning, he had set out intending to do something very different. He had walked to the boundary of the small Carrick estate, intending to call at the house and present himself. He had turned back. When he had arrived at his rooms in Falmouth, he had caught sight of himself in the mirror above the wash-stand. He'd stripped to the waist and passed a frenzied minute washing himself before putting a clean shirt on his damp body and setting out again.

There were times on that walk as the gloaming turned to pitch when he thought he would fall over the cliff edge. And deservedly so, he told himself, deservedly so. You have behaved irrationally towards Miss Carrick and too bad for you if you fall over the cliff and never discover her feelings. Too bad for you if you never have the opportunity to declare your own feelings. He had stopped at several points to strike a light, but the pathetic flare cupped in his hands had been blown out almost instantly by the gusts coming in off the sea.

How easy it was to allow events to overtake one's former intentions. It was a relief to discern the shape of the red brick summerhouse coming out of the mist, the wet dark slate of the roof almost a comfort to Edward as he rounded the corner on the steep path. In the far corner, he settled into the old armchair and pulled the musty blanket on it around his shoulders. It smelled strongly of tobacco smoke and the kind of smell Edward associated with cellars.

At five-thirty the crescendo of birdsong woke him briefly and he drifted back into the remnants of a dream. But he was cold and he woke again, the memory now of the real Miss Carrick stronger than the wisps of what he could recall of his dream. He looked at his watch and saw that it was almost six. He took another mouthful of whisky and decided that he would stay a while longer. He unfastened his breeches, pulled himself free and allowed the warmth of the whisky and the memory of Miss Carrick in the sunshine to run through his body.

By the time Gwen had been down to the beach and back up again, the mist had not lifted. The garden remained wet and veiled. The tips of her fingers inside her gloves felt a little numb. She could have a small fire in the summerhouse. It would likely be laid, and waiting for a match. She turned off the main path and made her way under the trees. The door had been left wide open. She could see that it had not been Murray opening the door. A man she did not at first recognise sat next to the unlit fire in the chair which Murray usually occupied to unknot string when it rained. For a second, she wondered if Murray had sent some younger chap in his place, but this man was not a gardener. Gwen's heart thudded. At first sight it seemed as if Mr Scales was asleep. His head tipped back in the chair, his eyes were shut and his mouth hung open. And she could see from the slight twitch in his arm that he was caught in a dream. His breaths though were not those of someone in a restful sleep: they were rapid and laboured. Gwen hovered in the doorway, unsure of whether she should make a noise to wake him, or leave him to sleep.

Down at his feet on the floor of the summerhouse was his old knapsack of heavy canvas with leather straps; the only worn-out thing apart from Mr Scales himself. Gwen wondered briefly if Mr Scales had been there all night. A sharp whiff of stale sweat hung in the room, even though the door stood open. As she was about to leave, Mr Scales stirred in his seat—but he did not open his eyes or close his mouth. Nothing about him changed but for his left arm, which began again to twitch. Perhaps he was suffering a fit, like the ones which had eventually killed her mother. In which case she ought to do something.

He didn't appear to be unconscious though. She stepped quietly inside the room, her view slightly obscured by the blanket draped over the arm of the chair. As the whole of him came into view, she saw that his breeches, the same ones he had been wearing when she had shared his beer, were open and pulled down around his thighs.

The drag of her heavy skirts was like the wash of a strong tide against her legs. By the time she reached the house, her back was studded in sweat, and her gloved hands were very hot and moist. She stood in the hall, listening to the ticking and grinding of the clock which struck the quarter hour. It was still only six-fifteen. Her gaze came to rest on the coat-stand. A large, old overcoat was hanging there, and on the tiles, next to the skirting, a pair of old boots she hadn't worn for a while. She was still standing there thinking about the last time she'd worn the boots when Euphemia bounced down the stairs at six-thirty.

"Oh, are you back from your wandering so soon? I didn't hear you come in."

Gwen flexed her fingers. "The mist hasn't lifted yet. I'll go out again later."

"Are you going to have breakfast?"

"No, I'm going upstairs for a while."

Gwen relaxed behind the closed door of her bedroom. Slowly, she began to undress. She traipsed over the carpet towards the adjoining bathroom. She stood shivering in her chemise beside the large white tub and turned on the tap. She watched the level of cold water rise, concentrating on its growing depth whilst trying to imagine what it was that Mr Scales had been doing to himself.

She tugged the bell-pull to let the maid know that she needed a bucket of hot water, turned off the tap and sat on the edge of the tub to wait.

Susan did not look to see which little bell was pinging away on its spring. She'd watched Gwen coming up the path to the house. She liked to think she could anticipate what either Gwen or Euphemia might want next, and it was a bath for Miss Gwen. She'd come hurtling up the path at just gone six that morning, tugging her outdoor things off, all puce in the face from the effort.

Susan calmly put a damp cloth over her bread dough then took up the padded mitt and lifted the kettle. She poured the steaming water into a bucket, refilled the kettle and set it back on the stove before taking the hot water up the back stairs.

Susan had not told her mother about the bathroom at Carrick House. She knew that the idea of long mirrors in a room just for washing yourself would make her mother think unfairly of the Miss Carricks and the late Mistress.

Not long after the funeral, when Mr Carrick had gone back to America, and the girls were staying with the Fernlys, Susan had taken a bath in the long white tub with the mirrors glinting at her from all sides. Susan had set the copper boiling and then emptied it quickly into buckets so that she might have a proper good hot soak, like the Mistress used to.

Breathing in the emptiness of the place with just the ticking of the tall clock for company gave her a jittery feeling under her ribcage. If Mistress Carrick had died in the house Susan would not have agreed to go back there on her own. Susan thought about her sometimes. About her being grey and cold out on Rosemullion Head and no one knowing; the liver-coloured bruise as they'd turned her over. They said a fox had pissed on her, but Susan didn't want to believe that was true.

Gwen sat on the edge of the bath tub, the skin on her arms like a plucked songbird and her face pinched. Susan put the bucket of hot water down and went to close the window.

"Thank you, Susan. I was very hot, but it is cool enough in here now."

"Would you like an extra bucket of water, ma'am—I mean, miss?"

"That's all right, Susan. I'm sure you've got better things to do."

Susan expected this answer, and knew it had nothing to do with what she had left to do. "Let me help you off with that chimmy, miss. You're all fingers and no thumbs."

Gwen let Susan help her out of her underwear. Susan said, "You've let yourself get too cold this morning." She lifted the bucket and poured the steaming water into the bath. Gwen climbed in, totally unselfconscious of her naked body. Gwen's breasts were firm and rounded; they did not swing or fall with her movements. Susan turned to go, picking up the empty bucket.

"Stay awhile, Susan, will you? Perhaps you could talk to me. I feel I should like to talk to someone."

Susan put the bucket on the floor again and clasped her hands in front of her. She could not avoid her reflection so stared at her feet.

"Move those things from the chair and sit down, if you like."

Sitting down meant that Susan had to face Gwen washing herself. "I won't stay more than a minute, miss. I've got bread rising."

"I won't keep you, Susan. I wanted to ask you something." Gwen soaped her leg with her foot propped up on the edge of the tub. Susan looked away as she caught a glimpse of pubic hair. "I wanted to ask you, because I know you have brothers and you are older than Effie and I. The thing I want to ask you—" She stopped washing and looked directly at Susan. "You mightn't know the answer, of course."

Susan stared at the soapy foot and then at her own hands. "You'd better ask the question, miss, or I'll not be able to answer one way or the other."

"Whilst I was out this morning, I came across something. Someone. I'm sure now that what he was doing was meant to be private. But, having seen it, I want to know whether you think it might have been rather unhinged."

"Are you telling me you saw a madman this morning, miss?"

"I don't know. I don't think so."

"What was he up to?"

Gwen lathered her other leg. "I'm not sure I can describe it properly. He was in the summerhouse. I thought Murray might have sent someone. I thought he was asleep at first."

"A tramp?"

"No, I'm sure he wasn't a tramp. In fact, certainly not a tramp. Susan, is it usual for a man to do . . . things . . . to himself?"

"Did this man do something to you, miss?"

"No. He didn't even see me. And when I saw, when I realised which . . . part . . . of himself was in his hand, I came back."

Susan bit her lip. "Maybe you should keep that summerhouse locked up."

"What *was* he doing, Susan. What did I see?"

Susan breathed in deeply, and let her breath out slowly. "Some would say what you saw was an awful, horrible thing, miss. But I'm sure it's no sin telling you I reckon it's a normal enough thing for a man to do sometimes, if he's not got a wife." She glanced at Gwen.

"But *what* was he doing?"

Susan looked down at her hands in her lap and told her.

"Whatever for?" Gwen began to wash the rest of her body.

"For the relief of it, I believe." Suddenly Susan envied Gwen's ignorance. It seemed peculiar to her that someone could read Latin, and not know about *that*.

"It looked quite brutal," said Gwen. "He looked uncomfortable or even that he might have been in pain. Do you think it hurts, to do that?" She was lying down in the bath now and splashing water over her flat stomach.

She's still like a child, thought Susan. Anyone else might think what she's just asked would be some sort of trick, some sort of tease. But she's asking me like a child, Susan thought. Who else might she ask anyway? It isn't the sort of stuff you could talk about politely.

Gwen said, "I'm glad I'm not a man, Susan. Aren't you?"

"Well, you couldn't change it, miss, even if you wished it."

After that, Gwen had avoided going to the garden so early in the morning, waiting long enough to be sure that she would not come upon him again in that way. She was uneasy with her intimate knowledge of Mr Scales' personal habits. It seemed impossible to reconcile the sight of him, the deep mauve of his—she didn't have a name for it, a word for it and this also made her perturbed. Of course, she knew the biological term for that appendage, that necessary organ to the male, from the beetle to the horse to the man in her summerhouse. But the purely biological was not enough, did not explain the emotion she now felt. The smell of him had worked its way into her dreams and tonight she had woken drenched in sweat, a noise from her own throat bringing her awake. And the rippling of that sensation. Yes, it was there, still there, but ebbing away as she lay in her sweaty sheets, coming awake. She brought her hand up to her face, listening intently to the quiet of the house, to the distant chiming of the clock in the hall, telling her that it was about to strike the hour. Gwen counted the twelve chimes and threw back her sheets. She had gone to bed just before ten and to be so wide awake at midnight disturbed her; she knew that she would find it difficult to go back to sleep and that she would have a bad temper in the morning. It put her on edge to be tired in the day when she wanted to be busy but found herself stupid and clumsy. Gwen got up and went to her bathroom to wash her hands and wipe her neck with a cold sponge. She did not take a light with her, feeling her way instead with her feet and her hands outstretched. Back in her bedroom again, she went to the window and pulled back the curtains. She raised the lower section of the window quietly, the sash cord working smoothly as she put her weight to the task and felt the cold draught against her thighs and stomach. She crouched on the floor, her face level with the open air, and listened to the night. The familiarity of the garden was made alien. She listened, cupping her hands behind her ears, to the very distant sound of the waves breaking on the beach and the play of wind in the trees. Below her she heard the crunch of careful footsteps on the gravel path as either Euphemia or Susan made her way to the privy. Gwen left the window open but pulled the curtains back together again.

Chapter IV

Edward Scales had sent Gwen a letter, and it was in her pocket, but she hadn't opened it yet. The thrill of seeing his handwriting for the first time had made her nauseous with excitement. Euphemia had again slept in very late and her usual habit of being first to sift through the morning post had been abandoned.

Taking the letter from the table in the hall, Gwen had felt an intense lurch, then a tightness in her shoulders threaded its way through her torso, down to her thighs, and back up again to the back of her skull. But she hadn't wanted to hear his voice in the hall where she stood resisting the urge to rip the letter open. She had met him first on the beach at the foot of her garden, and that seemed the most appropriate place to read his letter.

On the beach Gwen lay down on her stomach. She didn't linger to examine the seal as she broke the wax in half and pulled out the stiff laid paper. She felt her body thrumming to the rhythm of her pulse against the pebbled ground, heard the crash of the waves behind her, saw the bright sunlight on the paper, registered the unsteadiness of her hands as she straightened the single sheet, bending its crease back on itself; all of this crammed her senses as she began to read his letter. His handwriting was singularly awful. A great deal of care had gone into the addressing of the envelope, but the letter itself was a different matter.

"*My Dear Miss Carrick . . .*" Gwen studied the stroke of his pen, the urgency of the formations, the haste, the going over of certain letters where the ink had run dry, the fine spatters from the nib. On the corner of the paper there was a smudge of fingerprint.

The contents of the letter were very formal; he promised that he would send a copy of the Burns poem as soon as possible and that he admired the watercolour painting very much. He also told her that he was writing from his address in London, and that he would be travelling back to Cornwall within the month. He hoped that she was in good health and hoped that it was not too much to hope that he would have the pleasure of meeting her again. There was something touching in his repetition of the word 'hope' and the fact that he had been in such a hurry to write to her he had forgotten to write his London address. His feverish scrawl affected her more than she had expected. To know that while she'd been anticipating his return to her beach, he had in fact all the while been in London, made her grab a large stone and place it on the letter, haul herself from her position and walk to the water's edge. She let the waves come to her feet and run over her toes several times before she stepped back out of their reach. Within the month, he had said. He had left her no option but to wait for his return and whilst she did very much want to see him again, she felt trapped by her emotions, by her personal geography. Her world was this place, this brackish river from the shore of which she could stare out to sea. Her beach was officially part of the Helford river, but its waters were that of the wider ocean. He could come and go as he pleased. He could choose his place. She returned to where the letter lay and folded it back into the envelope. She walked up and down the beach from one end to the other until she could not face taking another step. In her exhaustion she sat down on the pebbles again and let herself weep. Nothing came but dry sobbing. Her lungs and ribs ached, and she swayed back and forth as if in a state of intense grief, yet there was nothing but lightness inside her.

★　　★　　★

On her way back up to the house Gwen saw a familiar young man come slithering down the shady path towards her in finely tailored clothes and a shiny top hat. Freddie Fernly batted at the overhanging ferns with a lacquered cane. She hadn't seen her cousin all winter and spring. He was as dapper as ever. His voice rang out as he noticed her.

"You know, it's an absolute bore having to chase after you all the way down here, Gwen. Mother has been waiting up top for at least an hour and your dear sister hasn't yet deigned to emerge."

"Freddie. How lovely; I didn't know you were coming today."

"Hello, old thing." He took off his hat and gave her a kiss on each cheek. "You look wild," he said, "like a tempestuous creature from a novel."

"Idiotic fellow, you look expensively over-dressed."

"Vulgar, as always. I have so missed your tenacious wit."

"And I yours. You should have told me you were coming."

"And if I had, you would have put us off."

"How is your mother, Freddie? Is she well?"

"There must be another way back up without having to go through all this verdant jungle."

"No, there isn't."

"Oh. Well, you know, I am her biggest frustration, and having given up on me for the time being, she thought she would make an impromptu call on the most eligible young lady in all of Cornwall."

"I'll see if I can persuade Effie to come downstairs."

"Not her, you gorgeous goose. You know Mother's opinion of ghosts and rappings and shaded lamps well enough. You and I are now at the top of her list."

"But she has given up on you."

"In a manner of speaking."

"I see. Ask me quickly, Freddie, so that we can get it over with."

"This suit is brand new. Mark my words, I am not getting down on bended knee in the mire."

"Ask."

"Gwen Carrick, will you be my wife?"

"Certainly not. Never in my life, Freddie Fernly."

"Thank God for that. Well, let's go and tell Mother the good news."

"I can't believe she really thought it would come off."

"No. I think it's a mark of how desperate she has become to get rid of me once and for all. She has already been through every possible candidate this season and I have refused every single one of them. We are back early because she is in a fit of pique."

Gwen laughed. "You should just tell her, Freddie, in simple words that even she can understand."

"What? Dearest Mother? It would finish her off. In any case, I am glad to see you more cheerful."

"I'm not unhappy."

"What tosh. You've turned yourself into a veritable hermit. No one can be happy living like this. Which reminds me, we are having a little gathering, Tuesday week. Do say you'll come."

Gwen had no desire to spend an evening with Mrs Fernly, despite her affection for Freddie. They arrived at a level path, halfway up to the house, where they stopped to get their breath back, Freddie more than Gwen.

"Euphemia won't be able to call off her engagements for that night."

"I know, that's why I fixed it for a Tuesday. I found out, you see, which nights your sister entertains her ladies."

"So very wicked of you, Freddie. There are male clients, too, just occasionally."

"Pooh to them all! So, now you will accept?"

"You won't let your mother make me sing, and you won't let some horrid crony of hers corner me."

"I promise that Mother won't even be there. It will be fun. And perhaps you can wear that lovely blue silk, because it will go very nicely with my new waistcoat and everyone will leave us both quite alone, because we shall strike such a stunning effect."

"I don't have it, Freddie. I sold most of my gowns."

"You do know that you have committed a mortal sin? That blue was heavenly on you. Never mind, whatever you shall wear will be irrelevant. You are truly the most eligible young lady in the entire county."

"If it weren't for my so-called hermitism and the fact that I can't sing."

"That and your love of stones. If you would just love the shiny kind."

"I do, just not in that way. And you've forgotten something."

"Of course. I am sure there is a perfect match for you out there. If some gentleman were to present you with a big shiny beetle I am sure your heart would melt at once."

"Don't tease. I can't think of anything more hideous than handing over my future and property to some—"

"Pax! I won't tease you any more. Do come Tuesday week."

They moved off again, going slowly up the steep path arm in arm; Freddie cajoling Gwen until she agreed that she would go to his party.

"Ha! I knew you would," he said, as they reached the house. "I'll send you a lovely present—but you must promise not to sell it. At least wear it once."

"You mustn't do anything extravagant on my behalf, Freddie."

"Not at all. I have something perfectly exquisite in mind."

"Your mother will have entirely the wrong impression if you send me gifts."

"I don't much care if she does. I want you to sparkle and be happy. I've neglected you, old thing; I want to make reparations."

Chapter V

London. May, 1859.

Edward had suffered a long and uncomfortable journey; dirty, tired and hungry, he'd been so dispirited on his return that he had considered booking a room somewhere for the first night back in London. He wished that he had decided after all to tear up his ticket and stay in Cornwall.

He had been back in London for about ten days but he had lost sense of the exact date. During this time he had witnessed his wife miscarry her child. The pregnancy had been troublesome; Isobel had lost blood on and off throughout, both from her womb and through leeches on her arm, courtesy of some quack in Edward's absence. She had been determined it would go to the full term and had neglected to continue the treatment he had secured for her. Now, Edward found himself organising a minute coffin and a funeral to go with it while also sourcing the right concoctions to dry up the milk which now leaked from her swollen breasts. Already it was all becoming too much again. He didn't know how many days he would be able to stand it.

After his supper, Edward took a cab to Leicester Square. To walk and to think—or rather to lose himself in the cacophony of sounds and smells, to see the sights, and be thoroughly revolted by all of it, so that he could go back to the miserable house and try to find something living there, some small remnant of the positive feelings he had once harboured for his wife.

He stood on the left-hand flight of steps leading to the entrance of the insalubrious Saville House. Beneath its three storeys of shabby late-baroque grandeur, Edward recalled snatches of his times with Natalia Jaspur. The memories of her person, her voice, and the physical presence she had. The way she owned the air in the room. Edward hesitated on the steps. Should he go up to the door and go in? What kind of tricks would he see there now? Would she still be there, or would she have moved on, as she had promised she would? There were few who could deny the quality of her voice. She was the kind of person to somehow always find a way of getting what she wanted. Notoriety of the right kind would surely fall her way. And what about him? There was a time when he had believed that Natalia Jaspur's medical condition was going to provide him with the evidence to make his name. That the condition had already been scientifically described had not prevented this belief for a while.

There was loose change in his coat pockets and in his trouser pockets. He couldn't remember putting the coins there. Some was change from the cabby. Some must be kept for the ride back home. Edward advanced a couple of steps higher but found himself clinging to the newer memory of Gwen Carrick, both in the summerhouse and on the beach. Such an extraordinary woman; so complex, so intuitive and so angry about the world. Why could he not have told her more? Did he really have to know her deepest passion and she his? He knew the answer to that. Edward looked up and tried to focus properly on the crowd of night-time revellers, the shadows from the lamplight making their faces ugly, every one of them.

Edward pushed his way down through the people now crowding up the steps to Saville House. They were welcome to their cheap entertainment. He found a cab and gave the address of his club. There he found Alexander Jacobs looking morose and staring into the fire, swirling a full measure of whisky, his half-bald head catching the warm glow from the grate. When he saw Edward he perked up, stood to shake his hand and offered him a drink.

"Hell, Scales, where the devil have you been hiding yourself? I was beginning to think you must be either dead or in the West Country."

Edward tried not to recoil. "I'm very much alive, as you can see. What makes you think I'd be in the West Country?"

"I didn't, not really. It's just that a lot of people have shot off there at the invitation of that Fernly."

"Who?"

"Don't know him? I thought everyone did."

"But you didn't go."

"Christ, no. I have my patients to consider. What *are* you doing with yourself though, Scales. When are you coming back?"

Edward was grateful for the fact that Jacobs had pretended not to know what had kept him away from London for so long. He couldn't remember if he had ever talked to Jacobs about his interest in the West Country, or that he'd considered looking for a small property there. Never mind if he had or had not. The fossil hunting was common knowledge.

"I don't think I shall. I've been considering a change of scene."

"But you've *had* a change of scene. You ought to come back and finish training. I always said you'd make a damn fine surgeon. We could fix you up in next to no time. Damn sight more talent than Jeffreye and I have put together."

"I don't know about that; rather late in the day. I don't think I shall ever elevate myself beyond general practitioner."

"Nonsense! This is unwarranted modesty. You still have youth and your health on your side. Jeffreye's gone off for that Fernly's Ball, you know; wanted me to join him. Had the devil of a time myself trying to persuade him not to go."

"Indeed."

"By the look on your face I can see that you two are still not reconciled. I don't know what your quarrel was, but if you'll take my advice, you should patch things up. It's a terrible thing to lose a true friend over a squabble."

"It's no simple quarrel. No doubt he's gone off in search of another self-indulgent medieval dose. Pity the unsuspecting in the West Country."

"Of course, I'm intruding where I've no business. It's between the two of you. Have another?"

Edward accepted a second whisky and decided not to mention Isobel. Now that the drink was loosening his wits, he didn't trust himself to remain neutral after Jeffreye's name had come up.

Jacobs moved the conversation on and went along quite happily without much contribution from Edward. He talked about his horses and his dogs, and invited Edward to dinner the next week so that he could show them off. Then he talked about a difficult skin case at the hospital, and tried to elicit some advice from Edward on the matter. It was an attempt to try and prove to Edward that his proper place was by his side, at the hospital, that his talent in medicine was being wilfully squandered. But Edward was noncommittal, and kept the talk moving without promising Jacobs anything definite. The pair talked until after one in the morning and Edward took a ride back to Hyde Park in Jacob's carriage.

"Good night, then. Give my best to your wife. How's she coming along?"

Edward jumped down to the street and steadied himself, clinging to the cabin door. "Isobel lost the child a few days ago."

"Oh. Bloody bad luck."

"Yes."

"Still, early days yet. There'll be others. Don't give up."

"No."

"Good chap."

"Good night, Alex." Edward shut the door and the cab pulled away. He took his shoes off in the entrance hall. In the dark, he twice missed the peg on the stand before his coat found its place. He blundered as quietly as he could, but his head was thick. He found a lamp and managed to light it after rummaging a long time for the box of matches in his trousers. He hadn't smoked in a long while but kept up the habit of having matches about him. He came to the bottom of the winding flight of stairs and gripped the turned end of the banister. He put his foot on the bottom step but then changed his mind. He didn't want to go and lie in bed wide awake. He just didn't want to go upstairs at all. Edward went to his study and turned the lamp up full. He poured himself another drink and pulled open the drawers where he kept his case-study papers. Perhaps Jacobs was right; he'd allowed himself to wallow for too long. He had once believed in himself as much as Jacobs now pretended to. He shuffled through them, looking for the file he'd kept on Natalia Jaspur. He could not find it; his mind was fixed on the naked body of Natalia Jaspur, and the extraordinary effect it had produced in him. He'd felt his whole being punched alive; a spark, a jolt, something unexpected. The revulsion he'd anticipated, and had been prepared to hide from her, had not been there. The sight of her naked body, so completely covered in hair, had caught him so sharply, so intensely that he had been afraid of his own desire. The papers were gone. He had no recollection of having destroyed his work, but, then again, he had not been terribly well. He could not settle. Seeing Alexander Jacobs again had caused the feelings he'd buried to migrate to the surface of his mind. When he closed his eyes he could not fully conjure Miss Carrick's face; the restorative effect she had brought to him was obscured by the too-familiar throw of the lamp's shadows in the room and the memory of Natalia Jaspur, the countless hours he had spent in her company, and then the striving to release himself from her hold. Meeting Miss Carrick had opened up something better in him—something he now knew that he valued above everything, and that he had never thought to own. There was no word nor expression that matched what he felt for her, and so he let the nameless thing exist without trying to pin it down. The torture he had minutes ago felt in remembering Natalia Jaspur dulled, and he fell asleep in the chair at his desk.

When he woke in the morning he was still drunk. He roused himself and looked at the chaos of paperwork he had strewn about the night before. He knew he could be better than the sum of these papers. It was just a matter of finding his own truth. Miss Carrick seemed to be aware of her own truth; she seemed to have a clear sense of purpose and a fierce determination, in spite of the hand that had been dealt her. He went upstairs to bed where he slept until late morning. Waking for the second time he threw himself out of the covers. He stood still for a moment at the bedside and reeled at his hangover, determined not to throw up. The pressing thought that he must find the Burns poem before he went back to see Miss Carrick was clear in his mind. As he splashed water on his face at the wash-stand he knew, suddenly, what the inexplicable feeling was. The thing he had been unable to name was simple. He was in love.

Chapter VI

"They are taking advantage of your vulnerable state, Isobel. These people are the lowest sort."

"Then you should be happy that I shall find myself in suitable company, Edward."

"Those are your words, not mine. What is done is done, but this will only serve to compound your unhappiness, not cure it."

"I am not looking for a cure, Edward, I am looking for my child."

"We buried him. Two days ago, we buried him; you know where his body lies. Wherever his tiny spirit has gone, I can guarantee that you will not find it in some spinster's *parlour* overstuffed with horsehair, velvet and threads of manipulation tied to hidden china bells."

"They say the spirits sometimes bring gifts from the other side. The Enderby sisters say—"

"All of it is nonsense, Isobel, and if you were not in this unfortunate state you would say the same yourself, without any doubt. Pure nonsense; it is nothing more than cheap trickery."

"And, of course, you are an authority on that particular subject. Why can't you let me grieve?"

"I wish you would grieve, but this is no way to go about it."

"You are punishing me because of the child."

"I have no wish to do any such thing."

"And yet, had he lived, I think you would have punished me more."

"Isobel, you are not yourself. Let me take you home."

"No."

Isobel's comment about his authority on trickery had pricked him, but he felt it unjust. Spirits quite simply could no more be conjured than congealed blood be made liquid and life-giving. Life was governed by the function of a body. Its deterioration to the point of cessation of functioning parts stopped the flow of blood. It—the flow of blood, that ordinary substance in veins—this in Edward's mind was where the spirit lay. Blood became infected with disease, and the body still living could exist for a time with the process of decay. He glanced at his wife, whose expression was unreadable. After the last breath, thought Edward, blood congealed, and then decayed. Once the body was dead, the spirit too was dead. He had watched, in his observation of patients' deaths, for evidence of the departure of the spirit. He could not attach to the process of a human death the sentiment enjoyed by those zealous purveyors of idiotic lies.

Their carriage came to a stop and Edward opened the door for her. He got out and helped her down. She was pitifully weak on her feet.

"We did not bury my child, Edward. You had him put in a box lined with lead and locked him into a cold, dark place. He will not be happy, and I need to let him know that it was not me who put him there."

"Your father and I did what you yourself asked us to do. You did not want him to be under the ground."

"I did not want him to be dead; I did not want to let him go anywhere. At least allow me this."

"I will be here again in one hour."

He took her up to the house and surveyed its facade with distaste. The afternoon light made the masonry glow, and a black-bird sang in a branch somewhere above his head. It was very ordinary. In spite of everything, he did not want to leave her here, but he did not stop her. He reached up for her and knocked on the door and watched her go in. My God, he thought, this is ridiculous. And where was Charles, in all of this? In Cornwall, in exactly the place Edward wanted to be. Edward felt he had more right to be in Cornwall at that moment than any other man. He told the driver to take him to the park.

"Which one, sir?"

"Oh, just any park, I don't care."

"Right you are then, sir, won't take five minutes."

When he went back to collect Isobel he could see that she had been weeping. They travelled in silence. He didn't know how to tell her that he would be returning to Cornwall the next week. She went to her room and he followed her.

"Isobel, I can't stay here and watch you do this to yourself."

"Don't use pity for myself or my child as your excuse, Edward."

"I am sorry. I must go."

"Curiosities again, is it? Or some other brilliant new *idea* of yours?"

"I know that it might seem—"

"Edward, stop now. I am tired."

Chapter VII

A Masqued Ball. If he was trying to make up for having neglected his favourite cousin, Freddie was doing it in the only way he could manage. His house in Falmouth town was overspilling with guests when Gwen arrived in the carriage Freddie had sent for her. Freddie leaped down the front steps of the house to greet her, wearing a grotesque *papier-mâché* grimace on the top of his head and waving an elaborate feathered mask in his hand.

"No one but I shall know who you are. There will be no introductions, no ghastly formalities. We are going to have so much fun. No singing for those who don't want to. No polite trivialities."

"This isn't a little gathering, Freddie."

"I've a wicked mind, dear Gwen. Do put this on." He tied the tapes at the back of her head and admired her hair. "The beetle looks lovely on you."

"It is too extravagant, Freddie. I can't keep it." The brooch he had sent her, a brilliant green beetle, was stunning in its design and the delicate craftsmanship of the goldsmith. Freddie had no regard for the amount of money he spent. It was only money, he always said. Happiness and love are more valuable. But Gwen knew that the money Freddie spent so easily was minted from the sweat and degradation of human beings he never had to see and never chose to dwell upon. It was the only subject which they could never discuss. If they did, then they would lose each other irrevocably.

"Such rot, of course, you shall keep it. No one else could wear it with such an audacious charm. Besides, it was made for you. Now, come with me. All these people think that they have abandoned London mid-season for a bit of riotous sensational whatsit, so we had better give it to them."

"You've been planning this for weeks."

"Months, if we must be truthful. I have missed you so much, and I know how you hated the way those half-wits swooned over you at my mother's gatherings. But I know you too well to know that you can't actually like the way you've gone and cut yourself off from the whirligig of life."

"Don't let's get into that again."

"But this fixes everything! You can say whatever comes into your head to whomsoever you choose. No one can form an opinion of your opinions, if you get my drift."

"I think Effie would be better at this than me."

"Your sister has chosen her own amusements. She prefers mothballs to masqued balls."

Gwen laughed, and Freddie pulled his own mask down onto his face and put his arm around her corseted waist.

Some of the guests had already spilled out onto the lamplit lawns of the garden and were having a treasure hunt among the topiary. The drawing room was set up as a gambling parlour and was a clamour of noise—music, the rattle of the roulette wheels, the chink of crystal and money, and shrieks of laughter. Everyone was playing Freddie's game to the letter and wore a mask of some kind; even the musicians.

Freddie spoke into her ear as they walked past a roulette table. "You see, dear cousin, we all need a mask to be our true selves. Look at them all, having such fun. In two days' time they will be back in London; the last thrill of this mid-week excursion to the precipice of debauchery will be the rattling speed of the express locomotive, and when they alight at the station they will pretend it was all just a dream. Now, come and trot a *gavotte* with me."

Three men sat at one piano playing the music to which Freddie and Gwen began to dance among the crowd of guests. Freddie's mask was the embodiment of the frustration Gwen knew he suffered in real life; the mask he was forced to wear and could never remove in the company of those who believed they knew him so well. Gwen was whirled about and lifted from her feet by Freddie's exuberant interpretation of the music. She felt herself swept along in thrall to his enthusiasm. She glanced at the other masked guests in the confusion of costumes around them and recognised no one at all though she knew there must be people in the room who were known to her besides Freddie. When the *gavotte* came to an end another man took Gwen around on the next dance until someone else cut in halfway through. Over the next hour, Gwen drank punch and danced with more strangers; she lost sight of Freddie. The mask's feathers stuck to the sweat on her face. She eventually went outside to find a private place to take it off and cool down. Others had the same idea, and there were several ladies wandering about fanning themselves among the tightly clipped hedges. She couldn't find anywhere private enough and so kept her mask on.

"Marvellous stroke of genius, wasn't it?"

Gwen turned to face the man who had obviously crept up behind her. "You refer to our host's flair for entertaining."

"I do, indeed. I've been trying to work out which mask is Fernly's ever since I arrived. Dark fellow."

"I think you mean that he has entered fully into the spirit of the evening."

"Absolutely. Yourself likewise. I may not be permitted to ask your name, but may I bring you some refreshment?"

"A glass of water, thank you."

He left her, and Gwen finally lifted her mask away from her

face and craned her neck up to the night sky. Some of the lanterns hung about the garden had burned out; where she stood, another guttered its last as she waited for the man to return. She heard the approach of a voice and put her mask back on, even though there was not enough light now to make out more than the outlines of figures backlit by the bright windows of the house. But it was not the man bringing her a drink. She heard Freddie's voice and was about to come out of the shadows to greet him when she heard that he was speaking to another man. She pulled her mask off again and stayed out of his sight. The punch had made her woozy; away from the swirl of the company of others she felt it more acutely. She tried to listen to what Freddie and his companion were saying on the other side of the hedge. It seemed that at last Freddie had found someone with whom he could wear his ideal mask. Gwen leaned against the thick hedge, slightly jealous of his romantic success and his utter disregard for rules. Freddie and the other young man moved further on into the deeper shadows where they would not be chanced upon by anyone.

Gwen retied her mask, but, unlike Freddie, she didn't want to go through life feathered up in an elaborate disguise. She loved Freddie for his sincere and elaborate efforts to make her happy despite his own deeply melancholic nature, but he didn't understand her desire to be treated with respect when she spoke openly about the things she cared for most.

The man who had gone off to fetch her a glass of water now came holding it out in front of his person, his view of the ground limited by his mask. He picked up his feet and raised his knees in a very comical way. Gwen thought he looked like a grey heron.

"I am very much obliged to you, sir." She took the glass and drank all the water.

"The lamps are going out. I'm afraid I left you standing alone in the dark longer than I anticipated."

"I didn't notice. I was looking at the stars."

"Ah, a romantic nature. Much like myself."

"Actually, I was reflecting on the fact that I so rarely take the trouble to study the night sky, and that I can't distinguish between the stars and the planets."

"I don't bother about it myself. They all twinkle, and they are all a very long way away, so I understand."

"Yes. A long way away. Perhaps tonight is not the time to be thinking about the planets."

"They are playing a waltz, madam. Would you do me the honour again?"

Gwen was disconcerted that she hadn't remembered dancing with the man and that he had taken the trouble to seek her out in the garden, but she agreed to dance with him again. As she waltzed she wondered how long Freddie would spend out in the dark with the other young man and whether either of them would take off their *papier-mâché* masks. She thought of Edward Scales and wanted to know what he was doing at that precise moment. The sudden thought that he might even be there, at Freddie's Ball, gripped her mind and would not leave her, even though she was convinced that a place like this was the least likely venue in which she would ever find him.

Chapter VIII

It was seventeen days since Gwen had received the letter from Edward, and she had heard nothing more from him until this morning. His short note told her that he would be taking a walk and begged for her company on the beach. Gwen picked up Freddie's beetle brooch and fixed it into her hair; then she took it out again and put it back into the velvet box. She changed her clothes again, swapping her good dress for the things she had been wearing the first time and looked at herself in the long mirror. The feathered mask she had worn at Freddie's ball hung by its tapes from the frame of the mirror. She unhooked it carefully and found some tissue to wrap it in. She placed it inside a hat box with some sachets of cloves and rosemary. When she picked up her jacket, her hands were shaking.

"I know I promised to send the poems to you by post, but I wanted to give them to you myself." He presented the book wrapped in paper to her. She opened it.

"Thank you."

"I hope you haven't minded the wait too much."

"It's a very handsome volume." In fact, it was a very tiny volume covered in a loud, blue-and-green tartan silk; it slipped into her pocket very easily.

Edward was relieved and sighed through his nose as he opened up his knapsack and began to spread out on the beach a lunch better prepared than their first picnic. The giving and the receiving of the gift was over. It had troubled them both, and they were both glad that it been done. The pebble containing the ammonite was still there in the bottom of his bag; he took it out and tossed it up and caught it, before putting it down next to the bottle of wine and the corkscrew. Gwen picked it up and ran her finger over the ridges.

He opened the wine and unwrapped wine glasses from newspaper. Gwen was touched by the effort he had gone to. He had brought delicacies and silver cutlery and starched fine linen serviettes.

"Tell me why you like fossils so much, Mr Scales."

"They intrigue me. They are a conundrum. And I like to discover them, to uncover a creature never before seen . . . At Lyme, in Dorset, it was possible to pick up glorious specimens from almost any random part of the cliff or the beach. Yet, here in Cornwall there seem to be no fossils at all."

What he had really wanted to say was that he believed he could find something new, and that he constantly hoped for this because he wanted to name a creature himself. He'd even gone so far as to write out invented names of half-imagined curiosities. They came out as badly as the shapes he couldn't quite fix in his mind's eye, always ending with 'scalesii'. He burned the scraps of paper afterwards. It would be as mortifying to be found out at that as— no, not today. He concentrated instead on Miss Carrick's voice, the pleasant breaking of the waves, the sun on her skin.

"Yes, they *are* very rare so far to the west," she said, "though not entirely absent. It is possible to find trilobites, for instance, at a place further west from here, but I would be surprised if you were able to find one after six months of searching. But, surely, it isn't so much of a conundrum, Mr Scales, since the geology of Dorset is quite different to that of Cornwall."

"Now you have stoked my attention, Miss Carrick. I was under the impression that your area of interest was the live flora and fauna of the region."

"But one specialism cannot exist without its complementary subjects, Mr Scales."

"Although, a creature like the ammonite, long since made extinct by the Great Flood, surely has but a slight connection to the live creatures with which we now inhabit the world."

"Mr Scales, I do hope you are being deliberately provocative."

"I am not insincere, Miss Carrick. I am impressed by your scope."

"You misunderstand me. I meant that I hope you don't really believe that Noah's Flood was the agent responsible for the distribution of fossils?"

"I take it you do not."

"Mr Scales! Good heavens. People once believed that the earth was flat and that the sun moved around the earth. Scientific thought, experiment and deduction always bring us closer to the truth. Have you not read Mr Smith's *Strata*?"

"I have not. I wish that I had."

"I would lend you my own copy, if my library had not recently suffered fire damage." Gwen had not been able to stop herself. She was aghast to find that Mr Scales' interest was based on the assumptions she so despised in her own sister.

"I'm sorry to hear about that. I hope no one was hurt."

"The damage was limited to a small area. It was caught in time."

"But, still, it must grieve you."

"It does. Books may be replaced, though. And you may find a copy, I am sure, quite easily in London."

"And when I do, I shall send it to you immediately."

"There's no need, Mr Scales, though your offer is very kind. I would rather you read the book for yourself. It is a revelatory volume."

"I will make it my priority, Miss Carrick."

"I'm glad. But, Mr Scales, you must have had cause to wonder about the geology of this place, as opposed to that of Dorset."

"Your knowledge of rocks is superior to mine. I must confess that, before this year, I have never had reason to study them in the way you obviously do."

"I have lived with these rocks all my life, Mr Scales. Perhaps my advantage is unfair."

"But I think life cast you an unfair disadvantage, Miss Carrick. I have thought about what you said to me about the beetles you study and paint. If you had been born male, you would have been sent to university. You would have had an even greater advantage. Yet, that also would have been to my great loss."

"I wouldn't wish to be a man, Mr Scales. Only that I should have the freedom to expand my knowledge of the world at first hand without attracting derision from all sides."

"All but one, Miss Carrick. I admire you a great deal."

"Thank you, Mr Scales."

"One very rarely meets a person like yourself. I consider myself extraordinarily fortunate."

Gwen could think of nothing to say to this. She was annoyed with herself for having been harsh with Edward. His ignorance was perhaps not his fault. Why should a man have cause to stop and wonder about the strata of rocks when he had, as she assumed Edward must have, spent his life in the city. And now that she had told him he would be unlikely to find any more fossils in Cornwall, he would have no reason to visit again. He said he was glad to have met her, but she knew that he must have a life of some kind outside her own world and that he would not be able to accommodate a passing interest at the expense of his other commitments, whatever they may be.

All of the food and most of the wine had been consumed. Gwen was drunk. She let Edward pour her a last half glass of wine.

"I consider myself fortunate, too, Mr Scales. I hope you will write to me again when you return to London."

"I have no need to return to London for a good while, Miss Carrick, though that shall not prevent me from looking for the title you recommend."

"I expect that you shall return to Dorset and continue your search there."

"Indeed not. I believe I have finished my search for fossils, at least for the time being. There are only so many one may find room for in a cabinet."

"But your collection from the south coast of England will be incomplete. Perhaps I can help."

"Miss Carrick, you have already inspired me more than you can know."

"Rubbish. I have told you to read a book. Anyone could have done the same, and you would probably have found Mr Smith's *Strata* without my help."

"It is by no means a certainty. What I have been trying to say, Miss Carrick, is that my interest in fossils has been supplanted by a much greater passion."

"Then you must pursue it, as fully as is possible. There is nothing worse than a pursuit for knowledge left to wither and atrophy. I think it sinful."

"I wouldn't dream of letting it happen."

"That is good to know, Mr Scales."

"Please understand me, it is my passion for you which over-shadows everything else."

Gwen stood up; Edward scrambled to his feet.

"Stay a while longer," he said. "I have wanted to tell you this— please don't reject me. I want so much to prove to you that I can be more than the person you must think I am."

"I'm not leaving yet. The tide is coming in, we must move

further back up the beach or we shall be cut off here and have to climb the cliff, which I wouldn't recommend, the topsoil of the overhang is—"

The energy contained in his kiss, the taste of his wine-tainted saliva on her tongue and the force of his grip as Edward put one hand behind her neck and the other around her waist pulling her close to his body so that she smelled his sweat—wasn't this what she had tried and failed to imagine after she had seen him in the summerhouse that morning? His own lungs seemed to be sucking the air from hers. His eyes were closed, and the image of his left hand working away at himself flooded her mind. The vivid colour of it. She found herself fighting for her breath, and he stopped the kiss but did not release her.

"Will you reject me, Gwen? Will you tell me to go away and leave you alone?"

"No, I don't want that. But my feet are getting wet, and so are yours."

Edward picked up his knapsack, which was also wet, and put it over his shoulder, carrying the two wine glasses in one hand. Gwen lurched up the beach, hauling herself in sodden skirts, trying to gather them all in one hand, Edward holding her by the other. The wine bottle, the corkscrew and the empty caviar pot and serviettes were all left to the incoming tide.

Edward and Gwen collapsed side by side onto the pebbles beyond the high tide mark. They watched the advance and retreat of the abandoned picnic articles. The waves churned the serviettes into the seaweed and they were lost from sight.

"I'm sorry about your dress, and your good shoes. The salt will have ruined them."

"Yours, too."

"Yes, never mind it."

Edward's second kiss threw Gwen off balance, and he clasped

her so hard that she could do nothing to stop herself from being made to lie on her back. Edward's mouth pressed to hers as the mussels stuck to crevices in the rocks. It did not frighten her. She felt that she was somewhere above her body, looking down at what they were doing. Just as suddenly as the kiss had begun, Edward finished it. He kept his face close to hers, so close that she was unable to focus, and after a minute she pushed him away, smiling at him. Her bottom lip had split and she tasted her blood.

"I've made you bleed. I'm sorry."

"It doesn't matter. But talk to me now."

"What shall I tell you?"

"A secret."

"I have none worth the telling."

"Everyone has a secret. Don't be miserable about it. Tell me something about your distant past if you like. Then it won't matter."

Edward looked at her and was stumped. He didn't want her to become bored but what on earth could he tell her? He cleared his throat.

"When I was nine, perhaps ten, my father took me on an expedition. Days of travelling. I was quite ill by the end of it all—the suspension of the carriage, the rocking and jolting. It was almost this time of year. There was hawthorn blossom in every direction. The scent of it; such a simple thing, but in such profusion. My father was a keen angler. He had a box of the most exquisite flies, which he made himself from feathers. I was clumsy as a child. Nervous. I wanted to please him. My feet were unused to the loose pebbles at the riverside, and my boots slid. I upset the box, almost crushing it, and the flies were scattered amongst the pebbles. I ran away down the riverbank after he had chastised me. He did not strike me. I ran away to the shade of some alder trees and brooded there.

"And my eye came to rest on a strange thing: an insect, quite large, but almost completely transparent in a pool of sunlight, clinging to the overhang of a large rock by the water. I leaned down to look. It did not move. I don't know how long I was like that, watching it. Eventually, I put out my finger to touch it, and it partly came away from the rock. I realised that it was not alive. I bent closer, and saw that it had an opening on its back. For some reason the thing frightened me."

Gwen sat up straighter. "You had found the empty skin of the mayfly."

"Yes, I understood that much later." He had been about to tell her the rest and then held back how he had taken the thing between his fingers and crushed it. Over the years, Edward had remodelled this memory; telling it now with only his father and himself in the frame made the recollection easier to live with.

"I don't think I would recognise you if I were to meet you as you were then," said Gwen. "Children can be so strange, can't they?"

Chapter IX

THE TIMES, Tuesday, October 2, 1866.

MURDER TRIAL AT THE OLD BAILEY.

IT is anticipated that The Crown v. Pemberton will prove to be a most interesting case to observe. Mrs Pemberton (26) is accused of murdering Mr Edward Scales (38) on or around the 6th of August. The gallery in court was swamped with a surfeit of spectators by 8 o'clock this morning, some of whom had to be removed in the interests of public safety and decorum. The prisoner, when asked to declare how she pleads at the opening of the trial, said, "Obviously, I shall plead Not Guilty, my Lord. I may say I had supposed I would not plead at all, as I am affronted that I should even *be* in this position, and I do not wish to give one iota of credence to the charge by answering it. However, I feel even more strongly that I must dissociate myself from this dreadful affair by stating the plain fact that I am Not Guilty. I do not know what else I can say to support my case other than to look every single person here in the eye and say that I did not have a hand in this awful deed."

Detective Sergeant Gray, of the Metropolitan Police Force, gave evidence of his discovery at the Hyde Park residence where the body of Mr Edward Osbert Scales was discovered.

"I attended the property of Mr Scales, on the morning of Tuesday, 7th August, accompanied by Constable Winters, and by Mr Pemberton, the husband of the prisoner at the insistence of Mr Pemberton. On entering the property, Mr Pemberton advanced before myself and my Constable, and began to open doors of the rooms and call to Mr Scales, whom I presumed to be still living at that time; that he must come out and answer for himself and that his time was up. Well, we soon after that found the deceased Mr Scales lying in the middle of the carpet in the morning room. Mr Pemberton spoke loudly to the tune that Mr Scales had better wake up. Constable Winters went to Mr Scales and turned him over whereupon it was obvious that the man was some time since passed away. Around the body were various bottles of spirits and spilled decanters of red wine. The room itself was in a state of great untidiness. At this moment, I had no reason to believe that Mr Scales had succumbed to anything other than a natural death. I sent Constable Winters for a doctor, and standing then in the hallway of the residence, I became aware of someone standing halfway down the main staircase. This person said he was Mr Morrisson, and that he was valet to Mr Scales and how could he help us. I informed him of his employer's demise, at which he did not so much as blink an eye. He came calmly down to the hallway and proceeded without hesitation to the very room where Mr Scales lay. Asking him how he could know where the body lay, Morrisson answered that Mr Scales had kept to that room all the previous day and night, and had not moved from it."

Mr Probart asked why the prisoner's husband had insisted the Police attend the property of Mr Scales.

A: "It was some domestic

matter, which did not seem to make any sense to me, and so to straighten it all out, I agreed to go there."

Q: "Could you be a little more specific as to the nature of this domestic matter?"

A: "I believe it was some quarrel that had occurred. Mr Pemberton made an accusation against the man regarding his wife's—the prisoner's—honour, sir."

Q: "Which part of the dispute did not make sense to you?"

A: "Mr Pemberton seemed to think that a murder of some sort had been committed."

Q: "Which, it so happens, had, in fact."

A: "Aye, sir. Unfortunately, it turned out to be so."

Chapter X

Helford Passage. June, 1859.

There hadn't been a single moment when Gwen had found herself thinking that she ought not to carry on. She did know, really, that this sort of encounter, might, in certain circumstances be dangerous but she didn't care. He was more than she could have ever hoped for. Better than that, he made her feel—without sliding into cliché, she thought to herself, as she slipped on the steep path between the bamboo thicket and grabbed at the yielding green poles—alive. It made her laugh, to think of all the ridiculous introductions she had been through under the gaze of the Fernly household. Pointless, all of them. Apart from the fact that she had used the money from the sale of her gowns to buy the microscope. Freddie would never have understood her attraction to Edward, and she was glad that she hadn't told Freddie about him, though there had been several times when Gwen had found herself almost on the point of confessing her secret.

No one was watching her. No one knew. No third party expected anything, and nor could they disapprove. He wasn't exactly any kind of romantic hero. For one thing he had the most peculiar sticking out pale hair she had ever seen and his skin was pale: freckled under his shirt and blotchy where the sun had caught his forearms. She stopped where she was amongst the stands of bamboo. This garden, she thought, we're hardly managing to keep abreast of it. In fact, there were parts of the garden which were virtually impenetrable. Murray and his lad, they kept the paths down to the beach clear; and they kept the top lawns well. But still, more than three quarters had run wild. She was trying an experiment with two goats, tethered under a massive magnolia. They looked like stupid animals and by the end of each day they had managed to get themselves tied in knots under the tree but they did eat everything. There was a sort of scruffy clear patch now. This was where she was heading, along a winding path which took her in a zigzag of steep gradients to the place where there had once been a lawn, nestled in the scoop of a valley. It was sheltered from the wind but rather too much goat manure had spoiled the ground, so they couldn't sit down.

Last time, they'd moved the goats away from the magnolia and tethered them in a very wild patch, so that they'd been hidden. Only the goats crashing about and their silly bleating disturbed them for a while. They'd talked, exhaustively, about the stupidity of goats until the animals had settled.

He'd pinned her against the tree, because of the ground being so littered with the dark pellets. Well, not pinned exactly. More supported. He'd kept her there anyway (perhaps, yes, she had been pinned, now she thought about it, because of her skirts being pushed up and to either side of her); and his head, she'd gripped his head to steady herself. None of it seemed wrong. The thrusting and the panting and the wetness between her thighs afterwards. He explored her with his fingers, running them back and forth until she was slippery and pliant in his hands and eager for anything that he would do, that he might think of doing; and then he would slip himself between her thighs. Make her keep them together, very tight, and he would delve there, and moan words in her ears that she hadn't heard before she'd met him, and still didn't know the meaning of.

She didn't like the smell. The runny then glutinous liquid which came out of him. It was too earthy. It caught in her throat like the smell of hanging poultry, and reminded her of certain flowers which attracted flies.

As he tightened his grip on her, and breathed into her, Gwen remembered one of the young men she'd been introduced to. His own body odour had been strong. They had been dancing and even out on the balcony in a stiff breeze she had smelled his sweat. The pressure of Edward's body reminded her of how the young man at that Ball had leaned in close; his breathing had been almost exactly like Edward's was now. What hindsight was, indeed, she thought.

"I was sorry to hear about your mother," he had said to her, and she had pretended not to hear, but he had carried on. "I had the good fortune to have been introduced, once." Still she had pretended not to hear, as the orchestra was very loud. "I am not one of those—" here she lost his words in the crescendo of the music "—you know, Miss Carrick." She had thanked him for his company and had never spoken to him again. She couldn't even remember his name. Charles somebody. A nobody.

Edward clamped his mouth over a tender part of her neck near the collarbone and sucked hard. Gwen looked up into the branches of the tree as she tried to twist her neck out of his mouth. Edward's groans were muffled; he let go briefly and then clamped his mouth again onto her neck, at the same time thrusting between her legs more furiously. Gwen concentrated on the sharp pinpricks of sunlight bursting through the leaves above her as they shifted in the breeze and made different patterns.

Edward released her. He said, "I have found a place in town. I mean to establish a practice."

"A medical practice?"

"Yes."

"You're a *doctor.*"

"The idea disappoints you."

"It surprises me."

"Oh. I had hoped to be able to see you more often. I hope I soon shall."

Gwen walked away and brushed down her skirt, buttoned up the collar of her blouse. She was upset that Edward had kept the secret of his life from her until this moment. How could he do this? One instant to be spilling himself between her clamped thighs, the next to be discussing some business arrangement. She had once asked him for a secret and he had told her some *thing* about a mayfly. He's made himself out to be ignorant about science, she thought, and yet he must have spent years in his medical training. Edward came after her, tucking himself up.

"I should have introduced myself in the proper way. For that I am sorry. It has been on my conscience. I would like to make amends."

"Why did you not?"

"I have never thought myself particularly worthy of the title. Call it self-doubt."

"And now you are confident."

"My mind and attitude have altered considerably since meeting you. You must know that you have had a great effect upon me."

"I am disappointed by your secrecy, Edward."

He slid an arm around her waist. "I am sorry to have hurt your feelings." He kissed her while he grabbed at the fabric of her skirt and pulled it up, slipping a hand underneath. He let his fingers rest, poised until he was sure of his impact through the kiss, and delicately drew her forgiveness from her as inevitably as the yolk in a blown egg must burst though the tiny aperture made by the pin.

★　　★　　★

"We simply can't afford anything so ridiculously extravagant. What on earth possessed you?" The irony of her own words were not lost on Gwen who looked at her sister across the breakfast table with cool fury.

"He's a gift."

"What? Oh, that makes it so much better. For heaven's sake. As if it wasn't already—"

"Yes? You were going to say 'bad enough', weren't you?" Euphemia's lips were parched and cracked and as she pursed them into a thin line of satisfaction, Gwen saw a beading thread of blood ooze over the papery skin.

"You are making us ridiculous, agreeing to have a pastry chef, of all things, in the house."

"I'm sorry, Gwen, to arouse such passion in you, but I can promise you that Mr Harris will do his best not to appear to be ridiculous under this roof."

"What kind of person, or mayn't I ask, sends a, a *dwarf* pastry chef to a household such as this?"

"An appreciative client. I knew it was his size which irked you, and not his culinary expertise."

"An appreciative—who exactly, which of them would—"

"I have not the faintest idea."

"He'll have to go back then; he'll be poisoning us at the first opportunity. We simply can't."

Euphemia threw back her head and shrieked like a herring gull. Gwen leaned over the table to slap her cheek and felt the smarting of it in her palm. Euphemia straightened up, instantly silent, glaring at her sister.

"He comes with the highest recommendation," she said. "From the housekeeper of a very good address in London."

Gwen regarded her sister in mute defeat for a few moments before telling her, "You appall me." She left the table, snatching up the daily newspaper and stalked out with it, rolling it into a baton as she went down the passage to the kitchen to inspect this new servant.

Chapter XI

"Let us be clear from the outset, Mr Harris—" Euphemia had invited him into the morning room to compliment his pastry, but a fever had lodged in her mind between the invitation being issued and her reading the letter Fergus Harris had given Susan for the post box that morning. It had been addressed to Mrs Isobel Scales in London. "Whilst you live under my roof, you are part of my household. You do not answer to anyone living in the establishment at which you were previously employed. Do I make myself quite understood?"

"Ma'am."

"You will not write letters of any kind to my clients."

"No, ma'am."

"And you will not make secret reports of any kind to any of my clients, nor to anyone else, about the private lives of people living in this house."

Fergus Harris looked up from where he had been staring at the floor. Euphemia saw no register of change in his expression as he replied that indeed he would not.

"Furthermore, you will not accept gratuities from any of my clients nor from anyone else, for any such undertakings. As you have so far surmised, we lead ordinary lives here, and there is nothing so remarkable about us bar that which is already known and appreciated by my clients."

Fergus Harris said, "No, ma'am. But is this you telling me to pack up and go?" Euphemia set her jaw and drew out the document she had prepared. "This is a new contract of employment, which you may read now and choose to sign. If you sign your name there, you will abide, absolutely, by everything which is set out, in plain English on that paper."

Fergus took the contract from where she had placed it on an occasional table beside her. She watched his eyes run over her tidy script. Here and there in his concentration he raised an eyebrow. When he came to the end he said that he would sign. Euphemia stood up and asked him to follow her through into the library where the ink and blotter were ready at the desk. Fergus Harris signed his name with the same flourish he had used to sign his letter to Isobel Scales. He rocked the blotter over his wet ink and handed the paper back to Euphemia.

"Thank you, Mr Harris. You are a most valued addition. Remember where your loyalties now rest and we shall all enjoy a peaceful, harmonious existence in this house. And, I almost forgot, your pastries are indeed quite excellent. That will be all for now, Mr Harris."

Married. Of course, he was married. His hand was practised; his touch was sure. Bella. The exceptionally quiet one. She could not credit the woman with such an extravagant habit. But there it was. She turned her attention to the pile of letters brought in from the table in the hall. The usual drift of thank-you notes and exclamations of gratitude. Among them a letter to Gwen in a hand she did not recognise. She put it to the side, and attended to things in an orderly fashion. Every now and then, between replying to her own letters, Euphemia's hand went out to touch the envelope addressed to Gwen. She picked it up, and turned it over and put it back down again just as her sister came into the room. She jammed the door wide open with a wedge. She brought the outside into the room with her.

"Effie, Susan tells me there is a letter for me this morning." Her whole self smelled of the hot weather. Of dust and pollen. And wine. Gwen came over to the desk. "Have you got it? Yes, there it is."

"A commission?"

"Perhaps."

"You were expecting it." Euphemia smelled the gritty earth on Gwen's hem as she swept around the back of Euphemia's chair.

"Hope for everything, and expect nothing, Effie. Isn't that the best way?"

"You have been taking our wine into the garden."

Gwen had been about to leave but she turned back again. "Honestly, Effie. It is such a glorious day, please don't try to spoil it for me."

"I hope the commission is a good one." Euphemia thought, I despise this buoyancy of yours. Please leave.

"If that is what it is, then so do I. It's very stuffy in here, Effie. You should go outside once in a while. More often than when nature calls. You go to bed too late and get up too late. You miss half the day. In fact, you have missed the entire summer. We may not have many more days like these."

"I miss nothing I do not wish to miss, much less than you might imagine."

Gwen went into the dining room to find the carafe, picking it up and then replacing it before going to the cellar instead. On the way down the path past the top lawn, she wiped the dust from the bottle on her skirt, holding the letter from Edward in her teeth. Edward, not Susan, had told her that there would be a letter waiting for her that morning. He had begged her not to rush off and fetch it but to read it after his visit. Seeing Euphemia with that pile of dull letters from her clients and her own placed there beside them had made Gwen suddenly sick. What if Edward one day forgot to put her full name on the envelope as he addressed it in a hurry. Miss G. Carrick. In a hurry, a "G" could be scrawled badly by Edward to look like an "E". The eleven o'clock sun was fierce out of the shade, and Gwen hurried back along the paths, under the wall of the kitchen garden and under the beech trees where she continued along one of the higher paths, past a wasps' nest and on to the boundary of the Carrick estate where she could look out over the fields if she chose, or out over the water where tall ships cut across the horizon of the glinting sea. Gwen opened the bottle; bending over, holding it between her feet. The noise of the cork coming out of the neck was satisfying in her solitude. She twisted the cork slowly from the screw with the letter laid across her skirts.

Dearest Gwen,

I am so happy with you. Does it seem like a monstrously obvious thing to say? To lie with my head in your lap and listen to you talk so seriously—these things matter enormously to me. You have no idea what a refreshing blast of goodness you have done to my soul. I have often wondered how any man could be content to loll in acres of petty small talk and twiddle flowers between thumb and finger when there is a universe of feeling to be communicated on all things—and you do so in such a fine and generous manner that it makes my whole self weak in admiration for you. Can you bear to read my inadequate missive? Perhaps you may think my words empty or second-hand when I have told you that I am inspired by you. It might seem too much to say, and yet I cannot say it enough— you must believe me when I say that there is no other person in this world near to you in your capacity for the extraordinary.

Do you see that full stop? I had to put down my pen and take

a walk into town to prevent myself from spilling a torrent of cliché
onto the paper. This is because there is no arrangement of words in
any language which may adequately express the depth of my feeling—
it gives me a sorry pain to try to make my brain and pen work in
harmony. You are an inspiration and yet inspiration renders me
speechless. Perhaps it is a mark of the truth of my feelings for you
that they cannot be expressed in words. Would that I could kiss your
mind, taste the light on your furrowed brow, swallow your every
thought . . .

Gwen took a swig of the wine and wiped a drip from her chin
with the back of her hand. She looked at the letter again and
laughed. Edward, she said to herself, you are utterly incorrigible.
He had engineered the manner of their meeting that morning so
that when Gwen read his letter the two would match exactly. He
had steered the conversation. Gwen had been talking about ordinary
things: Murray and his arthritis, and how she didn't want to have
anyone else, but knew that he was finding the work too much.
Edward had teased her mind away from that, by talking about Eden.
It was not a subject she could remain quiet about, and he had
known it. So, while she had talked about her ideas on the impossibility of a species derived from a limited source, he had lain his
head down in her lap and relished her impassioned speech. But
the letter did not mention how after a while with his head in her
lap, he had blown hot air through the fabric of her skirt, his mouth
firm against the layers of cloth at her crotch, his hands gripping
her at the hips so that she could not move. Yes, thought Gwen,
there were some things which could not be written down.

Chapter XII

Autumn, 1859.

He had been to the summerhouse only twice since the spring of that year. Between those visits Euphemia had waited there for him every night. Each of those times he had come, she had failed to accost him with her findings. Frost underfoot. Rime touched the edges of every leaf on the ground. As she left her mark on them, treading clumsily in the old boots she had slipped her bare feet into at the back door, she thought of the wasted hours she had spent waiting for him to arrive when she could have been sleeping. It was all made worse by the fact that what Gwen had said was true. She had been sleeping away the best of the day, every day, because of this man. No more humiliation on his account, then, she told herself. His wife may come to her meetings again, if she chose. Euphemia would not approach each evening with dread, hoping that the woman would not arrive to taunt her. She could give the woman what she wanted with a clear head. Mr Scales could scuttle off to wherever he had come from.

"If he is not here tonight," she said, "you will never come back to this summerhouse after dark. You will keep better hours and no one will have cause to scorn you. You will stop punishing your health over this man." And yet she still could not prevent her mind from skipping back to the details of those visits.

The first time she had met him in there she had been practising Gwen's voice. Euphemia had made the most of her awkward situation; it had been dark enough not to have been recognised. At first she assumed it must have been Murray, and after the surprise of finding him there, she managed to talk with him as carelessly as if she might have done in broad daylight. She knew that on the days he came, the gardener spent a great deal of time in the summer-house. It had seemed entirely logical to Euphemia that the man should still have been there at midnight because he spent so many hours in the old chair sucking on his pipe. Murray didn't like her, she knew that. He suspected her of being a fraud. But he liked Gwen because she spent so much time out of doors scratching away in her sketchbooks and collecting murky water from the ponds.

"I'm sorry to have disturbed you, Murray," Euphemia had said. "But you are aware that it is midnight?" She had been delighted at the way Gwen's voice was coming on and she smiled in the dark.

"I am the one who should apologise; I don't know who your Mr Murray is. I fell asleep in here, I hope you don't mind—there was no one here before. I must introduce myself; I am Edward Scales. You won't have heard of me, I shouldn't have thought."

And so the confusion had been eliminated. But Euphemia had enjoyed masquerading as Gwen and prolonged his stay. Letting Mr Scales believe she was someone else extinguished her sense of propriety altogether. It was just the way it was in the dark with the ladies and the spirits. She could do and say anything that came into her head. Mr Scales had advanced towards her as he introduced himself. He had obviously wanted to take her hand, politely, but they were standing closer to each other than he had judged. His hand touched her breast through the thin fabric of her nightdress where the overcoat was not buttoned down. Euphemia had remained absolutely still for a moment because, on touching her breast, Mr Scales did not take away his hand but kept it there. In the dark, in those slight seconds, Euphemia felt the pulse from his heart beating down his arm and joining itself to her own body.

Euphemia had thought that she had begun to see how her talents could be employed beyond the confines of her drawing room; that she would take her ability out into an altogether different sphere of experience. Some of the words he had spoken into her ear as he'd touched her on those other visits were not to be found in any dictionary. He had opened her eyes to the true meaning of delirium. But, in her craving, she had found that she was in control of nothing, and now, finally in his company again, Euphemia was determined to straighten everything which had become crooked. She had been feeling cold, but now she found herself at a perfect temperature.

"Who's there?" Edward's voice was uncertain, but his tone was proprietorial, indignant.

"What audacity, sir. This is my property, and you are the trespasser."

"Miss Carrick? My apologies, to you and your companion. I meant to startle no one."

"There is nobody here but me."

"Then, I—Gwen, are you quite well?"

Euphemia paused at the sound of her sister's name on his tongue. Images of the summer cantered before her eyes like the flicker of a daedalum. The memory of what he had done with her there suddenly sickened her. The slotted drum of illusion spun around in her mind. She heard her own heavy breath as if it did not belong to her. And it did not. What on earth had she wished for? If she met this man in daylight, she would not even know him until he spoke.

"This charade cannot go on, Mr Scales. Whatever would your wife have to say about your behaviour, should she know the truth of it?"

"I cannot say that I have not expected the event of this conversation."

"There is no conversation." Euphemia began to walk away from him and heard him take a few steps out of the summerhouse to follow her along the path.

"Gwen, please stay and listen to me. I must explain."

"There is nothing to explain, and nothing I wish to hear from you. I am glad I will never have to look into your eyes and see the arrogance there. Shame on you."

She left him standing in the dark and walked quickly, the cold in her lungs a relief. Physical exertion and pain were a liberation. To get away from him, to leave him there. She would go straight to bed and in the morning she would rise before her sister and this would end.

Chapter XIII

Carrick House. Christmas, 1859.

Whilst Euphemia's meetings went on in the drawing room almost every night, Gwen vanished to parts of the house where she could not hear her sister communicating with the departed on the 'other side' in various odd voices. She went, despite herself, with a plateful of sweet almond pastry and pored over Darwin's text, getting sugar between the pages, finger marks on the green cloth covers. Some of it she did not understand, and she read again until she thought that she had it. Not that she believed any of it at first, she was merely trying to comprehend the argument. She believed that to believe in anything she had to be true to what she saw as her duty of doubt. To try to comprehend evidence from every angle. This was difficult because the evidence had been collected by this man Darwin, not by herself. And the arguments he put to her were from his head. She always came up against this problem, of having to assimilate the ideas of others, always other men without ever having the opportunity to question the man who spoke to her from the page. She did not want to be lectured to; she wanted to have a conversation. But in between trying to grasp whatever Darwin was talking about and hiding from her sister's clients, she agitated over Edward. He came and went as he pleased. Over the summer and into the autumn her life had been turned inside out, and yet on the surface nothing had altered. She made her studies and kept herself to herself. Once, on a November morning, he had surprised her with an outburst of anguish, and it had taken some hours to persuade him that nightmares were only nightmares and that they meant nothing, and that whatever he had dreamed in his sleep could not possibly have been real. Here they were, she had said to him. Were they not happy together? Of course, they were. But still she felt that she might have been consoling him against her better judgement. The pain of being apart from him was real. He had seemed to read her thoughts, but then his absences were more protracted than ever. I will find you something extraordinary, he had told her. He brought her books, including the Darwin, as though it was enough. As though it would sustain her through the uncertainty of his long absences. She chided herself for being pleased when he did come, yet, she was pleased, she really was. The pleasure of finally seeing him standing under the big magnolia, after weeks and weeks, almost choked her. Knowing that it was childish to say that it wasn't fair didn't make it any less so. Freddie had almost given up trying to persuade her to quit her quiet habits and become the lively, sociable creature he wanted her to be. His invitations had become much less frequent. Sometimes, Gwen had wanted to go away, spend a week in London with her cousin, but the thought that she might miss one of Edward's visits while she was out riding with Freddie, or going to the opera, kept her to the confines of her own garden.

This, she thought to herself, is what women do. We wait, seemingly endlessly, without complaint, and without adequate solace, for men whose lives are too busy, too full, for them to stop and consider what degrees of frustration they heap thoughtlessly upon us.

Chapter XIV

Carrick House. March, 1860.

"Oh, please, not this again."

"I didn't tell her 'yes' outright, I only hinted."

"I'm not doing any more blasted portraits of that overfed lapdog."

"I think Miss Lotts has her nephew in mind."

"Exactly so."

"It will look bad if you don't at least come down and say hello."

Gwen narrowed her eyes at her sister. "Five minutes and not a second more. But, please, do not bother to introduce me to any of your clients. I will only be tempted to snub them and that will make you feel worse than me."

Gwen was becoming increasingly agitated by Edward's absences, which left her feeling hollow and without purpose. The thought of being forced to mingle with her sister's clients for the evening, while Euphemia proceeded to tie her to promises to paint pug dogs or nephews on cushions was too infuriating to handle with decorum. She felt sure that she would offend someone in the next thirty minutes.

They were mostly middle-aged women that evening, and Euphemia, for once, did not try to introduce Gwen to any more of them. Some of them clucked around one of the newest hopefuls, down from London, mid-season too; and the *petites bouchées*, a particular speciality of Fergus, were gobbled up appreciatively before the proceedings began. The sour-faced lady, in her late twenties, perhaps, seemed to take an especial interest in the tiny pastries but was the only one of the clients who did not sample them.

Gwen made polite conversation with the dreaded Miss Lotts, trying to undo the promise Effie had made on her behalf.

"I must apologise, Miss Lotts," she said. The woman took her arm and began to walk a few steps over to the large oval table where there was a gathering hush.

"Oh, call me Fanny. I am Fanny this evening, my dear."

"My diary is already very full, Miss Lotts. I have a very busy few months ahead of me. Now, if you will excuse me I—"

The lamp had already been turned to its lowest flame, and sputtering feebly, it went out. Gwen peeled Miss Lott's fingers from her arm in the sudden dark, thinking, I don't care if I offend the old bat.

Someone said, "Oh, that's a pity."

Euphemia cleared her throat. When the shuffling of expensive cloth let up, Euphemia began to go into her trance. The lamp going out was a great disappointment as the clients liked to see her eyes roll whilst the spirits took possession of her body.

Gwen squirmed in the dark and closed her eyes as her sister spoke in various pinched baby voices before settling on the one which a lady recognised.

"I'm here, my little dumpling," the woman called out.

Gwen's heart thudded; she didn't want this. It wasn't right. But she wasn't going to be weak about anything this evening.

It took some time, as there were a number of obstacles in her path. When at last she reached her sister's side at the head of the table she put out her hands to feel for her. She took a large handful of hair and tugged it. Gwen had been wondering what she could do to stop Euphemia's performance. When it had no effect at all she grew angry. She pulled very hard this time, and Euphemia let out a squeal, but continued to talk in the baby voice. Completely enraged, Gwen pinched her sister's arm through her silk shawl. As Gwen held on to her flesh, Euphemia cried out and in a pathetic voice murmured, "Stop. You're hurting me."

A low wail began from the lady's direction. The wail was punctuated with sobs and half-uttered, unintelligible sentences.

Gwen let Euphemia go.

The woman slid off her chair in a faint.

Gwen fumbled for the matches. As the wick took the flame the scene came into view. Someone ministered a bottle of smelling salts to the already recovering client who heaved herself back up onto her chair. Satisfied, soothing noises came from all directions. The evening had been a success. The woman, whose name was something like 'Bella' was moved to a more comfortable seat where she could be crowded and petted some more. Gwen whisked up the decanter and went off to fetch fresh water, saying to no one in particular, "If she hadn't had herself so tightly laced then there wouldn't be all this fuss."

Euphemia was still at her place at the head of the table, apparently in the last stages of recovering herself from the trance.

Did this woman do what she had once done? Euphemia shivered, remembering the sensation of cold air on the soles of her feet and the warmth then, between them, as this woman's husband had pressed his hands against her arches, the insteps slippery in that particular brand of intimacy. Was that, and the other thing, what married women allowed their husbands to perform on them? Or were those things especially reserved for another kind of woman? She remembered the taste. The pungent saltiness and the slime in her throat. How idiotic she had been, to have imagined herself any different from the kind of woman she knew she had imitated. Euphemia made another little groan. She had been surprised to see Isobel again, and immediately reminded herself that nothing should be surprising any longer. She had been right to end it. Trust no one and nothing but your gift, she said to herself, and Euphemia opened her eyes.

Chapter XV

June, 1860.

Gwen's face turned up into the deluge of rain and her long hair, undone, loose at last, was plastered over her naked body in thick strands which trailed off over the ground.

She stood up and peeled her hair from her body to plait a dirty rope, then wrapped it up in a shawl, a turban of silk dirtied and wet. They were both suddenly aware of the cold summer climate now. The rain continued to pour down through the trees and landed large droplets onto her clavicle and onto her breasts, which were firm and rounded on her chest. He pushed away the question of her age as he brushed at the leaves stuck on his own thighs. Oak, elm, ash. He gathered her up into his arms and kissed her neck, sucked at the rain which pooled on her collarbone but the moment was gone now, and she was cold, reaching for the damp blankets. He hated this parting. He both loathed and loved this weather.

Gwen was laughing now, as she dried herself, her jaw juddering in spasms. "I don't know how you can stand there," she said, wrapping the blanket tightly around herself, shutting out all sight of her body. She craned her neck, holding the weight of her hair with one hand and gazed up into the latticework of branches, then closed her eyes. The sensation of the spattering rain on her face.

When he had days like this, he could imagine himself doing something unthinkable, just so that he could have her to himself, all the time. For a split second, he held the image of Isobel, drowned at his hands in her rose-spattered bathtub, and this girl forever in his arms. A moment of intense ecstasy, which made him hard again, and which he did not bother to hide as he reached for his own grey blanket.

He ached to pull her onto the ground with him then, and just as she let her head down again and opened her eyes, the words spilled out of his mouth. He couldn't stifle them.

"I want you. I want to take you. I want to do, to do other things to you. I need to, I need to so very badly, to have you for my own and I can't—I'm—it's all impossible and horrible and wonderful all at the same time."

He saw her face collapse in disgust.

"Don't spoil it, Edward. Why do you have to spoil it now? There's no need to make excuses. I can well imagine." She was rubbing herself more thoroughly now and struggling with the inconvenient reality of being naked and filthy wet in a hidden spot of her garden, trying to rub some warmth back into the numbed parts of her. "I've known long enough and only too well that you and I would never cross paths in normal life. We occupy different spheres." She gave up trying to talk and manage the task with dignity.

"I'm sorry."

"Don't ever be sorry; I couldn't stand it."

They both rubbed their bodies in silence and then walked a short distance up a steep path to the old schoolhouse where they had left their piles of clothes forty minutes before.

It was a tiny building, once used for summertime lessons a dozen years before, disused now and crammed with old bits of garden furniture, bird baths, broken tools, mouse-traps and garden machinery. A gin-trap hung from the wall, its crushing teeth feathered with spider-webs. There was a small, wooden dovecot in there, and a perfectly good, sturdy table which had been cleared of broken plant-pots and brushed clean and now had a striped blanket over it. This was where they had laid their clothes. Gwen had found a serviceable chair amongst the tat and used it sometimes to watch the rain from the open doorway.

They shut the door now, closing themselves into the peculiar stuffiness of the schoolhouse. Something small scuttled in the rafters. They looked at each other. Her mind was empty except for the thought that she needed to wash herself. The rain came down around the schoolhouse, falling onto the old thatch and pouring off in noisy splashes. It was as well that there was some kind of noise for them both to focus on because neither had said anything yet. Edward was trembling. She couldn't tell whether he was over-come or just plain cold. She certainly felt clammy. But it was impossible for her to leave him there yet; he had a vacant look in his eyes and seemed rooted to the spot.

"Edward," she almost whispered, afraid now of what was happening.

"I have failed you," his voice cracked.

She stepped up to him, careful not to crush his naked toes under her shoes and grasped him with both hands. She felt annoyed, suddenly, that the aftermath of this event, which had come to its conclusion only ten minutes earlier, had opened a chasm between them that she alone was now compelled to dispel. She shook him slightly, not caring if it seemed odd. "I'll see you in two weeks."

"Tomorrow," he said. "I want to see you tomorrow."

"Tomorrow I'll be busy. I'll be just the same in two weeks' time."

"The day after tomorrow—will you see me then?"

She let go and turned away. She put on her ankle-length coat and finally unwrapped her hair, and put her hat on before taking up her bag of sketching things and paints and her old umbrella. She let herself out into the rain without looking back, pulling the door shut behind her with her head bent against the drive of the rain and wind.

Gwen made herself stay calm. It was nothing. It was everything. For more than a year she had lived in perpetual waiting. The ache in her groin spread down her legs and she powered them forward and up along the overgrown, meandering pathways until she reached the tended areas of garden nearest the house.

It would come the next day. There would be nothing until the morning except this growing ache, like a goblin's fist in her muscles, here and then here; reducing her by degrees to a knotted heap of pain and subdued only slightly by bags of hot wheat. She could never have agreed to see Edward in that state. Sweating and rushing to empty her bowels every half hour. Sometimes when it came, she vomited, doubled over the chamberpot. It came alternately less and more. The last month it was less. She braced herself now. Whatever it was, that had made Edward react in his peculiar way could wait— and she certainly didn't intend crying herself silly over it.

A hot bag of wheat clutched to her belly, she remembered the flash of bizarre scientific inspiration which had occurred to her as she'd lain on the blanket. She placed a glass trough on the table in her room next to her microscope. She squatted, rummaged with her fingers and then wiped the result into the trough. Quickly she put the trough into position and looked through the microscope at her specimen, focusing in disbelief at the frenetic movement of undulations in the tails, like eels of an indescribably small size.

Chapter XVI

July 8, 1860.

She said, "You probably fell asleep, and dreamed it. You'll have to tell me what you think you've already asked me." Her heart pounded, in a way which made her feel nauseous, which made her feel like an idiot female. He'd never asked her anything. This was what it felt like, she supposed. Or did it? The wind was getting up again in the trees; its sound crammed her ears and knotted her brain. She knew that she would accept, having never dared to even think of this kind of conversation happening between them. She watched his face; he looked so confused.

"I am quite certain that I came here, two days ago. We met in that very heavy storm. You were hurrying away and I caught up with you. I can't have dreamed it, Gwen. I was soaked to the skin. And you had forgotten your umbrella—you were wearing that huge hat. Rivers of rain fell off you, as though you were a—"

"I didn't go out that early, Edward," Gwen spoke slowly, tried to keep the anxiety out of her voice.

"Well, in any case, let us not argue over it. I was inconsiderate to ask you in such a way in the first place. But you must have received my letter by now? I sent it the same day."

"No, I haven't had your letter. Ask me again, Edward. It isn't raining yet. Besides, you must know by now that I'll accept."

"I have been making preparations," he said, "to go to Brazil, and I would like you to consider accompanying me, as illustrator of the natural world there."

Gwen's heart thudded in a different way. Don't let him see, she thought. But she fixed her gaze on his face, and as she did, she knew that she didn't want the thing she'd imagined. It was only vanity, and it made her cringe to think of it. "You are asking me to go with you to a place that is very far away. I have lived all my life here. I would leave my sister alone. It is a large house to be alone in. There are other things to consider, besides." Inwardly, she leaped in excitement. Stuff the silly thought that he was going to ask for something different. Now her garden seemed to be a gate, not the prison she had resigned herself to. She would be with him every day, and those interminable weeks of waiting to see him would be over—perhaps for years.

"These are not insurmountable obstacles." He faltered. A sister? She'd told him that she lived alone, hadn't she?

"This has come out of nowhere. Why Brazil, of all places?"

"Because of you. Because when I visited the Glasshouses at Kew, I was constantly reminded of you, and this place. You *in* this place, and you painting away at your beetle studies, and what you said, about beauty and science." He did not say that it was also because of something she had once told him about there being more insects in the world than any other kind of creature. Edward had discovered, during a conversation with Jacobs one night, that some believed most of the world's insects had not yet been named. He thought if he was to stand any chance of finding an insect as yet unknown to science, then the Brazilian forest seemed the best place to begin. He had begun practising his *scalesii* inventions again.

"You want me to run away."

"Think on it," Edward said, his voice flattened. Their meeting was over. He began to move away. Five paces. He stopped, half turned. "I have already bought the best-quality artists' paper and some vellum. Sketchbooks. I would rather it was your work filling the pages than that of some stranger." He felt inside his jacket, brought out a folded document and held it out to her. "Look."

Well, that's still not good enough, she thought. Can you not tell me now that you love me, after all? But she held onto the papers for long minutes, reading off the list of provisions and equipment. So many different items. Her brow wrinkled in concentration. "What are the numbers, the codes beside each entry?"

"Let me see. Ah, yes. It is to indicate which crate each item shall be packed into."

"This," she said, her finger on a line of script. "Surely, this is not right."

He came closer to her, and she smelled the sweat of him in his ungainliness.

"Oh, yes. That is quite right."

"*Such* a size. Will that be necessary? What on earth could one find to preserve—or is it meant to be used the way one packs fruit, I wonder?"

"Well, one never can quite predict, but that is the thrill. Don't you see?"

"The weight would be almost immeasurable."

"I had to have it. I went to the glassworks and there it was, and it—well, it inspired me. Yet not half as much as you."

Half an hour later, he was getting ready to leave again. He picked up the lacquered bamboo sticks which had held her hair in place and handed them back to her. He turned away while she twisted her hair into a knot.

"Did you hear that?" Gwen touched Edward's sleeve. "I thought I heard it before; I'm sure I'm not mistaken this time."

Edward looked at her, and as their eyes met, they both heard the noise, louder this time and undeniably there. "Some kind of animal? Perhaps a weasel with a rabbit," he said.

"No," Gwen shook her head, and looked away into the middle distance, scrunching her eyes into slits as though that might make her hear better. "No," she said again, the blood gone from her face. "It's more human." Gwen was yards away from Edward, before he realised that he was running after her.

Edward did not want to go into Carrick House now. He'd thought about what it might be like in there often enough; conjured up a picture of something extraordinary, even though he knew that in all probability it was the kind of house you would not remark upon except for its occupants. Now he had discovered that his wife had been there. Spiritualism and hokus pokus; Isobel was mocking him again. He'd been so sure that she had been lying, calling his bluff. He knew for certain that Gwen was not a Spiritualist. The very idea that she would indulge in that particular abomination was so preposterous. He'd laughed in Isobel's face. But she'd described the house in such detail. What was he to do? He thought of Gwen with her furrowed forehead scuffing the ground with her foot and imagined that he knew what it must be like, to be her. Waiting for him to appear. Looking under the tree, not letting herself hope that he might be there. And then the chill from the ground penetrating their bodies. No wonder she was guarded, angry. She was besieged by his long absences, and now Isobel, too, with her silly games. He'd meant to ask her to come away with him in a different way. He'd meant to use different words, but they'd rolled around at the back of his throat. His apology for his inconsistencies; it was a bolus refusing to be anything but that.

The house appeared from behind the screen of tall laurels: red brick, amongst so much green. Edward stopped in his tracks to admire it. Gwen caught his arm and pulled him forward into its shadow. "This house," he said to her, "it's barely twenty years old, is it?"

"What? Oh, yes. The other one was demolished to make room for it. I'm told it was a scandalous thing to do. At least they left the garden—"

It began to rain. Hard spittles smacked the windows at his back as Edward suppressed his desire to flee the place. Gwen turned to the bundle propped up in the chair. "Mr Harris, help is here now. I'm sure Mr Scales will be able to get your eye open."

Edward hesitated, concentrating on the pool of light at the table.

Gwen went outside and pumped a jugful of water. She brought it to the table with a glass. Edward looked critically at the dwarf. His eyelid was swollen, and where Euphemia had stitched the lids together, there was a general crustiness of blood mixed with yellow secretions. Edward glanced at Gwen, wishing that some of her apparent calm would settle on him.

"I can remove these, but, as for the rest, I am no specialist. I will be as careful as possible."

"I'd be much obliged, sir," said Fergus.

Edward said, "We'll have to bathe it first. Some boiled and cooled salty water would be best, I think."

As Gwen moved around him organising things, checking the water was at the right temperature, spooning salt into it, Edward wondered at her composure. Bed sheets tied around a man, pinning his arms to his sides, fixing his head still—he couldn't imagine the terror of it. He couldn't imagine why this man had not been able to save himself. Did she pounce on him? Did she trick him? Somewhere in the house Euphemia was locked safely away in her room. Edward recalled Gwen's face as she'd led Euphemia away from the scene. Euphemia bedraggled and wild-looking, slumping into her sister's arms, letting herself be moved away. Madness. There were all kinds of madness. Perhaps this was what Gwen had meant when she'd told him that there were other things to consider. Not the shame of being the mistress at all.

As he worked gingerly at the threads of silk, Edward's own eyes pricked with exhaustion and he battled to keep them open. Gwen stood behind Fergus with her hands on her servant's shoulders, her body pushed up against the chair.

No one said anything. The atrocious task in front of him seemed to demand an equally atrocious silence. Here I am, he thought, picking thread from eyelids. It was all too much of a mess, yet he had to find some way of persuading her to accept his offer. His hands fumbled. He thought of the wasted hours young women like Euphemia spent bending over needlework; it'd be enough to drive one to madness, perhaps. He wiped his face on his sleeve. If he could have bright daylight he could get this done much quicker. But the lamplight made everything uncertain. Was that silk thread or was that a bit of flesh? He had to decide. The blood oozed out of the puffed-up lids, and Fergus sat tight, bracing himself against the back of the chair. He'd be a mess in the morning. Gwen was watching Edward. He wanted to know what she was thinking. Was she making her decision, or was she lost in some other place not connected to where she stood? Edward cleared his throat several times just to make a noise. An hour passed and he wanted to rest, but it was better just to get on and finish the job.

Chapter XVII

THE TIMES, Wednesday, October 2, 1866.

MURDER TRIAL AT THE OLD BAILEY.

ON the second day of The Crown v. Pemberton, a veritable rumpus was observed outside the Central Criminal Court, as members of the public, keen to obtain entry to the gallery, had gathered in large numbers.

Witnesses for the Prosecution were called after the opening. The first, Mr James Morrisson, said, "I was valet to Mr Scales since the date of his first marriage up to the time he went away. I was never given notice to leave the house, and I carried on there until the present time, or near enough."

Q: "And how did you become aware of the untimely passing of Mr Scales?"

A: "I heard the noise, downstairs, in the morning. As I came down, I came upon the three men that I know to be the two police constables and her husband."

Q: "Do you mean Mr Pemberton, the prisoner's husband, Mr Morrisson?"

A: "I do that."

Q: "You had been at the deceased's residence the night previous to this?"

A: "Yes, and most of the day as well. Mr Scales was in town, and I knew that he'd be in need of my services. As it turned out, his wants were not many, and I had not much to attend to, so I retired. I was aware of his having visitors— a lady. I saw her enter the house about three in the afternoon. From an upstairs window I saw her approach the house, and Mr Scales let her in himself. He'd already said that he wouldn't want to be disturbed at all should he get a visit from anyone, so I kept to the back of the house until I heard the door bang shut about seven or so. He did not ring for me all night, so I did not go near his room."

Mr Shanks for the Defence: "Is it not the case, Mr Morrisson, that you were not wanted by the deceased Mr Scales in the days leading up to his death, but that you forced your way into the property, in your own words, 'to make his life a misery'?"

A: "I never said so."

Q: "We shall see, Mr Morrisson."

Other witnesses included staff from households neighbouring the Victim's address. Mrs Peters gave her evidence thus: "I have been housekeeper at the property adjoining the Scales' residence for some years and have always noticed the quantity of visitors, or lack of them, going into that house. On the morning of the last but one day of July this year I saw a man approach the house and I heard his knocking. I remember this quite clearly as it was so persistent. I also recall it in detail as I remember wondering at the time that a person should knock so when the house was empty. Then, on looking out more carefully, I saw who was there, and, of course, I was surprised to see Mr Morrisson returned after such a long absence. Well, naturally as his banging and knocking was a nuisance I sent out Smythe, my footman."

The footman, Mr Smythe, then later gave his evidence: "I am Smythe, footman to the

Picard household, and on the morning of July 30th I was instructed to go out and tell the gent making the racket that the house he was banging on was empty. I went out and I said to the man, who I knew to have been valet there long since but knew not on common terms, 'Here, the place is empty, sir.' In reply, he said to me that he knew Mr Scales was in there for certain and that he was d—d if he wasn't going to get in there and have words. He was very agitated and of a very high colour in the face, and persisted with his banging. I stood there some minutes and tried to persuade him that his racket was useless, when, all of a sudden, the door opened, and I saw Mr Scales himself. Mr Scales did not seem at all pleased to see who was stood on his doorstep. 'What the D— are you doing here?' he says to Morrisson, and Morrisson says back to him, 'More to the point, what the blazes are you doing here?' except stronger words than that was used, sir. 'I've more right to be in this property than you,' says Morrisson to Mr Scales, and then he pushed his way over the doorstep, and Mr Scales done nothing to stop him. I asked Mr Scales if he would like me to assist and he said he'd deal with the matter himself. Just before he shut the door, I heard Morrisson telling him he'd stay there whether he liked it or not and that he'd make his life a misery while he was at it."

Doctor Alexander Jacobs gave his evidence: "I attended the body of Mr Edward Scales at around ten o'clock on the morning of the 7th of August. The body had been turned over, but, other than that, had not been moved. Evidence of the body having lain face down on the floor for some time was immediately apparent. Because of this effect, it was not at first obvious that any trauma had occurred to the body. However, on detailed examination later in the day, it became clear that death might have occurred through strangulation by application of a ligature to the neck."

Cross-examined by Mr Shanks:

Q: "You said just now, that 'death might have occurred by strangulation'. And yet you were not so reticent when you stated at the inquest that you were of the 'firm opinion that the man had been strangled to death'. Are you saying that you have changed your mind? Or that you were not really sure in the first place?"

A: "In retrospect, sir, I conclude that the amount of alcohol present in the body of the deceased could just as easily have caused death to occur. I do not, in retrospect, believe that the marks to the neck, which were slight, corresponded with other, more conclusive, cases of death by strangulation that I have attended during my career."

Chapter XVIII

Carrick House. July 9, 1860.

Edward woke to the sound of a mistle thrush. Its song just beyond the window joined with the last of the dawn chorus. Lying there, listening to the burbling melody, he remembered a comment of Gwen's one morning; that the dawn chorus must be a wave of birdsong, as it moved from east to west, following the break of day in a relay of sound all over Europe, perhaps even the world, as it turned on its axis; and then, at nightfall, the sound coming back as a kind of inverted echo, west to east, the pinking and chipping sounds announcing the end of the day. Can you imagine, she'd said, if one could *see* it, as God must. It would be a tidal surge of sound, moving in an endless ripple of song across the globe.

His body felt clammy and cold; he shifted around under the covers and tried to plump up his pillow. He'd asked her where she had read this theory. Damn. That a mere girl should happen upon a thought as profound as that. He'd taken her rather too roughly some minutes afterwards. And then when he had left her, he'd written down everything she had said in his notebook, suffused with a surge of love.

There was the most God-awful smell in the room and the fust of mildew. The blankets felt heavy. He felt around underneath his hip for the hard object pressing against his skin. It slipped around in the folds of the rucked-up bed sheet. Edward listened to the thrush for a short while, turning the object in his fingers, wondering about the best thing to do. He did not turn his head to the left where he knew Gwen's servant, Harris, lay sleeping next to him. By God, of all the things that had happened to him, waking up next to a dwarf had to be one of the most novel. The object in his hand was about the size of a robin's egg, its surface both smooth and pitted. He couldn't think how a marble could have wound up in bed with him. But then, by the smell of the room it had not been in use for a long time. He couldn't stay there. He heard stifled strokes of a clock somewhere striking five. Getting into his clothes haphazardly, Edward skimmed over what he could remember of the night before. He stuffed the marble into his waistcoat pocket. In the dim light he tried to check his own time against the chimes he thought he had counted. Edward sighed heavily. Gwen would not be swayed, he thought, now that this had happened. The situation was only slightly better than if her servant had been dead.

As he tiptoed towards the door with his shoes in his hand, Harris spoke out from the bed. "Much obliged to you, sir, for all that you have done."

Edward paused. "Ah, yes. Don't mention it. Take care of that eye," and out of curiosity, he stepped back onto the square of carpet and moved over to the bed to peer at Fergus. "Look here, um, Harris. About this business."

Fergus hauled himself up and spoke as if he'd rehearsed his lines all night. "She hadn't slept for about three or four days by yesterday, and I ain't no medic, but I'd say that was half the problem, sir."

Edward sat down on the end of the bed, keeping his face turned away, so that he would not have to breathe in the rotten air expelled by Fergus. He felt sure his own breath smelled just as bad. He needed to spit and gargle.

"Has she suffered from insomnia—I mean to say, been like that before?"

"Not since I was at the house, sir."

"And do you know by any chance what the other half of the problem would be?"

"A romantic involvement."

Edward frowned. "You know this for certain?"

"I do."

"How unfortunate that she should take it out on you."

"It was an accident."

Edward was about to ask what kind of accident could possibly have resulted in the man having his eye sewn up when Fergus said, "You've your own romantic involvement, as well, sir. Though I think you've picked the more sensible of the two of them."

"What? Don't presume to speak to me of things you know absolutely nothing about."

"Well, I doubt Miss Gwen is ever likely to try sewing your eyes up and leaving you in a cellar to freeze half to death, now is she?"

"Have a care, Mr Harris. You've no business speaking about Miss Carrick like that. And I'll thank you not to speak of her in those tones again."

Fergus shifted against the bolster. He breathed deeply through his nose. "South America's a long way to go."

Edward narrowed his eyes, "Watch your tongue, Harris."

"So, did you never finish your *special* medical studies then? Last time I heard, you was going to be a famous doctor. Writing some big paper, she said, all about her. And then *pouf!* No more. Now, correct me if I'm wrong, but I don't think you abandoned Miss Jaspur for lack of interest. So, as I say, South America is a long way to go."

Edward stood up. "Who in hell's name are you?" He reeled, felt himself sway.

But Fergus had not finished. "Not saying I blame you, mind. Natalia snared all her men, including me. Don't know though, what Miss Carrick would think about that."

Edward found himself grasping the little man's neck and squeezing. "Tell me how you know these things." Fill his vile little mouth with feathers and let him choke. He released the pressure, eased himself back. "How dare you." Edward forced himself not to shout. "How dare you speak that woman's name in the same breath." He stared at Fergus. He's lying, he thought, he's lying. He must have said something to Euphemia; he must have done something, known something. Perhaps he'd been taunting Euphemia with information about her sister's reputation. He'd infuriated Euphemia and she had acted on her anger. Edward breathed heavily, waiting for the impulse to grind Fergus into nothing to subside as the extent of Isobel's involvement became clear. Edward knew he'd be a fool not to recognise it. Waiting for him to answer when he could see that he would not. "I should kill you now," he said, "but I'll not be a murderer for her." He glanced at Fergus. "Yes. I know. I can see it." He lowered his voice so that it was barely audible. "My wife sent you here. But mark my words, whatever she's promised you, she will never honour it. You are out of your depth, and you'll do well to keep your mouth shut. By God, you will."

The door handle turned, followed by a faint knocking. Edward went and put his ear to the door before opening it a crack.

Gwen pushed open the door and pulled Edward into the corridor. "How is Mr Harris? Is the swelling very much worse?" Gwen's own eyes were dark-circled and bloodshot.

"It looks worse than it really is. A lot of bruising, that's all. Your poultice has helped enormously."

Female hysteria, he thought. Common enough. Easy to handle that. Get some sedatives into the girl. But, by God, who was he trying to fool? He needed to get Gwen out of the house, away from everything. Isobel's hand was all over this. Her poisonous tendrils had spilled over the boundary he had constructed and were threatening to choke everything. He turned the object around in his fingers, not realising that he'd taken it from his pocket. He could still persuade Gwen to go with him to Brazil. He felt Fergus' presence in the closed room behind his back and he dropped the object into the folds of his pocket again and bent to tie his laces. As he straightened up, he saw Euphemia running at him. She had on a soiled nightdress and was screeching as she wielded a knitting needle in her hand.

"For goodness sake, Euphemia," Gwen bellowed, adding to the din. "Pull yourself together and stop behaving like such an idiot. This really is too much. Especially before breakfast—"

As Edward stepped neatly aside to avoid Euphemia, he stuck out his foot and tripped her up. Her face was stuck all over with matted strands of hair, glistening with fresh mucous; and her features swollen and red-blotched from weeping. Her nightdress was unbuttoned down to her navel. Edward looked away as Gwen bent over her sister to try and tidy her.

Edward helped Gwen take Euphemia to her bedroom. There was a strong smell of shit-filled chamberpot in there; it shrouded them in a clinging gossamer of stink as soon as the door was opened. Shafts of light hit the heaped chaos of clothes and torn papers. Gwen made her sister get into bed. Edward watched her tuck Euphemia into the covers as though nothing much more than a cold in the head had aggravated her temper. She'll not come with me, he thought. I'll not be able to drag her away from this.

Gwen pulled the window down on its cord, letting in a gust of fresh air.

"You didn't by any chance mention my travelling plans to that Harris, did you?"

Gwen picked her way over the mess on the floor towards Edward. (She stooped to pick up a visiting card. The photograph showed a beautiful, clean-shaven young man. She turned the card over. The printing was scratched out.) Distractedly, she said, "No, I never discuss private things with—Why?"

"Oh, nothing. He was mumbling something last night, probably just talking in his sleep. I may have got the wrong end of the stick."

"Susan will deal with all of this." Gwen waved her arm over the mess, letting the card drop. "Let's go downstairs now."

"By the way," Edward said, "I came across this in your guest room—an artefact from your childhood, perhaps?" He took her wrist gently and put the marble into her hand. Puzzled, Gwen glanced at it briefly before shutting the door behind them.

Fergus heard the commotion outside the bedroom door but did not pay much attention to it. He had drawn the curtains wide open and pulled back the covers from the bed. It must be hidden in a fold. He turned both pillows out of their cases and shook everything. He scrabbled around the mattress like a terrier looking for its rat. Then he got down and inspected the underneath of the bed. He lifted the carpet at its edges. He shook out all the bedding piece by piece, and folded every sheet and blanket in turn. Not an easy thing to do. His arms ached. He tussled with the panic bubbling in his throat and sat down on the heap of folded bedding to get his breath back. He began to doubt the memory of putting it under his pillow in the small hours before dawn. Mr Scales had been snoring like a drunk. He had not imagined it. He had fallen asleep with the balas diamond in his fist. He got up off the pile of bedclothes and began to unfold and shake out the sheets again, though he knew it was now a waste of time. His tears stung, and they blocked his already impaired vision. He poured the salty water from the jug into the bowl Gwen had set down and then put on the clothes which had been laid out for him the night before.

It was time to reassess his situation. This bit of theatre was over; there were better things to worry about. Bugger. He had to find it. He couldn't leave without it.

Edward looked about him in the library where he was waiting for Gwen to return after speaking at length to her maid. It had become clear to him that Gwen's sister had chosen the maid's one night off in the month to cause her havoc in the household. His own brief first appraisal of Susan at Carrick House that morning had been that she was not the kind of woman you would want to have about the house if you chose to misbehave in such a manner. Her hands were large and square. And she had an attitude he would never seek to cross in a month of her days off.

The library was at the front of the house and its window had an excellent view of the drive; the fields either side of it with their crops of barley and flax were full of flowers; swallows skimmed low for insects over the heads of the colourful blooms and ripening seed heads.

Gwen shut the door behind her, and Edward turned away from his gazing. He had been lost in his situation for a moment, but now he tried to guess what Gwen had to say. He waited for a moment and when she said nothing he asked if there was anything more that he could do to help. She shook her head. "I'll go with you to Brazil, Edward. You need not worry that my sister's hysterics will detain me here."

"Thank God. Thank you, I hardly know what to say."

"I am sure you're tired, and want to go to your own house and sleep properly."

"You are exhausted."

"Yes."

"But you are sure that you want this?"

"I am. It is not because of what my sister has done, or only partly. It has become impossible for me to live with her, but it is also impossible for me to continue to live the way I have been since the day I met you. I want to be with you every day, and I want to expand my scientific knowledge. So, yes, I am sure I want this, because I want you."

Edward lunged across the room and smothered her in a tight embrace. "You can't know how glad that makes me."

"I can guess."

"I have almost seven weeks to make the last arrangements. I must return to London for a short while. I have been given the name of a gentleman who will verify and buy specimens and I must meet with him to discuss terms. And there are other matters to tie up. But these things are routine, I should be able to return in three weeks' time. Our ship embarks from here."

"You mean from Falmouth?"

"Yes. I thought that if you did decide it was something you wanted, then you would not want to travel all the way to London or to Liverpool."

Gwen nodded and closed her eyes. She was sure that this was what she wanted. It frightened her more than anything and it gave her a thrill it was difficult to conceal. It was worth enduring the next weeks, no matter what kind of hysterics and difficulties Euphemia devised, when afterwards she would be able to be true to herself and to be with Edward.

"This is what we were always meant to do," he said. "Our joining together, in this way, is more divine than anything ever imagined."

Gwen opened her eyes again to find that he was leaning in; before she could speak he had clamped his mouth around her partly open lips.

Chapter XIX

Helford Passage, Cornwall. September, 1860.

Susan stood with her hip against the kitchen table in Carrick House and rubbed at the brass key with her apron. Fergus watched her bring the key up to her face and blow the last bits of soil from its crevices. She was calming herself after all the bother with the large crate of glassware which had arrived that morning from town. There had been some wrangling, but Susan had managed eventually to persuade the deliveryman and his lad to get the thing down the outside steps to the cellar. She eyed Fergus over the jumble of things on the kitchen table. He had been emptying another cupboard, and was halfway through examining the contents. The stone jar of flour was half sifted into a large bowl and a white layer of dust covered everything else. Susan cleared her throat and rubbed harder.

"I usually do that kind of thing in the springtime, Mr Harris," Susan met his eye, "and that flour was only bought very recent, as you well know. You won't find no grubs in there."

"I ain't looking for grubs, Miss Wright."

"Then what are you up to? It's making such a mess."

Fergus put down the sieve with a resigned huff. "I'm sorry, Miss Wright. I thought, with all the house being so upside down, I might have found—"

"Yes, Mr Harris?"

"You've been at this place a while, Miss Wright. Do you think—I mean, does this business seem out of the ordinary to you?"

"I never do the spring cleaning like that, if that's what you mean, Mr Harris."

"No. I mean the thing with the key. Her hiding it all over. And the other things, as well."

"You mean has Miss Euphemia done this before?"

"It is her, then? Not the other?"

Susan pulled out a chair and sat on it, holding the brass winding key in her lap. She looked at him square in the face. "Mr Harris, Miss Gwen would never do anything to annoy me, she'd never do anything to upset me and she'd never ever make extra work for me. I know that girl. She's as true as the day is long."

"And what would you have to say if I was to tell you that Miss Gwen has been making plans to go away?"

"Don't be daft now, Mr Harris. Where would she go?"

"I ain't being daft, Miss Wright; she's going," he lowered his voice, "to South America, Miss Wright. Yes," he said seeing her expression change, "Brazil."

"I swear, Mr Harris, you shouldn't tell tales on people like Miss Gwen. It's not nice."

"Maybe, but it's true."

"How come you know all about it?"

"Walls and doors have lugs, don't they?"

"Why? Why would she do that to us, leaving us with her batsy sister?" Susan covered her mouth with her hands still holding the key. "I never said that."

"Yes, you did. And it's right enough. She is barmy."

"We'll never manage her in this house on our own, Mr Harris. I'll have to have words with Miss Gwen."

"You won't change her mind." Fergus laughed under his breath.

"I might; she's a good girl. She's not like most people."

"She's running off, Miss Wright, with a man. The man what sorted this out," he gestured at his bad eye, still very much bruised and sore. Fergus closed his good eye, and he sighed deeply. He felt so bad this morning, awful. His head throbbed. He knew that a fever was building up. He poured himself a drink of water and wiped the sweat from his face with his sleeve.

"I never heard anything so out of character in all my life, Mr Harris. Are you sure?" Susan put the brass key on the floury table and stood up to tower over Fergus. "You don't make no sense at all today, Mr Harris. I reckon you've got this all wrong. I reckon what you heard is that Miss Gwen is having her sister put somewhere for a while. Though it would be a shame for the family, it wouldn't be no shame for this house. I could do without all her ghostly visitors, all them ladies in their black lace and musty taffeta. Now that *is* extra work, having them in the house four or five times a week. Wears me out—I never sleep when they've been."

Fergus gave a wry grin, and stopped himself from swaying. "You should have told me before, Miss Wright; I'd have set your mind at rest."

"How's that?"

"Ghostly visitors, Miss Wright? It's nought but a trick. Well, maybe a gift, in her case, she does it so well."

"And what would you know about ghosts, Mr Harris?"

"Nothing; but I know a damn, pardon me, fine ventriloquist when I see one. And not just that, the voices, my word, she does the voices."

"But that's just it, Mr Harris. The noises that come out of her, they don't come from this world."

"You're right there, Miss Wright. They come straight out of another world. I've often wondered where she learned it. I mean, I've seen it done often."

"At meetings, in that big house you was at, in London?" Susan sat down again and shoved some of the jumble of jars and bowls to the side to lean over the table and fix Fergus in an avid gaze.

Fergus shook his head. "No, Miss Wright, nowhere as nice as that house. No, I saw it done in Saville House, in Leicester Square, years ago."

"At a Spiritualist meeting," Susan said.

Fergus laughed through his nose, shaking his head; his brain felt as though it was coming loose. "Saville House was a den of infamous beings, that's what they called it. I used to go there, I used to go there an awful lot."

"You saw spirits there, Mr Harris?"

"Oh Lord help me, no. What I saw was—" His tone softened, seeing Susan's expression. "What I saw was all kinds of trickery, Miss Wright. Like Miss Euphemia does, with the voices. Some was so lunatic you wouldn't believe it."

"Mad people?"

He smiled. "It was mad what they believed they was paying for, in some of them rooms. Learned Pig was one. There was a pig kept in a cellar that was supposed to be able to read and write. And the lady who had her head cut off, every night, every half hour."

"Oh, my word, how awful."

"But you see, Miss Wright, it were a trick. There was two of them, the same, or almost. But see? I almost told you how it was done, and I ain't supposed to."

"Who'd know?"

"Me. Or take the Horned Lady. She was a friend of mine. She wouldn't mind me telling you, she showed me her scars on more than one occasion."

"I'm not sure I think you should be telling me anything about that, Mr Harris, if it's all the same to you."

"She weren't no lady friend! She was a pal, like. Like you and me."

"Are we, Mr Harris?"

"Well, I should hope so, Miss Wright. See, what I'm saying to you is, there ain't no need for you to bother about ghosts, and what have you. It ain't real."

"I'm sure I want to believe you, Mr Harris, but on the other hand, I'm not so sure. It might be nice, in a funny kind of way, to think you could get messages, from the other side."

"But the dead can't talk. Once you're gone, that's it."

"This has turned very gloomy indeed all of a sudden."

"Then we shall talk of it no more, Miss Wright. I shall undertake to divert, delight or charm you in more light-hearted ways."

"Mr Harris! Whatever shall I do with you?"

The bell pinged and bounced on the wall. Susan started, half jumped out of her seat. She gathered the tray of breakfast things and hurried out of the room with it. Fergus gave up the search in the kitchen. He felt very bad. He felt that he needed to lie down, and so he did, right there on the floor. The cold stone was like a balm to the fire that now engulfed him. He hadn't the strength to loosen his shirt; he just let the weight of his head press against the cold floor and waited for Miss Wright. Fergus wasn't sure if she would come in time. He let his mind sink a little further as his temperature raged. Here was something to hang onto. Something real, something that had been good in his life.

London: May, 1858. He'd been at Saville House in Leicester Square, that den of infamous beings which changed like the weather. He'd been there, as usual, to look out for an interesting angle, a new trick to add to his own tired repertoire of regurgitating objects from his stomach at will. Saville House: it could send your head into a spin if you didn't know what to expect. If you wanted, for sixpence, you might watch a lady have her head cut off and suffer no ill effects. You could go to the North Pole in another room, or see a diorama of gold-diggers in California. From dingy corners, ventriloquists would send a whisper into your ear, making you jump half out of your skin. Jugglers were two a penny. Fergus saw living serpents wrapped around a lady's naked body. And another lady whose enormous snake might have swallowed him whole. Its huge body rasped as it moved slowly over her skin and between her thighs. He saw her muscles quiver at the feat of holding the beast up for so long, but she was not at all afraid of it. This was the place where he met many other people who were like him, though he never spoke to any of them. They acknowledged him in the staircase and in the corridors. A nod, a pat on the shoulder, a quiet bustling family of strangers. No one asked Fergus for his money. His size was his ticket in Saville House. He moved unseen through the hall and down the cellar steps to see the learned pig, which seemed to have lost the will even to grunt. Once, he had seen hens' eggs being hatched out in a steam-filled cage in one room up the stairs, while in the adjacent chamber the lady was having her head cut off again. Above the disgusted gasps and muted shrieks he heard singing. Distracted, he had watched the exhausted chick still with its shell stuck to its rear end. It panted heavily. The singing was so light and airy it sounded to him like a nightingale—how he imagined a nightingale would sound. He watched the chick roll onto its side and flex its tiny legs. He didn't wait to see what happened next. He knew it already. The feathers would not dry out in the steam. He walked away from it.

The Horned Lady was having a break. A bright, jade-coloured turban of silk covered the lumps on her forehead where the ivory had been pushed in under her skin.

"Hello, my sweetheart," she said from behind her thin cigar.

"Madam, good evening." He bowed low, making her laugh.

"You little ones are a caution." She drew heavily on the cigar and blinked her eyes through the thick smoke. "You're always on the lookout. You lost somebody?"

"Who is that singing?"

"Mysterious Lady. They say she's so flippin' ugly, she'd turn you into stone, so she keeps her face hid—well, she ain't so much ugly as just covered in hair. Sings like a lark, though. As a matter of fact I was meaning to go and have a proper word with her. See if she wanted to pair up. But you know how it is." She took another long draw on her cigar and tapped off the ash, spilling it over her silk gown. "Looks like she's worked her spell on you." She blew smoke over his head and grinned. Her perfect false teeth gleamed in the lamplight. "Go on, I don't mind. Upstairs on the right. Now, I'll have to get this off my head and earn the rent."

It was late; almost chucking-out time. Fergus climbed the stairs. Narrow and steeper than the staircase leading up from the hall, they curved as he followed the sound of her singing. There were so many bodies crushed into the small room Fergus couldn't get a peep, but her voice wound over heads and through legs to reach him.

"Look at her shoulders, then. That little lady is hairier than what I am."

"Show us yer face, love."

"Shut up, I'm listening to her singing."

"Show us yer bits then, luvvie."

"It'll no' be a lassie at a', maybe."

The singing went on, unwavering through all the catcalls until the room began to empty a little. Fergus found spaces. He wriggled his way to the front, squashed next to the wall. The singing was pure and light, unchanging. The black veil over her face fell way below her chin. It billowed when she took a breath. The song finished, and she remained in position, with one leg stretched out, toe pointing.

Fergus dawdled his way down the staircase. Saville House was now closed to the public, but there were still plenty of punters milling around in the larger rooms downstairs and the main gallery. The sounds of their voices permeated the rest of the building. Fergus looked through the balustrade on the first-floor landing and surveyed the scene below him through a thick haze of tobacco smoke. One man stood out from the rest. His coat was long, almost touching his unfeasibly shiny shoes, and he stood right next to the main entrance. He looked as if he was waiting for a cab. People less conspicuous pushed past the man now and then, and he was obliged to make way. Every so often he took out a large handkerchief to wipe his top lip. Either he was suffering from the effects of over-dressing for the occasion, or he had smelled something disagreeable. Both seemed likely to Fergus. He couldn't see much of the gentle-man's face behind the upturned collar of that long coat. After a couple of minutes another man approached him on the step. Fergus recognised Miss Jaspur's assistant. The two men exchanged a few words whereupon the gentleman took off, turning on his heel so that the hem of his long coat flared out. As he turned, Fergus could see that the gentleman carried a large leather bag.

"He has come this night, asking for me again, the man down there at the door, the Doctor Scales." Miss Jaspur's voice lisped; Fergus noticed that her breath smelled faintly of aniseed. "Mr Scales wants to interview me. I cannot decide whether to make him wait a few more nights or put him out of his misery tomorrow."

"Would you like my opinion, Miss Jaspur?" He wondered if she had been sucking on a bon-bon, or drinking that French stuff—what was it called?

"It would do no harm."

"Make him wait, Miss Jaspur, for a week. If he's a genuine type, then he won't give up. Whereas if he is looking for a quick—if his intentions are less than genuine, he'll move on sure enough."

"Well, I should think his intention is genuine; that is not the question."

Perhaps she had been drinking after all and had suddenly grown tired of the charade. Only a few people now were left to be shepherded out of the building.

"If you have far to go, I should be happy to take you in my cab. It is waiting for me."

"But you barely know me, Miss Jaspur."

Her throaty laugh rang out too loudly. "I don't suppose you will prove troublesome, will you?"

"Wouldn't want to put you to any trouble. I ain't got far to go. Only just a couple of streets."

"Forgive me, but you are not a very tall man, and at this time of night there are all kinds of unmentionable, horrid people out there. Come." And she slipped her arm through his. Fergus was swept away down the wide staircase amidst the flurry of Miss Jaspur's rustling cape, her forearm jammed up inside his armpit.

"You'll tell me everything he says, Susan."

"Yes, ma'am."

Euphemia sat up with a posture of renewed force, "Everything; I won't stand for any mishaps with your memory, Susan. None."

"No, ma'am."

Susan told Euphemia about Saville House, but not the part about the trickery. Euphemia sat back a little and waited for her to finish. Eventually, Euphemia sighed with impatience.

"Yes, I know all about Mr Harris' low beginnings, Susan. Did he tell you nothing else?"

Susan said that no, there was nothing else Mr Harris had told her.

When Susan went back into the kitchen she didn't see Fergus on the floor. She thought he had gone off to create another bit of chaos elsewhere in the house, and she cursed him silently for leaving all that mess on the table. He'd had long enough to clean it up. Miss Euphemia had kept her back for an hour. Everything covered in a shower of flour. She began to clear it up. When she moved to the sink she tripped, and the armful of crockery she carried flew into the air as if time had stopped. Later, she didn't think that she could remember the sound of the breaking things all around her. In the instant before they hit the ground, Susan Wright turned her head just a few degrees and saw that she had tripped over Mr Harris. He was gone.

Chapter XX

September, 1860.

In the last moments of daylight, Gwen wrote hastily.

September 27, 1860.

Dear Effie,

I feel no compunction in my leaving, as I think it would do more good for me to do so. You must see now that your efforts to thwart my plans will go no further—stealing and hiding my correspondences from Mr Scales will not help you at all in whatever scheme you may have devised. But I will not admonish you further.

On a purely practical note, I suggest that you take on another servant. I cannot say more, Effie, as I write in haste, other than to say that as your sister I have to forgive you, as I hope you will be able to forgive me. I remain, forever, your loving sister,

Gwen.

The tide had long since begun its climb up towards the place where she sat when Gwen heard Edward's approach over the pebbles. In the last of the gloaming she had stared intently at the place he would appear from, and regretted not asking him to come earlier. The failing light played tricks, and once or twice she had started, thinking that a shadow among the rocks was his human form. Now it was unmistakably him.

He greeted her and wanted to hold her, but she asked him to

stand still. Suddenly, she was breathless. She didn't want him to understand her surprise until he could see it. She didn't want to let him anticipate what she was about to do. The waves lapped gently, hardly making a ripple as they hit the shore. Gwen could not have hoped for better conditions.

"Are you ready?"

"Yes, though I hardly know what it is I should be ready for."

"Close your eyes."

"But it is dark."

"Close them in any case. Do it for me."

"Will you tell me when to open them?"

"Count to ten very slowly, facing the water, then open your eyes again."

Edward began to count too fast. She flung off the coat she had been keeping wrapped about her and ran into the water. She let out a gasp as the chill touched her thighs but she plunged on further into the water up to her shoulders.

"Gwen! My God, what has happened?" He had run to the water's edge.

"Be calm, Edward. Look at the water. Look at me." She ducked her head under and resurfaced, beginning to swim back to the shore. The pinprick sparks of unearthly light, grouping in thousands, flaring in the water around her body like waterborne fireflies had silenced Edward in his cry of panic. Gwen thrashed the water and lunged, throwing up armfuls. "Can you see it, Edward. Do you see?"

"Yes," he said. "I am dumbstruck. I have never seen anything like it in my entire life. You have brought the heavens down into the water. There are entire constellations falling from you. You are lit up, like a miracle, like Venus."

"Take off your clothes, Edward."

"What? Oh, no. I couldn't."

"Yes. Take them off, come into the water."

"But the vision of you is so lovely. I don't want to spoil it."

"Rubbish. Come in!"

But he would not be persuaded. Gwen swam out in the dark, where the water was colder and where the lights no longer burst so readily about her. It gave her a thrill to be utterly suspended in the dark water, with the dark night above her. She turned on her back and looked up at the stars coming out in the sky, then, suddenly too cold, she began to swim hard, back towards Edward. The eerie, bluish lights in the water began to stream into life about her again as she neared the shore, and as she stood up, her legs weak, gravity pushing her down, she laughed as Edward caught her in his arms, wrapping his own coat about her, pulling her into his warmth.

"I have a towel, Edward. There is no need to make your clothes wet."

"Look, the light is still falling from you, from your hair and, my God, it is truly astonishing."

He cannot swim, she thought. That is why he wouldn't come in, why he did not rush into the water after me.

Part II

Chapter XXI

October, 1860.

Gwen leaned on the rail of the ship and held her head over the water, the spray stinging her eyes. She tried to imagine what it would be like to lean over a fraction more and then more—and then she tightened her grip. What was she thinking? That she had come unprepared for the boredom as well as the enervating effects of excitement. And where was her travelling companion? She saw him once or twice a day gripping the rail of the ship with a grim face, and the desperate character of him got on her nerves. That he was so sick at sea seemed such a miserable outcome. His greenish pallor had settled after a week to a general debilitation and waxiness. It was not fair. The bilious nausea she felt herself on waking was soon dispelled by rising and taking exercise on deck. When the captain asked after Edward at the dinner table in his scruffy quarters the compulsion to ridicule Edward almost overtook her sense of loyalty towards him. She looked down at the stained tablecloth and tried to make herself remember how much she had felt about him that had been revelatory in a very different way. Her recollections made her blush at the table, so that the captain imagined that his conversation was too much, and became solicitous, which made her agony even worse. Trapped in the conversation she wished herself outside. Outside she dreaded seeing Edward being ill over the side of the boat, the force of his vomiting not strong enough to get past the updraft, sending his expulsions back up to his face. This had happened only once; but it was the way she pictured him now at every hour of the day. It wasn't fair.

If she had been his wife she would have asked the captain for advice; or she may have felt obliged to stay at his side. She did neither.

Under her blankets at night the press of the vast water bothered her sleep. The groans of the ship, and the activity of the men who marshalled the wind to her sails and got her across the unimaginable depths swam with her jumbled memories. She went in and out of sleep each hour, and once she thought that Edward had come into the tiny room. She thought that he had heard her muttered misgivings, but she couldn't face him and turned her back to the cramped space and buried her face in her hammock. When she next saw Edward he seemed slightly better. He met her in the sunshine and blustered out something, but she misheard, or thought that she did, and so they tried to talk until the embarrassment of having nothing new to say to each other was overtaken by Edward's embarrassment at having to excuse himself.

When they arrived in New York and spent the day and night there together, Gwen's spirit was repaired by Edward's brief recovery. For the rest of the voyage she tried to hold on to the memory of those hours. But having to dine alone at the captain's table every evening did test her.

Swithin knew he was ugly. This woman was lonely, and he liked to see her smile. Her husband was in a bad way. Swithin couldn't get much of a hold on his character. You couldn't tell a man's character from the way he wrote a letter or through the woman he chose. There were moments when Swithin almost became jealous of the fact that this pair were newly wed. But this eased off, and his sympathy for Gwen came back again.

★   ★   ★

Gwen had spent as much time on deck, away from her own cramped quarters, as possible. One hour into the voyage she had begun writing in her journal.

This barque is primarily a vessel for goods, for things; & I think that I am but a very small thing amongst the boxes in this makeshift cabin. Despite staring out to sea for much of my life, the fact of its vastness had somehow, somewhere slipped from my imagination: now I am surrounded by this ever moving, ever changing & never changing grey swell of fathomless water, without the security of a rock at my back. The wind, a different animal out here, tugs from all sides—and I had never imagined how swift the shift in temperature might be. A penetrating salty chill to the air, even on a day so warm on land—Land & the people upon it seemed so insignificant & small very rapidly as we drew away from everything solid & still. The elements rush us all along on this unknowable voyage. Level with the Manacles & I spent a quiet moment in contemplation and prayer, strangely wordless, but more prayer than I have ever made, for the souls, past & future whose lives were & are yet to be lost there. Past the rolling breakers, crashing over the hidden treachery, I could not turn to look at the last view of our small river; instead determining my gaze on the horizon I saw a host of white gannets plummet one after another into the waves at tremendous speeds. Our course altered very slightly & as we neared the birds, the glistening bodies of dolphins broke the surface all around us, leapt along the rolling push, & I am sure I could spy as much joy in their dark eyes as there must have been in mine . . .

Edward read this passage two days after it had been written. Looking for Gwen one morning, and finding her little space empty, he'd

put his hand into the neatly folded blankets in her hammock.
Perhaps, he told himself, to feel some of the warmth her body
might have left behind. His fingers discovered her journal and
closed in around the newness of the leather binding. How could
he help himself from opening it? He'd only wanted to see some
part of her. And so it was in that cramped space he had first seen
that Gwen was happy to find a substitute.

And now at the end of this journey he watched Gwen with
the captain. He was tutoring her on the correct way to use a
telescope. Edward watched how Gwen covered one eye with her
hand and gave the captain her full attention.

"The city of Pará is seventy miles up the river of the same
name," The captain spoke with his face close to her ear—he brushed
Gwen's elbow. "Although, as you will have noticed, there is still
plenty of wind to carry us along." Edward thought of moist breath
on her earlobe: the captain's, then his own.

"Then where is the Amazon river, Captain?"

"In the simplest terms the Amazon proper is two hundred miles,
or sixty Spanish leagues from here."

She fingered the leather pouch at her neck and appeared agitated.
Perhaps, thought Edward, she is recalling the scene she had imagined waiting at her destination as described to her by Swithin.
Faced with the enormity of scale, he felt painfully aware of the
smallness of the life she wanted to discard.

"The largest river in the world," Edward forced a cheerful note.
He grasped the rails, inhaling deeply and leaning back, trusting his
weight. "Good morning, Swithin."

"A good morning to you, sir. I trust this day finds you well?"

Gwen murmured a greeting and did not look at Edward as he
stood beside her.

"Perfectly, thank you." Edward's hand slid along the rail and as
he clasped her hand briefly, he noticed the appalling state of her

kid gloves; they were stained with salty watermarks, smudges of dark stuff and paint. He suddenly felt that he should have thought of something as simple as gloves. He'd only thought of getting her enough good paper. And then, in New York, trinkets; he couldn't remember what. He'd never thought of the look of her hands, only of what they might give him.

Now that they were beyond the reaches of the open sea, Edward felt his nausea vanish. It was strange to be beside her on deck again. It had felt as though they had made the journey across the Atlantic on different boats.

"You must excuse me, madam. I will leave you in the capable hands of Mr Scales."

"Your telescope, Captain." Gwen offered it back, but Swithin put up his hand, glancing quickly away and then back to her. Edward noticed how the captain's gaze flitted back and forth, landing on anything except her face. Edward revelled for a moment in Swithin's discomfort.

"I have another; don't be concerned. In any case, this part of the river contains no surprises which may be detected by telescope. Besides, that kind of event is to be avoided, I should hope, by the skill of our pilot there."

Edward caught her eye and saw the look on her face. He saw the satisfaction in Gwen as she breathed in the knowledge that land was not an impossible distance from her.

The wind dropped slightly for a moment, and Gwen shut the telescope. She opened the small bag at her feet, putting the telescope in there for safekeeping, and took out her paint-box, brushes and sketchbooks. She sat on a coil of rope and began to make a sketch of Edward's profile as he leaned on the rail. He let her think that he was oblivious to her endeavours, but he noticed how awkwardly she sat.

Captain Swithin approached them again to tell them that the

Opal must wait awhile as the customs officer cleared it for docking. Gwen stopped drawing Edward and held the telescope out to Swithin, but he declined again, saying, "Please, I would like you to keep the glass."

"I couldn't possibly steal a piece of equipment from you, Captain."

"Please," Swithin insisted. "A memento of your first voyage across the Atlantic."

"Jolly decent of you, Captain," Edward said. "A most essential piece of equipment, indeed. I'm sure it will prove very useful."

Gwen flushed. "Thank you, Captain. I hope you realise that I will have developed a squint by the time you make your return."

"That may well be; but I tend to think—and you may agree—that one should always have an alternative view at one's disposal."

Chapter XXII

Pará, Brazil. Late October, 1860.

Just look at him. Seeing Edward prancing about among the crates being landed was something of a shock. It was a wild, bare-headed, leggy kind of dance under the flattening sun. All trace of his debilitating aversion to open water was miraculously vanished. Only the spikiness of his frame, his bony wrists, jittery as a cranefly, gesticulating at everything and nothing, spoke of his month-long ordeal on the Atlantic Ocean between Cornwall and here.

Gwen thought, Great men, great thinkers, have suffered the same; and look at him, he's well again now.

Edward grimaced against the glare and picked his teeth with a long fingernail. Gwen turned away. The telescope in her hands slipped. Her palms were slick against the warm metal; its topmost section came to a slithery halt as she tightened her fist and sat down on one of the crates.

It was a vast array of collecting equipment—Edward's announcement of his unfailing enthusiasm and faith in himself and everything he turned his hand to. She remembered the list, four columns deep and two pages long. Inside the crates were Wardian boxes, elegant insect frames and cabinets, glass jars of all different dimensions. Gallons of formalin. New books.

But Edward's optimism was infectious, too. And as she watched him again, the pale hair flaming from his scalp, she remembered the lick of fire in her bowels and gut. She stood, feeling her petticoats clinging to her sweating thighs. Someone, a man, came up to her.

"Grindlock," he said. "Consignee of the *Opal*." Mr Grindlock grasped her hand as if she were a man and pumped her arm. Grinning like a lunatic, he let go of her. Oh, God, let him not be a lunatic, she thought.

"Mr Scales!" Mr Grindlock lurched towards Edward and clapped him on the back. Edward flinched in pain.

Gwen said, "Mr Grindlock, I was about to buy some oranges, I wonder—"

"No need to waste your money, good lady. There are fruit trees aplenty at my humble abode. You may pluck as many oranges as you fancy." He ushered them away from the quayside up to his townhouse, talking all the time about how wonderful it was to see them. "My home is, of course, at your disposal. Consider yourselves most welcome whilst we look for something suitable in the suburbs—it being more convenient, I'm sure you'll come to agree, for your collectings. Do you have a particular area of interest, Mr Scales?"

They followed Mr Grindlock and tried to keep pace with his banter. She felt her underwear becoming soaked with sweat and then, by degrees, the rest of her clothes. Struggling to keep up, she bumped her parasol against several people; one of them was a priest.

"I beg your pardon, Father." Drips from her forehead ran down between her eyes and off her nose.

"*Senhora*." The priest barely turned. He touched his wide black hat and disappeared.

By the time she entered Mr Grindlock's cool house, every part of her body was running. Her clothes clung and dragged, and she felt as if she was drowning. Edward and Mr Grindlock were both drenched. Their host wiped his square, flattish face vigorously with a large handkerchief and kept the soggy material in his hand. Several children shouting, *"Pai! Pai!"* ran up to Mr Grindlock as they walked in.

"Hettie," Mr Grindlock called into the gloom of the house, over his children's heads, "I have brought two fine young people to keep us entertained."

One of the smaller children tugged on Gwen's sleeve and spoke to her in Portuguese.

"Remember to speak English to our guests, Pippi. It is polite. Now, here is my good wife. Hettie, I have brought Mr Scales, a naturalist, and his lovely wife. Mr Scales wanted to oversee the unloading of all his boxes of equipment, but I've put one or two of my men to the job."

"Another scientist!" Hettie clasped her hands in front of her large bosom. "Mrs Scales, you are the first lady I have heard of to accompany her husband. And I don't blame you. If Mr Grindlock had to travel again, we should all have to go with him."

Hettie's skin was mottled with a blue tint and quite dry. Gwen was conscious that her tendency to stoop was becoming more pronounced. She was a good head taller than Hettie.

"But Mrs Scales is an *artist*, my dear." Grindlock's words echoed off the cold walls. "Very sensible of Mr Scales to bring her along. Keep it all in the family, much the best way. Now, let's see about something to drink. We almost lost Mrs Scales in the market for the sake of an orange but what about some cold tea?"

"Don't worry, Mrs Scales," Hettie said. "It's not as bad as it sounds. We have it weak, with a slice of lemon. I have never acquired the habit of coffee. Mr Grindlock is partial to a cup in the morning, but I find it compounds the heat somewhat."

Hettie took Gwen by the arm and guided her through the hall and into the drawing room. Pippi was still hanging onto Gwen's other sleeve. The house and its people were swallowing her; this unconditional acceptance and the solid ground made her dizzy.

Gwen could not catch what Pippi was saying; the child was asking her something. She smiled down at her, and the girl scampered off.

"Very cooling, you'll find, Mrs Scales," Mr Grindlock said. "Come and make use of the coolest air, over here." Gwen looked up at the ceiling where she saw the contraption. She followed its cords away into a corner where a man sat working rope pedals with his feet.

The children were all over the place; on and off the chairs and up and down off their parents' laps. Mrs Grindlock was doing her best to be firm.

"Mrs Scales will not appreciate it. Take it away."

"But, Mama, I have it on a string."

"A monkey?" Edward asked.

"A spider. They are taking it away. Aren't you?"

"A spider monkey, now that is something I should like to see," Edward said.

"No, no, Mr Scales," Hettie said. "A spider."

"Well, I am interested in all creatures." He walked across to peer over the huddle of children's heads. "Ah, goodness me, quite a monster."

"I think, for the sake of Mrs Scales, these little revelations must come by degrees. Children, I really am going to become quite stern with you. That is better."

But Gwen's attention was still drawn to the fan working away above them all. The man, half obscured by a screen, silently pedalled, as if none of them were in the room with him. Gwen tilted her face upwards and closed her eyes, feeling the currents of air stroking her neck.

Later, while everyone in the house dozed, Gwen was alone in the room where she and Edward were to sleep. Edward was below her in the citrus courtyard, writing. She stepped away from the window. She'd been spying on the way he hunched over the papers perched on his knees, his ink positioned precariously on the tray at his side. She couldn't see anything of his face; he was wearing a straw hat with a wide brim. She could make out the faint, feverish scratching of his pen mingled against the peculiar and penetrating scrapings of insects. The noise of them got into her head and stayed there. Grasshoppers and hearth crickets would be as whisperers now.

There had been a package waiting for her on the cane chair beside the wash-stand. Earlier, when Edward had been in the room very briefly, she'd made a point of not acknowledging it.

"Better than you thought. The arrangements suit us."

She'd gaped as he turned his back and left her alone in the room. She eased off the string and paper.

It was a small, half-bound volume of tan calf and marbled paper with a swirling amber and bronze design flecked with touches of black. Gwen turned it over in her hands, reading the gold lettering on the spine. She ran her finger over the words indented slightly into the surface of the leather: *Eternal Blazon*. She frowned; it wasn't a romantic novel, was it? Sent by her sister as some kind of pathetic joke. It would suit her sense of humour; the carefully blocked name on the packet label which was only half her own, with merely, "Pará, Brazil" as the address. Gwen flicked the pages casually and found them unslit. Holding it away from her body, she read the frontispiece: "Eternal Blazon, or, Confessions of a Nondescript". So, not one of her sister's books after all. Who else? She blanched at the thought of Edward giving her a book with such a title. Whenever he'd given her a book, he'd given it into her hands and watched her face intently for whatever it was that he hoped to see.

Two-thirds of the way down the page there was a line which read "Printed and Bound for the Author, London 1859". Rather strangely, there was no mention of who had provided this service.

Gwen's stomach flipped, and she snapped the book shut. She worried at a tiny flap of sore flesh inside her mouth until she tasted her blood. *Eternal Blazon*—Eternal Truth. She knew it from somewhere, but her wrung-out brain wouldn't let her place it. It'll come, she thought.

Sunlight slashed the room in half, and a small, brown lizard spread its body against the wall and sunned itself. Gwen watched its barely perceptible breaths and dropped the book silently onto the bed to fetch her drawing things. She worked several sketches over the page, making enlarged details of its mottled, nubbly skin, its head and its feet. The lizard moved every now and then, allowing her to make studies of it from different angles. And then, it was gone. Shooting out of her sight, along the wall and over the edge of the window frame as quick as a bird. Gwen tidied up the sketches, adding areas of shading, giving more weight and substance to the creature. She put her things away and stretched. Hearing someone's footfall outside the room Gwen shoved *Eternal Blazon* along with its packaging into her sketching bag.

The girl with the pet spider—Pippi, was it? —came into the room, and Gwen scanned the floor around the girl's feet in case the spider had come in with her.

"Shouldn't you be resting?" Gwen didn't feel comfortable alone with the girl; she didn't really know how to speak to her, or what to say. The girl shrugged her shoulders and jumped onto the bed. Gwen watched as Pippi sprawled on the covers, rumpling them, and then pulled herself to the edge, hung her head over, arms falling down by her ears.

"I lost Hercules. He likes to hide in dark places." She raised herself up with a solemn look on her face, but then broke into a grin. "Your face is a picture." She laughed. "You're scared of spiders. Most people from home are scared of spiders."

"But you have an affinity with them."

"What's that?"

"You like them, as a friend."

"Almost."

Gwen relaxed a bit and sat down on the cane chair. "Almost. Then why do you keep the spider?"

"To watch it."

"And how do you watch it?"

The girl narrowed her eyes and frowned. "Like this." She put her elbows on the bed and supported her chin in her hands and opened her eyes wide.

"I see. I like to watch things, too. In fact, I was watching a little brown lizard a few moments ago. Here." Gwen pulled the sketch-book out of her bag and flicked the pages to the right place. She held the book out for the girl to see.

"Gecko."

"Is that its name?"

"Yes. You shouldn't keep your things in bags like that. Hercules might crawl in. It needs to have a tight string or lots of buttons. Hercules can do this . . ." She made her hand into a tarantula and lifted the edge of the bed clothes before making her hand crawl under the sheet.

Gwen's body jerked quickly, in a shudder of revulsion. "And what would be your advice, if I should meet Hercules, or one of his kind inside my bag?"

"Don't squash him."

"And after I haven't squashed him?"

The girl rolled over and stared hard at Gwen. "Find someone who isn't scared of spiders."

Chapter XXIII

Edward wrote in his small pocket diary by the light of a single candle, so as not to disturb Gwen's sleep.

The relief of being finally on dry land again, for both of us, is unquestionable. This evening I felt it as a palpable entity. The landing of all my equipment will take a few days at least, as the ship is anchored some distance from the port due to the fast currents and the silting bottom of the river. The landing stages seem hardly fit for the purpose they were made, but I must trust to those with greater knowledge and experience in these matters for the time being. Meanwhile, we are commodiously accommodated by Grindlock, merchant of cocoa and other such goods. His family and house being large and almost as riotous as the auditory assault emitted constantly from a plethora of faunae so new and alien to us. That is, the house does seem to have its own character, if that is possible. Everything about the place excites me. My brain is overloaded with senses, questions, possibilities, desires. I wish I could say the same for my ~~concubina~~ companion. I would not have imagined her to be so beset by an apparent misery. Perhaps it is merely the heat and humidity—it can be a shock if one has never experienced it before. However, a niggling doubt creeps, and I suspect that it is more deep-seated than that. On arrival, we were introduced to the entire retinue of the Grindlock household including giant forest spiders, and a small monkey which bit Grindlock on the hand (he made very light of it saying that the creature has never liked him). Also the servants. I did wonder that the lady of the house did not discreetly offer my companion a chance to freshen herself. We were fairly dripping with sweat from head to foot. We drank some cold tea, which I gathered was offered quite genuinely in place of a bowl of water and towel. Gwen hardly touched her tea. She kept looking up at the ceiling fan with quite an addled expression and stared at the negro fellow operating it for so long that I thought she would draw attention to herself. I made a buffoon of myself with the children, and so Gwen was for the most part left alone. There was an absolute downpour after a light lunch of cold ham. Some of the children ran out during the rain into the courtyard where there are growing several different kinds of citrus. The Grindlocks indulge their progeny somewhat. Gwen ate two oranges and a few other fruits which we do not see in England, their skins quite deformed with uneven knobbles, their colour quite unappetising. Her mood was lightened a little, I think, watching the children getting drenched, and she was more the person I left England with for those few moments. But on our ramble about the town (escaping the Grindlocks' offers of attendance with good grace), the mood darkened again. I did my utmost to cheer her spirits. I fear I annoyed her a little, or perhaps a lot. It is so difficult to know how to behave with her. ~~Sometimes I think perhaps I made a mistake.~~ There are certain fundamental aspects of her character ~~which I know nothing about.~~ The attraction of this state of affairs is no longer a sufficient basis for our project here. Coaxing her along the crowded streets was almost akin to cajoling a reluctant and grumpy child. It occurred to me this afternoon that I have no firm idea of how old she is. This thought kept me preoccupied for such a length of time that I did not notice when she fainted at my feet on a street none too salubrious, to say the least. Some of the natives living in the hovels there procured a cart and we arrived back at the Grindlocks' abode amidst much fuss (to the apparent amusement of all the small Grindlocks). Thank God, none but servants were there to greet us. We have managed to pass it off as an adventure, citing sore feet, which, I believe was not untrue. When she took off her boots, Gwen's feet did seem to be in a hideous state, and I have put cushions underneath them as she sleeps to drain the fluid. It would seem to work.

Now, I am concerned for her. Gwen has never been the type to faint; she even said so herself. She tried to dismiss it as a reaction to the heat, but the heat had passed; the air was much fresher after the rain.

Swollen feet and fainting do not bode well though; am I to have to search for another assistant before we have even begun? Perhaps it will not come to that.

Edward snuffed out the light with spit on his fingers and, having no blotting paper, waited for the ink to dry in the dark, listening, for the first time, to Gwen's breathing as she slept.

Chapter XXIV

Apart from a limited and limiting wardrobe, Gwen had brought with her two sets of watercolour paints, several good brushes of different sizes, leather-bound journals of good paper to paint in bought by Edward in London, as well as her smaller sketchbooks, and her most treasured possession, her microscope. Edward was convinced that the end result would bring some reward. There were already some studies: good likenesses of Edward reading on the boat—on the rare occasions when he had not felt ill, and there were a couple of impressions of Pará, done before the lighter had been ready to take them.

However, she felt no inclination to begin work right away. The idea of kudos did not greatly concern or excite her. She was perplexed by her own reaction to having arrived, which was so different to Edward's. She was aware of a vagueness, as if she saw everything through a mist. I am suffering from apathy, she thought. It puzzled her.

Mr Grindlock had found them a *casinha*, a little wooden house in the suburbs. Finally inside it, with her things around her again, Gwen wanted immediately to lie down. It had been a very strange experience, that first night in the Grindlock guest-room, where being suspended was forsaken in favour of more solid furniture. The enormous bed had allowed her to sleep, eventually, without having to touch Edward. In the dark of the room with only a light coverlet over their bodies, she'd sensed Edward's heartbeat: it had reverberated softly through the mattress. Being flat on her back had not dispelled the sensation that her body was still at sea. As he'd fallen asleep

Edward had begun to snore. Gwen had sighed loudly and plumped her pillows vigorously, banishing all thoughts of eerily articulated and oversized arachnids roaming free of restraining tethers. Even so, she hadn't slept well after the first night. Bad dreams had woken her, the details hazy but still disturbing as they persisted, festering in the hot, damp space between Edward's body and hers in the foreign bed. She had seemed to keep her sister company all night.

A verandah encircled the whole building of four rooms under wide eaves. Here, as the cookhouse was not yet ready for use, Gwen found Maria. She was already boiling water for tea on a small stove.

Gwen thought she would like this woman. She was glad that Maria had none of the deferential habits of Susan in Cornwall. If anything she had been relieved to get away from the "Yes, ma'am" and the bobbing Susan insisted on, even though she had been told not to.

Bearing the tea tray in front of her Maria said, "There are people in the town who could build a bed quickly."

"I'm not sure if our budget extends to large pieces of furniture," said Gwen; a proper bed was too much of an extravagance, and she didn't know whether she preferred the idea of big spiders hiding under her bed-covers or not.

Maria poured the tea and flicked the leaves from the strainer out over the verandah palings. "Wouldn't cost much." She poured two more cups of tea, drinking one before Edward left his unpacking and came out to join Gwen.

"Mrs Scales," she said, before Edward was within earshot, "I know how you Europeans like to have your babies."

Gwen laughed. "We are certainly not planning to start a family here, Maria. We have work to do. And, in any case, a bed would take up far too much space."

Maria looked her up and down, and said nothing.

No, Gwen definitely didn't want to share a bed with Edward. A bed was far too much like a statement of subservience, somehow. Gwen still felt uneasy about her status. She felt that she had to find her own way of existing in this set-up. It was a game, after all, what they were doing. Some of the rules had been foisted upon her, but the rest were unwritten, unspoken, unknown. She could pretend that she was his wife, but she didn't think it was necessary to have her sleep disturbed at quite such close range.

In the night, Gwen was woken by a thump from Edward's study and a faint trickle as he relieved himself over the edge of the verandah. She listened to geckos moving across the walls, and tucked her muslin net in about her more securely. The strange lizards were a delight to her; it was the large hairy spiders, whose nests she had seen under the eaves, which bothered her. Knowing that the ones living under the eaves were now secured in labelled specimen jars did not help. Edward, still unfailingly exuberant, had enthused about the proximity of nature in all its variation. And where a vacancy existed, she had reasoned, it would immediately be filled.

"Such a small creature," he had said, and laughed.

"I would say it was anything but small."

"It's smaller than you. It isn't poisonous . . . All the best houses in town have them, you know. Think of the Grindlock children."

"I would rather not."

"Well, this one is dead now. You can come out of the mosquito net. Besides, if it fancied biting you its fangs would go right through that muslin. Sorry, that's not at all funny."

"If it wasn't poisonous, then why did you use a pencil to poke it, and not your finger?"

Gwen's skin crawled; she was embarrassed for Edward because he didn't quite know how to behave with her. Standing next to him, looking at the revolting spider, and listening to the rising pitch of his voice, she wondered if he had ever really known how to behave with her. Before settling down to sleep again, Gwen made sure that there was no part of the muslin which touched her; she had already lined the rest of the hammock with a thick blanket. Dear God, she thought, but the rest of her plea was wordless.

Alone and naked in the dark, Edward listened to the sounds of the night. He shifted inside his hammock, aggravated by the image earlier that evening of Gwen with that thing at her neck. It was already very grubby. Like a sickly fetish. She touched it, fiddled with it, could not seem to leave it alone for a minute. Though the temperature had dropped considerably, it was still too hot for his blanket.

He could not help but recall the effect of a similar pressing heat. For much of that indelibly marked, and unseasonably hot week in May 1858, the closed stuffiness of the little rooms kept by Natalia had produced in him a state of lazy and surprising contentment.

God damn that woman. But even as he thought it he retracted it. He could neither resent nor condemn her, only his own stupidity. He got out of the hammock clumsily and went to relieve himself.

Chapter XXV

Carrick House. October 17, 1860.

Euphemia woke at six in the morning and sat up remembering where she had stuffed one of Gwen's letters in a hurry the winter before. Its place in the library was too tantalising to ignore, and in the dark she reached for her dressing gown. While Euphemia lit the lamp in the hall, she heard the barely perceptible clatter of Susan riddling the grate in the kitchen. Holding the light to the bookshelves Euphemia let her fingers run along the spines until they came to the place. She pulled out the thick volume, made very slightly thicker by the papers she had hidden there. Her fingertips lingered for a moment over the broken seal before she pulled the letter from the envelope.

November 13, 1859.

My Dear Gwen,

I have made, already, several different drafts of this letter, which have all found their way to the fire. I feel that I owe it to myself, and, of course, to you, to write this letter to you, and to send it. Please, when you receive it, do not keep it. After you have read it as many times as you need to, please destroy it in the fire. I could not bear to think that the words I am about to put down on this paper should lie in a drawer as a testament to my failings.

I know that I have not behaved properly with you. I know that I have not been the gentleman that I would have wished to have been with you. You were absolutely right to be angry with me. But can you believe me when I say that I am more angry at myself than you could ever be? In time, I hope that I may be proper and chivalrous towards you, as you deserve nothing less. You are the most extraordinary person I have ever met, and I would like you to know that in being my friend and my secret companion you have saved me from a certain kind of madness. Gwen, when I am with you I am whole and unmarked by my past.

You have been so very patient with me and most extraordinarily kind in every way imaginable. You have accommodated me in your splendid grounds without complaint. And the few nights that I have spent with you, when we have come together in the most secret of places, I have been beside myself with joy. I know that it is impossible for you to take pleasure in these particular meetings, but I wish you to know that I am most humbly grateful for them and that I will never embarrass you, as you have requested, by ever mentioning them to you again. They remain, those nights, our most secret and most blessed times.

But I must now speak of my past and indeed of my present. I am husband to a woman called Isobel—but husband in name only, as the marriage is not, has never been, consummated. It is for this reason that I have tormented myself over our friendship. I have omitted to reveal myself in my true colours, and for this I remain deeply ashamed. If you can bear to read it, let me tell you now that preceding our first meeting, I was entangled with another person. A female whose personal attributes I cannot bring myself to describe but for whom I was nevertheless bent on destroying myself. Please be assured that she was nothing compared to you and that my wife is nothing compared to you.

Truly, I feel that I have been saved by you and that you are the one person, the only person whom I should ever be able to call my own. You, and only you, have shown me what it means to be a whole man, unfettered by the ridiculous, stringent constrictions of our society.

If you still feel, after reading this letter, that you are able to allow me to continue to see you, then you must do no more than behave as if you have never received this letter. I hope that you will still accept me, as you have done so far, without judgement. If you will still allow it, let us meet, in darkness, as we have done before when no words have been needed except those which feed my all-consuming desire for you.

I seal this in haste, lest I should again waver over my conviction that I may remain, for ever,

Your Own Edward.

With a shiver of intense and exquisite satisfaction, Euphemia slid the letter back between the pages of the almanac.

Chapter XXVI

Each time he went out with his insect net, Edward seemed to come back with his collecting tin full of specimens he had already collected. For he would take not just a male and female specimen of every possible species, but several, arranging them in rows to show off minute variations in pattern and colour. And then there were those which did not make it into the collection but were discarded for slight lack of lustre or a small section of wing which had been broken off. There was a midden heap under the house outside his room. In varying stages of rapid decomposition, butterflies, spiders, beetles and other small fauna Edward did not wish to transport back to England soon became indistinguishable in a friable mass.

But her painting things stayed untouched; she worried vaguely that the humidity might be bad for them but she did nothing about it. The scents from the flowers in the garden and the undertones of decay were quite overwhelming; in part she blamed it for her inactivity. Sometimes, she would realise that she had been reading the same sentence over and over in a loop which made no sense, the magazine almost dropping from her hand. She felt herself sweating into her clothes and waiting for Edward to come back with his tired but joyous step and full of it all. What is wrong with me? she thought. She got up later than usual one morning, and was cross. It is absurd, she thought, that I should be here and not see for myself the walks he tells me about. She spent the rest of the day with the sticky shadow of an ill temper and hardly spoke to Maria.

When Edward came back she jumped up. "At last," she said.

Edward frowned, and then smiled. He put down his heavy bags. Bottles inside it clinked. He blew his nose through his fingers onto the ground and then after wiping his fingers on his trousers, he looked at her, holding her out at arm's length by the shoulders. She felt uncomfortable in his gaze, imagining herself as him, coming up to herself through his eyes to see that he hadn't thought of her all day. He never thought of her during any of his rambles. Since they had stepped off the boat he had been on the edge of something approaching ecstatic rapture. Gwen was aware that her eyes were staring and wide, and she bit her lip. Edward put his hand to her chin, and he squinted at her mouth where mango fibres were trapped between her top front teeth. "Has something happened?"

"No, no, nothing, nothing at all." She disengaged her chin from his fingers. "I should really like to come out with you tomorrow."

"What about your feet? Hmn? I thought we agreed that you should keep those ankles up."

She shrugged off his hands but she recovered her attitude, slipping her arm through his. "I'm not suggesting that I should be out with you all day. Perhaps a short walk." Do not treat me like an imbecile, she thought.

"Well, I had rather imagined that you would like to make a start on some of the specimens I have collected so far. But I can see that you are restless. It's understandable, of course. Nothing too taxing."

Gwen struggled to hammer down her frustration and fury as they went into the house.

Edward chatted for the entire ramble the next day. They had agreed that they would go out early, before breakfast. This is not what I had meant, she thought, as she listened to his incessant commentary. From the humidity (which she was already familiar with), to the height of the trees (which she could see for herself), to the insects in the leaf litter under their feet. Edward filled the air with his voice. They stopped once or twice, and she dutifully craned her neck to admire the height of the canopy. Edward took out his pocket knife and gouged into the side of a fallen tree to show her a beetle grub.

"See how its fat body writhes so slowly in my hand, Gwen. It would have stayed inside this rotting log for years, perhaps, before finally pupating. It's one of the longhorn beetles. I'll find one for you." My God, she wanted to say, I know a beetle larva when I see one. Who on earth do you imagine you are talking to?

She tried to hear the forest around them under the sound of his voice. It seemed incredible that a man who had not even known the Cardinal beetle in his own country should now be telling her about exotic Coleoptera. The morning chorus had calmed some time ago, but around them here and there were isolated bird calls and the ever present hum of insect life in the air. Gwen played a game with herself. How many things could she spot before Edward pointed them out to her. She knew other people used these paths. There were villages deeper into the forest, though what she regarded then as deep forest would be as nothing by the time she would have finally left Brazil. It would not be unusual to meet someone, even though they had not, so far. I am being silly, she told herself. But the sensation that she was being observed, like the squirming fat larva in Edward's hand, would not leave her. She watched, rather repulsed, as Edward put the larva into a small vial of preservative and straight into his collecting bag; its final moments dismissed to the dark pocket of red leather.

She could not believe what he was doing, treating her like some silly young girl out for a walk in the park, pointing out the greenness of the grass or the song of a blackbird. How could this be

the same man she had wanted to spend all her days with? She
wondered what it would take to have been able to make him
understand her desire to see everything around her in the same
state of awe that he had enjoyed. His being able to name some of
the flora and fauna was a clever kind of trick, but she couldn't see
that it served any particular kind of usefulness to his understanding
of the place. The flora specimens they took were identified, housed
and despatched to England in the Wardian cases. The butterflies
not for his own collection were wrapped in triangles of paper and
sent off to be set by others and placed in private collections. No,
she thought, in naming these things, in speaking their names, he
is claiming them. As they stood on the high ground and looked
down into a swampy hollow filled with huge arums she tried and
failed not to mind as Edward's tremulous voice told her that they
were standing under a Cassia tree. A surge of desire rushed down
through her legs, but it was undirected and confusing. It was not
Edward she desired. The heat prickled her neck and back, and her
head felt hot in irritation. She grasped his arm, and he patted her
hand saying, "Time to go back? Better not overdo it."

She clenched her teeth and watched where she trod, and noticed
little more than the mango trees lining the road. The feeling that
she was being watched disappeared slowly. Perhaps it was just a
monkey, or some animal like that.

After a couple of days, Gwen followed the road again away from
the direction of town. She went alone, taking herself into the
nearest edges of the forest. She did not tell Edward about her plans.
She told Maria that she was off for a little stroll, that she would
not be long. A rush of excitement came over her, and as she turned
off onto a path leading into the forest itself, butterflies danced in
the patches of sunlight around her.

Now the light changed; a diffused green was cast over everything. She dared to look up into the canopy. She was at the bottom of a pond and she reeled. Her bowels fluttered. She bent over and took deep breaths, and stared blinking into the shadows, which somehow contrived to surge before her eyes. The white tips of wings danced in and out of the islands of shade, the rest of the insects virtually invisible to her unpractised eye. They never went very high. It was, she thought, as if they were pretending to be moths. Upside down, some rested beneath wide, waxy leaves and she put out her finger, almost touching their closed wings before they took off again to settle out of reach. She retraced her steps back onto the sunnier main path through the forest and was mesmerised by the sight of several different blue Morphos. There was a very leisurely, luxuriant pattern to their flight; the way they seemed to know where the warm air would facilitate their desire most effectively. They would twist, mid-glide, like a seagull. No wonder Edward came back so frustrated sometimes. The changing hues of iridescent blue flashed in the sunlight as if they were taunting her. It was lovely to see these things in their proper context, and she was more than sorry for the burgeoning collection of butterflies in the wooden cases. And yet she wanted to hold one, to see it as closely, she thought, as the Creator in that moment of inspiration. And then she checked herself, remembering Darwin's theory. Her feelings and thoughts and learning were tangled and knotted, so that she didn't know what she should think or feel, confronted by the magnificence of everything surrounding her. How was it possible to believe and doubt at the same time, to see connection and disconnection in every object. She was completely overwhelmed—and burst into tears.

And now there was that suspicion again that someone was watching her. She had tried to dismiss it as a benign sensation in her brain. But she felt it more in her back; not only out here on the forest path but around the house she felt it sometimes. Some days, it was more acute than others. She could not talk about it. Every time she had felt like saying something about it, there had been the notion that Edward would not take her seriously or think that she was, after all, of flimsy character; a silly female, unable to function satisfactorily in this new environment, suited only to exist on the banks of the Helford in Cornwall. And sometimes she allowed herself to think that this was true. It must not be true, and yet while she was in awe of her surroundings she wanted to escape them. She found herself wishing that she would not have to speak to Edward when he returned. Already his voice grated in her mind and tipped her nerves. I am just his facilitator, she thought. He would not be here without me; no self-respecting man would have agreed to my unequal share in this endeavour. She wondered if this was the real reason she had been reluctant to begin her part of the bargain here.

She unlaced her boots and tossed them into a corner, pulled off her silk stockings and rubbed at her ankles, then she went barefoot through to Edward's room and rummaged in his closet. Maria's voice at her back remonstrated, and Gwen froze, her hands clutching at the waistband of Edward's trousers. "You can't wear a man's clothes, Mrs Scales. I've got a better idea."

Chapter XXVII

THE TIMES, Wednesday, October 3, 1866.

MURDER TRIAL AT THE OLD BAILEY.

MR Probart for the Prosecution addressed the Jury: "The prisoner is a woman, as we shall see, whose enthusiasm for immorality in her younger days persists into the present. Following her ill wonts has led her here: Murder. Gentlemen, why are we never surprised in this city when foul murder is committed by a female of low morals and even lower reputation? Perhaps it is because these two thrive together. Be not deceived by the prisoner's apparent stature, by her—notable—command of language; and nor yet by her insistence of guiltlessness. This, gentlemen, is a wily female cornered, who would stop at nothing to get what she wants."

At this last, Mrs Pemberton leaned forward. "I will have you retract every last slanderous word, sir," before she was reminded by Mr Justice Linden that she must, "internalise her outbursts, however well founded she believed them to be". The Clerk was not asked to strike the prisoner's remarks from his notes, and nor were the members of the Jury advised to ignore them.

In response to the Prosecution's statement, Mr Shanks for the Defence said: "Observers of this case may be forgiven if they have thought, up unto this moment, that what we are trying to set out for examination is a simple case of a lovers' tryst gone horribly, murderously wrong. The murder victim, the late Mr Scales, as you will come to see, treated the prisoner, Mrs Pemberton, with deviousness and subversive intent from the moment he laid eyes on her; this, you will see, is true. He lured her away from her family home, from the security and safety of her known world under false pretences. We know this to be true, for we know that Mr Scales was already a married man, and having no intention of enlightening the young Mrs Pemberton to this fact, allowed her to believe that in travelling with him to Brazil, she would eventually become his wife. It is a familiar tale, but in finding herself unwittingly cast in the tawdry plot, Mrs Pemberton, her passion high, one might assume, would, one might assume, seek revenge at the most convenient time and not, Gentlemen, wait, wait, wait and wait more long years until she was under the gaze of the entire City of London to commit a murder she might so easily have done many years before. Think on it, if you please, Gentlemen. In attempting to untangle the ghastly threads of any murder, one must cast his mind in the role of the perpetrator. A cold and calculated act, from a person as level and as intelligent as the prisoner, Mrs Pemberton—would it result in such an obvious mess? Would she have allowed herself to have no alibi? The obvious answer, of course, is that a woman as level and intelligent as Mrs Pemberton is not the murderous type. The crime, Gentlemen, does not fit the accused, and it does not fit the accused in such an obvious manner that I wonder, like the prisoner herself, and indeed many others, that she was charged with the crime—if there was a crime—at all. Life, real life, is not always as neat as we would like it to be. Mrs Pemberton was unfortunate in her acquaintance with Mr Scales from beginning to end. It seems that, even in death, Mr Scales has contrived to leave his mark upon her. Mrs Pemberton happened to have called upon Mr Scales on the day preceding the night he was, allegedly, murdered. This small fact has cast such aspersions on her—and why?"

Witnesses were then examined before it was stated that the Jury should be taken to see the house where the body of Mr Scales was found.

Chapter XXVIII

Gwen could barely breathe in the only evening gown she had brought with her. It had seemed such a ridiculous thing to pack into her trunk. It dug into her armpits, and her bosom was pressed painfully inside it.

"Mr and Mrs Scales! Marvellous! Hettie will be so pleased that you have been able to come to our little gathering."

"Mr Grindlock, good evening. We could hardly not have come; it was very good of you to invite us." Edward's speech was as stiff as his collar.

"Not at all, it's a pleasure to see you again. How are you finding your feet? Getting the feel of the place yet?"

"Absolutely, yes, absolutely." Edward cast a sideways glance at Gwen and placed his free hand briefly under her elbow. "Collecting's been most productive."

"Mrs Scales!" Hettie's voice floated in a sing-song warble over the room, closely followed by the woman herself, diaphanous and fluttery, in a muslin confection with a silk stole. She beamed into Gwen's face and prised her away from Edward's hands. "Do give Mr Scales a drink, Tristan. Mrs Scales, do come with me, and meet the ladies of our little amateur operatic society," she said, steering her away. Leaning into her she said, "It's such a pity my brother can't be here—I hope he will be with us by Christmas. I'm sure you'll adore him to bits. Tristan," she called over her shoulder, "you did say, didn't you, that Marcus Frome will be coming tonight?"

"Indeed, indeed I did, my dear," he said, "many, many times." He

caught Gwen's eye and gave her half a wink. His wife caught the
tail end of his action, and he hastily poked a finger to his eye to
brush away an invisible fleck. It was misjudged and he injured himself.
Hettie admonished him from across the floor with a hint of a frown.

"Someone for your husband to talk to, my dear girl. Marcus
Frome is a doctor of medicine, poor man. He has been travelling
to the interior, back and forth, back and forth. We could never pin
him down—so committed to his work, you see. Always writing up
his papers. Lost now, of course. Here we are. Ladies, you must make
our newest member very welcome."

They had arrived at the far end of the room, where a gaggle of
pouchy-looking ladies opened their huddle and drew Hettie and
Gwen into the circle.

The names were rattled off like a peculiar mantra, and Gwen
regarded each one in turn with a polite smile.

"What are you, Mrs Scales? Wonderful, to have a 'Mrs Scales' in
our society."

"I paint. I'm an artist."

"Oh, yes, we know all about that," one said with a dismissive
air. "But what are you—contralto, soprano?"

"I'm barely passable, is what I am," said Gwen. "I don't think I
would make a very useful addition—quite apart from my, from our
routine being very rigid. Though it is very kind of you, of course.
I am very flattered."

"Oh, but all the ladies from home are in our society, Mrs Scales."

"I'm sure I—"

"Marcus Frome has arrived at long last, the dear soul!" Hettie
exclaimed and clapped her hands. "Ladies, do let us give him an
impromptu musical welcome."

Gwen did not know where to look. She could sense the hilarity
of the situation unfolding as the gathered ladies began to twitter like
syncopated chickens whilst they decided which piece would be best.

She moved herself a little apart from the group and then, sure that she would not be missed, went back to where Edward stood, still talking to Tristan Grindlock and now the eagerly awaited Mr Frome.

"Is everything all right?" Edward asked.

"Yes, of course."

"Mrs Scales," said Tristan Grindlock, "may I introduce you to Marcus Frome, who is just regaling us with his tale of woe."

Marcus Frome looked to Gwen like a toad. She gave him a pleasant enough smile and let him take her hand and press his lips to her fingers, glad that she had worn the lace cotton gloves after all.

"Enchanting wife, you have, Scales," he said with a wet smile on his lips. "Enchanting."

"Mr Frome," Gwen said, unable to find anything pleasant to say to the man as she felt his saliva soak into her glove and between her fingers.

"Frome, poor chap, was just telling us how he's lost everything in a gale," said Tristan Grindlock.

"Yes, I'm making arrangements for my passage back to Liverpool. Can't get the stuff, see, out here." He rolled on his heels. "Got to hop back and stock up all over."

"How terrible," Gwen managed to say without irony.

"Yes, it's a blow." He turned away from Gwen to address the two men: "Two years' work sunk. Capsized, see? Not enough ballast. I expect you, Scales, I expect you've seen to it that you're properly kitted out?"

"Properly, indeed!" said Tristan Grindlock. "Took a week to land all those crates. Well, near enough anyway, eh, Scales?"

"Entomology? Almost my line."

"Indeed, Mr Frome?" said Gwen, still put out by the saliva which lingered on her glove.

"Yes, Mrs Scales," he said, very deliberately turning to address her, but finding that he had to look straight into her eyes, lowering his gaze to her bust and addressing her there. "Mosquitoes." He turned away again to speak to the men.

"Mr Frome!" Hettie floated herself up to him. "Do forgive us, we are ready now." Quite unselfconsciously, Hettie Grindlock took his hand and pulled him to a sofa where she made him sit down. Ranged in front of him now were the ladies, some of them breathing too rapidly to be able to sing effectively. Gwen thought, I do hope this turns out to be truly dreadful; he certainly deserves a good blast of bad notes.

Hettie ushered everyone else into seats, and Gwen noticed that all the Grindlock children were now present. Her eyes widened in search of creatures on the ends of strings. There were none.

"A little bit of 'Lucia', we have decided upon, in honour of Marcus Frome, who will soon be leaving for England, and will be very much missed. We give you 'Spargi d'amaro pianto'," Hettie declared.

It was as Gwen had hoped and more so. She revelled in Mr Frome's discomfort and, when it was over, stood up to give her very enthusiastic applause to the ladies. She beamed at them all with genuine smiles of appreciation.

Edward muttered in her ear, "You do know that was a dreadful rendering. A cat, a dead one, could have done better."

"Of course," she said, still smiling. "It was most extraordinary, and I would not have missed it for anything."

"Are you sure you are quite all right?"

Gwen didn't have time to reply; they were called to dinner and spliced to different parts of the table. She was happy to note that Marcus Frome was nowhere near her and that she wouldn't have to speak to him. Gwen was amongst the ladies, who having delivered their masterpiece, now wanted to know all about the young couple. They began to quiz her in earnest. Gwen gave vague replies and picked up her glass of wine.

"French," nodded a woman called Mrs Trisk, whose top notes

had been delightfully grating. "They have it shipped twice a year. Royal stuff, royal." Mrs Trisk gulped at her own glass. Gwen sipped and felt a rush of energy swoop down her arms and rest in her elbows. My God, she thought, I'm absolutely drunk on one mouthful. Her plate of meat and fruit danced on the table, and she gripped the edge of her chair with her free hand. She took another sip and the same rush powered its way to her elbows, but she steadied and let go of the chair.

"Eloquent, isn't it?" said Mrs Trisk, studying Gwen's reaction.

"Very."

"So, do tell me again, your family are Cornish?"

Gwen sliced at a bit of meat.

"Why, that's extraordinary good luck!" Everyone at the table stopped talking or eating to look up and direct their attention to Marcus Frome who had just shouted the words out and was standing up to lean over the table and shake Edward by the hand. He pumped his arm as though he would never stop.

"Mrs Scales, you were saying?"

The noise of resumed conversations rose to fill the air again, and Gwen couldn't catch what Edward had said in reply to Mr Frome's outburst.

"My family? My family is my sister." Gwen did not want to get further drawn into the conversation.

"And she is married, too?"

"No, she is not. What do you know about Mr Frome?" Gwen looked past Mrs Trisk towards Edward and strained to hear how his conversation was developing. His words were muffled, but Mr Frome's were not.

"Absolutely, my dear fellow! One cannot allow these matters to flourish. In my opinion—"

"Not married?" Mrs Trisk engaged her again. "How on earth does she live?"

"Quite well, as a matter of fact. What do you make of Mr Frome?"

"Oh? Ah. I am sure I am not as well acquainted with Mr Frome as our dear Mrs Grindlock."

"But why do you think he must go back to England, when, surely, all he needs to do is send for whatever he requires?"

"But, my dear Mrs Scales, the man lost everything, everything, you understand. He had not even a full set of clothing on his back when he was rescued, you see."

Gwen pushed the food around her plate, slicing it up into ever smaller and smaller pieces until it resembled something indescribably horrid. She stabbed a flake of meat and put it into her mouth.

"Can't let them loose amongst such dangerous subjects," Mr Frome said, and Gwen tried to hear the rest. "Consequences dire, I may assure you."

"Is he married, Mr Frome?" she asked Mrs Trisk, "Is he perhaps returning to see loved ones?" The very idea struck her as unimaginable.

Mrs Trisk tucked her chin into her neck and tried to sip her wine. "I think he is a confirmed bachelor, Mrs Scales."

"Really. How interesting."

Later during the meal, Gwen heard Edward's voice raised. He was being too loud because of the wine. She heard him say, "Of course, the country offers a vast opportunity, as you yourself are aware, Frome, to make one's mark, to secure one's place in the annals of history and scientific endeavour. And, in entomology, especially so."

"And what of the opportunities of the land itself, eh, Scales? What do you make of the fertility of the place?"

"Obviously, the verdant nature of the forest points to all kinds of opportunities, indeed it is so. If one were to cultivate the land in the civilised way—"

Gwen listened to Edward's talk with a growing sense of disbe-lief. Everything they had talked about before they had come here was being flayed. Knowledge for its own sake, not kudos; the value of pristine nature and its role in the search for that truth which was as yet incomplete. In her bleary, tipsy state she saw Edward in a moment of intense clarity, and she hated it. She blanched and then felt suffocated as the talk went on. Edward's voice pitched over the clusters of babble going on around the table.

"From what I have seen so far," Edward was now saying, "the local way of cultivation is very primitive. These fellows don't seem to take much pride in their kitchen gardens; weeds choking things, nothing in any discernible order, a hotchpotch. From what I have been able to gather, the attitude is just the tip of the iceberg—"

The evening had to end, and it did, and Gwen was very glad of it. She couldn't wait to get back and take off her clothes, breathe again, eat something, empty her bladder. Stop talking, stop trying to both hear and blot out what the men were saying. To just get away.

"There'll be a slight change to my routine tomorrow," Edward told her as he unfastened her gown, his breath hot on her neck. "I've invited Frome for breakfast. Well, he's invited himself, actually. Nothing I can do about it now, of course. Still. So, formal for breakfast. Apologies." He let his hands fall away from her.

Gwen stood still for a moment, and then without a word went to her hammock and dropped her clothes to the floor, too tired to care about what might crawl into the folds of it all.

In the morning, she chose from between the layers of tissue and mothballs in her trunk a good dark skirt. She struggled to fasten the skirt's topmost hooks and eyes. As long as I don't sit down, she thought. She undid the last four fastenings and tied a sash over the gape, its tail hanging down over her hip. To make up for it, Gwen fixed her hair into the neatest, most severe style she could manage on her own, using every pin and comb she could lay her fingers on.

"You won't mind if I don't wait for Mr Frome," Gwen said as she took up a cup of pale tea and stabbed at the lemon slice with a small fork. "Only, I didn't eat last night."

Edward coughed, and Gwen froze, looking up at him.

"Carry on," was all he said.

Marcus Frome was an hour late. They received him on the verandah where he arrived in a burst of noise. Gwen wondered how anyone could be so consistently obnoxious.

"Capital morning, Scales!" he said. "Capital morning! My God, I've hardly slept a wink all night. I've been revising everything. Up to here I am, up to here," he said, his hand jabbing at the air above his head.

"Good morning, Mr Frome," Gwen said. "May I get you something?"

"Enchanted again. Enchanted." He turned to Edward. "Listen, old chap, I can't tell you how much I appreciate this."

Gwen moved towards Marcus Frome with a cup. "Your coffee, Mr Frome." She put it into his hands so that he had to take it from her or risk scalding himself. Marcus Frome was also forced to acknowledge her. "One gets frightfully jungly," he said, looking her over, "but that's to be expected. Shall we get on with it, then?" Marcus Frome put the cup down untouched and walked off into the house. "Ah yes," he said through his nose, "standard set-up. Though, of course, with me, there were no females to complicate the situation. Through here then, is it?" He busied himself into Edward's workroom and stalked about, surveying the room and its contents, touching things with an offhand flutter of his fingertips.

"It's, er, not exactly. No, not in this room at present," Edward said quietly as he followed him.

"So, let's see the thing then, shall we?" Marcus Frome's eyes widened in impatient expectation.

Gwen stood in the doorway and leaned against the timber with her arms folded. Edward turned to her, his face pale. "Gwen, I wonder, if you would mind very much, if Mr Frome were to have a look at the—at your microscope?"

"I beg your pardon?" Her arms unfolded.

"Microscope, Mrs Scales; not a plaything but an instrument of science."

"I'm fully aware of its function, Mr Frome."

"Let's have it, then, Scales old boy, and I'll see what I think of it and write you out the note."

"Would you mind stepping outside for a moment, Edward? Do excuse us, Mr Frome." Gwen trod heavily to the verandah and turned on Edward. "What is going on? What does the man mean, 'Let's have it'?"

"Gwen, I was meaning to—I would have liked to have had more opportunity to discuss the matter."

"I'd like very much to know what there is to discuss."

"Nothing to discuss, Mrs Scales." Marcus Frome had appeared behind them and picked up the cup of coffee to blow noisily over it, grinning at them. "Scales is selling me his microscope, see. But I can't very well buy the thing if I haven't seen it first."

"Mr Scales doesn't have a microscope to sell," she said, not taking her eyes off Edward.

"Ha! What did I tell you last night, Scales, eh? Got a pair of trousers on under that skirt have you, Mrs Scales?"

"You'll kindly leave at once, Mr Frome." Gwen's voice was level. "Good day to you."

"Sorry, can't do that. See, Scales here made me a promise."

"Mr Frome! You appear to have been labouring under the misapprehension that Mr Scales is at liberty to sell my property without telling me and without my say-so. Allow me to divest you of this misguided notion."

"The modern woman, eh? Well, let me tell you, Mrs Scales, when you made those vows, you relinquished all rights to your property; Mr Scales is your protector and keeper. He has promised me a microscope, and, by golly, I'll have it."

"You are not having my microscope, you impudent toad of a man; get that plain fact into your fat head."

"Gwen," Edward's voice was quiet, "perhaps if we take a moment to discuss the matter—"

"I'll be discussing it no further, Mr Scales."

"For God's sake, Scales! See to it that your obstreperous woman here understands her obligations."

"This man is offensive, Mr Scales; invite him to leave immediately."

"You see, the fact of the matter is this. Frome was in the middle of some very—" Edward's manner was irritatingly calm and reasonable, and it stirred up a turbulent fury just underneath Gwen's breastbone.

"Will you, or will you not, tell this person to leave?"

"He was telling me about his undertaking some research, you see, into malaria, and—"

"Malaria? He said that he was interested in mosquitoes."

"Madam, I most certainly did no such thing. I—"

"Mr Frome, I am not stupid, and I am not a liar. You told me your interests lay in mosquitoes."

"I didn't! I said no such thing at all. I assure you both on my life that I am not interested in mosquitoes and I have no reason to be interested in mosquitoes. I am not an entomologist. I am a medical man; I am a doctor of medicine. It was not mosquitoes, not at all."

Edward and Gwen both regarded Mr Frome with great interest as he gave his fast, stuttering speech on his lack of interest in mosquitoes. Gwen was the first to cut into the silence which followed.

"I believe, Mr Frome, that you are indeed, very, very interested in mosquitoes." She paused, expecting him to deny it further, but his chest heaved as he drew out a grey handkerchief to wipe over his forehead. "And I shall tell you what else I believe, shall I? I think that you lost your last chance in that squall to complete whatever research you were engaged in. I believe, Mr Frome, that you are penniless now, and that in returning to England you will be permanently terminating your secret relationship with the mosquito."

"Preposterous!" A shower of spittle caught the light, but his protest was feeble, and Gwen continued regardless.

"However, hearing that Mr Scales and I had recently arrived in the country, fully equipped for entomologising and so forth, you sought immediately to make our acquaintance with the sole intention of stealing some instruments of science from us. From *me*."

"Absurd woman, your mind is no doubt affected by the humidity, I—"

"You know, Frome, I don't think Gwen's mind is affected by anything at all but good sense. I am inclined to agree with her. It does seem a trifle strange that you have not chosen to resupply yourself with a microscope by the more reasonable, by the more *usual* process of writing off for one to be shipped out here to you."

"Are you to tell me, sir, that you will stand in the way of a major scientific breakthrough? The biggest medical discovery of this century?"

"Well, I suppose, given that I only have your word for it," said

Edward, rather thoughtfully, scratching the back of his head, "it rather looks like I am."

"You what?"

"I concur; I'll not let you have that microscope. You'll be obliged to locate another or return to England."

"There is no other! There is no other microscope in this place that I might have."

"Oh, come now, Mr Frome," Gwen said wearily, sitting down, tired of it all now that Edward was on her side again. "I'm sure there are other, more gullible people in possession of a microscope whom you may yet endeavour to hoodwink."

"No," he spat, "there are not!"

Gwen laughed and kicked off her fancy house slippers, leaning back to put her feet onto a footstool. She wriggled her bare toes.

"Then we must, Mr Scales, declare this breakfast party over and done with. I do hope, Mr Frome, that your return voyage to England is uneventful."

"You sly bitch."

"How dare you!" Edward shouted. "Apologise immediately, sir, or I'll see you."

Gwen sat up, astonished at Edward's swift change in tone and, moreover, dumbfounded that he—had he?

"Edward," she said, standing up and putting a hand lightly on his arm, "I don't think it very wise."

"No, you are quite right," he said, relaxing as Frome backed away clumsily. "He is no gentleman; I'll just fetch my whip."

"Are you threatening me, Scales?"

"Indeed, I am, although I perceive you are something of a coward, and I may not have to act on it."

"You'll regret this, see, you will."

"I doubt it most wholeheartedly."

Gwen and Edward watched as Marcus Frome marched away

from them, turning back every now and then to glance over his shoulder to convey what they supposed were meant to be sneers of contempt. Edward put his arm around Gwen and raised his hand in farewell. As Marcus Frome disappeared from their sight she rounded on him.

"Hypocrite," she said separating from him. "You're as unspeakable as that wretched man."

"It wasn't as it seemed, Gwen. I made no promise of anything."

"Don't make things worse. I am not an idiot."

"I know that."

"Then please do me the honour of not behaving as if you didn't. Furthermore, I wish to make it abundantly clear that my few possessions are mine and mine alone."

"Absolutely; Gwen, please forgive me, I should have given you fair warning."

"And you had ample opportunity; but whatever promise that Frome man thought he had extracted from you last night, you were too much of a weakling to put him right."

"The Bordeaux was very—"

"It was certainly far more 'eloquent' than you. Don't ever let anything like this happen again, Edward, or I shall follow that odious creature back to England."

"You can't possibly mean that."

"Can't I?" she sat down, loosening the sash at her side and breathing out.

There passed some minutes where they would not look at each other. Edward paced up and down the verandah, and Gwen put her slippers back on her feet. She fiddled with them, slipping them half off and on.

Presently, Edward came to a halt. "I have excused your behaviour this morning for two reasons. The first being, as you quite succinctly surmised, Marcus Frome is an odious creature—of the lowest order. The second being that I excuse you on account of your condition."

Gwen's slippers fell to the floor. "I beg your pardon?"

"Which part?"

"All of it! I can't believe what I've just heard. *My* behaviour? Have you forgotten, Mr Scales, that I am not, in fact, your wife? You have no business excusing or not excusing me. Almost selling my possessions. You have no business treating me so—"

He caught her up by the arms and pulled her close to him. "Haven't you understood? At all?" His eyes roved her face. "You're tied to me, whether either of us likes it or not, by your *condition*. And I'm not asking you, I'm telling you now. Don't make a fool of me again."

"If anyone has made a fool of you, Mr Scales, it is only yourself." Gwen picked his hands off her and sat down, utterly livid.

In the aftermath of Frome's attempt on her microscope she couldn't sustain the bravado she had felt in his presence.

I just don't have a single thing to say to him, she thought. And she slithered down into a capsule of loneliness. A crushing wave of homesickness came over her. All she wanted to do was stamp off and tell her sister what a thoroughly annoying and bumptious man he was; that perhaps she had been right to try and stop her from leaving Cornwall. She couldn't think how Edward might have arrived at the conclusion that just because she had agreed to this *condition*, as he called it, to be his mistress, he had the right to fume over her with his idiotic words.

The humidity gathered around Gwen and Edward; they were deadly silent with each other until Edward left with his nets and other equipment. I am leaving, she thought, watching the stiffness of his gait as he walked away from her. I shall go home. She pictured herself packing up her few things, nesting the microscope in its box amongst her clothes. Infernal man, she muttered, but she made no move to do anything except kick her fancy slippers across the floor and let down her hair. Slowly, she began to plait it into a thick rope, and when it was done, she spent a long time wrapping the rope of it around her wrist and along the length of her forearm.

Soon after turning in that night, she heard the shuffle of Edward's bare feet on the floorboards as he scuffed his way towards her in the dark. She lay still in her hammock and did not speak.

"I must apologise," he said. "Everything I said before, in England, everything I told you, it still holds true. Please forgive my unutterably dismal attitude today. I couldn't bear it if you went away. There would be no point." There seemed to be a moment in which he intended to tell her what, exactly, there would be no point to. The space for the words was there—and then it closed. She heard him turning blindly in the dark of the room and his retreating footfall to his own hammock.

Gwen lay awake for a long time wondering to which conversation in England he could have been referring. After a while, she heard the alarming, deep choking rattle of Edward's snoring. She muffled her head with a blanket and tried to sleep.

Chapter XXIX

Pará, Brazil. Old Year's Night, 1860/1.

Of course, she had known. She must have, mustn't she? No, she still didn't think so. The knowledge sickened her and tore at her. She felt shredded and raw under Edward's gaze and Maria's solicitations. And fat. And stupid. And desperate. What was to be done about it? Nothing. Her half-formed plans to return to Cornwall were as substantial as a drop of ink in a barrel full of water. And so she'd started work.

Gwen arranged the first insects she intended to paint into her book. Very delicately, she reached into the middle of the wooden case and tugged a pinned butterfly free from its base of cork. An afternoon breeze caught the edges of the stiffened wings and the insect twirled around on its axis like a vibrant miniature windmill. Cupping her hands over the insect she brought it away from the main thrust of the breeze, and she stuck the pin into another piece of cork set onto a wooden wedge.

She began to sketch out very lightly the outline beginning with the bulbous eyes and delicately furry thorax, down to the abdomen, which was as brightly coloured as the rest of the butterfly. She imagined it alive, its fat pulse. It was now thin and pinched, the result of its handling. Edward did not collect every single insect himself. Sometimes children came to the house with things they had caught. One of them said he had collected for another Englishman a few years before. He brought Edward some specimens which he said the other man had not been able to catch.

Gwen stared hard at the butterfly. Making the thing properly, *scientifically* symmetrical was a challenge in itself. At home, she'd always accepted her slight mistakes as part of what it was to spend time staring so hard at one creature or landscape. Now, she felt entirely useless. She lightly sketched out the first half on the left of the insect. She shifted in her seat. Her internal workings were not her own. There seemed an awful lot of wind to pass, and at frequent intervals. And she had become terribly constipated. These things were easy to deal with when Edward was not at the house. She put down her pencil, got up and expelled a lot of wind loudly. When he was there, she spent as much time on the verandah as possible; it gave her the most dreadful stomach ache, trying to hold it all in. Maria had told her to eat lots of fruit from the garden. The mangoes were very sticky and drippy. Maria laughed at her complaints, saying that as it was she had an easy time of it.

Maria sat with Gwen, it seemed to Edward, for most of the day. When he left the house after breakfast and his first morning ramble, they were sitting in hammocks slung under the verandah; when he returned, they were in exactly the same place. Yet, he knew this could not be true because each evening there would be a new set of studies in her painting book. The first time he leafed through her paintings he had been beside himself with expectation. He had put off looking because she had not offered to show him anything yet. He was disinclined to ask her while the prickliness of the atmosphere over Frome and the microscope had not quite been smoothed over. But, one evening, she said casually, "Did you see what I have done today, Edward?" and continued to swing in the hammock with her eyes closed.

So, after he had organised his day's quarry—he fiddled about with the mangled bird he'd shot for quite a while—he stepped cautiously over to her workbench by the window as if the insects inside the pages might suddenly detect his presence and fly off.

They were better than he expected. Better than he had hoped for. He took a pocket magnifying glass and held it to the page. She had painted the individual hairs on the thorax of a butterfly. It was modelled in gouache so that it seemed to stand proud of the paper, even hover just slightly above it, the tips of the wings coming down to touch the paper. He went out onto the verandah with the book in his hands.

"Gwen, these are magnificent."

"I wish there was a way of painting them to look the way they do when they are alive. Feeding on nectar or floating along."

"These are marvellous things."

Edward had worried that she might not be up to the task, or that her condition would become her priority. She seemed these days to be as focused in her work as a man might be. The sheer body of it was testament to that. Her condition seemed to be irrelevant to her.

Gwen had been learning Portuguese from Maria. Keeping her feet in the air, propped up inside the hammock made her restless. As the heat gathered between eleven and three there was little she felt like doing, anyway. As the temperature soared, the silence of the place was absolute, only punctuated now and then with the odd penetrating whine of an insect.

Every day, it was as if the oppressiveness had been only a part of her imagination as the rain, suddenly released, poured down to enliven her spirits, and sharp cracks of thunder erupted overhead. And every afternoon, she doubted the relief which was to come. In the stillness, she doubted the ability of the birds to start up their calls again. And over each new tree bursting into bloom in the morning out of the blanket of green she was as surprised and delighted as she had been the first morning she had seen it.

"You are fighting, fighting all the time."

Gwen looked up from the letter she was trying to write. "What?"

"The heat, Mrs Scales. You have to let it through you. You have to let it soak you up."

Maria observed the Christmas festivals in the town, leaving Edward and Gwen to themselves. They did not exchange gifts, and they did not attend any services at any of the churches. Without Maria, they got on with each other as well as they could. In England Edward had once remarked that he couldn't imagine Gwen inhabiting an interior. He couldn't imagine, he had said, what it would be like to see her contained within four walls. And he still could not, for there had not been many occasions when he had been inside a building with her. And that seemed as if it was another life, anyway. He looked at Gwen and at the rain falling off the verandah roof. The clothes she wore concealed her shape. They were an odd combination of styles. Maria had brought some items to the house, and together the women had connived and contrived to transform Gwen's appearance, slowly. Now, when he looked at her properly he would easily have mistaken her for—what? Not quite a native. Her skin had changed, too. He pictured the dark line of melanin, which he assumed was marking her belly, and almost wanted to take her there where she stood. She wore her sleeves short. The slippers he had bought for her spent most of the day under the hammock. The sight of her toes and their new colour drew him out under the eaves. She loved listening to the noisy frogs and toads. Pointless to try and talk, even with the shutters closed inside the house. The frogs had released them both for the time being of the arduous business of making conversation which did not include references to the past or the future. This had been one such evening. Edward had gone into his room to try and write up some of his notes but he'd been unable to concentrate. His jagged writing skittered and meandered over the page; the ink was blotted badly, and there were smears made by his grubby thumbs. Out collecting, if he had a thought to put down he'd get distracted before the words were formed on the page. He'd found himself, some days, trying to write with the insect nets still gripped in the same hand, his fingers contorted.

Edward looked at Gwen. Why shouldn't he just go to her now? No words would be needed. He felt a familiar drawing in, as though he were a hawk moth, in awe of her scent, unable to resist. He came up close to her, his fingertips touching the bare skin of her arms, and she gave a half jump, half shiver of surprise.

"Won't you let your hair down for me again?" He spoke the words right into her ear and pulled the thin, ebony rods from the coils piled onto her head. The rope of hair fell heavily down her back, but she hardly moved, barely gave any indication that she had heard him speak or that he had touched her. After half a minute her head turned in his direction. He saw her lips moving, the words lost in the amphibious chorus.

"In London the bells will all have rung out." His lips touched her face. "Loosen your hair for me again. This rain is perfect for it; do you remember what you said?" He grasped at her and fumbled underneath her clothes.

"Do you think about England that much?" She pulled away from him, detaching his fingers like so much sticky cobweb. "What is that?" They were roaring at each other now. The moment, if it had indeed been a moment, was gone. They both strained to hear. Edward cupped his hand around his ear, and made out two distinct male voices, one Scottish and one American.

The Scot was saying, "I keep telling you why it's Old Year's

Night, and yet you still insist on calling it New Year's Eve, which any reasonable man would agree is tomorrow night—tomorrow being the first day of the new year."

"Oh, indeed; just as you like," came the other voice.

Gwen and Edward both tensed at the sound of the heavy treading on the boards of the verandah. What must we look like? she thought. "Give me those," she said and took her pins back and piled up her long plait, jabbing everything into place. She tried to alter her features into something resembling a welcoming gaze. But still, she thought, we must look like two startled rabbits. The men careened around the corner.

"Ah. A Happy New Year's Eve to you good people both."

"I must apologise for Mr Coyne. He means to wish you a good Old Year's Night."

Their arms were draped around each other's shoulders; it was impossible to tell which man was being supported or if the stance was of mutual benefit.

Inside, with the shutters closed, it was just about possible to converse properly. The younger man spoke first; he wore a pair of spectacles designed to shade his eyes from the sun. The glass was tinted Madonna blue, the frames sparkling slivers of silver. They gave his eyes a most astonishing aspect. Gwen had to acknowledge the effect, even though it did seem a little bit affected.

"Vincent Coyne, glad to make your acquaintance, sir, ma'am, on this fine New Year's Eve."

"Gus Pemberton, also pleased to meet you, madam, and sir, on the last night of the Old Year." His voice was playful, like a rolling sweep of cool air.

"Scales. As a matter of fact you are both wrong."

"Wrong? Hey, we got the wrong day. Ha! Sorry to bother you. We'll just go squish some more of those toads and come back tomorrow."

"No." Gwen said. "Don't go now that you are here. We just meant that clocks at home have already struck the hour."

"Have you been to every house in the neighbourhood?" asked Edward, a little warily.

"Oh, no, sir, indeed we have not. We have been sent by your friends in town. Mrs Grindlock is a fine, fine lady, for whom I have the very highest regard."

"Excuse him, he isn't always like this."

Gwen said, "That's perfectly all right, Mr Pemberton. I'm sure half the population of the town is in much the same state."

"I can assure you the numbers amount to more than half."

Edward breathed in through his nose. "Perhaps some coffee."

Gwen looked away and grimaced inwardly at Edward. Mr Coyne slithered into a lacquered cane chair. Pemberton turned to Gwen. "I'm sorry we startled you. We did call out but the frogs—"

"—drowned us out." Vincent tried to sit up. "*O da Casa.*"

"O of the house?"

"It's the proper thing to do, in the jungle you know."

Gwen suspected that Vincent was suddenly not quite as drunk as he had been outside. She smiled at him. "I haven't been into the jungle yet, so I am still ignorant about that kind of thing."

Vincent's eyes made an unabashed tour of her person and stopped at her middle, just for a second, before slewing his gaze around the room. "You speak the language, not quite so ignorant."

Mr Coyne was extraordinarily beautiful; he wore the whiskers on his chin clipped to a neat point, rather than cultivating the bushy side-whiskers, which, Gwen thought, made most men who wore them resemble guinea-pigs. Not handsome. Mr Pemberton was handsome; Gwen registered it. The two men were like a pair of elegant butterflies, opposites but perfectly matched; whereas Edward, in comparison, was like the longhorn beetle grub. She watched his squirming accommodation of the unexpected guests with cool fascination.

Pemberton cleared his throat. "You really don't have to trouble yourselves with the coffee."

"Please, it's no trouble."

"We don't like to impose," said Pemberton.

"You are not imposing. Really, we have made ourselves such hermits; of course, we must offer you something. It is the thing to do, in the jungle, I believe."

Gus Pemberton laughed. "Yes, indeed, Mrs Scales." The chorus from outside almost swallowed his words completely.

"Mrs Scales," Vincent sounded very serious, "I have had a letter from a good friend of mine who tells me that—"

"Later, Vincent, later," Gus Pemberton said.

"Here we are then, gentlemen, a pot of coffee for the weary and travel-worn."

"That was very clever of you, Edward." Gwen couldn't help it, but he didn't seem to notice.

"I had made it before, and, would you believe it, the pot was still hot."

Thank God for these people, thought Gwen. She studied Mr Coyne's profile. I feel that I know him; or rather, that I am meeting him at last. Mr Coyne's blue spectacles glimmered in the lamplight as he pushed them up the bridge of his nose. A beautiful young man—but for all his show, perhaps a bit nervous. The air between the four of them felt charged with something alive. Gwen felt its invisible form move between them, sinuous, shifting, elemental. She thought, this is the creature which has been following me and watching me. It knows my heart, and it knows too that my heart is leaving Edward.

Chapter XXX

They were still drinking coffee, and Edward had grown tired of his guests. Still, he listened to the conversation to which he felt he could not contribute.

Gus Pemberton took out a fat cigar and asked if anyone minded if he stepped outside to fumigate the frogs.

Gwen watched Gus Pemberton and Edward go out onto the verandah. Then she said, "Mr Coyne, you mentioned a letter earlier."

Vincent cleared his throat. "I believe we could be of mutual benefit to each other regarding the person you wish to find." He lowered his voice a little and glanced in the direction of the verandah where Gus Pemberton had managed to get his damp cigar to light. In a confiding tone, he said, "I have only mentioned to Gus half of what it could mean. You've read Darwin, most likely a given that you are aware of his sparrows." He paused, and Gwen nodded, mentally correcting him, unsure of how finches could have any relevance. He continued, "It all has to do with isolation. I have been paddling through the forests, and to cut it rather short, Mrs Scales, I believe it is perfectly possible for an isolated tribe of a type of *pre-human* people to exist within." Gwen raised her eyebrows but remained silent. It was beginning to dawn on her that perhaps Mr Pemberton's friend really was mad, as he had jokingly suggested. She wanted to ask whom the letter was from. She remained politely and silently attentive, but she didn't want to appear complicit, and certainly didn't want to prolong the discussion.

Vincent took her silence as a cue and continued, "With no contact hitherto from the outside world, what's to say that a missing link can't in fact be found right here in the Amazons?" Clearly, he expected her to say something.

"Mr Coyne, are you saying that you think there exists a living example, a specimen of *proof* that human beings are descended from apes?"

"Yes! that's it," Vincent almost squealed. "Wouldn't it be the most fantastic discovery? Darwin provides the theory; and Vincent Coyne provides the proof."

Gwen swallowed. "Mr Darwin, if my memory serves me correctly, has not exactly, not quite yet, at any rate, proposed the theory you suppose he has. And, in any case, I am sure you are aware that others have already said it. The person, for instance, who published *Vestiges* almost twenty years ago." Vincent stared at her. He seemed baffled. Gwen thought, He doesn't know about that book. In fact, she hadn't read it either; she only knew about it because of a similar but less personal discussion with Captain Swithin. She said, "Perhaps it was not available in America." Vincent seemed not to have heard her.

He said, "It is only a matter of time. Everyone is aware of what he is getting at. Everyone is talking about it. He's testing the water. He's making little amendments here and there with every new edition. Eventually, when he thinks we've had time to adjust to the idea of natural selection—he'll put in a new chapter about Man."

"Mr Coyne, I think if and when that chapter is written, then it will be proposed, as I understand it at any rate, that you cannot prove the theory by finding living specimens. I think that, perhaps, in time, Mr Darwin may suggest that apes and humans have what we might call a, a common ancestor, who has long since been laid down in the stones of time. As far as I can see, during the process of natural selection, if you choose to take up the theory in earnest, the links are changed with each generation, so that we are a long line of descendents and ancestors. We cannot live at the same time as our ancestors, Mr Coyne." Gwen felt herself becoming breathless. "An isolated tribe of people, however primitive-seeming, cannot be our ancestors; they would merely be an isolated tribe of people with certain attributes, probably attributable to external circumstance." Gwen felt that she had tied herself up in a tangle of theory she knew little enough about, but she hoped that Mr Coyne would understand that she wanted no part of his plan. He was unnerving her. She threw up her hands in feigned defeat and looked to the verandah to see whether Mr Pemberton was coming back inside.

Vincent Coyne laughed, and Gus Pemberton stepped into the room saying, "He at least had the sense to do that."

Chapter XXXI

Cornwall. February 16, 1861.

Euphemia's meetings were reduced to two or three evenings a week. Isobel Scales came once a month. The unbridled and undiminished audacity of the woman. Once a month Euphemia's Spiritualist meetings morphed into a game of Cheat; only two of the players were aware of the game or the lack of rules and the other players concealing tricks or double bluffs. Euphemia's contacts with the other side were leaving her uncharacteristically ravaged with fatigue.

Isobel Scales brought with her a variety of new clients in various states of mourning and others with a nose for something a little sensational. She had a reputation for punctuality and preciseness in everything. So, it was with some bemusement that Euphemia found herself entertaining Isobel Scales at ten-thirty in the morning in the middle of the week. It was shocking to see her so garishly dressed. She wore the front of her skirt flat in contrasting layers of mauve and yellow silk, whilst her rump displayed a voluminous puff of satin and taffeta ruffles in alternating rosettes. The whole thing jarred on Euphemia's eye, and she wondered what kind of imbecile could design such an outrage.

"I'm disturbing your reading," Isobel perched her puff, settling herself into the nearest chair. Euphemia followed her gaze to the book lying splayed open on a small card table. She took it up and closed it, not bothering to mark the page. The polished calfskin felt cool.

"It's just a trifle. I haven't managed to get along with it yet.

Epistolary novels!—I have it on loan from Mrs Coyne. She was anxious to hear my opinion of it."

"Mrs Coyne, you'll have to remind me if I have made her acquaintance, I—may I?"

Euphemia pretended not to have noticed Isobel's request and kept the book in her lap, covering it with both hands.

"Oh, but you must remember poor Penelope Coyne."

"Perhaps I do. I must confess that I have an ulterior motive for calling on you like this."

Euphemia relaxed and her fingers stopped palpating the embroidered hem of her napkin. Perhaps Isobel would soon go away. She hadn't taken off her gloves.

"I have a little occasion to organise at our London house next week and I wondered if I might borrow your cook. Of course, we can come to some sort of agreement; I would be happy to do a fair swap, if you are willing. It is just that none of the staff have your cook's particular talent in the art of *petites bouchées*, and I did so want something a little more extraordinary—though all of my kitchen staff are quite excellent in their own ways."

Euphemia did not know whether to be flattered or outraged. Instead, she sat in a fug of agitation and listened to the cranking internals of the hall clock mark the half hour. If she did not manage to get the tonic into her tea in the next ten minutes she would have to excuse herself. Her fingers tapped out a syncopated tinkle on the saucer.

"I have no need of a confirmation immediately, of course. Has your cook ever been on a locomotive, to your knowledge, Miss Carrick? I am afraid it inspired in me a fit of terror the first time I stepped up into a carriage. Heaven knows we should be used to them by now."

Heaven knows a lot, thought Euphemia, putting her hand into her pocket and fingering the stopper on the bottle of laudanum.

"My dear, don't rouse yourself on my account. There is plenty of time, after all."

"I have a cramp coming on in my foot; the exercise will get rid of it."

"Oh, that is a nuisance, isn't it? Why don't you walk up and down?" Isobel got up and put her arm under Euphemia's elbow. "You seem a little clammy, if I may say so." Looking at her closely she said, "You are in a state, Miss Carrick. I think I will go and find that girl of yours—Susan, isn't it?

"Now, wriggle your feet whilst I find some brandy, I won't be long." She peered at Euphemia's eyes. "You look ghastly. I always used to get the cramps down my legs. Of course, all this sort of nuisance just disappears when you get married and—" She gave a nervous giggle. Perhaps it was a snort.

Euphemia closed her eyes and clutched at the bottle. Isobel Scales was already at the door. Euphemia watched in fascination as the train on her mauve and vivid lilac skirt with the yellow trimmings whipped out of sight.

When Isobel came back some fifteen minutes later with the brandy bottle (not the decanter which would have been easy enough to locate in the dining room) and a couple of glasses (not brandy glasses), Euphemia was almost back together again. She accepted the glass of brandy and drank it quite cheerfully.

"I do apologise, Mrs Scales. How dreadful of me."

"Let's not mention it. I'm not in the least perturbed by these mishaps. We are all human and subject to the whims of nature. And I think we are well enough acquainted by now, not to let that sort of thing embarrass us, are we not?"

And you are fairly well acquainted with my kitchen, thought Euphemia, as Isobel Scales sipped at the brandy she had poured for herself and fully occupied the chair.

"After all, I myself have fainted in this very house. If you don't mind my saying so, you lace yourself rather tighter than fashion absolutely dictates, Miss Carrick. I have always striven for the nineteen; you on the other hand really have no need to be so fierce. My husband, when I was first married, was constantly arguing the case for a more 'natural' figure. His head was full of scientific this and medical reasons for that. To be honest, I did not care for his arguments at all. Being looser around one's torso is in no way indicative of one's morals, Miss Carrick." Isobel Scales was in no particular hurry to leave. She gave another nervous snort. "This water is gone tepid, shall we ring for some hot? Then we can discuss my little plan to steal your dwarf away for a few days. Isn't this fun?"

There was no doubt in Euphemia's mind that Isobel Scales was having fun of some sort. She found herself unable, finally, to keep it up any longer.

"Mrs Scales," she said abruptly, "Harris has departed this world. It was quite sudden, and unexpected, some five months ago."

Euphemia watched Isobel's face moving. Flakes of powder fell from her face; spittle glistened on her teeth and made silvery strings as she opened her mouth silently and shut it again. Her hair was dressed so tightly that the skin around her temples forced her expression into something which was not natural. It was interesting to see her in daylight, and alone. Euphemia found herself wondering if Mrs Scales ever took her hair pins out.

Mrs Scales had satisfied her appetite for brandy. She dropped the Angel's fingers she had been holding to the china. "And so whom must I congratulate for those?"

"Susan, of course. She made a point of learning the craft very quickly."

"Quite so." Isobel Scales rose unsteadily to her feet.

Euphemia forced herself out of her chair to see her out. She did not want Mrs Scales wandering the wrong way.

Isobel Scales thanked Euphemia for the interview, but as she turned to leave what little colour there was in her face drained away. Euphemia was fascinated to see the grey skin clouded under the flaky powder and, sidling a little closer, waited to see what would happen next. Mrs Scales began to say something but it was incomprehensible; she raised her hands in the form of some gesture as the words refused to come out in the right order. Euphemia frowned. One moment there she was upright, the next moment she had fallen onto the carpet in a swoosh of silk and a small thud, which was made by her head, banging on the floor.

The fresh air assaulted Euphemia on the doorstep. It went into her ears and up her nose. It travelled along her sleeves and slipped into her armpits. Mrs Scales' driver got down from the coach when he caught sight of her. Euphemia said, "Fetch this doctor from this address. Are you literate, or do I need to read it out to you? Very good. Mrs Scales is gravely ill—do not come back without the doctor."

The coach bounced on its springs as he stepped up and settled himself, slapping the reins. The two horses touched noses and tossed their heads. The gravel beneath hooves and wheels crunched.

"She seemed all right before, ma'am," said Susan, who had managed without Euphemia's assistance to get the conscious but immobile Mrs Scales onto the day-bed and into a comfortable repose while they waited for the doctor. "But just because someone seems all right, doesn't mean to say that they *are* all right." Susan dabbed at Mrs Scales' forehead with a cool damp muslin and felt her pulse. Both of them were thinking about Mr Harris' sudden demise but neither wanted to admit that they feared a repeat performance.

"What on earth are you doing?"

"Taking the lady's pulse, ma'am. I learned it years ago."

"And what good will that do?"

"It won't do any good at all, ma'am, but it tells me how strong and fast her heart is beating."

"And how does she do?"

"She's in a bad way, ma'am. Like a bird that's been mauled by the cat."

"Oh, for heaven's sake, Susan." Euphemia got down onto her knees and spoke to Isobel in a businesslike voice. "The doctor will be here very soon, I should think. But, in the meantime, would you please let me know if there is anything you need. Is there a particular remedy, Mrs Scales, which you have been prescribed of late?"

"I don't think you'll get no answer from her, ma'am."

Isobel's breaths were shallow and laboured; her eyes were open and the lids flickered a little as she tried to focus on Euphemia. Under duress Susan took a pair of scissors to Isobel's corset after unbuttoning the silk jacket of her dress.

"Don't fuss, Susan; it can't possibly do any harm and it may do some good."

Cutting the linen tapes made no difference and Isobel's paralysis remained unchanged. Susan continued to dab at Isobel's forehead and now also at her chest with the damp muslin. Isobel continued to breathe but just as badly. Euphemia got up and went to stand at the front door. Isobel Scales' penchant for games had taken a turn for the worse.

Euphemia smoothed the already smooth covers on the bed in the guest room Susan had prepared in a rush while the doctor had examined the patient on the day-bed downstairs. Mrs Scales had been carried up to the room in the arms of her driver. She had recovered from her three hour-long episode enough to talk, though Euphemia wished that she would go to sleep. It had been a difficult day. Isobel slurred as if drunk.

"When I am dead, I want you to invite my husband to your Spirit conference. There are conversations I was unable to have. I would like you to help me."

"Your time is not now, not even close. The doctor has said so."

"That doctor is wrong."

"As you wish. I will do my—whatever I can."

Euphemia could think of nothing more horrible than being witness to whatever conversation Mrs Scales had in mind for her errant husband. She shuddered to think of it. The idea of the intimacy appalled her.

"It doesn't really matter how long it takes for you to accomplish my request. I will not mind waiting. Though I am concerned for your sister, Miss Carrick."

Euphemia drew back and released Isobel's hands from what she had been hoping conveyed tenderness or at least polite sympathy. "My sister conducts her own affairs in the way she has seen fit. I have no influence over her."

"She can't have known what she was committing herself to."

"Don't tire yourself, Mrs Scales."

"I have been battling with this—*malady*, for years, Miss Carrick. I am tired, indeed, of keeping up the pretence. You know what I speak of. My concern for your sister. Troubles me. I did what I thought I must. I tried to help. I have gone to lengths."

"It is so cold in this room, I must apologise."

Euphemia went to the small fireplace where the flames were failing yet to throw any heat into the room. She put a lump of coal into the middle of the fire. Euphemia pulled the cord to ring for Susan, and when she came, Euphemia told her to bring another bed-warmer for Mrs Scales.

"The cold does not trouble me. Death will be cold; I will have an eternity to get used to it."

"That's no way to talk, ma'am," Susan said. "I won't have you catching your death over the want of a bed-warmer."

Euphemia looked at her desperately ill guest. At least it is winter, she thought. As long as she dies soon, I will be able to send her body back to London. I won't have to see to her buried here.

The light went steadily from the window. The day had become duller and duller, the grey of the sky thickened, and in the gloaming, as Euphemia looked out of the guest bedroom window, she saw fat flakes of snow. Her heart sank.

That evening Euphemia looked for the book which had arrived months before, without a note. Penelope Coyne had not loaned it, but Euphemia suspected that under the quiver on Penelope's pout, there was a taste for something sensational. Certainly, a woman like Mrs Coyne would not forget to scribble a line or two when sending a book. Euphemia searched under all the cushions. Susan must have tidied it away. She sat down in the chair Isobel Scales had occupied that morning and closed her eyes. A vivid image of Penelope's son came to rest under her eyelids. It didn't matter that her communications with him had come to such an abrupt end. She trusted that he would make new contact with her whenever he was able and give her some positive news about the progress he must surely by now be making with her sister.

Susan checked on Mrs Scales as often as she was able that first night. She made the fire hotter and replenished the bed-warmers and found an extra eiderdown. She covered Mrs Scales' shoulders with a fur stole and made the lamps bright in the room. Susan did everything she could to banish death from the house. Every night and every morning for the past five months, kneeling at her bedside,

Susan had begged forgiveness for her part in Mr Harris' lonely passing on the cold kitchen floor. She closed her mind to the rest.

Mrs Scales had eaten nothing of the syllabub but had taken the honey from the spoon; she had refused the tincture left by the doctor, describing it as an evil poison and told Susan that the doctor was an incompetent fool, that all doctors were incompetent, and that she should never trust them, especially those who were the most trustworthy of all. Some of her talk was certainly muddled. At times during the evening, Mrs Scales drifted off to sleep propped up on the pillows. Then, she would open her eyes suddenly and begin to talk again. Twice, Susan had come into the room with a hot bed-warmer to find Mrs Scales having a conversation with the empty room. Susan did not like this. It was her firm belief that those close to death were able to see ghosts. In this case, she determined to make the room too bright and too hot for any ghosts to find agreeable for very long.

"When they lock my body away, in that horrible vault," she said to Susan, "you must make sure that the name carved is my maiden name. Fetch the ink and paper to me."

Susan filled the nib and wiped it carefully against the neck of the ink bottle and passed it to Mrs Scales. She spent some time over it. The pen had to be passed back and forth to be refilled, and Mrs Scales' hand was not steady.

"This is an instruction to be sent to my solicitor. I have put his address there." She asked Susan to sign her own name at the bottom of the paper as witness. "I had meant to do this. I have been forgetting and remembering too much all at once."

"I'll see that it's delivered, ma'am."

"I am very grateful."

Susan put it aside to dry as there was no blotting paper. Mrs Scales lay back again on the pillows and closed her eyes. Susan checked the time. It was almost ten at night. Susan was reluctant to do the usual things and leave the room. She looked at the messy scrawl and tried to decipher Mrs Scales' line of thoughts on the paper and was doubtful over it. She filled the nib again and wrote out on a clean sheet what she could make of the instructions.

At half past eleven Mrs Scales woke Susan who had fallen asleep in a chair near the bed.

"Miss, I'm sorry, I don't know your name. Will you tell me where he went? I came here to find him, but he wasn't here. I can't remember your name. Will you fetch Mr Harris? There is something I have wanted to ask him." She made a feeble attempt to throw back the covers from the bed and to get herself up. "I think he might be out there."

"No one is out there this time of night, Mrs Scales. Not in the weather we're having."

"Nonsense, it is the middle of summer."

"It's blowing a gale of snow, Mrs Scales."

"That's not my name. But, my manners, what do they call you?"

"I'm Susan Wright, ma'am."

"Very pleased to make your acquaintance, Susan Wright. I am Isobel Armstrong. Did you know that?"

"I saw you write it down, ma'am, and I signed my own beneath."

"So you did. They won't call me after him. I don't want his name after all."

"Ma'am, please let me put the covers back up."

"Did you just say it was snowing?"

"I did, ma'am."

"Isn't that a curious thing to happen in the middle of summer."

"We're in the month of February, ma'am."

"I see. Tell me about your sister."

"I have only brothers, ma'am."

"Of course, I remember now. And what about Mr Harris? Who has him now?"

"The Lord keeps him now, ma'am."

"Goodness, how the little man has progressed! Do tell me—Lord whom? Oh, never mind. The next thing we shall hear is that he has been employed to spy on the Queen."

Isobel sank into herself as she closed her eyes again. Susan turned away and busied herself with the coal bucket; she didn't want Mrs Scales to hear her weeping.

Chapter XXXII

THE TIMES, Thursday, October 4, 1866.

MURDER TRIAL AT THE OLD BAILEY.

WITNESS for the Prosecution, Mrs Fernly surprised the court with her statement. It was and, indeed, still remains unclear whether the Counsel for the Prosecution had prior knowledge of its content: "I have known the accused since the day she first smiled at a handful of May blossom with not yet a tooth in her dear head. What I shall say of my account of the accused shall be this: the dear child [the prisoner] was never an immoral person. Never. And nothing [pointing her finger towards the heavens] will induce me to say that she is an immoral person now. Her conduct throughout her life has been exemplary; her manner with all those around her fine and true, and she never acted on impulse or unkindly. Indeed, she took it upon herself to educate the children of the poorest families in the village, devoting many hours to Bible study with those little souls. To elope is not immoral— misguided in some cases, perhaps—but not the deed of a bad person as has been suggested here. In taking passage to Brazil with that man [Mr Scales], she believed that she was eloping—that she was deceived by him and others is no fault of hers. Her family, *and* the Pemberton family have a good standing, and I believe will continue to do so, once this ridiculous business is over. Murder! For goodness sake, I never heard anything so outrageous in all my blessed days [crossing herself flamboyantly] and I hope that the Gentlemen of the Jury will see good sense and find in Mrs Pemberton's favour.

Chapter XXXIII

Cornwall. March 6, 1861.

Susan showed a small, dark-veiled figure into the morning room. Euphemia sat with her back to the sun; the room was warming up already. The little woman positioned herself neatly opposite Euphemia. Both of them waited: Euphemia waited for the woman to lift her veil; Natalia Jaspur waited for Miss Carrick to speak.

When the carriage had drawn up outside, Euphemia had been pretending that she had not been up all night. She had begun eating a soft-boiled egg as Susan had rushed excitedly into the dining-room.

"Visitors, ma'am."

"Are you sure? It's barely eight."

"It's a right grand carriage, ma'am. Four-horser."

"Horses, Susan."

"Shall I ask them to wait, ma'am?"

"No. I'll receive them in the morning room, whoever they are."

Euphemia had bolted the last bit of egg and now it was repeating on her. Natalia Jaspur was the first to speak.

"I am sorry to disturb you, Miss Carrick, at this hour, but I have spent a good deal of time trying to locate you and I do not have much left."

Euphemia strained to hear every syllable correctly; the woman's voice seemed to be a hotchpotch of different influences. She cleared her throat quietly. "My usual hours for Contact are more frequently held in the evening, but I am sure if we were to draw the curtains—" Her hands had become clammy.

"I am not interested in Spiritualism, Miss Carrick. And, if I were, there is no one I would wish to contact. No, the reason I have looked for you is this." She produced a piece of flimsy paper from a small beaded pouch hanging at her wrist. "It was discovered by one of my staff and brought to my attention. I see from the look on your face you are a little confused. It is a personal advertisement from the pages of the *Evening Standard*. It bears my name, and also the name of a person I was once in acquaintance with. This is quite old." She flapped the cutting. "My housekeeper likes to waste nothing; it was packaging, but that is not interesting to you at all. I made enquiries to the offices of that paper which has eventually led me here."

Euphemia's mind was in turmoil and her stomach threatened to dispose of her egg. "You believe I may be of assistance in some way?"

"The person mentioned along with my name on this paper—that person was not the person who placed the advertisement. It is a delicate matter. I wish to contact the person who did."

"Being?"

"Miss Carrick, I do not have time for obfuscation. I would very much appreciate it if you would let me know the whereabouts of Mr Edward Scales."

"I did have the pleasure of meeting Mr Scales on one occasion, some months ago—just before he departed on a trip, an excursion overseas."

"Very good. You will give me his address."

Euphemia swallowed. "Mr Scales left no forwarding address. Perhaps his family—I believe they reside in London."

"I have been there. It is shut. Someone in that house died. The rest have gone."

"Then I, I can help you no further."

"Miss Carrick, if you please. I do know, for instance, that Mr Scales went to Brazil to catch butterflies and put snakes and other creatures in bottles, and I know that your sister, Miss Gwen Carrick, is an artist who travelled with him. I know that, despite differences, your sister will have sent a letter by now detailing her particulars of residence in that country." Natalia Jaspur breathed heavily after this, and her thick black veil moved a little. "I have no time to play any games with you, Miss Carrick. I am sure your sister is an honourable woman. I will leave you my card, in case you remember where you have put your sister's letters." She stuffed the folded piece of newspaper back into her purse and produced a small, white card, which she placed with a snap onto an occasional table. "Now, if you will excuse me, I must leave this moment to be in good time. The drive back to Exeter is tedious. I will see myself out." She stood up to leave. "Good day to you, Miss Carrick."

The sunshine had brought out a sweat on Euphemia. She wiped her face and neck, and waited until she was satisfied that there had been a crunching of wheels and the woman had gone. She eyed the card left by Natalia Jaspur for a few seconds then picked it up and took it to the study where she chose a book at random and slipped the card between its pages. That this strange, dark little woman had been right there in the morning room was not in itself the most extraordinary thing. If only she could find that missing book; Euphemia felt, for the first time in her life, that she had been speaking to a ghost. *Someone in that house died.* She went to look for Susan. The kitchen door was wide open to the morning, and Susan was on her knees cleaning the flagstones. Euphemia spoke to Susan's backside as it wagged back and forth with the effort of scrubbing.

"Spring is here then, Susan."

"Yes, ma'am, and about time, too." Susan did not stop scrubbing.

"I'd like a cup of tea, and some more toast. You can bring it up to my room."

Susan's shoulders sagged momentarily, but she did not stop scrubbing.

Chapter XXXIV

Edward awoke in his hammock one April morning not knowing if he should concern himself over Mr Coyne's attention to Gwen. God knows, he thought, how physically lacking in seductive charm she had become in her present state.

Edward had seen Mr Coyne coming away from the house and walking down the road towards the town. He'd waited for her to mention it, and when he'd asked her how her day had gone she'd said that it had been quiet enough. Gwen still did not mention Coyne over the next couple of days, and he decided to leave it alone.

Sometimes, he imagined himself telling her that he made it all up. It was different each time. Sometimes, she laughed, and said that she knew and told him not to be a silly. Other times, his mind played out something violent. Gwen threw objects. Ripped up her work. Shouted. Or she packed her things quietly and calmly into her small trunk and left. When his thoughts ran this way he fixed on telling her the moment he next saw her. Things got in the way. She would be talking to Maria, or asleep.

Gwen did not talk about Natalia Jaspur to Edward. He was thankful for this. The idea of the two of them discussing her at length was too disturbing to contemplate. Edward thought that he must remove himself from the torment of it and the painful silence of avoidance in the house during the evenings after Maria had gone home to her own family.

Pemberton had told him about a small place, a village one day's walk away where he would find Morpho rhetenor. Perhaps, he reasoned, he should go there for a while. The thought of the rhetenor's alluring blue metallic sheen quickened his stomach.

He'd lingered longer than usual over his coffee and biscuit. As he readied himself, Maria arrived with the day's provisions and handed him a letter.

"I've brought you some American pork, Mr Scales, it came in yesterday. Won't you eat before you go?"

Edward wavered on the threshold at the thought of bacon. "Thank you Maria, but it will be better for the waiting, I should think."

"Letter from home, Mr Scales?"

Edward looked at the postmark and the writing. It was addressed to him and was from Cornwall. The hand was not his wife's, though certainly female. There were careful flourishes all over the envelope. He inspected the seal on the reverse, which was also flamboyant and depicted a ship with a "C" curled around it. He put the letter inside his knapsack next to the killing jars waiting for the post-breakfast entomological ramble. He hitched his collecting bag over his shoulder, picked up the birding gun and bid his perfunctory farewell to Maria. Gwen was still asleep.

Waiting for Maria to cook the bacon, Gwen noticed Edward's knapsack on the verandah. She picked it up, imagining it slung over her own back. Tucked in with the jars, she saw the letter and pulled it out. She looked at the fancy handwriting which she recognised at once as Susan's. Her fantasy evaporated.

Gwen had often found discarded or forgotten lists of things to do and things to buy, scrawled carefully by Susan. Sometimes the lists were personal, and sometimes for the house. She turned the letter over, thinking how long Susan must have practised to get her handwriting so neat. She looked at the seal. Susan must have been rummaging in the library bureau to have found that old thing. Gwen smiled at Susan addressing the letter to Edward, in an attempt to be proper. Gwen knew that the letter inside would be meant for her.

She tapped the letter on her knuckles before deciding not to open it. She would wait until Edward came back. She left the knapsack on its proper hook on the wall and replaced the letter inside. All through breakfast the thought of Susan's letter took precedence over everything else until Maria asked her what was wrong.

Curupíra, the wild man of the forest, mysterious being with various attributes: Edward recalled Gus Pemberton's description as he headed down the road towards the forest paths. He stopped himself from turning to look behind. Sometimes, he heard noises which he supposed might be attributable to the *Curupíra*. Gus Pemberton and Edward had discussed the propensity of primitive peoples to find unnatural causes to occurrences for which they could not account. Or, rather, after the disagreeable beginning to the conversation, Edward had listened to Gus Pemberton's ideas whilst trying to listen with half an ear to what Gwen had been saying to Vincent inside and wondering at the extreme effrontery of the man in turning up like that.

Now, though, as he walked, he heard only Natalia: "You are as curious to me as I am to you. Sometimes I have asked myself: why does a man with a pretty blonde wife spend so many of his hours here? And before my question is finished I answer myself. The two sides of my head in conversation." She breathed deeply at her own convenience which coincided with Edward's hand slipping between her thighs. "Because I remind you of what you are not and what your wife is not. It is simple, I think. You confirm our own place in this world by putting yourself inside me. You say nothing. This is because I am right. It is the same with all the people who must come to hear me sing and assure themselves. Your curiosity has never been any different to those faceless people, dropping coins, dropping their jaws at me. I am a freak; yes, I can say this word; but are you not a freak also?"

At the window a fly had buzzed; Natalia had risen from the bed and crossed the room to kill it. Edward watched her. Her backlit outline glowed in the dirty room at three in the afternoon. He had not cared that she mentioned his wife. That she knew her hair colour did not concern him. Perhaps one night he had told her, after too many glasses of stout. It did not matter, Edward was immersed. Natalia climbed back onto the bed with her fist closed over the fly. Its muted buzzing against her skin sounded in Edward's ear as he pushed her legs apart with his knee.

Now, the insects in the forest air butted his conscience, the high-pitched whine mirrored the protracted death of the bluebottle in Natalia's fist.

In the next moment, Edward's brief return from Lyme Regis to London filled his mind; the pile of letters, opened at random and scanned through, revealing nothing but that which he knew to already have been said or not said, left burning in the grate of his attic room at the hotel.

The surprised astonishment, embarrassment, and later, the disgust betrayed by Isobel's face.

Edward had arrived at his home in London at nine-thirty in the evening. His manservant still on extended leave as Edwards' had not been due back for another week or so, he brushed aside the feeble attempts made by some maid (whose name he did not know and forgot as soon as he learned it) to help him out of his overcoat and remove from him his travelling bags containing all his rocks and fossils. His intention had not been to see Isobel immediately, but the rather peculiar noises and furtive looks from the maid persuaded him to go straight to Isobel's rooms.

Edward had stood unobserved in his wife's bedroom as he watched her receive the attentions of his best friend, Charles.

He had assumed it was Charles; whose face was hidden between his wife's pale thighs; whose hair was being twined into knots by her dumpy fingers (he did not remember Isobel's fingers as ever having been dumpy). Edward thought that he would step out of the room as quietly as he had entered it, but the play of lamplight on his wife's skin kept him there. He saw Charles move his head up from between Isobel's thighs and over her belly, slowly licking her skin in a line up to her chin where she caught his mouth with her own. In quiet fascination Edward watched Charles take possession of Isobel, his eyes fixed on Charles' buttocks, reminding him of the young woman with the flushed pink cheeks in the hotel room below his at Lyme Regis.

He did not wait to see it end. He let himself out, allowing the door to make a noise, and returned downstairs, still grimy from his journey, where he poured himself a gin and drank it neat. He stared at a portrait of Isobel hung above the fireplace, whilst another servant whose name he had no intention of learning fussed over the fire which had been allowed to get low. Half an hour, perhaps forty-five minutes later, he heard someone leaving the house. Edward poured himself another gin and went back upstairs in the manner of someone who has only just that moment arrived to greet his wife.

She was sitting at a card table, wearing a green silk dressing gown, embroidered down the front with pale yellow butterflies. She was dealing herself a game of patience. She had dabbed cologne on her wrists, which did not mask the smell of Charles' own distinctive hair pomade, nor the acrid linger of his cigars in her silk. And as he looked at her he saw how plump she had become.

A loose sentence from the pile of burning letters skipped in his mind: "We have a new addition to the kitchen; he does not take up much space and so does not incur the wrath of Cook, but the best thing is that he makes the most delightful pastries." What pleasant words of greeting there might have been were obliterated by what had happened next. The shouting, and the bath water. Forcing his wife to wash herself, his hand gripping her neck and her fine pale hair coming loose. The way the bath water wicked into his dirty clothes as he rammed her head under. Hurt her, Isobel, his wife. And her placid face all the while despising him; her eyes open beneath the surface, bubbles escaping from her nose, just waiting for him to finish.

He let go of her when he saw her hands. The palms flashed up at him revealing the brown rash. He stepped back from her, as if that would have made any difference. Very slowly, Isobel got out of the bath, drew to her skin the green silk which clung and darkened against the contours of her. There, around her middle, obvious now, the swell in the candle light.

"You are finished," he'd spat out at her, pointing at her belly. "If that doesn't kill you, then those marks will."

"What are they?" she'd whispered.

"Hasn't he told you? A medical man. I suppose he thought to get himself a nice easy cure. Bit more palatable than mercury but, unfortunately for him, utterly useless."

"What is it? What do they mean? Please, tell me—" the whisper barely audible.

He'd backed further away from her, wiping his hands on his clothes. "I'll get you—" His voice fragmented and he struggled to contain the pieces. "I'll see to it that you receive the best treatment, but it's probably too late. For God's sake!"

"Please, Edward?"

"You have syphilis, courtesy of Mr Charles Jeffreye."

He'd turned and left her there, deaf to her calling him to come back. He'd rung for a maid, any maid, and told her to bring him some carbolic and hot water.

Afterwards, he'd gone and looked for Natalia, but he'd not been able to find her that night.

And how could he ever have thought of mentioning Natalia's name to Gwen? He cursed himself for it; and then he cursed Gwen for passing on the lie, for making others become entwined in a moment which had been so intensely private, tenuous and desperate between himself and Gwen. As he turned the thing over in jagged thoughts he remembered that Gwen had made such a play of not remembering that second rainy day in her garden. He could not fathom her game.

Edward took the letter from Cornwall out of his collecting bag and ripped it open.

Mr Scales,

My Mistress being unwell, it falls to me to write to you with the grave news that your wife, Mrs Isobel Scales, died here at Carrick House on the 21st February in the year of Our Lord, Eighteen Hundred & Sixty-One. Mrs Scales visited here & she was taken ill. She did not recover well enough to return home nor leave her bed here. I am sure it would be a comfort to you to know that your late wife was well cared for & wanted for nothing except to be able to speak with you at some time in the future, when, as she conveyed to my Mistress & to me, she hoped that you would attend one of my Mistress' Spiritual Evenings in order that she could talk with you. This was her dying wish.

We had a big fall of snow here, & we were not able to get a carriage through to take the coffin back to London. It must be my duty, also, to tell you that your late wife was buried here, at our church.

Another person has been here who was very interested to know where both yourself & also the late Mr Harris had got to. She payed my mistress a visit not long since & not so long after Mrs Scales had come here and passed away. This person said that she had spoken to your wife previous, & I thought that all in all you would want to know this as well.

Yours Truly,
Susan Wright.

Chapter XXXV

If this is what happens to every woman who becomes a mother, thought Gwen, then it is no wonder men want as many offspring as possible. A woman continually pregnant would make her forever stupid to the world and to her own thoughts. To her own self. Gwen thought of Edward, of his silly, purposeful stride, boxing up his specimens, busy, his mind uncomplicated by the kind of emotional demands her own body made of her. She thought that she could see his purpose in getting her with child. She did not need to *think* to be his illustrator; he did not want her as his assistant in the true sense. He had brought her here to be the skilled labour. She was becoming a kind of base animal, full of maternal instinct and nothing much else. It was a struggle to find herself each day, to carve out an inch of motivation. It was a battle of wills: her own and the will of nature. If I was not in this state, she thought, if I was not tied down by my 'condition' as Edward had referred to it, then I would leave. The fact that she could not possibly leave pressed a weight of almost unbearable discontent into her being. She steeled herself against it, washed her brush and carried on with her painting. All thought left her. She lost sense of where and who she was as she entered the topographies of the creatures before her.

Gwen looked up from her half-finished study of a large green caterpillar and met the amused gaze of Vincent Coyne. She regarded him for a moment, allowing a smile to curl the corner of her mouth, and then went about the business of putting the object of her study away. Here, at least, was another chance to take her mind out of the spiral of self-pity she had allowed herself to become

absorbed in that morning. The defoliated citrus twig went back
into the cage with the caterpillar. She wiped her paintbrush on a
cloth, and then wetted her fingers with spit to make a point on
the sable hairs. Gwen had not been expecting Vincent. He had sent
her a note a few days before, telling her that he would not be able
to come and visit. He had apologised and described how Mr
Pemberton had been struck with a fever. Now, he leaned over
the open windowsill.

"How can you do that when he doesn't keep still for one
minute?"

"Oh, it's simple enough. Far more agreeable than being presented
with an empty skin."

"People actually stuff those things?"

"Sometimes. Thankfully, Edward is far too busy."

"So, you've got him trapped in there, food plants on your doorstep. Will you let him go free, or is your plan to observe the whole
transformation and then stick a pin through him?"

"No, I couldn't do that."

Vincent brought up his closed fist and dropped a pale green
pupa attached to a leaf onto Gwen's workbook. "I have no idea
how old it is, or if it will hatch, but I think you'll be pleased with
it if it does. I believe that the mush in that thing is pretty damn
impossible to catch with a net."

Gwen eyed the gift without picking it up. "Are you an expert
on lepidoptera?"

"Is that what you call it? Well, you learn something new every
day."

Gwen took up the leaf and pupa and held it up to the light.
You are getting too familiar, she thought, but I like you. "You can
include moths in the order, as well. Thank you for this, Mr Coyne.
I'll keep it on my desk."

"I'd like to see Mr Scales' face when it hatches."

"That is probably unlikely since he has taken himself off on a little excursion. He should be back in a couple of weeks." Why on earth did I tell you that? Gwen blinked and avoided his gaze while making a show of examining the pupa more thoroughly.

"Are you comfortable, alone here?"

"I'm not alone," she said quickly. "I have Maria; she stays at night. I have no reason to feel uncomfortable."

"No, of course not. So. I'll let you continue."

"And what of Mr Pemberton, is he well enough?"

"To tell you the truth, I think he is malingering."

"The fever has eased off?"

"Some days it seems like he's just about himself again, and others he is the picture of woe. I'm convinced he eats hot peppers while I'm out to make himself come out in a sweat."

"But he has enough quinine?"

"Enough? He's using my supply now. We won't be able to make another excursion until the next boat comes in. Our search for your mysterious lady has been put back somewhat."

"These things are out of our control."

"May I come in? Where is your maid, by the way? I've been all around the house."

"I asked her to take a letter for me. I expect she has stopped to visit her family." Gwen felt suddenly uneasy; there was a kind of suppressed determination in Vincent's voice, which made her want to shrink into herself, like the mimosa leaves at the edges of the forest paths. She tried to make herself sound careless, but her own voice was now stretched with a breathlessness. "Do you know anything about Oxbow lakes? Edward is determined to find one."

"Is that where he has gone, to find one?"

"No."

"Just as well. Easy when you know where to look. They happen when the river changes its course."

"Have you seen one? Perhaps when Edward comes back you might show him on a map." Please, please, she thought, don't start on again about Darwin. She certainly wasn't in the mood for another convoluted conversation about the gigantic scientific discoveries Coyne believed he could make or prove.

"It's a possibility, certainly, but, you know, these lakes dry up. It may be that by the time Mr Pemberton and I are able to travel again, the lakes I know of will have turned to swamp. Of course, if Gus decides to malinger for much longer I may have to review my situation."

"You don't mean that. I think the pair of you are inseparable."

Vincent picked up the telescope from its resting place and extended each section. "Now this is something I never had the brains to think of acquiring. Perhaps I have gotten a little complacent and ought to put myself in the shoes of a novice, or semi-novice, and learn something."

"That spyglass actually had nothing to do with foresight. It was a gift."

"Then I wish I had friends like yours."

"It was a gift from the captain of the *Opal*. If I hadn't asked to use it so much, he probably would not have given it away."

"Ah." Vincent put the telescope back on the shelf and seated himself on one of the cane armchairs. "Don't mind me. Just carry on as you were; I don't want to interrupt you. I promise not to disturb you."

"You won't disturb me. I ought to move around a little, anyway."

"You look remarkably well, I must say. And your innovative style is rather becoming."

Gwen was suddenly annoyed at his candour. "Let me bring you a little something. I think we still have a drop of *cashaca*, or I could make some fresh coffee."

"No, no thank you. I don't need anything."

"Are you sure? What about some fruit? I am going to have some. Will you take an orange, Mr Coyne?"

Gwen went out to the next room and came back with two oranges. She sat in the chair opposite Vincent Coyne and began to peel one, dropping the peel into a handkerchief. Vincent played with his orange. He prodded it all over and sniffed the skin. He dug his nail into the zest and scraped off a tiny amount.

For goodness sake, she thought, just peel the orange. When Gwen had eaten half of her segments, he had still not begun to peel the fruit, nor had he said anything. Gwen noticed that a dullness had come over his expression. She let him be for a few minutes more and then asked if anything was the matter.

Vincent sighed. "Rust."

"Pardon?"

He leaned forward, his fist tight over the orange. "Tell me honestly, do you have any problem with rust?"

"I don't quite understand. Rot, insect damage—these a little, perhaps. We manage to keep on top of it, just. The problem of rust is no more or less trouble."

"You admit that rust is a problem though. You must beware of rust."

She laughed, uneasy at his serious face, thinking that he was far more peculiar than she had imagined. "We keep everything well oiled, you may be sure, Mr Coyne."

"You do understand my meaning?"

"I think I do."

"Fine then, that's settled." He peeled his orange. "Mrs Scales, I would have loved to see you in English society, hosting one of those 'at homes' which people seem to go in for."

"I doubt you would have enjoyed yourself, Mr Coyne, even if I had. I think you would have found yourself in rather boring company."

There followed an awkward pause and then he said, "What do

your family make of your leaving England for such noble causes as art and science?"

"I have only a sister. She thinks very little of any of it."

"I'm sorry. I didn't mean to open wounds."

Gwen had been avoiding his gaze; now she glanced at him, "You haven't."

Chapter XXXVI

The morning was fresh as they set off along the road. Gwen tucked her arm into Maria's and they walked like that all the way.

Maria bought bread, dried saltfish, bacon, a jar of oil, tomatoes and peppers. Gwen stayed at her side trying to catch phrases and words of what was said, but she was distracted. Being part of a crowd again after her quiet months with only Edward and Maria for company made her edgy, alert. She was thrilled at the variety of different faces, all absorbed in their own errands or conversations. Her gaze darted, unable to rest on a single thing or person for very long. Her arm was growing tired from holding the basket of Maria's purchases, but there was nowhere to put it down safely. The ringing of church bells filled the air as it had on her very first morning in Pará: some festival was going on that week, Maria had told her. Would she like to go to one of the services? Gwen had been unsure but now she thought that if Maria mentioned it again perhaps she might, after all.

"Mrs Scales, may I?"

She started at the sound of his voice and turned. Gwen looked up into the smiling face of Gus Pemberton. His pale linen jacket, newly pressed and reflecting the light, made her shade her eyes with her hand. She let him take her basket.

He said, "Are you here alone?"

"Mr Pemberton. How well you look. I came with Maria, I fancied a walk." She was conscious of herself beginning to babble. She was blushing. She teetered on the heat of it, and chided herself for being so pathetic.

"I always get the day's provisions myself. I can't be sitting around in the morning waiting for my breakfast. I'd much rather go out and buy it myself."

Gus Pemberton's talk was easy and he smiled again. She felt stupid under his gaze. Gwen saw that he had some packages under his arm. "I was under the impression—" She felt confused; he didn't seem like someone recovering from an illness at all; certainly not the malingerer that Vincent had reported. She said, "I mean, it's very lively, for such an early hour. We have a rather more sedate existence."

"Yes. I do prefer it after the detachment of an excursion. Will you have breakfast? You can enjoy the scene from my windows without having to be in the middle of it."

Gus Pemberton's apartments were on the corner of a long row of imposing but dilapidated buildings near the port. Its first-floor windows gave an aspect out over the port and across the streets. Gwen looked down at the market vendors in the sun and the sharply contrasting shade cast by the buildings. She could see how easily Mr Pemberton would have spotted her parasol in the crowd; how quick he might have been in going down there to buy himself a loaf of bread before accosting her. The smell of toast, bacon and coffee mingled with Mr Pemberton's cigarette smoke and drifted around her. It was not an acrid smoke but pleasingly sweet; not the tobacco smell she was used to. Gwen's stomach rumbled loudly. She was glad that he had no servant. His preference, not a circumstance. His preference then, had given her the opportunity to compose herself.

There was something about his unspoken experience which left her feeling even more intimidated now that she was alone with him. And she did not want to admit that Vincent had been to see her. She looked over her shoulder towards the open door. There was nothing about the man to suggest that he was capable of malingering. He was whistling a tune. Though perhaps malingerers whistled: she did not know. Something complicated, and too high for his mouth and tongue to register. Perhaps it was part of an aria from an opera; and a giggle rose uncontrollably in her throat as she recalled the amateur operatic ladies' performance. She was reminded suddenly of the surprise she had felt, a long time past, it seemed now, when she had learned that female voices could break. And the remembered surprise could not be dissociated from the look of bewilderment on her mother's face. Gwen let her mother's face slide away. She had not said yesterday to Vincent that her mother would have revelled in her daughter's desire to travel; nor had she said that her mother would have made it impossible to leave Euphemia behind. She told herself Euphemia would never have come with her, even had she been asked. Had she been different.

She would have liked to ask Gus Pemberton things that she had not thought to ask Captain Swithin. But, in between sips of coffee, black and punchingly bitter, she was still paralysed by this shyness. He smiled at her. Gwen consumed her breakfast in a state of extreme hunger. It was difficult not to appear ravenous as she bit into the crisp toast and salty bacon. He squeezed oranges over a greenish glass tumbler on the table. He pushed it over to her. "Mind the pips, you can spit them out onto your plate." Gwen gulped the juice, swallowing the pips.

He said, "I admire your tenacity."

She laughed, dispossessed finally of some of her shyness. "For not spitting?"

"For not staying in England; for following your husband in his work. And, I may say, for your reputation. It precedes you, Mrs Scales." Gwen blanched a little at the connection of Edward to work. It had not occurred to her that what he was doing was associated with the word. A vocation. "Of course," he continued, mistaking her discomfort for something else, "it is yours as much as his. I have known couples whose combined efforts would have amounted to nothing without the female part of the equation."

"In our case that remains to be seen."

"Forgive me, that did not sound as I intended it. I don't mean to cast any doubt over your husband's own tenacity. But do not take this the wrong way. As amateurs you have set out on an equal footing. You have an enquiring and, I believe, determined character, Mrs Scales, that I know already. And talented as you are with the paint-box, I cannot imagine that your part of the venture will ultimately be restricted to such."

"Mr Pemberton, may I ask you a personal question?"

Gus leaned back in his chair, and crossed his ankle over his knee.

"Have you ever had malaria?" She watched his face for a sign.

He uncrossed his ankle and reached for the coffee pot. "Fortunately, not for a long time. You mustn't worry about contracting it here, if that is what the question is about."

She watched his hands and then met his gaze. "It wasn't."

"I was wondering if you might mention the rather famous tussle over your microscope."

"Famous?" Gwen was at once mortified and confused.

"Oh, perhaps not famous—you mustn't worry about it. You are held in very high regard here, you know, for standing your ground. Marcus Frome was never an easy person to get along with."

"You know him?"

He paused. "Ah . . . not as such. I don't think anyone could ever have known him, really."

"Well, I am glad that he went back to England."

"Mrs Scales, did your husband not tell you? I'm sorry to have brought it up. I thought you knew."

"Knew about what?"

"Marcus Frome went missing from the ship. No one can be sure of the precise point of the voyage, but, two weeks out, some other passenger was in need of a doctor and—he simply wasn't to be found."

Gwen gazed at Gus Pemberton in mute disbelief. It seemed too ridiculous. She'd thought of him sometimes, and wondered if he really had been as desperate as he had seemed. "Mr Pemberton, I'm—thank you for telling me." Gwen sat in stunned silence for a moment.

"I came with the news on Old Year's Night," he said gently. "I had thought that your husband would have wanted to tell you as soon as possible."

Gwen recalled the excuse Mr Pemberton had used to get Edward to go outside. Fumigating the amphibians.

"A lot of news escapes my attention, Mr Pemberton. *The Times* frequently has sections missing before it comes to me."

"That's—regrettable."

"I can't believe that a man would do such a thing over—such a *dreadful* thing to do, Mr Pemberton, over a microscope of all objects."

"Please, you must not think for a minute, Mrs Scales, that it was for want of a microscope that the man threw himself overboard."

"Well, whatever am I to suppose? He made it very clear that he believed—"

"What Marcus Frome believed and what was fact did not always sit harmoniously; you must not dwell on it."

"I can't help but dwell on it. Mr Frome was convinced that he was on the point of a momentous discovery."

"Suppose then, that he had been. Giving him your microscope would not have helped him. He would have needed to borrow everything you have, and more." He leaned forward on the edge of his seat, resting his elbows on his knees. "And, frankly, Mrs Scales, he was not a lucky man. Do set your mind at ease."

She wanted to change the subject. "I have been —" she said, her voice rising. "I was led to believe that you were very ill."

Gus threw himself back into his chair, "Ach, this is about Vincent. I knew he had been to see you yesterday. I think you came into town to find me?"

Gwen shrugged her shoulders. "Perhaps I did."

"Whatever he has told you, you mustn't feel let down by his inconsistencies. He means well, I can assure you of that."

"You are not hurt that he has lied about you."

"He meant no harm by it. But I feel I must be straight with you. He and I have come to blows over the direction of our own travels. We have agreed to go our separate ways."

"Then why did he not tell me that?"

"It may have been my fault. I told him to say what he liked about me. That he only cites me as being ill is reassuring."

"Your disagreement was serious."

"In the light of day, on a morning such as this, it would sound petty in the retelling."

Gwen was surprised that a man like Gus Pemberton would admit to describing a disagreement like that. His openness pulled her in. "I feel deceived. I feel now that I have spent hours talking to an actor."

"Well, we are all actors, Mrs Scales—whether we think it or not. Even as our truest selves, even when alone with our thoughts." Gus Pemberton took up a piece of rind and nibbled off a small portion. He played it around his mouth for a while. Gwen waited. After some time, he said, "In essence, it was about our authority, as outsiders, to disregard boundaries. I, I should say no more about it." His smile was apologetic.

"I'm sorry."

"Ach, no need to be." Gus Pemberton paused. Then, "He and I were not simply exploring. We were prospecting. Diamonds, gold.

That is our business. Partnerships like ours, they come to blows sooner or later." His tone was light. "It is no great tragedy."

"What will you do now?" Gwen felt small in the light of his candid speech. A man can be more than one thing if he chooses, she thought. He does not have to define himself by his means of survival.

Gus said, "I am undecided. There is some property in Scotland, which I must dispose of, and then, after a suitable period, perhaps take my stick to pastures new. Maybe New Zealand."

"And what do you think Mr Coyne will do, without you to guide him?"

Gus Pemberton hesitated. "I think he should go back, precarious as times are. Perhaps in twelve or eighteen months he will be ready to return if he wishes."

"Mr Pemberton," she said.

"Gus, please. Call me Gus, won't you?"

"Gus. Mr Coyne has said that he will help me find someone."

"Indeed, he has."

"I don't know how to put it, but I don't wish to find anyone. And I don't quite understand how."

"How?"

"I have never mentioned anything about finding any person, ever, to anyone at all. Not a soul. And as far as I know, neither has Edward. And so—"

"He's talked to me, on occasions, at great length about this. I have understood that it has been widely known."

Gwen's hands fluttered at her throat and then fell back down to twist in her lap. "Mr Pemberton, Gus. If I tell you something, I believe you will preserve the integrity of that thing. I don't know you at all, but I have to tell you that this person, the search, is just a fabrication. No one needs to find her. In fact, I don't believe she even exists. At least, not in the temporal world."

"I can see that it upsets you. Would you rather not speak about it?"

"I merely wanted one other person to know." She searched his face for any glimmer of amusement. There was none. "Gus, how could Mr Coyne possibly have come to believe anything so ridiculous and so specific?"

"That, I can't pretend to know the answer to."

"He is your companion. You must know each other very well."

"Mrs Scales, please understand. I will keep this to myself, I fully comprehend your anxiety—but Vincent, he . . . Look, we met, quite by chance, some few years back in Australia, and I took him on. He had a letter of recommendation from a fellow I used to know. We travelled, prospecting, and then later here, in Brazil and after, we parted ways—I had thought for good—until we met again, quite by chance in the spring of '59 and—it really isn't important. What is important is that Vincent will be leaving again, quite soon, and so you will have no need to bother about anything but your work."

His face was open, eager for her to be appeased. He leaned towards her and took her hand. His speech became low, a whisper. "Don't let him travel with you, under any circumstances. Say nothing; he is here. I saw his shadow." Before she could say anything, Gus had planted a kiss on her lips and pulled her towards him. She resisted him as she felt her big belly making contact with his body, but he made her stand up, still firmly connected by the kiss and then ushered her into his small sleeping quarters where he closed the door behind them.

"Forgive, please forgive me, Mrs Scales. I didn't have time to think," he whispered.

"Will he go away now?"

"Yes, I think so. We'll let him have a few moments." They looked at each other. Gwen tried not to notice that Gus Pemberton

favoured a firm bed over a hammock or that the impression from
his head was still left in the pillow.

Leaving Gus Pemberton, Gwen wondered how much influence
he held over Vincent Coyne. What kind of influence was it that
allowed one man to send another back home? Despite everything,
and in spite of herself, she still liked Vincent. Or was it just that
she liked him to speak to her. His attention. To look at him, he
was so beautiful; that he was mad did not always seem to matter.
Conversation with Edward was not stimulating, only irritating.
In conversation with both Mr Coyne and Mr Pemberton they
had both treated her as if her opinion mattered, as Edward had
once done.

    The rain came down so forcefully in the afternoon that each
drop seemed to have its own precise destination. The first drops
fell on the leaves like fleas against newsprint gathering in numbers
exponentially, swelling rapidly to a fully liquid sound.

    Gwen felt that the weather's exactness was sharpening her senses;
she let herself believe this for a while and revelled in her indulgence.
What is there to stop me? she thought. Who is there to accuse me,
if I never speak of it? The rain plastered her hair to her skull, and
she felt the drops mapping its surface, washing all trace of Gus
Pemberton from her skin.

During the night she woke and thought that Gus Pemberton was
beside her, somehow, in her hammock. She put her hand out into
the dark of the room; a pair of frogs called to each other. She heard
the soft snoring of Maria in the next room and closed her eyes
again. But the image of Gus Pemberton was still in her mind. His
words, the pattern of his speech, the touch of his hand on her sleeve.

"Don't worry, Mrs Scales. I'd never ask you to compromise your integrity, but I'd like to let you have my address. Please, you must write to me, tell me how things progress, regarding everything."

"I will."

She shifted in her hammock, smiling to herself that she would be able to write to Gus Pemberton and ask him to explain properly the things he had told her about Marcus Frome and the mosquitoes, and his own thoughts about how it might have been connected to Frome's research—his great discovery. She relaxed back into a sleepy state, but then suddenly became wide awake again. Gus Pemberton had not given her his address at all, not asked her to write to him. And they had not, she realised now, talked in any detail about Marcus Frome's mosquitoes.

Chapter XXXVII

THE TIMES, Thursday, October 4, 1866.

MURDER TRIAL AT THE OLD BAILEY.

HUSBAND of the prisoner Mrs Pemberton today gave evidence in the form of a statement read out to the court. The body of the statement was in effect heavily redacted by repeated objections from the Prosecution, all of which were upheld. Being frustrated in his attempts to read out Mr Pemberton's account of his involvement in the case as a witness, Mr Shanks called Mr Pemberton himself, to the great surprise of the court.

Mr Pemberton said, "I wish to make it known to the Jury that important information pertaining to this case has been omitted from the evidence so far submitted or allowed by this court. As the first person to enter the room where Mr Scales' body was found, I can tell you, Gentlemen, that it was not an ordinary scene, if any scene of supposed murder may be called ordinary. What Detective Sergeant Gray and Doctor Jacobs failed to communicate to both the inquest and this court I shall now divulge."

Mr Pemberton went on to say that upon turning over the corpse, all three men noted that certain mutilations had been done but that there was no evidence of profuse bleeding, which, Mr Pemberton surmised, indicated that such mutilations had been carried out either post mortem or in some other part of the house at the time of, or close to, the time of death. Mr Pemberton went on to state that he spent some time searching the house for signs of such mutilation having occurred, and that although he found no direct clue, he did notice that the large table in the kitchen had been recently scrubbed clean, and that a copper full of articles of clothing was in the process of being boiled. Mr Probart for the Prosecution made objection to the nature of Mr Pemberton's evidence, but the Judge overruled, and Mr Pemberton was permitted to continue. He said, "My wife's clothing from the previous day had not yet been laundered, as I found to my relief when I returned home. Her clothes had not a single sign of blood spatters on them anywhere; this fact will be corroborated by my servants whose attention I called to this fact in a discreet manner. Therefore, I must ask the question of all assembled here: that perhaps some other person was responsible for those mutilations. Some other person whose motives, however obscure to us now, may soon become clear. I put it to the court that whomsoever perpetrated this ghastly detail upon the body of the unfortunate Mr Scales was also the perpetrator of his murder.

"I might add further details of the general scene, if I might, of the room in that property. There was, attached to the back of the door in that room, a substantial hook, the screw of which being very long protruded an eighth of an inch to the other side of the door. The hook was a crude one, and its presence there was incongruous with the rest of the furnishings. On close inspection I found traces of fresh sawdust on panel beadings directly below its point of entry. I made several and exhaustive notes on everything I witnessed in that house the same day, which I shall be happy to submit to the Jury for their considered inspection. I feel that such details are pertinent to this case and that without them no true conclusion can be made."

Mr Justice Linden allowed that such a diary may be submitted in its entirety with the redacted statement for the Jury to consider, with full copies to himself and to the Prosecution.

Chapter XXXVIII

Gwen lit a lamp and paced the rooms in her slippers and then kicked them off. Marcus Frome had actually thrown himself overboard. But why? Why am I anxious about it, when it is already done? The man has been dead for months. I am the last to know about it, when I—. But he was an obnoxious toad of a man, she reminded herself, and did not deserve my microscope, not at any price; even if he had been able to pay. But, she asked herself now, would I have let him take my microscope if I had known that he would do such a stupid thing. Was it stupid, though? How much courage does it take to throw yourself over the side of the ship?

Stop it, she told herself. But she kept running over the things Gus Pemberton had said and realised that he had been trying to allay any doubts she may have had about her own part in Frome's final act.

As dawn broke she got back into her hammock, wild through want of sleep, and she did sleep for a while.

Fitful on waking, she tried to work but found herself dull-fingered. She made errors which ruined whole pieces, and had to give in. I can't go and visit him again, she thought.

In town, she made no pretence of wanting to hang about at the market and went instead straight to Gus Pemberton's apartment. In her purse she had folded a piece of paper with a message, asking Gus Pemberton to come and visit her as soon as he was able. If he is not at home, she told herself, I will leave this. But she could not

decide. She stood at his door with her hand at the bell pull. She
was acting too hastily. He would think her demented. She turned
her back on the door and leaned on it, facing out towards the bustle
of the market. The sharp light stunned her eyes and she had to shut
them tight. I'll go and find Maria, she told herself. She leaned more
heavily on the door to propel herself forward and the door gave
under her weight. She turned and pushed on it, stepping into the
instant cool and quiet of his vestibule. She retraced her steps, remembered from the day before, to the rooms Gus Pemberton kept. She
paused, nervous suddenly of her assumption that it would be perfectly
fine for her to walk into his rooms unannounced. To her great relief,
the whole place felt empty, and she made to leave, pulling out her
note to drop at the threshold. A noise made her catch her breath.
A hard slap of a hand on solid flesh. It was quite unmistakable. Then
something softer, and with it this time a gruff voice. Gwen stood
there, unable to remove herself from the scene of something she
immediately knew was very private. Gwen's throat pulsed hard with
the beat of her heart and with it the repeated noise and what she
knew were moans of pleasure. You fool, she told herself, you were
completely taken up with your nightmare and you have delivered
yourself into another.

"You want her, don't you?" The voice was unmistakably Vincent's.

"Just shut up." The words of reply belonged to Gus Pemberton,
but they were hardly his; they were strained and hoarse.

"Say it. You want, her, so much. That—belly of hers. You're.
Thinking. Of. It. Right. Now. Aren't. You?"

Gwen clasped her hands over her mouth and turned to leave
in a hurry, knocking into the doorframe, hearing Gus Pemberton
yelling, "Shut up, shut up, shut up."

Remove yourself, she told herself. Get out, before you are
discovered.

★   ★   ★

She woke streaked in sweat, gasping, fingers digging into the flesh of her palms. Maria stood over her. Gwen struggled to compose herself. "What was I saying? Did I speak in my sleep, Maria?"

Maria shook her head, "No, you were fitful, that's all, Mrs Scales. I thought I should wake you."

Gwen rubbed her face with her hands as though she had come up from under water. "I have to go into town again today, Maria. I must call on Mr Pemberton."

The baby turned over in her belly; putting her hand to the unfathomable, undulating writhe of it, she remembered that in her last dream, there had been no child inside her.

In Gus Pemberton's apartment Gwen was breathless, hot, thirsty. Gus looked at her for a second but didn't do what she dreaded him doing. He didn't treat her as a flustered and confused woman standing inside his door, clutching at the huge belly she bore.

"Who, exactly, is Vincent Coyne?" She had thought about how she might phrase this as the cart had trundled along the road, the bumps hurting her so much that she had asked the driver to stop so she could get out and walk instead.

"In what way do you mean?"

"I mean where is he from? Because he isn't actually American, is he?"

Gus raised his eyebrows and jerked back his neck in surprise. "I am not sure that I understand you."

"How can you be so sure that he is exactly who he says he is?"

"I met him through an acquaintance."

"And this man introduced you to him personally?"

"Yes, in a letter."

Gwen breathed, in raising the bulk of her belly. "But he isn't from America, I am sure of it. I am sure he is something else."

"*Something* else? That sounds interesting."

"It isn't really. Has he gone?"

"Yes. He will leave this morning. He isn't here; he has gone out to say his farewells. I am simply waiting for his return and then we will take his trunk down to the—"

"I need to see it. You warned me about him yesterday."

"Well, yes, but purely for selfish reasons."

"Gus, please, let me see his trunk."

It had been left open; Gwen got down on her knees to look at the things inside it. A man not expecting someone to come poking about among his things would not conceal his paperwork, she thought, and her eyes travelled over the pockets on the inside of the trunk lid. Her hands patted the satin and then rummaged into the opening. She pulled out a small bundle of letters and untied the plain cotton tape holding them together. She felt Gus at her shoulder, watching her, but she did not stop, either in embarrassment or in panic at the idea of Vincent's return. She no longer cared if he knew about her suspicions. Her body sagged a little when she did not find any familiar handwriting on the envelopes. She had almost given up, and was on the point of stuffing the letters back into the satin pocket when the last envelope, unmarked, came to the top of the small pile. She delved in and brought out a collection of calling cards. For a moment she was baffled. Vincent Coyne's whiskerless face in a fine photographic representation stared out at her from the flat of her palm. On the reverse was his name, nothing more. She put it back with the rest and replaced them. She tied up the tape and after putting the letters back heaved herself up off the floor.

"I knew that I had seen Mr Coyne before. The first time I met you both, I had the oddest feeling—the feeling that you have lived that moment before and that everything you see and hear is, in fact, just a memory."

"I know the feeling; there ought to be an expression for it."

"But it was not in the normal way. I felt it only when I looked at Mr Coyne. I felt a peculiar connection to him."

"You found him attractive; well, that is understandable enough."

"No, it was because of that card," she gestured at the trunk.

"I can't say that I have seen it before."

"But I have. On the floor of my sister's bedroom, just before I left. Do you see?"

"Perhaps."

"Yes, perhaps? Yes, certainly. He knows my sister. He has let tiny things slip. Things which I would not usually have noticed if it had been only once."

"Can you be sure of—what is it that you *are* sure of, Gwen?"

"That my sister has sent him on some errand to drive suspicion and enmity between Edward and me. She has sent Mr Coyne with false information, which she hopes will destroy this venture."

"You are talking about this phantom woman, the one who does not exist."

"Yes, some hideous thing—I don't know, I can't even imagine what she can have concocted. She isn't sane. I mean to say, she isn't a lunatic, but my sister was always jealous of everything I did, of everyone I saw, of everyone who wanted to speak to me—though latterly there were very few, if any. I left my home, a place I have loved, to get away from the stifling atmosphere my sister created. And yet I can travel thousands of miles, and still she persists. I sound ridiculous to you. I must be pathetic to you, standing in here, going through these belongings. Like a thief."

"I led you to this room, remember. But Vincent is leaving, Gwen. He has not succeeded, even if your suspicions are correct. Neither Vincent nor your sister have driven anything here to destroy your marriage."

Gwen turned away at the mention of that particular lie. She hid

her face from Gus for a moment, then said, "It was his blue spectacles, as much as his whiskers. He never takes them off, and they
altered his features just enough to have thrown me."

"Oh, well, that he probably didn't mean to do. He has sensitive
eyes. I've never seen him without his spectacles."

"And you will be going away as well?" She couldn't say what
she needed to express. That one afternoon alone with Gus had
changed her beyond her own comprehension, that to see him
leave—she felt that she would not be able to cope in his absence.

"But we can write to each other," he said. "You can give me a
regular report on every new insect and bug that you find, and their
peculiar habits."

"Gus, I am afraid. I am afraid of—I didn't come here to have
a child. I came here to work."

"Maria is the best person in the entire world you could hope
to have in the house. Trust her."

"It isn't that. I'm afraid of the pain."

"She will help you."

Gwen wanted to say that she was afraid of death. That she was
afraid that the child would die, or that it would be born some
kind of monstrous creature, that she herself would die, that she
would bleed to death in that little wooden house on the edge of
the jungle. That her blood would run through the floorboards and
the insects would consume it. But she kept quiet. She let Gus hold
her and stroke her hair and lead her away from Vincent's emptied
room into his own.

Lying on her side, with Gus curled around her awkward, naked,
pregnant shape, she wanted him to beg her to leave Brazil with
him. She waited on every breath he took, and listened for the
change that would come in the deepest part of his chest. But his

breathing was regular and easy, and she knew that he was too good a person to try and take her entirely away from the man he thought of as her husband, no matter what else he may privately have thought of Edward. Gwen had to resign herself to the fugitive nature of their time together and the fact that she would never be able to tell him the truth. And while she lay there with Gus, the trickle of his semen running down the inside of her thigh and cooling on her skin, she couldn't even bring herself to ask if he would ever come back to Brazil, or if he thought that they would ever meet again.

Chapter XXXIX

Pará, Brazil. June, 1861.

Edward was carrying a brace of limp parrots over his shoulder as he leaped up the steps of the house. He had been out since seven. Gwen saw the blunt grey tongues caught between the open beaks and turned away. Edward didn't see her revulsion; he was too excited. The birds were a pair, a fine pair which had been flying together, and he had brought them down without needing to reload his rifle.

It had become apparent that skinning creatures near the house was contributing to the ant problem. No specimen or part small enough was immune to the ants' own predilection for collecting. Maria had smeared bitter sticky stuff on the table and chair legs and the ropes suspending the food-sacks. The birds he carried were already empty of their internal organs. He was so pleased with himself he whistled an improvised tune as he dusted the skins and wrapped them in paper. He thought of his waiting breakfast, and the thick coffee. Killing the birds so cleanly, and being able to retrieve them on his own, made up for the terrible experience beforehand of trying to secure a monkey. Nausea fingered his throat. Why had he done that? Monkeys of virtually any kind were easily obtainable in the city. But then there were the parrots. When he saw them, all the sickening guilt over the ruined and wasted monkey fell away.

His boyhood days spent skinning and stuffing crows were paying off. He finished the parrots, and packed them away. Gwen would not paint them unless they retained their living form. Squawking, defecating, flapping and intent on destroying everything with their beaks. Gwen seemed quiet this morning. Perhaps it would be better not to talk about parrots. She was not even talking to Maria. He was glad. All that Portuguese being spoken in the house made him feel more keenly that he was on the periphery of the world that Gwen constructed about herself. He slurped noisily at the coffee and looked out across the garden. It was so fantastic to have fruit growing right there. He'd found a use for them. Every day he took the discarded skins to the same part of the forest, a sunny glade where he had first seen the large blue Morpho butterflies. His idea was to create a kind of feast table, to attract them. So far he had collected an incredible number of different lepidoptera species from that one spot. He finished his coffee and called out his farewell again to Gwen. Her reply came to him as an offhand mutter. He took up his insect equipment and bounced out of the house.

By two in the afternoon his tin collecting boxes were full. He rested his insect nets carefully with the rest of his equipment in a heap on the floor of the verandah. He had come back an hour earlier than usual, full of excitement, eager to show Gwen what his boxes contained. He finally had an excellent specimen of a male Morpho rhetenor, which had eluded his net during his solitary two-week trip, and a slightly less brilliant but no less exciting pair of M. Menelaus, caught as they'd tasted the banana skins.

One by one, the birds gave up their noises, trailed by the scraping of the cicadas. They stopped and started, stopped and started again, like a partially jammed clockwork toy. The bellies of the clouds amassed overhead were bruised with the swell of rain. As Edward stepped towards Gwen, he felt the first rustle of wind, signalling their release.

There was an extra stickiness about the house, and the pungent smells of childbirth hung in the air. He felt light-headed, knowing that this scene of the simplest domesticity was a world away from his old life. He stepped closer to see the small jaw, the half-extended tongue, fluttering in sleepy rest against her breast. He tried to imagine himself, for a fleeting instant, making the place where he stood his permanent home. The wind grew stronger, making the slack leaves in the trees talk. He had an impulse to step out into it as the thunder cracked. The child opened its eyes, and he thought it perceived him. It had Gwen's mouth and nose; Edward's forehead and brow in miniature wrinkled back at him. A tiny fist had come loose from the cloth bindings and he went to touch it, drawing back at the last moment, remembering his ramble through the forest. He wiped the imagined traces of butterfly onto his trousers. He knew that Gwen loved this time of day best; she would often come out onto the verandah and stand motionless to see it all pouring down off the thatch overhang.

Gwen woke up; the child began to feed again. She didn't notice him standing there. He couldn't bear it; he felt he must break the silence. "Is it a girl, or a boy?"

Gwen dragged her gaze away from her child, but she was not really seeing him. "A girl."

Edward breathed out. Had he been holding his breath all this time?

She smiled at the child; its jaw worked away drawing the milk down. That strange sensation, that strangest thing which Nature had provided for. She felt sure that she would never get used to it.

He bent over her and she accepted his kiss on her forehead. When he took his mouth away, she kept her head tilted up as though she expected more than a simple peck on the forehead. Her eyes were closed. He quickly checked the corners of his mouth to see that no dried spittle had collected there before bending forward again to kiss her on the mouth. He had taken too long. She was moving her head back to a more natural position. Damn it. He kissed her anyway, on her cheek. It reminded them both of a place almost forgotten, that bumbling botchedness which had passed for passion in the beginning.

He would bring back some of those moody birds from the dingy parts of the forest in a cage. She would paint them, and he would let them go again.

He needed to wipe himself down, and change. He could feel bits of forest caught inside his shirt and ears. He always checked for ticks; he couldn't stand the way their heads would bury right under the skin. He'd found that a well-heated specimen pin applied to the abdomen did the trick. He gathered himself together, "Have you thought of a name. Perhaps a family name?" How strange, he thought, for her to blush at such a simple question.

"Augusta."

"Augusta," he repeated, trying it out on his tongue. "It seems very severe. But it has a certain quality about it. Is it a family name?"

She shook her head. "I just like it. I thought something would come to mind when I saw her face, and that came to my mind."

"You know," he said hesitantly, "if I could have foreseen this moment, that first night I spoke to you in your little summerhouse, I would have arranged our passage the very next day."

Gwen's forehead wrinkled in concentration. He could not tell whether she had heard him properly until she spoke. "We met on the beach, Edward. In broad daylight." Her eyes were still fixed on the face of her child; it was as if she spoke to the baby, not Edward. "I never spoke to you in that summerhouse. I have never told you, but I found you there one morning. You were—you were asleep, and I thought you looked so exhausted I did not wake you." She laughed. "At first I had thought you were some kind of vagrant; in point of fact, I was a little afraid of you." She turned her face up to his and met his gaze.

He said, "But I remember it so clearly; we spoke for some forty minutes. It was midnight, and you were wrapped against the chill in a very thick old coat and boots which were too big for your feet by far. You mistook me for your gardener. But you were very different from the way you were the next time we spoke on the beach. And I *distinctly* remember being glad, that next time on the beach, that I could see your face properly and that your attitude towards me was much lighter, much more natural. And I remember thinking what a fool I was to have avoided that part of the coast, fearing that I had offended you." Edward watched a wave of realisation sweep across Gwen's face as it dawned on her what he was saying.

"You could not have known that I had a sister whose most prized possession was her ability to impersonate any being, living or dead, animal or human, including myself."

"Gwen, I—"

"It doesn't matter; not now."

Again, she was speaking to him but looking all the while intently at the baby. He almost backed into Maria. He'd totally forgotten about her.

He opened up his collecting tin and paused, remembering his jubilation at having the specimens in his possession. He wavered, half turning, deliberating over whether he should not show them to her anyway. As he picked them over, looking for flaws in the iridescent patina, that shocking, crackling blue, he let the knowledge of what he had done with Gwen's sister that dank morning, and, he now admitted to himself, those other times, wash over his conscience. He'd wanted it not to have been so, and therefore it had existed in his mind as something malleable as putty. A memory reshaped; a physical act becoming a conversation; one person becoming another.

He looked down at his hands and saw the ruined Morpho butterfly wings spread as dull dust across his fingers. And he knew that Gwen was innocent—she did not know about Natalia. He was safe. He found the key to the writing slope and opened it up. There was the letter from Gwen's maid lying on the top of his papers. He walked out onto the verandah on the opposite side of the house from Gwen and their child and Maria. He struck a match and set light to the letter, holding it by the corner so that it drooped down and the flames licked up the words. A mimic. He did not know whether Euphemia's talents extended to mimicking others' voices on paper, but as he could not be sure, he felt it was better to burn it. He had made a note of the date of Isobel's death. He still felt lighter in the head when he reflected on the fact that he was now free of her. He dropped the charred paper to the floor of the verandah and stamped on its glowing fragments. No more recriminations, no more hysterics, nothing of that; even in his absence she had tried her damnedest to reel him in, through the pity of strangers. But she had failed. There was nothing more Isobel could do to him. She was silenced for all time.

Chapter XL

As the months went on, Gwen was submerged by the routine of feeding her baby. It would latch onto her breast with a mouth as wide as a cat fish and just as strong. It sucked the juice from her, and Gwen felt herself shrivelling. The clarity of the last two months before the birth left her; she was befuddled and dazed, propped up half conscious. She was either feeding the baby or being woken to feed the baby or falling asleep feeding the baby.

Her world had diminished to her breasts and whether or not the baby was sucking on them. It was so boring. It was everything she had not wanted or asked for. The initial euphoria of having survived it, of having this miraculous tiny human come from her intact and also alive, had evaporated. The momentary surge of warm feelings for Edward had receded, too, as quickly as they had come.

She looked at her drawing things in a state of listless exhaustion one afternoon. The baby was cradled in the crook of her arm; its head moist with her sweat, the bright fuzz which passed for hair, dark and slick against the skull. She caught sight of the fontanelle pulsating on the top. That thick membrane stretched over brain. Maria had told her to make sure it never dipped into the skull; if it did, she'd told her, the baby was not getting enough to drink and might die. This information both fascinated and distressed Gwen. She'd pass her fingers over the patch of soft head and hold her breath.

With one hand she pulled the things out of her bag to air them and to check for signs of mould or insect damage. She wiped over the surface of her books which had been treated with kerosene. It kept away some of the insects; others didn't object to the stink and burrowed holes into her pages. Then there was the novel, still unread. She'd treated that as well, and now idly she checked for insect damage. She shook the book, knocked it on the surface of the workbench. The baby stirred and fell asleep again instantly, her eyes rolling glassily.

She opened the book wide, so that she could look along the hollow of the spine and knocked it down on the bench again. A single beetle fell out, something small and brown. Before, she would have caught it with a pooter and then trapped it in the live box for observation under the microscope. Now, she watched it, her naked eyes stinging with fatigue as the beetle trundled off and hid itself in a crack on the bench.

The book had creaked a greeting at her. The fanning sections had kissed the air, the open lower edges sucking in space. When she closed the book with a disregarding flick, the cover said *fphphphf*. Gwen no longer cared who had sent her a novel to read. She kept the book in good condition because that was what you did with books. And if she never read it, then someone, at some point, might want to; she would have been ashamed to own an unslit book which was falling to bits. Unslit books had once excited her beyond the limit she believed they ought. As a child she had loved slitting pages more than eating, or sleeping between fresh sheets. More than her paint-box, even. More than her sister, sometimes.

She had owned a paper knife made from a very thin piece of bone. She'd loved that instrument, too, until she'd overheard what it was really made of. Then, she had taken it to the kitchen and opened the range door. The smell of the burning slave's rib had escaped into the room and she'd run away to be sick in the pantry.

Gwen doubted now that it had really been a human rib; much more likely, she thought, to have been a sliver of ivory, or something more prosaic like beef shinbone. The baby's head lolled and slipped a bit in the pooling sweat. Gwen fingered the binding on the novel and stared some long minutes at the swirls of colour on the marbled paper.

Edward had bought her a letter knife of carved horn in New York. She hadn't thought to take one with her. It pained her to think of the two of them; awkward strangers seeing the sights, buying trinkets.

Her scalp crawled, the beading sweat masquerading as a legion of lice, and she thought, Where did I put that letter knife? She didn't think, I'm going to slip the knife in and hold the paper firm as I slit it through.

The letter knife was an awful-looking object; it had a pattern of roses, a sort of grim and mawkish posy on the handle and an attempt at a thorned stem along the spine. He'd bought her a pair of combs, as well, but she'd made a show of liking the plain ones. Edward had wanted to shower her with gifts: useless articles, or garish, horrible American hats. She'd needed gloves. All the time, it had been so obvious, she had thought. Perhaps gloves were too mundane. Too ordinary. Too intimate. Too much like a thing to buy for your wife. She couldn't imagine wanting to wear gloves now.

She held the ugly letter knife in her palm. It wasn't nice to handle. It was as if the person who'd carved it had never opened a letter with anything other than their fingers. Or never opened a letter at all.

Gwen laid the baby in the hammock. She slit the first page, and the last page. Her rule was, had been, that if the first page of the book was terrible, she was justified in skipping to the last, just to see how it ended. If the first page was any good, the last page would taunt her. But she had grown out of that kind of nonsense now. She slit the pages, one after another. Everything about the construction of the book screamed money: the calf, the extraordinary marbling, the thick, creamy pages of Dutch paper which behaved so beautifully under the knife, the green silk headbands, which seemed an odd choice of colour. Everything about the book made her want to read the first page.

Chapter XLI

Eternal Blazon
or
The Confessions of a Nondescript
Volume I.

I am, in all outward appearances, the antithesis of you. You know this; you know that I am not beautiful to look at. My body is not silken soft in the same way as yours, and it is not as pale as veal flesh, as wan and ghostly as mare's milk. Have you ever wondered over the fact that your husband might want—need—to plunge himself with such force, such consummate desire, at a woman whose body is dark with hair. Whose face, bearded and defiant, stares out at you from the *carte de visite* you so unfortunately found amongst your husband's possessions. My image is everywhere in certain circles. I am scattered on the dirtiest streets of the most unwholesome districts of this city. My face is hidden by respectable men, whilst their good, honest, faithful wives are awake, and then it is taken out to be slavered over in the darkest places, in the deepest part of night.

I am not sixteen any more, yet that image of me as I was then still circulates. As I cover my face with thick veils in public places, my image is there to be appropriated in any which way, by anyone who may choose to do so. I was sixteen. My voice had not thickened with regret; I knew nothing. I believed those who told me when I arrived in this dreary country that the paying public would not care what I looked like; that it was my voice they came to hear. I could not understand, on my first night at the Empire Theatre, why so many people who had paid good money to hear me perform my repertoire should be so noisy. I expected hushed silence. And that I did get: a hushed silence of awe and repulsion. I managed that first night to sing despite the crowd. I never imagined that I would ever have to sing like that; to fold in on myself; to forge my voice into a steely thing. The liquid slipped away.

Will you let the tarnished liquid of your life slip away in your state of ignorance?

When the concert was over, on that horrible night, I was taken by a man to his shop. A man who had sat brooding over my countenance during the concert, his mind silently acting out the delicate, intricate manoeuvres his hands might make if only I would come away with him. The price surprised him. My "chaperone" allowed him a small discount, enough to pay a cab fare. I was taken out by a side entrance of the Empire Theatre, used only by the rat catchers and the night soil collectors. My chaperone, Mr Helson Blackwater, told me nothing. He avoided my gaze. He handed me over like a skinned rabbit at Smithfield's, and wiped his hands on the tails of his coat.

He did not speak to me, this man who took me away to his shop. He sat opposite me and studied me in the dark interior of the cab as we jolted over the streets, the doors shut to the outside. The cab seats were not quite clean. The floor was grimy. There was a faint odour of vomit, and I put my shawl to my face, thinking I might not be able to control my stomach, though it was empty, as I had not eaten that day through nervousness and excitement.

He leaned forward as our bodies jarred on the cab seats and he touched my free hand. The heat from his fingers seared through our gloves; his hand closed around mine, pushing my knuckles against each other. He slipped over to sit beside me, and I tried to wrench my hand free.

"Do I hurt you?" he whispered. "I don't mean to hurt you." His voice was soft, his breath fragrant with caraway seed as he lowered the shawl away from my face. "I shall not ever do anything to cause you to hurt, my dear."

But he still held tight to my hand, as though I might fall from the cab, as though he feared that someone bigger than he might jump up to the window of the cab and snatch me away into the horrid night air. I sparkled in his mind, Isobel. My knuckles ache with the memory of it.

The name of this man was Mr Abalone Wilson Tench. It was written in gold lettering above the door of his barbershop. It glinted in the sputtering gaslight, but I could not read it then. I could read and write only in Spanish when I was sixteen. I did not know that I was being led into an establishment that specialised in the removal of facial hair. Not at once. He lit a taper from a tinderbox, and proceeded to light a lamp and several candles.

I had till now imagined that the man was large only in my imagination, swelled by my own fright to a giant. His chest was wide, and his shoulders broad as a buffalo. I could see now that he had removed his coat and jacket his waist narrowed, like a dancer's. His hands were finely shaped, the skin and fingernails well cared for. He took care not to burn himself or get soot on his hands. He clamped the stove door shut and opened the vent to get the fire raging and hot.

"You are wondering, my dear, what on this earth you might be doing in a barber's place." His voice barely rose above the guttering of the candles and the hiss of the wet coals inside the pot-bellied stove. "Well, I shall tell you in good time."

He looked at me the way other men of his kind would come to look at me. Including, Isobel, your husband. It was a look of tenderness mixed with desire.

"I was sore angry at the way you were received this night, my dear. What animals live in this city. Rats, dogs. Horrible beasts." He spoke my name. "Natalia." Only once. He uttered it with such profound sensibility, his tongue lingering on the middle syllable.

"But I am forgetful of my manners, my dear," he said. "I will provide you with refreshment, you must have a little something to drink. You must look after yourself. I see that your lips are dry. We must not let you become what they call de-hydrated. Do you know that word, my dear?" He did not pause to see whether I did. "To hydrate, my dear, is to wet something. And so it follows, or, *ipso facto*, as they say in those places what are higher than this, that to dehydrate is to become too dry."

Though I felt ill with hunger, I could not face the thought of eating; but I needed something to occupy me. I drank the stuff he'd given me; it burned my throat and my nose. My eyes watered, but he did not notice my discomfort. I fought back the urge to cough.

"My dear," he said to me, "are you comfortable enough? Have you want for anything more?" I shook my head. "Miss Jaspur," he said, sounding perplexed, "if you do no more than shake your head I shall not know whether to assume that you have enjoyed an elegant sufficiency or rather if you are not yet fully satisfied."

"I do not need anything more. I am very comfortable, thank you, sir." Though if the truth be told I was far too hot. Under my bonnet I felt the tickle of perspiration begin to agitate my scalp and I longed to tear out my pins and ruffle my hair with my hands, shaking my head between my knees as I had been able to do every evening before this.

His face had become very grave in the flickering light. "You must know by now, Miss Jaspur, that I am a barber by trade. I cuts the hair of gentlemen, and I shaves their faces. It is my passion, this trade. I might have been other things, a different kind of man, but this trade called on me the way a man of the cloth is called upon by the Almighty. I don't mean disrespect to them what's holier than me and there is plenty of them. My dear, I wish to impress upon you that this is not just a thing that I do to earn my keep. It is my life. When I puts my hands on a gent's head, when I lays my fingers against his cheek, all hot from my towels, I sometimes see great things. Sometimes the things I see ain't so nice. Now, I don't believe in no hokery-pokery. You must not get this wrong. I have thought hard about it for twenty years or more. A man gives himself away when he surrenders himself to the barber's hands. He is, what you might call, vulnerable in a special way. He lets his soul speak to me. I see it, there, a flash in his eyes, here, in a twitch beside his nose. The way his hands fall onto his chest as he lays back in my chair. The rest is what you might call elicitation. I knows how to make the gents speak. They think I am simple. They think themselves safe. And mostly they are. But your Mister Blackwater, he come to me not two weeks ago. And all he gives me, my dear, it is pure gold. I takes my time; I go slow, careful. He's telling me about a young lady. I gives his cheeks another, closer shaving. I works the soap up into a big, feathery lather, and then I hold his head." Mr Tench made a shape in the air with his body and his arms, his hands held the absent head of my chaperone and I shivered to see it, Isobel. I shivered because I suddenly heard Blackwater speaking about me.

Mr Tench became solemn. "You must feel liberated, Miss Jaspur, my dear. Liberated. Your Mister Blackwater, and believe me he is of the blackest, foulest, murkiest water what ever flowed through this city. Blackwater, he thinks one thing of my paying for you, and well I know it to be another. You have your freedom, my dear.

I will transform you. I will release you into a better life with my razor and my scissors."

"I see structures. I have studied the human skeleton in great detail both living and defleshed, and bleached in the anatomist's cauldron. And I see beauty hid behind your mask. If you will allow me, I will reveal you for the hidden beauty that you really are, my dear, my lovely, my precious, precious jewel."

I heard Mr Tench move around lighting more candles, refreshing those that had almost burned to nothing. He brought out another lamp. Gradually, the room was filled with an amber hue; I could sense shadows slinking back to the furthest recesses of the shop, and I opened my eyes.

Mr Tench smiled at me in the mirror. His sleeves were folded back meticulously to his elbows. He wrapped my face deftly, gently, without saying a word. He then took up a razor, its handle made from a deep chestnut turtleshell, inlaid with delicate silverwork. He grasped the bottom end of the leather strop, as though he was restraining the beast the hide had come from and slowly began to whisk the opened blade up and down the length of the hide. He laid the honed razor carefully down on a clean cotton cloth on the work shelf and walked the few paces across the room to the pot-bellied stove. He moved softly across the room, carrying out his preparations as though he was performing a religious rite. I felt myself being tipped back in the chair and discerned his breath again close by.

He worked quickly, finding the contours of my face, mapping the structure of my jaw through the round handle of the brush. Mr Tench curved around me, his hands splayed, making my skin taut as the blade moved over, guided by his instinct. In a very few minutes he had finished with my jaw and neck and was engaged in marking a new hairline on my forehead. He separated my eyebrows with one miniscule flick above the bridge of my nose. He rubbed something sweet-smelling into my skin.

"Almond oil," he told me. "With something of my own. A little secret that I have been working on for just this moment." He caressed my newly exposed face, my never seen cheeks, my until now hidden chin. He pulled himself closer to me pushing his belly against the top of my head so that I could feel the heat of his blood through my hair. I heard him sigh again and again. He moved around me fondling my face as though it was the first and last thing he might ever behold in this life. His hands on my face spoke of an aching desire I could not have imagined. I thought that he was done. But he was not finished in his work yet. He spoke to me, his voice cracked and strained. "I must let you up, my dear," he breathed in a tiny breath and held it in his chest as if he felt a great pain. I was confronted by a strange girl in the mirror; a girl with pink cheeks, glistening with the sweet almond oil. Her eyes were wide and I watched them fill with tears. Quickly, Mr Tench wiped my eyes with a pocket handkerchief.

"Now, my dear, what say you to this? You have seen my work. You have seen how I have the ability to transform you into a wondrous creature. Let me do more. Allow me to continue. And if your modesty is likely to be offended I will practise my art on the rest of your body with a blindfold. You may even tie it to my eyes yourself."

I felt my skin ripple in horrific anticipation and yet I knew that I would not be able to leave this man until I had allowed him to do what he proposed. I must expose my naked body in all the truth of its condition in order to satisfy this man's unfathomable desire to swipe his blade over my belly and breasts, over my arms and legs, even, as I was to discover that night, down to the hairs which grow on my toes. He was not a man to be dissuaded once he had set his mind on something. I cowered at the thought of this man thinking of me in such a way; not for a fleeting moment, something which might spark before the eyes and then be dismissed out of hand, but each day. Planning, mixing his special oil. Well, Isobel, what would you have done, if you had been so unlucky as to have been me?

There was nothing I could say.

As I lay there, Isobel, I found myself slipping into a trance, being conscious only of the sensation of those hands moving the blade across my skin; the quick, sure rub of his thumb where the hair had been removed and then moving on again, working around my arm in a spiral pattern from my shoulder down to my wrist. He wiped my arm slowly when he was satisfied that he had been thorough, and then embarked upon the right arm, after covering my left side. At this moment, Mr Tench spoke to me. "Are you well enough, my dear? Do you feel the air too cold? I must keep you warm, you see, for, if not, your skin will raise bumps like a plucked goose and I will not be able to continue."

In fact, I was roasting under the cape and the towelling. It was one of those nights when the air never finds its coolness, and there is no relief from the smothering atmosphere. I felt trickles of perspiration running down my sides, and I knew that my underarms were beginning to let loose the odour of stale sweat. But he was already employed in removing all the hair from under my arms.

You are blonde, Isobel. I wonder if you can sympathise at all with the story I am relating to you. You perhaps have used a weak solution of arsenic to make your underarms silky smooth, ready for your evening gown. Perhaps you have even used it on your long, slender legs. There is nothing I shall not tell you Isobel.

Your husband once told me that he liked the sensation of going from one extreme to the other. So, I assumed, as I still do, that your own body is as naturally hairless as mine is naturally covered in (the words of your husband) "a thick luxurious mane, a sumptuous, luscious, glossy fur". He would come to me after those tortured nights with you, in your enormous, bug-free bedroom. He would leave your house while your servants were sleeping, perhaps one boy still awake, polishing your husband's riding boots. He would carry his shoes and his clothes down the hall and go into his room to change into different clothes.

Afterwards, he would wash himself carefully with his own soap and his own washing cloth, which he kept in his doctor's bag along with the morphine and the smelling salts and the callipers and the glass suction cups and the jars of leeches and the speculum and the tweezers and all the other instruments of his trade which he was to abandon in favour of rocks and fossilised forms. But that was to come.

When Mr Tench came to that place between my legs he said, "This is a place where a woman should have hair aplenty. This is the place I vow I shall never ever touch with my razor." And he kept his promise. Do I shock you with these words, Isobel?

He smothered my entire body in the almond oil, the scent of which was overpowering now. Its cumulative effect and the lack of sleep made me very tired. I had not dared to fall asleep before, but now all I wanted to do was curl up and let myself fall into a deep and intense slumber. I felt I could sleep for a whole day and not feel refreshed on waking. But the man had to be satisfied. He worked his hands over my shaven body. His hands moved over the lubricated surface of my body in swirls and he began to knead my flesh like you must if you have suffered a cramp. His hands pummelled my body; my muscles at first felt soothed by it, but as his hands continued their journey over my newly revealed form it became more and more uncomfortable. And as the discomfort turned into something more sinister, Abalone Wilson Tench began to groan again. He squeezed and kneaded my skin and flesh as though it was dough on a baker's table. He began to push his weight into my shoulders. He lingered so long over this that he needed to apply more of the almond oil to my skin. The groans became longer and longer, more noisy and abandoned. The room was awash with his feral grunting and I thought that I would faint from the pain, which had turned into such an agony that I barely knew that I was still alive. He began to slap my body; lightly at first, and only with each new application of oil. I felt the palms of his hands burning into my unprotected skin and still I kept silent.

He stopped abruptly. My body was sore. My muscles protested as I slowly moved away from Mr Tench. With my back to him, began to dress myself, pulling on my stockings and my underclothes which clung to my bare skin. As I dressed, I listened to the room. I could not tell where he had gone. I had not been aware of his leaving the room. I did not try to look about me. I kept my eyes from straying into the mirror, and attended to the rest of my clothes. The fabric felt unfamiliar on my skin. As the daylight began to filter through the blinds, and the noises of the streets outside became more lively, what had happened to me seemed to become unreal. I allowed myself to look again in the mirror to fix up my bonnet, which was limp and bedraggled. I avoided my gaze, concentrating only on the business of hiding my unruly hair under the bonnet as well as I could. There was a hairbrush, silver-backed, right by my hand, but I did not like to pick it up. I did not want to touch anything connected with Abalone Wilson Tench. Whilst I looked in the mirror and tied the ribbons under my chin, my hands knowing the form but being surprised, all the time I did this I let my eyes dart about the room behind me. As my body became used to its new state, in all its hurt, in all its injury and its shaven state I noticed that I was hungry again. I looked at the door leading to the street. People's shadows flitted past under the small gap where the blind on the door did not reach. I studied the door for some minutes, remaining with my back to the rest of the room, unable yet to discover by listening whether I had been abandoned, even if only temporarily. My heart beat hard. I had only to walk three paces and turn the key, open the door and step out onto the street. I hesitated, my head in a frenzy of indecision before I felt my hands fumbling with the key, the door swinging open and my feet on the pavement outside. I pulled the door shut, leaving Abalone Wilson Tench inside, neither looking to see if he watched me depart nor waiting to wonder whether he might call me back or try to haul me back into his shop.

The sunlight was bright in my eyes. The stench of the night still hung on the air but it was as a sweet reality to me, then. I did not care to smell anything properly perfumed. I started walking, trying to find my way by keeping the sun on my right. My slippers had worn right through before I found a cab.

And so, as I sat in my room, scrubbing my skin which plagued me with the discomfort of the re-emergence of my hair, I thought of myself as a ghost who was no ghost. And yet unremarkable, Isobel. You will know this feeling. You, too, have harboured the desire to stare and take in your fill. I spent a long night contemplating my future, and with the first light on a chilly September morning I knew that I would have to turn to Leicester Square, not as a sight-seer, but to investigate the place as a means to my survival. So, Isobel, I come to the question to which I already have the answer; and it is not so out of the ordinary that one might be shocked. Yes, if I were to ask you, you would admit, perhaps after a little hesitation that you believe that the spirits of the deceased can manifest themselves in this world. I have not been entirely honest with you.

How did you feel when you faced the mirror image of your husband's newest mistress? You went there to Carrick House in search of your dead children, and you sat in the parlour, in its darkened state, waiting for Euphemia Carrick to drift into her trance. What were you hoping to see? What were you thinking? I could have told you that Euphemia was nothing like her sister. That you would not find Gwen. For what is the mirror image but the opposite of that object which you seek?

How can I know these things, if I was never there to see them myself? How can I know that Euphemia Carrick spoke in many tongues—incomprehensible gibberish which the newly bereaved allowed themselves to believe were the tangled thoughts and messages of those struggling to contact them from the other side.

And you fainted, Isobel. The spell worked on you. No bells tinkling, no table rattling, no pointer on a board twirling magnetically, no glass tumbler of water tipping over. No gifts dropped into your lap from the other side. Only Euphemia, Gwen's sister, babbling and burbling like the babies you once held in your arms whose lives were the briefest of flames, their sickliness only the fault of your loneliness.

You were never your husband's wife, Isobel, and neither I. The impossibility of perfection festers and cripples his mind. You hoped in the end that your presence at the table would be enough to stay the cycle of disaster. But, faced with those sisters, your efforts came adrift. Let a different wind fill your sails, Isobel, as you make that final journey. Not an abrupt end for you, Isobel. I cannot imagine that you would follow the cowardice of your *closest* friend, Dr Charles Jeffreye.

★   ★   ★

Forgive me, Isobel, for I get ahead of myself.

Should I go straight to the part now where I met your husband? Shall I describe what he did, or would that be too distasteful?

He came to Saville House one evening. The place was thick with tobacco smoke. People were leaving. It had been my first week there as the Mysterious Lady, though there was not much mysterious about me it seemed—other than whether or not it was me singing and whether or not I was a lady at all.

That night, I would not consent to see him. He gave me his card, or rather he sent it up to me, telling me that he was an admirer. I did not want to see another admirer. I fancied there was another Abalone Wilson Tench down at the grand entrance to that Den of Iniquity. No. That night, I took the advice of a little man called Fergus Harris. I think the name may be familiar to you, if you are the sort of woman who keeps track of her servants' names. Certainly, you will have remarked him; his size set him apart. I liked him instantly. He was direct; the only person in that stinking, louse-infested room who had come to listen to my singing. My voice captivated him, and he was persistent. I did not think that he would prove very troublesome if I invited him to dine with me—people like us, we cannot stand on ceremony, we must behave all as equals and not simper behind Japanese silk fans and parasols. I do not believe in a second sense; I never have thought that one human being may read the mind or thoughts of another, but there was something uncanny about that evening. A prickle shivered down my neck when I spoke to Mr Fergus Harris. It was I for once who felt that I must not let another out of my sight—and it was invigorating. I was exhausted after my long performance, but a new energy came over me.

Fergus Harris was very deferential towards me, though it soon became clear that his personality would have fit inside a body as large as Abalone Wilson Tench's. And so he became my eyes and ears in your house. When you finally became aware of his talents you sent him on his way to Carrick House. You were able to persuade him with a bigger purse and the promise of cleaner air; an easier life but a more demanding role. He took the challenge, he took it to his heart because he had something to prove and because he enjoyed the irony. He has proven his weight, Isobel, but do not forget that his loyalties will change with the prospect of better weather. His ambition is no brother to duty and the rewards for his endeavours cannot be measured in guineas.

Chapter XLII

Observations.
Pará, Brazil. 1861/1862.

Underneath, she was floating.

Her eyes followed the things around her before her brain had a chance to catch up. She managed, in ways which were not too strange, to look after her baby.

I didn't come all this way, she heard herself thinking over and over, just to be his unkissed mistress, to have a child, hidden away in the jungle under lies, swaddled in deceit. To think about Gus Pemberton was too painful and so she tried not to.

On the surface, she was still.

She watched her baby, whose name was Augusta—yes, she remembered that, though other facts were difficult to retain. She watched Augusta watching her with unfocused eyes.

First, the baby was like a grub; pale, and startlingly basic in her needs. Gwen learned how to anticipate the bodily functions of the grub, the baby, Augusta. There were no mountains of soiled napkins to launder or send away for laundering. Maria taught her things; and there was a small dog which came to live in the house and which removed mishaps from the floor.

But this creature was not interesting to Gwen. She never called the dog by its name or petted it in any way. Sometimes, Gwen saw Edward going through her things. He would stand for an hour, perhaps more, unaware that she was watching him read the notes she had made alongside the work she'd so far put into her sketchbooks. Occasionally, Edward would shuffle into his own room with her sketchbook in his hand and then write things down in his own notebooks while referring to hers. She didn't know whether he was transcribing or what he was doing; it was curious behaviour to her and only mildly interesting.

Gwen was aware that she did not speak. When he was out of the house, Edward couldn't hear her whispering to Maria.

The grub learned to roll over. The baby smiled. The baby became mobile. Augusta rolled and rolled across surfaces until she came to an obstacle and then looked about her, unable to roll back the other way.

By the time Baby Augusta had learned to crawl, and dribbled and began to eat plain things, like bananas and rice, Gwen had read the book six times.

There must be a hidden message, she thought, and I have to find that message, and understand it. But all there was to understand was that she could not understand him.

There are certain books, Gwen wrote feverishly, *which are all well and good for the lay-person vaguely interested, one rainy afternoon, in finding out about the secrets a microscope might offer. But they do not illustrate properly, or investigate fully, or show such possible investigations that they might, and which I think that they ought. By which I mean that the secrets of the microscope will remain secrets largely to the entire population of the civilised world, other than those with the time, means and inclination to investigate for themselves. This cannot be right. I do not feel that it is proper . . .*

My own purpose, then, is to create a kind of Atlas of the Insect World.

How frustrating, it is, as I know through my own experience, to see, "a fly leg" illustrated, for example, in amongst other, unrelated bits taken from other creatures and laid out prettily, without being able to ascertain from which fly the leg came and which leg it was which happened to be illustrated in isolation.

It is my opinion, which I am free to expound in the privacy of this journal, that there should be available to any adult person or intelligent and inquisitive child, the kind of Atlas that I mean to create. Moreover, in creating such an Atlas it should, in part, remove the need for the intelligent and inquisitive child (or adult) to plunder *nature so* unnecesarily, *and with such* careless *attitude in the pursuit of elementary scientific enquiry and knowledge.*

Of course, I could never speak of this to anyone. On the surface, my idea is to produce something which is instructive, as well as being a work of Art. I wish to make my work appealing to both the scientist and the art lover.

I think this Atlas might take up the rest of my days here. I cannot continue to make lovely representations of insects set in their ranks and be satisfied.

We cannot understand the truth of a creature and its place in nature, through the singular fact of its carcass.

And so I wish to say: let us be done with this obsession for collecting variations in a specimen to the last available insect, to be pored over by but a few and left forevermore to the darkness of the cabinet. (Is this Science? No, it is Vanity.) Let us try to understand Nature in a way that does not deplete Her, or ravage Her, or decimate Her. Because I think that this attitude which leads a man to take as much as he can, without thinking with due care for the result of his actions, will lead that man to no good purpose, and ultimately waste his whole life in the pursuit of false knowledge. I do not mean that Darwin's idea is false; I mean that for others to pursue what he has already proved is stupid. We do not need to replicate his work; we need to find other ways if we are to progress. I cannot condone wholesale capture in the name of vanity.

I have thought very much on the ways of the ants here. They are everywhere and there are many different species. We have had to protect our equipment and our food against the attentions of these enterprising insects from the outset, and must always be vigilant against their ingenuity.

Recently, I have been trying out an experiment involving the enticing of a small colony into a large specimen jar which I had prepared. After a frustrating start, I discovered that the ants will only begin anew where there is a Queen to serve, and that the colony is not merely a collection of individuals, but a collective; an organism made up of other organisms, with their beating heart, their Queen, at the centre. I now have a system of cords leading in and out of the jar, which are suspended by treated cords from the ceiling. I have taken the extra precaution of standing the specimen jar in a large bowl of water.

The most marvellous thing that I have found is that these leaf-cutting ants, which we had both assumed were consuming the leaves, are not. A kind of midden heap is prepared by the ants, and it is the resulting fungus growing there on the leaf cuttings which the ants eat.

I have not read anywhere of other observers of these creatures having come to the same conclusion. Of course, I would not claim to be the first to discover the true nature of their foraging habits and their purpose, however, I am still excited by this idea—of the ants' apparent knowledge of, or at least their harnessing of, the basics of horticulture.

I am still much given to spending long hours of thought on the subject of Mr Frome. His remarks, and his wildness, and his claims, and his final deed, seem, on the one hand, to mark him out as a singularly disturbed individual who perhaps spent too much time with his theories and not enough in the common pursuit of friendship and good humour. (Of course, I am an expert on this.) On the other hand, I wonder if, in his madness, there was some kind of logical reasoning. I have gone over it so many times.

Gwen stopped writing, remembering Edward's reaction to her experiment with the ants. He had stomped into her room, and she had listened to him quietly. The quieter she was, the more infuriated he seemed to become.

"There is not the room here, Gwen, for your school-room antics with these pests. Whatever you think you may have observed in these jars is irrelevant and highly likely to be wrong. Just stick to what you came here to do, namely, illustrate *my* findings. And clear up this dreadful mess. We'll have the blasted things in our food."

Who did this man think he was, to instruct her, to try to remove the one thing which allowed her to reconcile herself to this situation? Gwen did not clear away her ants in jars. She did not stop writing; her efforts were redoubled in the face of his attempts to obstruct her observations.

She began to keep her notes locked up in her trunk.

Chapter XLIII

THE TIMES, Thursday, October 4, 1866.

MURDER TRIAL AT THE OLD BAILEY.

MR PROBART for the Prosecution called as witness a Mr Harpe, who said, "I am a bookseller in this city and I am well acquainted with Mrs Pemberton, the prisoner in this trial. She has come to my shop on many occasions, asking for a certain title."

Q: "What is the title, Mr Harpe?"

A: "The prisoner has always asked for *Eternal Blazon*, sir, and when I have told her that no such title has come my way, the prisoner has always spent a deal of time lingering over other titles on display. Sometimes, she has bought a copy of obscurity, and most other times, nothing."

Q: "Curious, would you not say, for a lady to be perusing the shelves of an establishment such as your own, Mr Harpe?"

A: "Perhaps, at first; I wouldn't often get a customer such as the prisoner, but I came to expect her, sir, after a while. You never can tell what kind of reading matter a person will have in their house, sir, from appearances alone."

Q: "Please tell the court, Mr Harpe, exactly what kind of reading matter it is which lines the shelves of your shop."

A: "Everything I sell is absolutely legal and above board, sir, in my bookshop.

Titles are of a mainly scientific interest, a specialist interest, not novels or any such matter."

Q: "And yet, Mr Harpe, the volume which the prisoner, by your account, was so keen to obtain, it does in fact fit loosely the description of 'novel', does it not?"

A: "I believe it does, sir."

Q: "And yet you do not have any such 'novels' on display in your shop?"

A: "No, sir."

Q: "But if I were to pay you a large sum, perhaps to obtain a certain title, then you might be able to oblige?"

A: "There is no doubt that just about anything is obtainable in this city if the seeker is determined enough, sir."

Q: "Please tell me, Mr Harpe, what is the title of the last volume you sold to the prisoner?"

A: "That's easy enough, it was called *The Book of Phobias*, and I sold it to the prisoner on the 4th of August, the Saturday before the murder."

Q: "A novel, Mr Harpe?"

A: "A scientific book, sir. By Dr Charles Jeffreye. It is about certain maladies of the nerves and so forth."

Q: "Maladies of the nerves. Thank you, Mr Harpe."

The unfortunate fate of Dr Jeffreye, who was crippled by a fall from his horse and later died, was briefly discussed. More witnesses were questioned—all booksellers—all of whom said that Mrs Pemberton was a regular patron who always asked for a particular title. Mrs Pemberton had visited the establishments of each on Monday, 6th August.

Mr Shanks for the Defence then addressed the court in respect of the evidence given by the various booksellers: "Mrs Pemberton does not deny having been a regular customer at many bookshops in the city. Nor does she deny having sought a particular volume mentioned earlier. Her motives, however, for having devoted so much time and effort in her search were entirely honourable. The volume mentioned, was, some of you will be aware, of ill-repute. What you may not be fully aware of is the fact that within that novel lay certain unsavoury accusations against Mr Scales. Mrs Pemberton's brief was simple: to locate any surviving copies of that title and to destroy them. Why? Because she wished to eradicate foulness, however false, against her former companion. Why? Because she had forgiven him his falseness against her, and wished to do him well, not ill. This determined effort, sirs, is not the kind of sustained action of a murderess. Furthermore, the other volume, entitled *The Book of Phobias*, was obtained for the same reason. Spurious and lewd claims were made by its author against Mr Scales' reputation. No one, who had travailed so long, in such a manner, would then murder the very person whose name she desired to clear."

Chapter XLIV

Pará, Brazil. May, 1863.

Gwen, hunched over a pot she had just taken from the fire, was utterly absorbed in her task. The stench coming from the pot stung Edward's eyes. Augusta, unwatched by her mother, poked a stick into the fire—in and out—and then jabbed it inexpertly into the ground and tried to make a hole, immersed in the serious business of finding out what was possible with a stick. Gwen sat with her feet planted apart in a squat as though about to defecate. She stirred the foul brew, which Edward now realised was a broth containing fish skin and bones.

"Soup?" he ventured, little expecting any response; her muteness towards him was absolute. Gwen seemed not to have heard him, and so he continued to watch Augusta should she fall into difficulties with her stick, or the fire, or both. Then Gwen reached to her side and held a tatty book up and waved it, only a slight twist from her wrist. Edward didn't know what to make of this latest peculiar enterprise, but, at least, he had managed to get some kind of reaction from her, which might, at a stretch, be interpreted as communication.

Gwen's post-partum melancholia had been sudden and severe. It had not affected her ability to function as a mother, which surprised him, but she had suddenly one day taken ill and refused to speak or paint. She would spend long hours walking the perimeter of the *casinha* with the baby in a pouch, native style on her back. Or she would suddenly take instead to lying for days on end in her hammock. The malaise had not affected her appetite too badly. She seemed to be aware of the need to fill her stomach in order to nurse the child. She sang to it, whispered lovingly to it, but she would speak to no one else; not even Maria, who told Edward, without his asking, that European women always had some trouble of this kind and that he should keep an eye on her but stay out of her way. Edward resented the inclusion of Maria in their number, but knew that hiring anyone else would probably result in the same deluge of un-asked for advice. Sometimes, he did wonder if it was something more. He wouldn't put a name to it; he wouldn't call her mad. It was like no kind of madness he had ever seen. His entomologising rambles became truncated as a result. He scrutinised her, from a suitable distance, for signs of a change in her condition, either good or not so good. He couldn't even bring himself to use the word 'bad'. There seemed to be nothing bad about her. Occasionally, she appeared to be staring intently at something far away, and so absolute was her concentration, that Edward, more than once, fetched out the telescope to discover her object of interest.

During all this time, Gwen read and re-read a book. He was not permitted to see it. He knew that she kept it inside her painting bag, modified within the first week of their arrival to exclude tarantulas with an interest in art. If Edward came within twenty feet of the open book, it was snapped shut and tucked under Gwen's arm or inside the tight folds of the pouch across her breastbone.

Edward was sure that the tatty article she had just waved at him was the same volume which had received such intensive attention. It had a curious title: *Eternal Blazon*. He'd vowed to get at it one day and see what could possibly be written there which could be so consuming.

★   ★   ★

Augusta let a trickle of urine, travelling part of the way down her chubby legs, fall to the ground. She stamped gleefully in the wetted earth and squatted again to poke at it with her fingers. Edward cast a glance towards Gwen. She opened her blouse and placed the book next to her skin. Edward backed away as she got up and removed Augusta from the mess and took her away to clean her, murmuring that she was a rascal, in a voice so quiet no one else would have recognised it as speech. Gwen left the child with Maria and returned to the pot. Edward fetched his gun out to the verandah and began to clean it, taking extra care over each section. He was far enough away now, for Gwen to carry on without hindrance. She turned her back to him again and spent an hour doing something which Edward was not allowed to see. Eventually, she stood and stretched, and with the book in her hand went inside.

Edward went over to the pot. The concoction was beginning to congeal. It looked, for all the world, like glue.

Chapter XLV

Pará, Brazil. July, 1863.

The last of Edward's specimens had been packaged carefully and crated up, ready to be shipped back to England. Some were to be sold; the rest were to be kept safely in storage until their own return. Edward had decided that this was the best way to do things. They would now quit the *casinha* and take a boat up into the country to search for specimens as yet unknown to science. The Grindlocks had told him that Coyne, now back in the country, was interested in taking part in the expedition. Edward knew he needed a guide and so agreed to take him on. All this had been arranged, and Gwen had not spoken. Her manner was curiously ordinary despite the muteness. He had taken her silence to mean that she agreed with his plans wholeheartedly.

Now, she had broken her silence. Edward's mouth hung open, she thought, in quite an idiotic way. What was there not to comprehend? She waited whilst she folded the last of her moth-bitten clothes into her trunk. The only things which were not packed into it were her drawing things, and her tin of paints.

"What do you mean, what plan?"

"I have always intended to leave, Edward, when the child was big enough to stand the journey."

"But," he said, "if she is big enough to stand the journey, as you put it, over the Atlantic, then she is big enough to take part in this excursion. It is what we came here for."

"It is not the excursion, Edward. It's me. I don't want to stay here with you any longer. I have had my fill. I cannot continue." Perhaps, she thought, this is more arduous than the voyage I face, and she drew comfort from that.

"Who have you told? The Grindlocks, have you told them?"

"No, why on earth would I do that? I'll make my own arrangements. I can explain my return in terms which will cast no aspersions on you, if that's what worries you."

Edward threw his arms out, and Gwen stepped back, unsure the gesture was nicely meant. But Edward began to grab at handfuls of his hair.

"You have to come with me. I can't do the thing—not on my own. Those two weeks, remember, when we first came here. It was hell without you. You. You are—necessary."

"I'm not. You can collect things without me."

"We had an arrangement. An agreement. I trusted you, for God's sake."

"To do what? To keep on lying? To keep on pretending that we have some kind of affinity? We don't. Nothing binds us."

"Our daughter, Augusta. She binds us. She would be fatherless."

"She already is. It makes not a jot of difference."

"You can't take her. I won't allow it."

"You don't have to allow it. We are not husband and wife."

"The law favours me, as her father. You count for nothing. Nothing!"

"You have no interest in her. You can't collect her."

"I have every interest in her, and I will not permit her removal."

"We'll see about that. In any case, Edward, I can't be a part of this excursion whilst you persist with the idea of including Mr Coyne."

"I had every impression that you were rather taken with him."

"I'll not get on a boat with him, under any circumstances. He is altogether a menace."

Edward swivelled on his heel to face her, and his hands dropped away from knotting his hair. "Since when have you ever regarded Coyne as a menace?"

"From the moment I met him."

"This is just bluff. You had something with him, and now you want to hide it."

"Don't be absurd!"

"That is exactly the answer I would expect from a guilty party."

"Listen to yourself! You'll drive yourself mad over nothing if you keep this up. I'm going home, Mr Scales, and I'm taking Augusta with me."

Edward pressed his eyes with his fingers and for several long moments did nothing but breathe heavily through his nose, which made a dry whistle with every intake. Then he spoke from behind his hands: "Will you at least come and see us off?"

Gwen suddenly felt sorry for him. He looked, and sounded, so pathetic, "Yes, of course, I will."

"You'll want to have your luggage sent on to the Grindlocks, I suppose. I shall see to that for you."

Gwen gave a small nod.

"Gwen," he said. She was moving away from him, but he caught her by the arm. She stood and waited for whatever was to come next, but all he said was, "I do love you. You know that, don't you? Above all else."

At last, she gave another small nod and he let her go.

Vincent Coyne's blue spectacles flashed in the sun; his teeth seemed yellow beneath them in the harsh light. He strode up and down the deck of the two-masted boat, slapping its sides and slapping the crates of Edward's things like tethered beasts which had previously irked him. Still, Gwen looked on the scene with a glad sense of detachment. It was nearly over. She must have smiled as Vincent Coyne looked up and saw her.

"Hey," he shouted, throwing a clenched fist high in the air, his gaze fixed on her. "She's here."

Edward appeared from underneath the awning. He looked harassed. Augusta leaned precariously off Gwen's hip where she had been sitting quietly. She flung her arms out towards Edward.

"Bring her on board, just for a minute," he said.

"No. We'll wave from here. Here will be sufficient."

"Don't you trust him?" yelled Vincent, vicious, playful.

"We don't need to complicate her day."

"It's not complicated, Gwen," said Edward. "Just let her have a little inspection of the boat. Bring her aboard for ten minutes."

This will be the last thing, she thought, that he will make me do. In half an hour the boat will be setting sail, and I will be able breathe freely again. She relented and carried Augusta onto the boat.

Edward took her into his arms and held her high up above his head.

Had that been the signal, thought Gwen later, for the men to cast off? Around her, the scrambled activity, the sails filling, the ropes thrown, the men jumping here and there with careless concentration, calling to each other short words of affirmation: they were leaving.

Her heart pumped with hatred as she saw that it was useless to make a fuss, or to demand that she be allowed to alight. He had devised this, and she remembered now his warning to her after Frome had walked away; that she should not make a fool of him again. I'll wait, she thought; there'll be some chance later. I'll use this time to think of every possible pitfall. But the hatred surged through her like molten glass; its colours twisted and settled in her breast, hardening her resolve to one day be absolutely free of this man. She walked to the stern and faced away from him, alert all the while, to the presence of Vincent Coyne.

Edward wrote in his diary:

We resemble I don't know what as the boat goes along at a spanking pace. The wind smacks the canvas with a cheerful bite, and the child leaps about the place, her little eyes bright with expectation; and I dare say there is a hint of something similar in my own. All that has gone before was mere preparatory work. The child puts her fingers into anything she can. She investigates any available surface, or drawer, or book, with avid enthusiasm. Her presence adds another dimension to the excursion, which will be no less the richer for it.

In the absence of any practical measure to prevent it, and in the light of the perceived advantages of such a coalition, I have been obliged, after some lengthy discussions, to accept, under the unwavering and hearty recommendation of Mr Grindlock, the returned Mr Coyne as an addition to our party. The regrettable absence of Maria, who must return to her former duties at the Grindlock household, will be felt most keenly by the female members of the party.

Edward emerged from under the awning with an ink-laden pen in his hand. Gwen watched him with a certain amount of satisfaction as he gripped the rail and reached over to be sick before staggering back. And now, as she trailed her gaze back to the open water, she saw her trunk, tucked in with some of the crates.

Vincent Coyne stood at the bow, his arms pounding the air in time to a song he was singing. The wind caught it up and shredded it, the words lost as soon as they left his lungs. Phrases from the now unreadable volume preyed on her mind yet again. It was not only that the ghastly details of his past had been concealed from her but read about by others, nor was it that he had kept his marriage to himself—perhaps she could have found some way to reconcile herself to these things if it were not for the fact that her own name, and that of her sister, and of her family home had been so casually thrown into the pages of the book while Edward himself had never been named. In the whole damn compendium of confession, it was Edward whose identity had been protected. Gwen turned her face into the wind.

Chapter XLVI

Lower Amazons. August, 1863.

They were unpacking boxes properly for the first time since they had left Pará. Before this, they had worked and lived on the boat, stopping in a place for three days, a week, or ten days, and then moving further on, so that Gwen was never able to make any arrangements to get away. Now, she was in a small house rented from some person or other whom Vincent seemed to know. Setting up tables and trying to keep Augusta in sight, Gwen turned around for the umpteenth time to find that she had trundled off again. Following Augusta's trail of discarded objects, and piling them into her arms as she went, Gwen found herself confronted with the spectacle of Vincent rummaging through her field bag, as she had come to think of it.

Immediately enraged and finding herself incapable of finding the right sequence of words to whip out at him, she simply stood, with her arms full, waiting for Vincent to notice her. Outside, she heard Edward speaking to Augusta. She watched Vincent's hands.

He pulled out the stuck-together book, and Gwen made an instinctive move towards him, dumping her armful of things and stretching her arm out towards the book.

"That is mine," she said. The firmness, the tripping anger in her voice thrummed on the bare walls. "As is everything else in that bag."

Finally, lazily, Vincent looked up; his expression masked, as always, by the blue tinted spectacles which she had so loved when she had first seen him. But there was a fever over his top lip.

"Where'd you get this?" His question, demanding, arrogant. The way he held her property in his fist. He began to flick through the book but, of course, was frustrated. He knocked the stiff brick of glued paper against his knuckle. "What's the point in keeping a book you can't even read?" Tremulous, his voice wavered between incredulity, annoyance and laughter.

"I never throw books away," said Gwen, her voice gentle, its tone massaging Vincent's shoulders into a droop. She heard Augusta with Edward in the next room and stepped forward, taking the book from his hands as well as her bag. "Even when I have no intention of reading them again."

He pinched the bridge of his nose where his spectacles had made red dents on the surface of his skin. "Dumb name for a dumb book, anyway. What kind of dumb fool'd think up a name like that?"

"Shakespeare. It's the Ghost in *Hamlet*." She paused. "'I could a tale unfold whose lightest word would harrow up thy soul, freeze thy young blood, make thy two eyes, like stars, start from their spheres—'"

"Is that so?" His posture changed. He pulled himself straight and clicked his tongue at her as though he was speaking to a mare, pushed his blue spectacles up to the hilt of his brow and strode out of the room.

Gwen's gaze took in her child's pale ringlets and her eyes, which had miraculously changed from the deep obsidian of a newborn to the scorching light blue of her father.

Gwen squared the writing paper lying on the table in front of her, and gave her daughter a spoiled sheet of paper and a pencil to play with. She had not discussed the letter she was about to write. She was still furious and didn't know what to do with her anger. She avoided Edward, and her play with Augusta now came out as false jollity. She couldn't say anything without it coming out badly. The child's puzzlement at her mother's sudden ill temper made it all so much worse. Augusta had begun to draw in the middle of the page. Gwen noted with satisfaction that the child held the pencil correctly. A tight little scrawl of individual shapes began to emerge. Augusta's stomach was flat on the floor and her feet were in the air. Twirling feet.

Gwen cleared her throat as if she were about to address her sister in person, and dipped her pen into the ink. She knew she would not be able to send the letter. Everything in it bore resemblance to the truth—to some degree. A man had lost his life to an alligator in the dark but he had not been going for a swim. The other man had escaped unhurt. Missionaries lost in the jungle. Well, that was true, Gwen reasoned. They had visited a village where the people filed their teeth, but the missionaries had been missing for about thirty years. Edward's pet leech was already dead, and Edward was convinced that the mysterious fish did not exist.

But she couldn't deny that Augusta was her own child. She just couldn't. She couldn't add another lie to whatever she might have left with Edward. Lies can so easily dominate, she thought. Deceptively benign in their first instance, they leach the life out of you as they grow, like a tumour on your good intentions.

She folded the letter and stowed it away amongst her things. She looked at what Augusta had drawn, and wondered if she had been speaking out loud as she had written the letter. Augusta had scribbled a tangle of things, which might be fish, and she had made shapes which vaguely resembled alligators. The child could barely utter a few words but she could draw.

In the days that followed there were new varieties of Morpho butterflies, which had become something of an obsession for both of them: for Edward, because they were so impossible to obtain;

and for Gwen, because of the impossibility of rendering in paint the magnificence of that lustrous blue in flight. Their rigid corpses captivated her, but no other did now. The specimen boxes were filling up with an astonishing array of Coleoptera. Edward's interest in beetles grew steadily. Easier to catch and observe than butterflies, he said, and less easily damaged in transit.

Gwen and Augusta set off along the shore, stopping every so often to look at the drifts of butterflies feeding amongst the thick carpet of flowering shrubs. They had stolen away from that other leech, Vincent. He was making it his own little parlour game to know exactly Gwen's intentions for every moment of every day and to be there, to advise her. As Augusta slithered down off her hip, and stumped about barefoot, Gwen looked back over her shoulder for a glimpse of the man. Gwen had tried to teach Augusta not to grab at things. Plants had poisonous sap and thorns. Broken twigs might reveal legions of ants. Vines were sometimes a snake. Yet these dangers to her daughter's small chubby fingers were only part of Gwen's concern. She did not want her child to grow up believing that the natural world was her plaything. Now she smiled, as the chubby fingers cupped a flower. Their owner looked up for approval. This was a game, too. Everything was a game.

Later, when Edward had returned from his ramble, and with Augusta asleep, Gwen began to chew a piece of tobacco. Neither of them remembered encountering quite so many ticks as in the area around that village. Naked to the waist, Edward waited for Gwen to spit the juice onto his back to loosen the ticks; he was conscious of the effort she was expending.

★   ★   ★

Edward had referred many times in his field journal to his "assistant". He felt slightly uncomfortable in omitting Gwen's considerable contributions to his work but could not bring himself to name her, either. He had thought on it quite often, changing his mind every time. She was as competent as any man might have been in the tasks she set herself. She familiarised herself with everything, and her observations were meticulous. If she had been a man, he mused to himself, he would have been envious.

Edward sat at his makeshift desk, constructed from crates and rough planks, and opened his journal. On a fresh page he wrote:

A heated discussion on the very first day that lasted into the small hours has culminated in an unfortunate but illuminating incident. The main thrust of my argument that first night was that if a parasite caused its host to die and in the process its own extermination, then the species would not last long enough to establish itself as a viable Link in Nature's chain of Life.

In the days and weeks which have followed, the discussion regarding the candiru fish has re-emerged and re-ignited passionate debate several times. Until today, I believed strongly that the tales bandied about by the local inhabitants regarding this fish were entirely apocryphal.

It would seem that Mr Coyne has indeed proved his point by using his own body as example. Of course, now I see the inadequacies of my argument, but this would hardly merit such a blatant lack of regard for his own self-preservation.

Edward read over what he had just written and scored through it all, beginning again, incorporating what he could remember of Gwen's observations and conclusions.

The candiru is a phlebotomist, attracted by the urea of larger fish, excreted at the gills. The candiru would seem to follow this trail of urea in the water and attach itself to the inside of the gill belonging to the larger fish. This in itself does not cause the fish to die. When the candiru has had its fill of blood it detaches to digest its meal, functioning in much the same manner as the leech, with which we are all most familiar.

The rather stronger allure of human urea passed in water was attractive to such an extent that the confused candiru navigated Mr Coyne's trouser leg in pursuit of the source. The candiru is in possession of fearsome barbs which assist its attachment to its more usual host. I was able to remove the candiru from the patient's urethra by means of a two-inch incision, thereby limiting damage.

The patient has ~~successfully~~ passed water since the operation, but this caused loss of consciousness. The local rum has proved useful not only in the preservation of specimens, including the rather poor specimen of the candiru, but medicinally it has been of great importance.

I admit freely that, until the evidence before me is irrefutable, I am disinclined to alter my position, and remain sceptical of apocryphal tales. I claim no responsibility, for one must question such intractable determination on the part of the patient and balance it against an apparent underlying inconsistency of rational thought.

Edward closed his journal and set down his pen. Now his attention was drawn to the heaps of unsorted lepidoptera. He took up his pen again.

Infection, followed by fever, in circumstances such as these, is usually followed rapidly by a glissade into unconsciousness from which

*the patient is most unlikely to recover. The patient has indeed
spent two days in a delirious state (curious, indeed, how, suffering
from the effects of the barbed fish, the patient began to speak in
various tongues). However, frequent and assiduous attention to
the wound may have contributed to the patient's remarkable
recovery; although much weakened, the patient is able to sit up
and converse lucidly.*

During Vincent's fever, Gwen had tried to talk to Edward about the
practicalities of finding a way to separate themselves from Vincent
and continue their journey without the air being filled with the
sound of his voice. From sunrise to sunset. It was almost impossible
to find quietness, to be able to think. Even when Gwen and Edward
retired behind their makeshift screen to deal with the various para-
sites—or to pretend to, as they had begun to do—Vincent was audible.
He'd sing, if he couldn't think of anything to say, and when he'd run
his limited repertoire thoroughly ragged, he'd make up his own verses.

"We must leave him," she said. Her clear voice quivered, but
Edward said, "Irritating he may be, but the man is on his deathbed."

"I don't think so."

"It is out of my hands."

"Will you not consider an early departure from this place, without
Mr Coyne?"

"We have much to do here yet."

It was torture trying to speak to him. Gwen's chest rose and fell
with short and rapid breaths. She looked over to the hammock
where Vincent lay as another tirade of strange, uninhibited utter-
ances issued forth from his mouth. The blackest water, she thought.

Over the course of the next month, Vincent recovered fully, as
Gwen had known that he would. By the beginning of September
he was back on form; Gwen thought even more so. She had resented
the respect she felt for the way he had used his own body as a

subject for scientific study. She knew it had come from his madness, and she regarded it now as coincidence that his madness had manifested itself in such a logical fashion.

Edward heard her step and continued sorting his butterflies. "I do like collecting on the *campos*," he said to her, with his head still bent over the setting boards. "The thrill of being able to walk in an open space again is exhilarating."

Gwen waited for a moment to see if he would say anything else. She went over to the table to look at the butterflies. How strange it is, she thought, that we can continue to discuss insects in such a casual way. The accident had no place at the setting table, but she knew that she must speak. She said, "We have been very fortunate, Edward." He nodded, and she could see that he thought she was referring to his morning's entomologising. "But until today I did not appreciate our fortune. I have never considered my own mortality. Our mortality."

"Has something happened?"

Gwen said, "What will happen to Augusta, when we go back to England?"

Edward stood up straight and looked into her face. She saw thoughts of classification drop away from his mind as he comprehended her.

"What I mean is, Edward, if I were to die I don't want her to be near Isobel."

He stared at her incredulously, that woman's name on her lips. "I can't see that ever being an option, no." He half turned back to the specimens on his work table, and then looked at Gwen again. "Isobel was dying when we left England. I had word of her passing away not long after we arrived in Pará—and so, in any case, that person should no longer concern you." He studied her chin, and Gwen instinctively wiped it with the back of her hand. He licked his thumb and pressed it to her face.

Gwen waited for him to say more. I've finally been able to speak her name, she thought, and you brush it aside carelessly, as if I had known of her all this time. "Edward," she said, taking hold of his wrist and moving his skin away from her face. "You had a wife, called Isobel?"

He did not flinch. She observed him minutely, only the glimmer of a ghost across his eyes. She dropped his wrist. "You left her to die alone, and put me in her place?"

"You promised never to mention her name." He did not so much whisper the words as breathe them out over his tongue.

"Now I know it for certain. You have deluded yourself completely. If I had known that you were already married, I would have stopped meeting with you. Immediately."

"I put that letter into your hand—" But even as he said it, Gwen could see that he knew that it was not the case.

"No," she said slowly, eliminating any passion from her voice. "Even Miss Jaspur, especially her—" She couldn't go on. "What manner of deceit have you created, Edward? What kind of trouble have you peddled with your lies?"

As she came out of the room she walked into Vincent, but this time she did not care if he had heard it all. "Mr Coyne. At a loose end, again?"

"No, I'm wondering —" He looked past her into Edward's room and quickly back at her again. She knew that Edward was watching them. "I'm wondering if the Oxbow excursion is still on for tomorrow or —" He looked past her again. "—if plans might have changed?"

"Nothing has changed at all, Mr Coyne," she said. "You may assume that everything will go according to plan." She swept up Augusta and placing her on her hip walked out of the house.

Chapter XLVII

Pará, Brazil. November, 1863.

"Mr Edward Scales!" Tristan Grindlock grasped him by the shoulders with a happy grin. "How long have you been back? Hettie will be delighted. Come in, come in. Do they follow on? Are they waiting somewhere? Let me send someone for them."

The cool enclosure of Grindlock's house, the resonance and gaiety of the man's voice on the walls—Edward remembered his first entrance to the house with Gwen and knew suddenly that in a moment he and Tristan Grindlock would be surrounded by a clamour of excitement. He must say it now. He met Grindlock's gaze and stared unblinkingly into his grey eyes. Grindlock was no fool. Edward needed, in the end, to say nothing. He did not have to declare it in words. Tristan Grindlock pulled Edward into an embrace the like he could not remember having received since the very earliest days of his boyhood. The man was strong and did not let go for many minutes. Edward felt the sobbing from Tristan Grindlock spread through his own body. He was wrapped up in the man's grief and condolence in one never-ending squeeze and was enormously touched.

Later in the evening, after a faltering start, he told Tristan and Hettie Grindlock how he had left bait for the alligators and had stood ready with his guns primed. He had registered the broad, flat snouts on the huge beasts and had not been afraid of their enormous length or their girth, or the rows of teeth which he later hacked from their stinking gums. He had no regard for his

own life in those hours of killing and butchering as he had searched
for the remains.

"But you know the way they consume their prey, they rip and
churn; I could not discern from the mess. The abomination of it
was too much. I did not pause in my quest for twenty-four hours,
but then I was overcome. I had to leave the place. I brought their
belongings with me, and I left everything else."

He could not mention the fact that he and Gwen had spoken
words that could never have been undone. That she had chosen,
suddenly, to go with Augusta in the second canoe with Coyne,
leaving Edward to search for the black caiman with the hired men.

"I should have insisted that they stay behind. I told Coyne to
look for hatchlings only. Something for—" He had been going to
say that he'd thought the hatchlings would be harmless and easy
to secure with a woman and a child as company. "Coyne stayed
on, when I came away, to continue where I left off. He would not
hear otherwise. He claimed responsibility."

"Of course, he did," said Hettie. Her face had not lost the ashen
complexion it had assumed.

"I want to take a passage as soon as possible."

"Trust everything to me," Tristan said. "I'll find you a good ship."

Edward valued Tristan Grindlock's blunt empathy, and the softness
with which he had listened to Edward's guilt-ridden ramblings.
But now he knew he was making Hettie and Tristan uncomfortable. In their position, he might have felt the same. A mammoth
obligation surely, to console a man who has lost his wife and only
child when one was literally surrounded, overrun with one's own
progeny. The pressure of so many children at such close proximity
did not disturb Edward. They were not Augusta.

He tried to project himself a few months forward, sitting at home, attempting to make sense of his collections. But he could not even picture which home that might have been.

"Regret," Tristan Grindlock broke into his thoughts, and yet again Edward was grateful. They were standing together watching Edward's few belongings being ferried over the water to the ship. "Regret. There is no point to it, no usefulness to be had from it. If you give in to it, it'll drain you till there is barely any part of you not smudged by it. But, I tell you this for nothing, I'd hop on that boat with you in a trice."

"Your kindness has been immeasurable, but I couldn't let you part with your family on my account."

Edward smiled at Tristan Grindlock weakly and briefly. They were standing on almost exactly the same spot where he had greeted Edward so effusively. Edward caught something odd in the man's eyes.

Tristan patted Edward's shoulder. "There's no need to worry. I wouldn't burden you like that." His hand stayed on Edward's shoulder, and neither man said anything more as the time came for Edward to be taken across the water. The pressure of Tristan's hand on Edward felt immense.

Edward sat facing away from the steamer. He knew the sunlight glinting off the water into his eyes would make his smile seem grim. Tristan Grindlock held up a hand, half salute and half farewell, before he turned and walked away. Edward promised himself that he would write to the man, as soon as he felt able, on his return to England.

Part III

Chapter XLVIII

THE TIMES, Friday, October 5, 1866.

MURDER TRIAL AT THE OLD BAILEY.

EXTRAORDINARY scenes were witnessed at the Central Criminal Court today as the Prosecution called for Miss Natalia Jaspur to give evidence. Miss Jaspur, once notorious for her appearance alone, is well known these days for her vocal virtuosity as a soprano, having appeared in a number of operatic performances last season and due to do so again this year.

Mr Probart: "Did you know Mr Edward Osbert Scales, Miss Jaspur?"

A: "I did know him. I met him eleven years ago, when my life was hard. Life was difficult for me then. I took my living however I could.

Mr Scales was trying to be a doctor. I let him make observations of me. This led to many meetings with Mr Scales which grew sentimental, and eventually an attachment was formed between myself and Mr Scales. However, he was married, and his wife, a very beautiful creature, hated me, and I saw him no more."

Q: "Did the prisoner know of your former attachment to Mr Scales?"

A: "I do not know."

Q: "Were you aware, Miss Jaspur, that a novel had been written about you, in which details of your affair with Mr Scales were laid out?"

A: "I do not pay attention

to rumours, though to be quite correct, I do not believe Mr Scales' name was ever mentioned."

Q: "But you freely admit that you had an affair with Mr Scales which lasted—how long did it last, Miss Jaspur?"

A: "I saw him last seven years ago."

Q: "Two years, you say?"

A: "Simple subtraction suggests it."

Mr Probart then thanked his witness before going on to say that the so-called false allegations made against Mr Scales in the books Mrs Pemberton had been so keen to locate and eradicate were, in fact, true, and that, therefore, Mrs Pemberton was well versed in calling the truth a lie and then attempting to cover up the truth with more falseness.

Chapter XLIX

London. February, 1864.

On the ship to England, Edward had taken a grim pleasure in the special violence of his sickness. His berth had a bucket, which he slopped out only once a day. He took his meals in his cabin and never once took a turn on deck.

In the first days back, the extreme change in temperature, which had begun on the voyage, settled into his head. The cold winter air seemed to compress his skull as he walked and slipped on the frozen shit and mud on the streets. He had arrived back in England in the most shabby state imaginable, but he had not realised this until he was among his own countrymen again. He affected strangers in a different way. He had assumed it was because of his own misery—that others did not want to be infected with it—but catching sight of himself in the glazed shop-fronts he understood that it was because he looked like a vagrant. His face was shaggy with untamed beard, and framed with a mass of unkempt, dirty hair. His shoes were coming apart again because the string which had held them together had rotted and worn away. His bare toes were visible with every step he took. His clothes hung from him. He passed his nights in a cheap hotel, and the company of bed bugs had kept him from sleeping. There was something so vile about the bugs in the hotel bed, which burrowed into his conscious-ness as well as his skin; they were far worse than any of the leeches, ticks, biting flies or mosquitoes they had endured in Brazil. The thought of these bugs biting strangers in that same bed drove him

out, and Edward finally returned to his own house. Scratching his
bug bites as he looked for a cab, Edward saw a shimmering black
edge to everything in his path, and everything else around him.
And as the wind bit his face and gnawed at his exposed feet and
gloveless hands, he was aware of an aperture opening in his torso,
which grew with every step and let in the cold air. Fist-sized to
begin with, now as he neared the rank of cabs it felt large enough
to admit a small dog. He was embarrassed at this, and hoped that
the driver would not say anything about it. The black line around
the edges of the man fizzed, and as Edward saw the frightening
bulk of the horse gush its steamy piss onto the ground, simultane-
ously dropping its manure, he wanted to dive under it, make it
rear up and bring its hooves down on his head, and break his
spine. But the thought of what miscalculation might entail stopped
him. Edward got into the cab. As soon as they moved off, Edward
fell asleep, the dullness of his thoughts being composed of nothing
more or less than the knowledge that he would never be able to
put his name next to anything definite except the death of Augusta
and Gwen.

Many hours later, in his own old and unfamiliar bed the hole
in his torso had gone, but the black lines remained. He took
himself to a barber as soon as he could.

He knew that a letter would never do, but he still composed
them with the thought that he could pull it off, and not have to
face her. But the more he left it, the worse he knew it would be
when he finally did manage to get down to the business of breaking
the news. The bag containing the few things he had rescued from
the wreckage of the day he had lost them lay untouched. He took
it with him everywhere; he could not let the bag out of his sight,
because although he had not the courage yet to look inside, it had
slowly begun to dawn on him that Gwen's notebooks contained
his only chance of gaining some measure of scientific celebrity.

Edward packed an old overnight bag, musty from the back of a wardrobe. He took a cab to the bank and then to the train station, where he bought a third-class ticket to Falmouth. It would not do for this journey to be remotely pleasant.

Chapter L

Helford Vicarage, Cornwall. February, 1864.

"You feel that the air around her is filled with an essence that, once it has touched you, some small part of you, will forever be there to determine the course your life will veer down." Edward glanced at Reverend George Sparsholt who in turn repressed the urge to look at his pocket watch. "You have to imagine her as you would a large gilded moth under close scrutiny. The closer you get, the less of the initial attraction you see, yet still she pulls you in, inviting you to observe every scale. Under the microscope, the lustre disappears and yet you seek the brilliance that you know is there. She holds an illusion you must step back to appreciate, all the while longing to bring her up close to your face."

Reverend Sparsholt studied his cuticles; stiff and bored, he was not really paying attention to what Edward said. What little he had heard, he had not understood at all. When he spoke, he was alarmed at his own volume; it was almost a bark. "Moths! What wonderful creatures they are. I never tire of watching the hawk moths on the verbena just outside the study during the summer months." He took a swig of sherry and sloshed it between the gap in his front teeth before swallowing it. He knew it was not good for his teeth but he could not help himself in the company of this man. It was nervousness, and he stuttered a little. "In the late hours of a July evening, one can be induced into something almost resembling a trance; I have never yet been moved to still one, however. This may seem contradictory to a scientist like yourself, but I always feel that to stop one (he did not like to say "kill") would somehow diminish it, would remove some of the magic of our Creator's imagination. That is not to say I disparage your work in the least, I merely wish to say—"

Edward interrupted. "Reverend Sparsholt, I have managed to contrive a mess—an unintentional mess which I don't know how to untangle."

"That is hardly surprising, but you must not be disheartened. You must disentwine yourself in order that you may step back and view the situation from a more dispassionate standpoint, to which, I think, you were alluding. And, really, I cannot see how you come to lay blame on yourself when you were a thousand miles away."

"But that is precisely what I have tried to explain." Edward's voice began to rise. George began to sweat. Feeling the moisture accumulate on his top lip, he wriggled his nose and mouth, and raised his eyebrows in what he hoped was a sympathetic gesture. He was flummoxed. Edward went on. "It is all connected; it is all because of me."

George stood up and placed his sherry glass on the mantle-piece where gummy stains and other telltale rings marked the marble, now blackening with dust and a fine film of dirt. He caught sight of his reflection in the mirror above the fireplace. The mass of wiry greying hair he had tamed with grease that morning had become unruly, and fell into his eyes. He pushed it back and wiped his hand on the seat of his trousers.

"My dear fellow, Miss Carrick is, I am assured, merely suffering from a heightened sensitivity which is self-induced. I do not claim to have any knowledge in medical matters, but it seems pretty obvious to me that her problems are nothing a few months' rest won't see to. Ah, notwithstanding, of course, the, ah, period of mourning, which, understandably—"

"No! No! That is not it at all. I am to blame for the most part.

Oh, God, I wish I still had Susan's letter."

George Sparsholt wished that this twitchy, blasphemous man was not taking up space in his study. It had been something of a relief that morning to realise that here, finally, was another to take an interest in Miss Carrick. He had waved aside a disinclination to invite the man in; his Darwinist views and his adultery and his wild look—despite being clean-shaven—should not be impediments, not that morning, anyway. Now, it was afternoon, well into the afternoon. The sun had not only moved out of his study, it was beginning to set, and Mr Scales was still galloping through his sherry. He had missed lunch because of this man. Whatever had been intended would be served up cold for dinner. The man was obtuse. George wished Mr Scales would vanish like the lustre on the moth wing. But he would not. His eyes, rather disconcertingly, were glittering, and the prospect of George being able to relinquish some, if not all responsibility for Miss Euphemia Carrick now appeared to diminish by the second. George was now responsible; he now had two persons under his roof whose normal faculty for straightforward reasoning had abandoned them, or was severely depleted. With a feeling of hopelessness and a need to be in his kitchen where he might get some food, he grasped at the mention of Susan.

"Ah now, Susan. I know exactly where Susan is. She is with Mrs Brewin. I will go and fetch her." This piece of information seemed to shock Mr Scales out of his private reverie for a moment. He looked up at George, and George thought if he had told Mr Scales that the queen herself was in the kitchen, he would not have looked more horrified. "Well, I shan't be a moment then. Perhaps some tea, also. So, if you'll excuse me."

George swung open the door. He could not get out of the room quick enough. He was not sure whom Mr Scales had been likening to a moth. He had assumed that there was only one female now in the equation, but it would be better if he stopped assuming anything at all. Mr Scales' willingness to lay himself open, to disgorge his most secret, intimate feelings for a woman made George uncomfortable. It was too much. The nearer he got to the kitchen and its pleasant smells, the less irritated he became.

Mrs Brewin and Susan had their heads together over a large book on the table in the middle of the room. Every surface was sprinkled with grains of sugar and punctuated with drips of pulped fruit. Ranks of gleaming preserving jars were lined up, warming near the oven and a flupping, plopping sound came from the giant preserving pan on the hot-plate. He cleared his throat twice to get the women's attention. "Ah, there you are, Susan. I wonder if I might extract you for a moment. Mr Scales is most anxious to speak with you."

"Is he still here?"

"Yes. Yes, indeed, still here."

Mrs Brewin glanced at him, but there was nothing in her gaze except matters pertaining to jam reluctant to set. George liked his housekeeper a great deal. She was young but plain enough for George not to desire her. And he did not have to worry about losing her to another. She was faithful to the memory of her husband, lost in the Crimea. Initially, George had worried that this fact might inflame Miss Carrick, but Mrs Brewin had told him quite bluntly that she didn't go in for all that murmuring and nonsense. She was pleased, she said, to have Susan to help her; she was a good girl and pleasant company.

Whilst Susan washed her hands and put on a clean apron, George made a pot of tea and fetched the biscuit tin. Mrs Brewin was quite used to him bumbling about in her kitchen and ignored it, but Susan was perturbed by it. Susan tried to take over, but all he would let her do was fetch a small jug of milk. She had to follow on behind down the passage towards the study as he bore the tray in front of him. It had crockery for three. George could feel her alarm and agitation at his back. He had a large stride and the china rattled.

Edward Scales was poking the fire and adding another lump of coal from the wrong bucket. There were two buckets next to the fire: one with the wet stuff, and one with the dry. The fire belched thick, greenish smoke, and as George came into the room the draw from the doorway caused the smoke to guff out into the room. When Edward turned around with the poker in his hand, George had a strong impulse to reprimand his guest, but he did not. He asked Susan to bring up another chair.

"Yes, sir."

Susan wanted to rescue the fire but didn't. She watched the gobbet of smoke unfurl along the ceiling from the corner of her eye.

Chapter LI

Mrs Brewin was a religious woman but she did not believe in divine retribution. She felt a great deal of sympathy for Mr Scales, even though he had committed the sin of adultery. She did not believe in an Almighty who, having given Mr Scales the gift of a child, should then take it and its mother in such an horrific way. Accidents could happen, and these accidents had nothing to do with anything except extremely bad luck. Certainly, Mr Scales seemed to be a luckless man, if not perhaps perfectly stupid, as well. It wasn't clear whether Mr Scales was a bigamist; he had referred on more than one occasion to his wife, meaning the late sister of Miss Carrick upstairs, and not the late Mrs Scales who had lived in London and was now buried in the Reverend's church-yard.

Mrs Brewin and Susan had taken turns all morning to listen at the study door. If she had not heard it herself she would not have believed it. She had seen pictures of a crocodile once, and she imagined that an alligator was much the same thing. The crocodile pictures were in a large heavy volume belonging to Reverend Sparsholt; it had been left open on the settee, of all places. The vision she had then of George Sparsholt with a heavy book in his lap did not sit comfortably with the way he stood at the lectern in his study to practise his sermons. The picture now fullest in her mind of Mr Scales killing all those creatures and emptying their guts in search of his loved ones appalled and inspired her.

It went against her principles, to eavesdrop. She had always looked down on others who indulged and divulged, as she called it, yet it had been she, not Susan, who had started it that morning. As a result, there was no hot meal for the vicar and Miss Carrick, only some runny plum jam from her stock of bottled fruit, which should by now have set.

She had been George Sparsholt's housekeeper for some years. She liked the position; it was not taxing. He did not notice dust, and she had time to read novels. She had never done that when her husband had been alive. And though the sermons were boring and she was obliged to go and listen every Sunday (as well as through the week in disconnected dribs and drabs), she did at least get to sit in the pew usually reserved for the vicar's family (as he had none), and so did not have to spend the time looking at the back of people's heads.

Now, she felt herself somehow infected by the sudden rash of activity in the vicarage. Susan's enthusiasm for melodrama bubbled over. There seemed to be a surfeit, and Mrs Brewin absorbed it readily, like a sponge sopping a puddle leaking in under the back door. Poor Mr Scales. He'd spent the first hour of his interview with Reverend Sparsholt weeping. Mrs Brewin had never heard a man cry like that before. From the stuffy confines of George Sparsholt's study had come the sound of heaving sobs and hiccoughs. She thought it a very sorry state of affairs, that Mr Scales had felt compelled to remove himself and his mistress to such a remote corner of the world. She'd heard of Romantic Couples going off to Italy; surely, that would have been better. Elizabeth Brewin felt sure that the waterways of Venice were safer, being riddled not with alligators, but handsome gondoliers.

An hour had passed since Susan had been called into the study and she had not yet emerged.

Susan had told her all sorts of tales about the actual, Mrs Isobel Scales, and her visits to Carrick House. She'd nodded knowingly when Susan had mentioned the vast quantities of tonic previously consumed by Miss Euphemia Carrick upstairs. Elizabeth Brewin had suffered with the stuff herself for a short time—whilst her husband had been alive.

Now, she stood at the study door again, aware of the scum forming on the fruit pulp back in the kitchen but not moving to do anything about it. She heard Susan's high voice laughing nervously behind the door, and the rumble of Reverend Sparsholt's church voice. When the Reverend's voice vaulted through the keyhole Elizabeth Brewin retreated down the passage to the kitchen.

Among the mess of her jam-making on the kitchen table she began to draft a reply to a letter from her brother. The letter had been a little distressing, to say the least, and Mrs Brewin still felt that, compared to camels and mysterious Black Brethren of the Australian desert, life at the vicarage was unmentionably dull. Her brother's admonishing words filled her with sorrowful vexation, and she pictured her small letters of the previous months; how those small packets had braved tumult and tempest to arrive at last in her dear brother's hands, only to disappoint him. He'd said that her letters made him lonelier than ever. She dipped her finger into the pooled jam at her elbow and pushed it along. The jam made a wave at her fingertip and then settled back to its puddle without showing any sign of a skin. Not the slightest little wrinkle. She sucked her finger and began to write.

Dearest Brother,

How I dread to think of you alone in that tent all those long and strange nights. What you told me of the stars vexed me, and I can't stand to think of you under the peculiarness of that odd sky, like as if you were in another world altogether. If the stars are upside-down, then does not the blood rush always to your head? Since last I wrote to you two souls more bide here at the

vicarage. Miss E. Carrick from the big house on the river, and
her girl, Susan Wright, who is fine company for me; and I often
speak of you to her, and I know that you would find her a fine
person as well . . .

Elizabeth Brewin considered what she had put down, and thought
that it didn't much matter that the way it came out sounded like
matchmaking. Her brother would likely laugh about it; for a person
like him was never interested in taking a wife nor would he let
anything of the kind pass through his mind. Certainly, he wasn't
the sort to entertain beneath. It was true he thought himself better.
And what was it that he had written? "*Here, a man may be anything*
or anyone he chooses to be as long as he minds his way." Her thoughts
ran to the way her brother had been as a child. She remembered
the particular habit he'd taken a liking to, of clearing his throat
before speaking. He'd been a very dry little bodkin, even then, and
it pained her to think that he'd wandered so very far from her.
She looked about her and heard the tinkle of the bell, and realised
that it had been pinging for a while now. All this jam. If she could
just get the stuff to set, she could send a pot of it to her brother.
She would pack it tight in a box of straw. She was sure that Susan
would think it a fine idea. Very fine.

She looked up when she heard the click of the kitchen door
opening and Susan coming back in. Down the hall, the Reverend's
voice could be heard indistinctly.

"I'm to go up, and fetch Miss Carrick," Susan said.

Edward waited in the study, and the Reverend rocked back and
forth on his heels, his hands clasped behind his back, until Susan
came into the room with Miss Carrick, and then vanished.

"Miss Carrick," Reverend Sparsholt said to her, "do make

yourself comfortable. This gentleman whom I believe you have met once before, erm, has come bearing some grave news."

"Edward Scales." Edward bowed to Euphemia who stood apart from the two of them and refused to sit on the settee. She inclined her head to Edward.

"Susan has told me that you have come to tell me that my sister is dead, Mr Scales."

"I wish it were not so, but I must beg your forgiveness, Miss Carrick."

They each looked into the other's eyes. Then she said, "I am sorry for your loss, Mr Scales. I understand there was a child, also."

Edward hung his head. "My daughter, Augusta."

"That must be hard on you. I expect she was very lovely."

He could not think how this had happened. He felt insubstantial in the presence of this woman he had known so privately and so intimately. He realised how different she sounded from Gwen. He had been afraid of hearing her voice, but Euphemia looked and sounded quite different. Her movements and the clarity of her diction were a little slurred from a recent dose of tincture, but she was not as he had feared. And perhaps it was this which changed everything.

Chapter LII

Two Years Later.
Carrick House. June, 1866.

A hot day in the middle of June. Swifts flew overhead, almost clipping the man's wide-brimmed hat as he walked over the scorched gravel of the drive. The windows were all open in Carrick House, and a warm breeze lifted the edges of papers on the library desk. Susan watched the man make his progress up the drive. The rustle of papers distracted her for a moment, and she patted the paper-weight holding the pile of letters and bills in place.

The screeching of the swifts cut through the air as deftly as their scimitar wings. Susan left the room, giving it a cursory glance, and went to find her mistress. It would not be difficult, she had only to follow the sounds of the children playing. With all the doors in the house propped open, she followed the children's noises and their mother's voice through to the playroom. Mr Scales had insisted on the playroom being located downstairs with direct access to the garden. Susan had thought it strange. The new French windows let the twins career in and out at will. They had not employed a nurse or a nanny. Euphemia spent all her time with the children. She was sitting on the floor surrounded by snippings of paper and string. The twins ran clumsily up and down the room trailing kites in each hand. Susan eyed the mess with distaste.

"Ma'am, there's a gentleman coming up the drive. Shall I show him into the library?" Euphemia turned and stood, still smiling at her children, not looking at Susan. "Yes, show him in. I'm not certain when Mr Scales will be back, but it can't be any more than half an hour. Give him something to drink." She clapped her hands. "Let's fly them outside now, yes?"

As Susan stepped into the hall the bell sounded and she ran to open the door.

The man stood straight, clasping his hat to his crumpled, linen-clad chest. He was so tall. He bent down courteously. "Is this the home of Mr Edward Scales?" He gave Susan his card, but she did not look at it. She put it in her pocket.

"Please come in, sir. Mr Scales'll be back dreckly from his afternoon walk." She took his hat, but he kept his walking stick. He followed Susan into the study and accepted a brandy. There was something about his manner which made Susan want to stay in the room. "We're having such a blast of hot weather, sir. I hope you haven't had to come far." She put the glass next to Edward's armchair, hoping the man would sit down in it. The warm wind shouldered the smell more or less out of the room. Susan felt her spine ease. The smell from the cellar had come and inhabited the rest of the house; intruder that it was, greeting all at the doormat and on the stair carpet. It was the brother of mothballs and sister to the worst kind of sin.

"You're not so easy to find, out here on the river, are you?"

As if it was she, and not Mr Scales, he had come to see. "Depends on whether you're local, sir."

"Ah. Well, I'm not local." He sat in the chair and motioned for Susan to sit in the other. She remained as she was. The man swirled the brandy around in the glass and looked into Susan's eyes. "You say he's out for a walk. Does he take a walk every afternoon?"

"And every morning, too, sir. Since he come back, he's not able to—break the habit."

"No, I should think it would be hard. Is he well?"

"Very, sir. Thank you." Susan shifted, left to right and back again. She excused herself, dipping a curtsey, and left the room.

Alone, Gus Pemberton paced a circuit of the room, and stopped at the bookshelves along the back wall. He let his eyes wander along the titles without paying attention to them and then turned to look back into the room. It seemed dead. He faced the bookshelves again and made a couple more paces. He stopped again at a slim door set into the wall of books. The papers on the desk behind him rustled as he tried the handle and the door swung open under his fingers with the faintest of clicks. The smell of mothballs and some other kind of clinical taint he'd noticed pervading the air when he'd stepped into the house was now a suffocating fug of determined preservation. He whipped out a handkerchief.

Here then, were the things he had expected to see. A display cabinet, waist high, half timber, half glazed; it bisected the length of the room.

The walls were lined with cabinets and cupboards. Gus opened a drawer and looked down at the ranks of pinned butterflies: luminous, metallic, unearthly blue, shocking in their vivacity. He couldn't remember ever having seen them in flight. He remembered something Gwen had said about Vincent taking her a gift of a pupa. He'd never been much interested in butterflies. He understood that they were beautiful to look at. And, yes, they were like jewels; but no more or less significant to him than a cranefly or a wasp. In another set of drawers, he found bird skins. Hyacinthine macaws. Miniscule hummingbirds. Bright green things. More parrots. All the eyes padded out with cotton wool, the empty bodies stuffed so much like feathered lozenges. A milliner's wet dream, he thought. He closed the drawers.

Gus paced the room, his fingertips skimming the surface of the central display cabinet. He stopped short. There laid out were

Gwen's belongings. A pair of filthy kid gloves, which he had never seen on her hands. A pair of combs he had seen her wear on a couple of occasions, which had not suited or complemented her colouring. She'd worn them very deeply, probably aware of this fact. He remembered her hair had fallen heavily when he'd pulled the things out. A truly ghastly letter knife. Her paint-box, opened; the mixing tray still cupped the dried traces of her last study done in South America. There, next to it, her paintbrushes laid out in neat ranks like the insect specimens. Gus felt a wave of sickness and pity and guilt wash through his gut and end in his throat. What could it have been like, to have been Edward Scales? Was this an embodiment of his guilt, his grief? Was it here to ward off madness? Ghosts?

More; and worse. Scraps of paper, scribbled on by Augusta, precocious, of course, with such a talented mother. A tiny smock was laid out, still slightly stained with mud and clay around the hem and around the neck and down the front; the evidence of some dripping fruit, messily consumed. It was too horrible to contemplate, the care with which these artefacts of loss had been laid out. No labels, of course. These things were not meant for visitors. Gus felt his neck prickle.

At the far end of the room was a single armchair; an old thing, covered in worn, frayed and light-damaged watered silk with stains snaking here and there. Delicate structure. He went and stood next to it. He could see that it had once been a good piece. The chair was flanked by a pair of identical cupboards; deep-bodied, they seemed ill-matched to the rest of the room. Gus imagined rails full of Gwen's clothes hanging there, falling apart and still musty with the residues of the forest. He turned a key and opened one of the doors. It swung out fast on its hinge and Gus had to step back. At the same time he caught sight of the contents.

He swore sharply out into the empty room. A crude word to

match the raw sight. And then, more softly, "Jesus." He cleared his throat and peered into the chamber. The specimen jar was huge. He stood for some moments regarding the thing critically, and then had to look away as he composed himself. He turned again to the body in the jar. It had sunk down to the base, the feet turned in horribly under itself and one side flattened against the glass. The features of the face looked slightly swollen.

He found the edge of the cupboard door, pushed it home, turned the key. He left the room smartly and pulled the door closed. He wiped his teary hands on his balled handkerchief and his trousers, and poured himself another drink. The screaming of the swifts sliced the hot air. With the first mouthful of his drink, his pulse began to return to its normal and steady rhythm.

Gus Pemberton closed his eyes. It's all right, he told himself. It's all going to be fine now. But he knew that couldn't be true. All could only become much more complicated. He still had to speak to Edward Scales. He'd been prepared for it this morning. He wasn't so sure he was still prepared for it now.

"In a hurry again, Susan?"

"Gent to see you, sir." She gave him the card, aware that the man could hear her every word.

"He's not been waiting very long. I gave him a brandy."

Edward said quietly, "Good Lord, I wonder if it can really be him, after all this time."

"Madam said I was to give the gent a drink."

"It's quite all right, Susan. You did the right thing."

Susan followed Mr Scales down the hall and, taking her duster from her pocket, began to flick it at the stairs and banisters, climbing up a few steps where she knew the sound of Mr Scales' voice would still reach her.

"What the devil are you doing here?!" Susan heard Mr Scales kicking the wedge away from the study door. He slammed it shut.

Susan thought how odd it was, that a person could say what he was thinking but cover his meaning up with the way that he said it.

Gus stood up. "Been availing myself of your hospitality again, Scales, as you can see."

"My God." Edward shook his hand and clapped him tentatively on the shoulder. "What on earth brings you to Cornwall?"

"You, as a matter of fact. I've been sent to see you; I've got a bit of news."

Chapter LIII

Carrick House. June, 1866.

Edward stared at Gus Pemberton. The sound of his two small boys crashing about in the hall and playroom was muffled; audible, the sound of his wife's laughter.

Helpless in the face of Augustus Pemberton's news, he sat quite still. Gus, seeming to have anticipated this confusion, also sat quietly, moving now and then to take a sip of his drink and to cast a sidelong glance out of the window.

"Where is she? Did she come with you?" Edward pushed himself up from his seat and went over to the window.

Gus turned, half rising, to speak to Edward: "Gwen and the child bide in Richmond. She didn't want to come here. She and her sister—there are, shall we say grievances—"

"Does she know? Does she know? Christ."

"Come and sit down, man."

Edward's shoulders drooped, and he stood immobile. Gus got up, led him back to his chair and poured some more brandy into both their glasses.

Edward said, "When I came back to England everything was in turmoil without and within. There had been so much loss, so much death—there was a feeling, a need—in both of us, Effie and I, to salvage something." He rushed to qualify. "Of course, my own conscience, but also to do something good for its own sake. At first our own private griefs bound us, but it is so much more than that; especially, since the twins. My wife—my first wife—had been quite ill. An obstruction of the bowel. A rather twisted turn of events."

Gus Pemberton said, "Yes, I know. But your deed was an act of chivalry few would contemplate, let alone carry through."

Edward looked up at Gus questioningly and said, "It was not a simple case of finding comfort in shared grief. Euphemia was on the precipice of madness when I found her at the vicarage. Amongst so much confusion, the least I could do."

Edward began to shiver slightly and then his body shook, in quiet convulsions; he hugged himself to try and stop it.

"Have a drink," Gus said. "It's the shock, that's all. I should have written first, if I could have been sure that you'd have received it."

Gus waited for the shaking to subside, not allowing Edward to speak until he'd downed at least half the brandy in his glass.

"I've been alone with it. With how she is—potentially. I'd never, I couldn't ever have expected anyone else to understand the complicated nature of her. I've felt responsible, at every level. Will she want to, to see me, at all; what does Gwen say? Did she give you a message?"

"I can arrange for a meeting to take place, if that is what you would like."

"Say nothing of it to Effie. This, it will tip her over. I have to think of the boys. I can't have them being—" He was going to say "ruined", but let his sentence peter out.

"I'll be discreet."

Chapter LIV

THE TIMES, Friday, October 5, 1866.

MURDER TRIAL AT THE OLD BAILEY.

MR SHANKS, for the Defence, called the prisoner's doctor, Dr Rathstone.

Q: "You were called to the Pemberton family home on the morning of August 7th, were you not?"

A: "Indeed, that is quite so. I was summoned to the aid of Mrs Pemberton. I put off another call, as this call was urgent, but the nature of the call only became apparent when I examined the patient, Mrs Pemberton. It was rather a delicate matter. The patient was in a considerable deal of pain, and unable to rise from her bed unassisted. It was immediately apparent that Mrs Pemberton had suffered injuries to her torso, limbs and to her head and also to her face. There were abrasions and bruises which I tended first. But, as I suspected a broken rib and further examined the patient, I questioned her in earnest about the nature of her injuries. At first, she was reluctant to reveal how she had sustained the bruising and so forth, but after an hour or more, I learned that Mrs Pemberton had been beaten severely the night before. Of course, I did not want to press for further details, but Mrs Pemberton was anxious for the reputation of her husband. She asked me to pass the Good Book, lying at her bedside and told me, with her hand upon it, that her husband had not harmed her. She was most anxious about it. Then she asked me if I had spoken to her husband. When I told her that I believed he was out of the house, she became very agitated, saying that she thought Mr Pemberton must have gone to see the man about it himself and that the thought of the two men fighting over it was worse than the injuries. Mrs Pemberton said over and over again that she didn't want her husband to come home battered or worse."

Q: "It was Mrs Pemberton's impression then, that the person who had harmed her on the night of August 3rd was still alive?"

A: "Without a doubt, sir, indeed it was. She feared for her husband's life."

Q: "And she seemed in genuine distress over this last?"

A: "Sir, in my long career, I have seen many women make a sham over some thing or another, but I have known Mrs Pemberton some years now, and no doubt is in my mind that the fear she felt over her husband's safety that morning was genuine."

Q: "Please, Dr Rathstone, if you can, would you tell me what her exact words were?"

A: "She said, 'He'll kill my husband, I know he will.' She said it many, many times until I could persuade her to take a sedative."

Q: "And did Mrs Pemberton give you the name of the man who had injured her and whom she believed would harm her husband?"

A: "She did not; she was in great distress and would only repeat what I have told you."

Chapter LV

Euphemia laughed, showing all her teeth. Gus Pemberton smiled, joining his face to her laugh, but he could not meet her gaze. Trout. He attended to the food on his plate. Done very nicely by Susan, gutted earlier by himself and Edward, Susan quiet by the sink waiting to deal with the guts and cleaned fish. The task of taking the trout from the pool (it was not large enough to be a lake, not really) could hardly have been less satisfying. As Edward lowered the landing net into the water, Gus had heard the gentle breaking of waves, fifty yards beyond the garden wall. An unsightly and abrupt end to the amble down the paths. In his mind, he vaulted the mortar and stone, and stood looking out at the scene Gwen had once described to him. The wall must be new. She had never mentioned a wall. The innards spilled neatly, releasing a muddy taint into the air.

Gus Pemberton found Gwen's sister charmless. He tried to discover something he could like in Euphemia's character, so that he would not find himself being false with her. He thought that if he'd found himself married to such a creature, he would have spent twice as much time out of the house as Edward Scales.

Initially, he had been struck by her appearance. How like Gwen she was, in that first instant, despite the obvious difference between the sisters. He could see how Edward would have fallen at once into tying himself to this woman, rather than striving to extricate himself—and then forever regretting it.

Gus felt the tension creep down his back as Euphemia said, "You never did say, Ted, how the two of you met."

Edward's reply was a little too studious. "We have an acquaintance in common. A Midlander, now living in London—"

"What? Mr Coyne is Cornish—and he certainly isn't—"

Edward's cutlery clattered onto his plate. He placed his hands flat on the table. Gus had his fork midway between his plate and his mouth; pink fish flesh dropped with an almost silent splat back onto his plate. He looked from Scales to Scales' wife and back again.

Euphemia said, "What I mean to say, is—"

"Take the boys, why don't you, Euphemia, to the kitchen, where I am sure Susan will be only too happy to give them their milk pudding," Edward said quietly.

"But the thing is, obviously—"

"Take them, Euphemia."

Both men were quiet after the corralling had been accomplished.

Gus said, "Would I be right in assuming that your wife's comment just now came as much of a surprise to you, as it did to me?"

"If she had made that comment before I'd had your news, I would have wanted to know what she meant by it immediately. As it is, I can wait. And I am even more convinced that your news should be withheld from Euphemia, for the time being at least. She has not been very calm these past few days. Her chirpy facade seems egg-shell thin."

The next morning Gus held Gwen's notebooks in his lap. Looking into them by the open window of his room, he'd expected to see her watercolours and sketches laid out on the page in much the same way as the specimens themselves. Ordered by class, neatly labelled, a border of white paper between each regimented subject.

No. Her pages were, to the uninitiated eye, a jumbled, mixed-up mess. A morass of things, jostling for space. Her written notes meandered around her work: lines, arrows, and dates seemingly confused, overlapping; nothing was chronological. These were her private thoughts and impressions layered year on year. Gus supposed that her intention had been to sort through and make fair copies of the best of it. It was obvious that she had never intended these notebooks to be used by anyone but herself. With this in mind, he looked more carefully. He got up and went downstairs to the library to find a magnifying glass. He could not read her tiny handwriting without one. The house seemed deserted. Edward, out for his morning ramble. No evidence of Euphemia and the children: perhaps they, too, had gone out. Gus stopped to crane his head at the landing window and studied the sky. If Euphemia had ventured out like her husband, she would get wet very soon. The pallid grey of the early hours had begun to transform into something much more forbidding, though the air was still. On the cusp of something, thought Gus, waiting for the telltale sign, and the rush of wind in the treetops. Always expecting something grander than British weather could produce; he hoped that Cornish weather might prove a little different.

He went on down the stairs and to the library. He took a moment on the threshold. He had not noticed much about it the day before. It had been so terribly hot out, and he'd been so tired, so glad to be in a cool place, and only thinking of how he might tell Edward about Gwen and Augusta.

Edward had wasted no time in giving the heap of Gwen's sketchbooks to Gus.

The room seemed to say that its owner had gone out of his way to make it utterly unextraordinary, bland.

Gus found a magnifying glass on the desk and putting it into his jacket pocket made to leave the room. Susan was standing just inside the door with her hands behind her back, as though she had just shut herself quietly in with the guest.

"Good morning, Susan. I'm just stealing a magnifying glass. I'll not get in your way."

"It's all right, sir, I don't do this room today."

Later, he picked up the sketchbooks again and opened a page at random. A portrait of a girl wearing black and red face paint, bordered by a trail of crimson passion-flowers and studies of Heliconid butterflies and their larvae, as Gwen called them; not caterpillars. The sight of the girl brought a knot into his stomach. She was smiling, her gaze turned away from Gwen, unlike so many portraits of indigenous peoples of far-off places. Gwen's portrait of the girl had caught her in a moment. It was perhaps as contrived as any other portrait; no one could paint that quickly. Gus could sense that, to the girl, this had not been the most important part of her day. Something more engaging had caught her attention, and the viewer was not allowed to look into her eyes. On the same page, Gwen had painted the leaves of the tree from which the red dye had been extracted. There was an unfinished study of a minis-cule yellow and black tree-frog. Gwen's tiny script edged around it all, and Gus peered through the magnifying glass at her pencilled in words: ". . . each variant would seem to support its own kind of insect. A curious thing, for these relationships to be so special-ised. On each plant stem there are tiny nodules, different on each variant, positioned half an inch or so below the leaf and sometimes around the edges of the leaf itself. The nodules vary in size from the almost invisible to the size of a pimpernel flower-bud. These nodules, I have come to realise, are almost exact representations of the ova belonging to the particular Heliconids which rely on the plant as its food source. It is unclear in my mind whether these nodules serve to act as some kind of attractant, or a dissuasive measure. Is the plant attempting to repel the butterflies by announcing that there is already a crop of ova about to hatch and thereafter devour the food ahead of the new additions. Or is it a reminder to the butterfly to lay her eggs? Either way it is a remarkable example of a plant imitating its parasite. I cannot help but speculate that in some cases at least, nature is indeed perhaps as C.D. suggests, working independently of its Originator . . ."

Gus smiled to himself at Gwen's younger self and her tentative words. She was much more direct now, and unwavering in her conviction. The open window brought in a rush of cooler air and the first raindrops began to spatter the glass. With his gaze fixed in the middle distance through the gathering rain, he thought of her speculating, her imagination ignited by such tiny things as the almost invisible bump on a passion-flower stem. Gus spent the remaining hours of the morning lost in the pages of her work.

Eventually, he heard nearby the commotion of Euphemia coaxing the children, filthy by the sound of it, from exploring the midden heap, into being scrubbed before Susan took them off to have their lunch in the kitchen. Gus heard the resonant clang of an enamel bowl put down on the flagstones and a cloth being dipped and wrung, punctuated by aggrieved noises from both parties.

Two days after Pemberton's stay had come to an end, Euphemia was high-pitched and overly loquacious. There was a worrying shimmer in her eyes.

A darkening bruise spread out on the horizon casting a dull beginning to the day. As the sky turned a deeper hue of slate, the sea became pale and luminous under it. The wind frigged with Edward's clothes, and he decided to turn back before he was blown off the path. The house, which only a few days before had been open at every window, was now battened down, and seemed to be as hunched as he was as he came in the back door. He kicked off his boots and shoved them under a chair, fully expecting Susan to appear from somewhere and tell him off. She didn't. Edward poked around for something to eat, and finding nothing that wasn't rising or steaming in the deserted kitchen, went along, still wearing his outdoor things, to the library. He kept dry biscuits there. It wasn't exactly an appetising thought, and he was just considering the possible ramifications of ringing for Susan when he saw his wife.

She didn't see him; Euphemia was standing with her back to the door. She was busy searching for something to read. Edward waited for her to sense him there. She was leafing through a book; he could tell from her posture and from the tune that she hummed that she was unlikely to realise he was there unless he made a noise. He stayed perfectly still for a moment, enjoying seeing her absorbed in something so simple. The tune that she hummed was one that she had been practising on the piano very recently. The mistakes that she made over and over again on the keys had corrupted her memory of the piece so that she was humming it wrong. The wind hit the house in a smack of squall, rattling the windows. Edward took his cue and moved into the room, making a noise as he went.

Euphemia turned and let out a yelp like a puppy being trodden on, her eyes widening in alarm. Almost immediately, but not quite soon enough, she said, "Ted, you quite startled me. Goodness, a storm."

Edward waited patiently as she fiddled, putting the book back into the case. His wife slammed the doors shut over the books, standing defensively—protectively? Edward couldn't decide—with her back to them, her arms splayed out at her sides.

"What a silly goose I am. Are you wet? I think I can hear one of the boys; he's calling me." She walked across the room briskly, intending to go past Edward without another word. Edward stepped in her way, and she bumped up against him, recoiling fractionally. Hardly at all, Edward thought, but it was there all the same. Now, he thought, whilst I don't mind about it. "There is something I have been meaning to speak with you about."

"Well, I shall look forward to it over dinner, Ted."

"It is a private matter. A matter of great importance, which—"

"I must get on, Ted. We can speak later." She pushed him aside, and he let her go. As she left him, she gave him a parting kiss as an afterthought, her top lip beaded with moisture. There was a tang of ripe underarm heat in the space she left behind.

Edward swore under his breath and locked the door after her. Since the arrival of the twins—no, since the very beginning of her bearing them—she hadn't needed any medicine. The glitter of her eyes, in the first days of his taking her on, as he had come to think of it, had vanished. Her demeanour had changed. She was lighter; hadn't cared about his insistence on her not taking clients in, for those evenings to cease altogether. That part of her seemed to have been smoothed right away.

Edward couldn't be sure when this edginess had come back. It was not easy to pinpoint. He thought that perhaps he was being too hard on her. But then there was the comment she'd made about Vincent Coyne; she'd avoided answering his questions, despite his attempts. He didn't want to think about its possible implications. There were far too many little things that he wanted to avoid dwelling on.

He rummaged for his dry biscuits; cramming one into his mouth, he sloped over to the bookcase Euphemia had been rifling through. He didn't mind, on principle. The books there were as wallpaper to him. Certainly, he'd never read anything from those cases. Never even considered it. Euphemia had transferred her edginess; she'd left it in the room and it hovered right there at the bookcase. Don't be a stupid ass, Edward told himself, as he scanned the shelves. He made himself assume an idleness and was about to shut the doors again when he saw it. A book not aligned with its neighbours or the shelf, its lower edge hovering. Edward slid his middle finger into the inch of darkness and grasped the top of the spine with his other hand. The book was wedged tight and when it came out it spewed papers, which drifted in all directions to the floor.

Edward instinctively dropped to his knees to gather them up. It was as well that he was so near to the floor when he saw whose handwriting covered the papers. He read them hungrily, feverishly, spreading them all out on the carpet, sorting them into columns finding the chronological order, finding the extent of Euphemia's game.

Dear Euphemia,

I write this letter to you in haste, much weakened by a lengthy ordeal which had me laid down very low with a case of the ague. I would have travelled back instead of this letter but for my young companion, who has fared much worse than I with the fatigue and the debilitating effects of the ague. I shall wait here, in Pará, as a guest of some friends here whilst my companion recovers. Do not concern yourself, dear sister, I am all in one piece. But there was some confusion, to put it mildly, when I became separated from my party. I have learned since my return that it was believed that all members of my small party had perished.

Mr Scales has returned to England still under this illusion. I know that he would want to visit our house in person, to deliver this erroneous piece of news.

Please relieve him of this misapprehension as soon as the opportunity may arise either by letter or in person.

I hope to be able to travel home one month from now . . .

—

. . . I have managed to find a place to stay—temporarily, until I have sorted out my financial affairs, and until I am able to manage the final leg of the journey home. The voyage has taken much out of me, and, again, I am able to take advantage of the kindness of friends. I will need you to send me a cheque as an interim whilst you sign over the full amount of my inheritance to me. Please send it as soon as you are able . . .

—

. . . I have spent several days since your letter arrived redrafting my response. But I am now of the opinion, having had time to think on everything, that there is no response which would adequately encapsulate all that might reasonably be committed to paper. There was no need to include the cutting. I read the papers daily from cover to cover. At least, I know now that he is alive, safely returned to England, and that you are not unwell. Your timing, as always, is impeccable . . .

—

. . . Will you at least send on my work? I don't presume to ruin your happiness, as you claimed in your letter; I wish only to allow him to know that I did not perish, as he and everyone else had previously thought. Don't force me into the ridiculous indignity of having to beg you for something which would normally be given freely, without thought or preamble. I will be contacting the Bank, again, in due course.

—

You MUST inform your husband of my whereabouts. It is the only thing that I wish for, nothing more. I cannot see that any benefit can come from his continuing to believe that I am dead . . . As it would seem that I am virtually penniless, may I now, please, at least, have my work returned to me? There are a number of notebooks and sketchbooks which contain important notes in the work I carried out in Pará on some species of ants. You would find this dull, but it is most important that these books are returned to me.

—

Euphemia, you are and always will be my sister, but you leave me in an impossible position . . . Please be advised that I am not prepared to put up with this charade any more. Do what you will, and I shall do the same.

There were thirty-two letters in all, ranging in length, detail and tone. In none of the letters did Gwen mention anything of Augusta save for the mention of her "young companion", which he knew Euphemia would not have passed over lightly. Edward buried his head between his knees and rocked on the floor until he almost passed out. He wanted to smash things. If only. If only. If *only* he had stayed just a week more before leaving for England. He banged his head on the carpet until his vision was nothing but sparks of brightness, pinging back and forth, up, down. He didn't have the vocabulary to curse the woman. All words had gone from his head. All was vacant, leaving only sadness and regret and self-pity. And fire. A burning gripped his heart, and squeezed at the life of him as the possibilities of his future seized his imagination. He gathered the papers up to shove them back into the book, taking up another document thicker than the rest, which had slipped from its resting place. His own hand stared up at him: November 13, 1859.

He didn't need to read it. Snatches of phrases rose to the surface of his mind before he could stop them: "*. . . please destroy it in the fire . . . a testament to my failings . . . be assured that she was nothing compared to you and that my wife is nothing . . .*"

He screwed up the letter and threw it into the empty grate, scrabbling for matches, falling painfully to his knees at the hearth. Striking, striking, striking. The stink of the unwilling matches curling in the air.

When Pemberton had given him the news that Gwen was alive, that Augusta was alive, there had been a feeling of weird levitation—of his not really being a part of the scene. Reality, as Edward's father might once have said, had not yet jumped up and bitten his arse. Now, he wanted to go. Take a train to London, and find her. But he stayed rooted to the carpet, crawling, placing his hands on her letters, spreading them. In some, she asked for nothing: she gave Euphemia an account of a walk in a park, which Edward thought he recognised. She told Euphemia about a visit to the gardens at Kew, and her impressions of the Glasshouses. In another, she detailed a visit to the Zoo, with intimate observations of other visitors, which were both funny and poignant. Edward knew that there would have been a small hand in hers; that these were not solitary excursions. Some letters were posted all on the same day— and then there would be a silence which would last for months before the next letter.

Edward felt deeply ashamed at every mention in her letters of her missing work. It was his fault. He'd locked her things into cabinets, made a museum of her. He'd let Pemberton look at those sketches and paintings, and then he'd taken them back, locked them away again as if they still belonged under glass. The embarrassment of his having to be asked for them again, so that they could be returned to their owner. He might have pissed in his shoes for the shame of it if he hadn't busied himself with wrapping them in parcel paper and slipping in a note. And her lost money. Christ, her lost money. Euphemia had spent vast amounts refurbishing the house after the death of their father, and he'd never thought on it. Installation of the gas and a new bathroom with hot water. She'd employed an army of gardeners and had ripped out everything that was overgrown. And his extension to the library—her wedding gift to him, she had said. And he had accepted it. Too keen to believe that it was anything other than a romantic gesture.

And in amongst all of this extravagant activity she had steadfastly refused to allow Edward to erect a memorial to Gwen. Always claiming that she knew that she was still alive somewhere. Her genius; the simplicity of it.

He'd married Gwen's sister so that he might hear Gwen's voice again. It had been for the facsimile of Gwen, as conjured by her sister. And this was the only thing which had kept him from falling over the edge—a black pit in his mind or a real edge; he could have picked one of many along the coast. All he needed to do was go to her bed.

She wouldn't call him Ted. If she did, he shrivelled, and there was nothing to be done for the rest of the night.

He went to her room without a light, and slipped between the covers, pulled the hot body, stumbled into her. Re-enacted fragments of time spent with Gwen on damp ground, under trees and always in uncomfortable places. He pulled the body to the floor, or he made her stand, awkward against the corner of a piece of furniture. Or he'd just manage to pretend, for as long as he needed to, that this was her, this was Gwen's arm, hot against the cool, smooth sheets. This was her thigh, yielding under the pressure of his fingers. This was her, pushed up close to his face, her sea-salt, crusting on his fingers. This was her, the way he had always wanted her to be. The way she had been before she'd known anything about him. He held her and buried himself in her for as long as he could bear it.

He wouldn't ever have to go and do those things again. He wouldn't have to see, or puzzle over, her triumphant face in the morning.

Pemberton's promise—that he could arrange a meeting if that was what he wanted. Edward had said nothing at the time. If? Why should there be, how could there be, an "if"?

He rose unsteadily, and opened all the shutters in that little mausoleum. He shunted the windows open, each one a fraction to let in the air, the sound of the rain, and the sound of a thrush singing. He opened the cabinets where he'd laid all those things of hers, and removed them. The paint-box and her brushes. Living things again, because of the knowledge that her eyes would look at them again, and her fingers could turn these dry cubes of dust to life again. Everything was not as it had seemed. He laughed at the absurdity of it, that she could have come back from a certain death. That her mouth could speak. Yes, there was that. Her mouth could speak; her hand could write. He pressed his open hand to the filthy gloves she'd worn on the ship, which he'd never thought to replace. How could he scrape the pieces back? He was trying to stem the fury now. Trying to press back the need to destroy things and to cause physical, irreparable damage to the woman he must call his wife, who should only ever have been his sister-in-law. He hated her with every single cell in his body. He wanted to kill her.

Chapter LVI

London. Saturday, August 4, 1866.

In all endings, there are beginnings.

In this place, he looked so different. The years spent away from him had drawn him very differently in her imagination; and, of course, she hadn't yet managed to find the courage to look at her sketches of Edward to remind her of particular days or minutes she'd spent staring at him. In her imagination, he'd roamed faceless for so long. A peculiar ghost; even the vivid corona of pale fire had grown dim.

He'd spotted her first, so that she'd been caught looking past him until he'd been so close that she'd begun to move away from the man obscuring her view.

She couldn't ever have dreamed of him looking so—old; and tamed. She moved her hand to get a smut out of her eye, and he grabbed it, thinking she was going to embrace him, in this very public place, where no one would bat an eye at a man and a woman embracing on a station platform. His clutching instantly startled her and also reminded her of why she had liked him so much in the beginning, before she had known.

But what did she know, now, that would have made any difference to her back then? Everything, nothing; she mustn't let herself forget any of it.

Sulphurous pong, smuts, bodies pushing, elbows, smoke, whistles, shouting. I shouldn't have agreed to this, she thought. And then, but there was no other way. Edward held Gwen clasped to his chest, and she felt the thud of his heart through their summer clothes. She braced herself in the stiff shoes she still found so impractical and uncomfortable to wear.

"Edward," she said, pulling herself out of his grip enough to breathe, "perhaps we should get a cab."

He wouldn't let go of her. She hadn't imagined this kind of fever. She hadn't imagined anything at all beyond the simple fact that she would see his face again. He gripped her hand as though Vincent Coyne was about to abduct her again, even though it was absolutely and utterly impossible and quite silly.

Somehow, they both got into the cab, and the door was shut without trapping the yards of her dress. Straight away, Edward fell into a gush of sobbing. This is horrible, she thought. How can I get him to stop? But, she patted him, anyway, all the time looking over his shoulder out of the cab window.

By the time they reached the gardens, Edward was in a better state and only looked as if he had a mild case of hay fever.

They wandered aimlessly, Gwen knowing that Augusta was quite happily spending the day digging up an ants' nest in the garden with her long-suffering nanny. The thought of her daughter's interest in ants brought to mind the moment she had discovered what Edward had done with all her own work. The work she had done with the ants and which he had taken such pains to disparage at the time in Brazil had been written up in a paper and presented to the Royal Society under his own name. She had been denied recognition for her work. She had been denied the chance to prove that a woman might be a person of science in the field of Natural History.

She looked at him, and wondered if she still felt the same anger. She didn't know whether the time for accusations and recriminations was yet past. She had thought she would know it, finally, if she could have the chance to look into his face again. Now, when she looked at him there was nothing she could find of what she had thought of as his devious attitude; his features were a new canvas and he was so much the stranger to her that she felt some of the weight of fury lifted from her.

They came to the water-lily house.

"Shall we go in?"

"Won't you find it, the heat, rather uncomfortable?"

She laughed, "Come on."

But they both became very quiet as they walked in, perhaps both of them remembering Edward's exultation, that first day on landing at Pará.

It's just like the tropical Glasshouses, at Kew, wouldn't you say?

And her reply: *I wouldn't know, I've never been.*

It was nothing like it, of course. They faltered on the threshold and then they ignored the stifling, humid air and forged on. But neither of them bargained for the effect it would have.

Outside again, they walked until they found a niche to sit in.

"Those lilies, they were everywhere."

"On that day. Yes, I know." She almost took his hand and sat back, holding her gloves in her lap. They stayed there, like that, in silence until it was time for Gwen to go. Before she stood up to leave she said softly, "There is still the small matter of the birth certificate. You brought it with you."

"The— No, I'm sorry. I forgot."

Two days later, on Monday, Gwen took the omnibus to the address Edward had given her. She'd committed it to memory at the gardens, torn the slip of paper to shreds as soon as she'd been out of sight of him.

The house had the closed-up, musty smell of a place left alone for too long. Gwen wondered whether she would take the smell of it away with her on her clothes.

Edward opened the door to her himself and led her into the bowels of the place. In the morning room, a daybed was covered with blankets despite the heat. Under it lay glasses and plates. In a corner of the room, a pile of dust sheets which Edward had not bothered to have taken away.

"Edward," she faltered, shaken by this scene, "haven't you, have you no one here, to see to things? To look after you?"

Gwen made herself look at Edward in his pathetic state. He hadn't washed or changed his clothes since she had last seen him. His face was covered in rough stubble. From his mouth, a fetid cloud of breath which hung in the musty air. His lips were stained with streaks of dried red wine. Crusts of sleep at the corners of his eyes and amongst his lashes.

This man is stuck somewhere else, she thought; he's neither at the end of something nor yet at the beginning of anything.

"Tell me what you plan to do here, Edward."

He regarded her blankly, and then with an expression which asked Gwen why she was asking such a stupid question, he advanced closer to her. She had to move her head to the side and hold her breath. Gwen let Edward put his arms around her, let him put his face to her neck and snuffle into the delicate collar of her dress.

Then she pulled out of his grasp and stood apart from him again. "Edward, I think you need to make some changes here." She tried to sound comforting, though it resisted her.

"Changes. Yes, everything must change now," he said slowly.

"In the wider sense, they inevitably will. But, Edward, I'm talking about practical matters. I mean, for instance, that you must attend to your toilet; change your clothes. Have a hot bath—though if you have no one here, that may have to wait. Find a barber. Open

up more rooms. You need to be in a fit state, Edward. I can't talk
to you when you are like this."

"Like this?"

"Edward." She couldn't take it; she hadn't imagined it would be
quite so unpleasant. "You stink. Your clothes. Your breath is offensive—when was the last time you drank a glass of clean water?"

Edward stared at her. "I—you say I stink?"

"I'm sorry, I shouldn't have."

"No. You're right; I probably do. I must apologise." He swept a
hand through his hair. "What you must think of me."

"I think you have had a shock. I am standing here, with you,
when for years you have imagined that I was, that both Augusta
and I were dead. I think, when you saw me at the station and at
the gardens, it wasn't quite real for you. There were so many things
we thought of saying and couldn't say any of them. I think both
of us are wondering where on earth we should begin; what should
remain unsaid and what should not."

"You seem to know exactly what to say, and I—"

"I've had years to think of it, of this meeting, Edward. You have
had only a matter of weeks."

"You might have written to me." His voice was thick with
emotion and a sudden thirst. "I found your letters, to her."

"I did write to you, Edward," Gwen spoke very carefully. "I
wrote every week for a whole year until I was certain that they
were being intercepted."

"You could have," Edward grasped at the air as though it would
offer him some comfort, "you could have sent him sooner."

Gwen watched Edward begin to pace the room. How dare you,
she thought. How dare you blame me like this, as though it was
all down to me. You should have done more, she thought, when
Vincent told you I was dead. You should have noticed how mad
he was, how crazed, how false he was. You should have done more

to find out the truth of it, of what happened that day. You should have been able to find us, she wanted to scream, you should have been able to deduce what had happened in an instant. But, you were as useless as I had always suspected you were, and now you lay all the blame of your own hurt and misery on my shoulders.

Gwen said quietly, "You'll know her ways now, Edward. And you have those two boys. I think you know, really, that I could never have acted on impulse."

Edward stopped and turned, then he let himself slide into a leather reading chair, giving gravity the final decision on how he should land. "Her ways. Gwen, I am lost. The boys, yes; I think they are everything to her. Yet other times, when I see her, some days, it seems she hardly knows that they exist."

"Mr Pemberton told me that they looked like they were very happy, healthy children. Edward, I could never have acted selfishly."

"Why not? She has."

"That's always been her way, Edward. My sister has never done anything which did not benefit her. The rest of us, we have to negotiate through whatever she lays down in our path. Let's not talk about it until later. Why not show me the rest of your house? I'll help you draw up a list. I can help you find staff."

And yet all the time she was thinking, I must leave, I've made a mistake. I must go from here.

He brushed her words aside with jerking flicks of his hands as he advanced towards her. "Pemberton, Pemberton. Why was it him? What else, what did he tell you? To your face? In a letter? What kind of cosy discussion did you have, the two of you?"

"It's irrelevant."

"Look at me. No, somehow I don't think that it is at all irrelevant. It appears to me now, very odd, indeed, that a man you met *but once*, should be the one to come and deliver such devastating news."

"You're devastated that I am alive?"

"No."

"There was no one else; no one who had known us both. Honestly, I have tried to do the right thing."

"But where did you pluck him from? You don't know him!"

Gwen looked away. "He is Hettie Grindlock's brother. I thought you knew."

Chapter LVII

Richmond. Monday, August 6, 1866.

Gwen's hand hovered over the blank page for so long that the ink dried on the nib. She loaded her pen afresh and closed her eyes as she wrote: *I killed him.*

Opening her eyes, she looked down at her words. They were skewed and slanting, black and shining. She pressed the blotting paper to them; they had authority now. She added something to the sentence, gave the full stop a tail: *I killed him, the man called Vincent Coyne.*

So the letter became:

I killed him, the man called Vincent Coyne. One of us should have done it sooner or later, and since you were not there, the onerous task was left to me.

I can't say I undertook such a ghastly task lightly. It only sounds so, when you write it down.

He came back, to where he had left us. He came alone, and, of course, I never thought he intended to rescue us, or remove us to a place of safety after that first night. After those two days without shelter or food, perhaps he imagined a greeting different to the one he received.

Faced with such an intimidating prospect—left alone to perish through starvation or thirst, I never let myself believe that this was a certainty. I had Augusta to protect. I had the flint and the pocket knife, which Mr Coyne did not know about. He took everything else from us, as you know. But we were not weak with hunger. The place we had been abandoned to was favoured by the river turtle. We ate hatchlings roasted in their own shells for those two days. A happy coincidence while God had been averting his gaze.

Augusta slipped out of my hands, came out from our hiding place, running. He picked her up too roughly. He shouted that I should come out.

"Where is Edward?"

"My conscience is saved. However, you're still alive." His face for a second looked stupid with incomprehension. But he recovered himself.

"Mr Coyne. Two days ago, you told me that you would be gone for one hour, and that you would bring Edward here. Where is he?"

"You think he respects you. Do you really suppose that a man like Scales could ever respect a woman like you the way he respected Frome? And do you think by not being his lawful wife, you have elevated yourself to some higher position? Think."

"What? Put my daughter down, and tell me where Edward is."

"Go on, think. What promise did Scales ever make to you? No one is ever quite what they seem to be, are they, Miss Carrick? You should know that more than most."

"Augusta is innocent. You can talk to me, but put her down."

"Think, Miss Carrick. Thinking, working things out. That is your gift, isn't it?"

"Yes, it is, Mr Coyne. Please put Augusta down; you are frightening her."

"Miss Carrick. Which one of you did he really fall in love with? Do you think he really fell in love with you? Or was it the woman who would never question his authority, who would never be able to put his own intelligence in the dock? Which woman, Miss Carrick, do you think Scales really fell in love with—you? Or was it Euphemia?"

"Your mother was one of her clients. If you suppose that you

surprise me, Mr Coyne, with your little revelation, you do not.
Augusta, please, give her to me now."

"No. Euphemia hated you enough to employ my assistance. But
I don't believe she would bear a grudge against the innocent party.
Scales' bastard child is coming with me." Augusta, my child, the
only light I possessed. To hear that ugly word used to describe my
beautiful daughter. He turned his back on me and went to put
Augusta in the canoe.

These things are done without thought.

His guard was down for a second. Just a second.

I had been walking slowly towards him over the sand but now
I ran. I fixed my loose plait round his neck in a quick tourniquet.
He dropped Augusta. He tried to shake me off, and in his confusion,
and in the struggle, he and I fell.

He, face down in the sand; myself, landing on top of him. All of
my strength was taken by the determination not to let him free of
my throttling.

Augusta stood at the water's edge and screamed for her father.
Over and over. Bright macaws took off from the trees and called over
our heads.

After a while, he became still; I don't know if he meant to fool
me or not. I wrapped both ends of the tourniquet around my left
hand and brought out my pocket knife. And then a new vigour, I
didn't know whether he was trying to throw me off or if these were
his death throes. My knee in his back. All of my strength.

Being a mother, protecting Augusta. These were the things on
my mind as I pressed the point of the knife into his neck, just
below his jaw, turning the blade handle, driving it deeper. And I
thought of the stillness of oppressive afternoons as I dragged the
knife across his neck, messily, inexpertly, towards the other side of
his jaw. I thought of never having to wonder what he would do
next. What the next insane plan he might concoct in his addled

head or conduct on behalf of my sister would be. I shushed Augusta.
I waited.

When I rolled him over, I saw that his bladder had emptied. I
am ashamed now to say that I scraped a handful of sand and let it
drop into his open eyes; to verify his death, only to know, not out
of malice for the corpse. I washed my hair, face, hands in the river.

Her hands shook, her body convulsed, she poured with a sweat
that went cold on her skin. Her vision was blurred, the image of
his spectacles slipping down into the river, released from her fingers.
The silver frames and the blue glass catching the sunlight so briefly
before being covered completely by the black, tannin-stained water.
She wanted to run; her legs felt twitchy, and yet they barely
supported the weight of her. It was impossible to think that it
could have happened. Should a letter like this contain every detail,
she thought, it loses its purpose.

We drank some of his water, we ate some of his food. I covered him
with sand. We got into his boat. I paddled.

We came that night to the place where we had stayed. We were
ghosts. But ghosts who were clothed and fed and looked after.

You know the rest of it already. And now—

Gwen read it through. She was tired. Behind her on the bed,
Augusta shifted in her sleep—her legs and the sheets tangled,
her arms thrown wide. Gwen wanted him to know the depth
of it. Had to get rid of him herself; no one else was there to do
it for her. Gwen put the letter onto the table. She folded it up.
She unfolded it. She read it again. She cut it into flaccid spills
and fed them into the flame of her candle, letting them drop,
brittle, grey flakes of her confession, onto the rim of the candle-
holder. The top half of the window was open behind the thick,

heavy curtains. Gwen listened to the stillness. She looked over at Augusta. She'd agreed to take her to the Zoo the next day. It would be a day to make up for her long absence today, just the two of them. She crawled gingerly onto the wide bed, as though it were a trough of sinking sand, not wanting to disturb her daughter, spreading out her limbs, waiting for the tincture of morphine to work.

The afternoon she'd spent with Edward at his house drifted in and out of her mind as she tried to push it firmly out of reach so that she might be able to sleep.

Time and again, Edward had tried to pull her into an embrace, and each time she had evaded him he had become more determined. Eventually, stepping back, putting a physical distance between them, she said, "Because I don't love you, you see. And because I can't begin to love you. I know too much. Yes, once I was gullible, Edward. From before the moment you met me you were already hiding things, but I am not that girl. I have a different life now. The person you knew no longer exists. I'm sorry. I'll go."

Edward had made a show of intending to see her out, but at the door he was more insistent than ever. "A different life? What different life?" He grabbed her hands, pulled off the fine gloves, painfully tugging at her fingers, forcing them into his mouth where he sucked drily on them. She felt his teeth closing on her bones.

"You have no different life now," he said. "You are the same, just the same and more; you still wear that cheap ring I gave you. You can't bear to take it off when you put on your gloves. It looks better than I remember. It grows well on you. It used to slide between your knuckles, but now—"

Gwen tried to close her fist, get her fingers away from his mouth, pull free.

He pressed his cracked lips to her mouth and drew breath from her lungs. "Say the words," he said. "Tell me what you used to say."

In her corset, bound and stiff, she was unable to gather the wit of her strength to block him. She pushed her face aside, nauseated, gasping. "I can't remember any words, Edward. Let me go now." She reached out for the door handle, but he grabbed her wrist, holding her painfully, pressing skin to bone.

"Tell me about the weather. Make it the way it was."

"What?" She twisted her arm in his grip. His determination was manic; rub turning to burn.

"The rain, that we've been having this week. Say, 'This rain, this rain', say it to me."

"Edward, you must let go of me, you must stop this. I am married. Gus Pemberton is my husband."

"Whore." Edward shoved her against the wall and spat into her face. Her anger dug at her as his hands scrabbled at her clothes tearing a seam in the silk. He pushed her back along the dingy hall into the room across the floor and down. She lost her footing in her heels on the rucked carpet, and knocked her head against some part of the daybed as he thrust a hand up under the heaps of expensive silk, his fingernails scraping her, his grotesque heaving panting, shoving her into a corner of the bed, her legs parted now with the full weight of his hips bearing down on her. She took hold of his neck and squeezed. He slapped her across the face. A raw, flesh-stinging swipe, catching her lip against her teeth. She felt the swell of it, the butcher-block taste of it.

"Tell me about the foul weather, Mrs *Pemberton*, you obstinate bitch."

"I don't care to."

There came an enormous crack from somewhere. Gwen realised that her hearing had failed, and just as the black edges began to close in around her she knew that the crack must have come from her own head.

She woke face down. Her head throbbing, hanging over the

edge of the daybed. He wasn't finished. She made no sound, her eyes fixed on a plate of half-eaten food, a glass half full of claret gone to vinegar. For a long while, it seemed, she simply couldn't believe that it could have happened so suddenly, and without warning.

She remained immobile as he gripped the flesh on her thighs and pulled himself away from her. Thumbs pressed in, he ground the meat of her as he followed the contours of her lower back to her buttocks and hovered there.

"Do you realise," he murmured, "that I have not fucked you since that horrible day when I had to unpick your sister's needle-work?" He seemed not to mind that she made no answer or that she might be unconscious. Perhaps he wished it that way. Gwen felt the wet and cooling weight of him resting now between her buttocks. He pulled himself closer again.

"No," she coughed, and tried to right herself.

"I've always wondered," he said. And Gwen thought that he spoke through gritted teeth. She tried to edge away from him. He caught her up and pressed down on her back. Gwen yelled, angry at her incoherence, as he spat at her again; a great gobbet of phlegm landing on her buttock.

She twisted herself around, and flung her arm up, elbow jagged, catching him somewhere soft.

"Stop." She managed to get the word out as she heard Edward grunt in pain and swear, before he hit her again and pressed her back down into the daybed. "Don't, Ted," she said. "Ted. That's what she calls you now, isn't it? You have a different—" The thump from his fist into her side winded her completely. A searing pain rent through her as he drove into her and thrust harder, harder, shouting, "Tell me about the rain, you bitch," until his shouting became incomprehensible, the words catching in his throat until they became one long yell of anger.

He pushed her aside as he rose and left her, walking to the end of the room. She heard the cold, clear ring of crystal meeting crystal as he poured.

"Ted," she murmured, inaudible to him. She thought for the first time of her sister being his wife, letting him into her bed. She wondered what room Effie had now. Was it her old one or the one she had always wanted? She thought of Effie doing as she was told, and saying the words. Of Effie refusing and of her lying as she was, thinking as she was, that he might have cracked her rib. Concentrating on the bones. Just the bones.

The light had almost gone from the room. Her view of the floor, tipped on its edge, saw Edward's trousers and shoes pacing over the floor, coming to the fringe of the carpet and swivelling on the first inch of wood before turning. The different kinds of pain she felt astonished her. Her right arm was caught up underneath her ribcage, a dead limb. I can't leave, she thought. I shouldn't even move, until I have my arm back.

"Drink?" he said. "You've got to tell me now, how did you survive? You were thrown from the canoe. The river was teeming with alligators." Edward did not seem to be talking to her now, and when she replied, Gwen was not sure that he heard her.

"Vincent Coyne was a parasitic lunatic," she said, and studied the pattern in the carpet as she felt with her good hand for her hair. He was a lunatic, she thought. But you, Edward, are just a disgusting parasite. Letting her hair down slowly, the pins collected in her fist as she unwound the coil.

As she began to fall asleep, the pain of it played over and over in her mind, ghastly and dulled now by the tincture, still present and

livid in her mind. She wondered in her stupor on the nature of
pain embedded in the memory, trying still to distance herself from
the thing which kept her from sleeping.

She'd waited a long time for Edward to get drunk enough to
become enfeebled. And for the life to come back to her arm so
that she could begin to plait her hair.

Her mind had been clear.

Gus Pemberton smiled at his wife as she lay sleeping with her
daughter on the big bed. He'd come in and drawn back the curtains.
The window had been left open a little all night, and the room
was only slightly fusty with their sleep. He bent over to kiss her
forehead and stopped. There was a large bruise above her nose, and
the swelling had spread down, puffing up her face. Her lips were
misshapen and dark with the lively purple of trauma.

Gwen opened her eyes. Seeing him standing over her, she moved
without remembering and winced.

"You've suffered some kind of injury," he said. "What on earth
has happened?"

"I stumbled," she said, her voice masked with a dry tongue.

Gus passed her a glass of water. "Tell me," he said quietly, helping
her to sip it.

"I lost my footing. On the omnibus. People were very kind. I
ripped my dress. It wasn't so bad at the time. But —"

"You'll be feeling it now. Oh, dear, poor love. My poor dove."
He cupped her cheek with a soft hand, and she closed her eyes.
"I wish you'd have said yesterday."

"It seemed just so silly. I didn't want to wake you."

"Here, let's get you sitting up." He tried to ease her into a heap
of pillows. She tried to keep the extent of her injuries hidden from
him but she couldn't stop herself from crying out at his touch.

"Don't move me, please."

"No Zoo today. Not for you, anyway. I'll send for Rathstone."

"Don't bother Dr Rathstone, I don't want to see him. I just need to sleep."

"But, surely, just to see that nothing —" He stopped as she shook her head.

"I look as if I've been knocked rather badly, I know, but don't waste money on it."

"Hell! Who cares about that?"

"Just a drop of tincture."

"That will not do, you know it. See sense, let me send for the doctor."

"Bring the scissors from the table, will you please? I'm so hot, and my head hurts."

Gus put his hand on her forehead. "Now, why on earth do you want the scissors?"

When she told him, he wouldn't do it.

"But it is matted, and I shan't be able to dress it; no one shall. It is better to cut it off to my shoulder. My head aches with it, the weight of it is too much."

"When the doctor has seen you, you will feel differently."

"I don't think I shall."

Gus glanced at the sprawled child who was beginning to wake. He scooped her up as she became instantly conscious. From the child's hand he saw a pale grey, pearlescent sphere drop to the folds of the sheets. It was a very good example of a balas diamond, the best he had ever seen. He had no idea how Gwen had come about it. She had never said that she knew what it was, and had given it to Augusta to play with a long time ago. Gus jollied Augusta out of the room, making trumpeting elephant noises. It had always been on the tip of his tongue to say that she had given her daughter a small fortune to play with.

Now, as he looked at his wife in her state of distress, just as during the voyage back home on the steamer, he knew it was better to drop all thoughts of probing her deeply over things he could see she did not want to discuss. He knew that she must have spent the day with Scales again; Gwen taking the omnibus was unusual. But here she was, home again. And he knew that whatever she did, wherever she went, she'd always do the right thing. But he couldn't bring himself to cut her hair.

He handed Augusta over to the nanny and sent for Rathstone. While he waited for the doctor to arrive, Gus went back to his rooms to inspect the map of New Zealand he'd recently acquired. As he took the map from its paper casing, he remembered the way the servant girl at Carrick House had shut herself in the study with him.

"You're a detective, sir, aren't you?" she'd said. "From Scotland Yard."

"I'm sorry?"

"Aren't you, sir? I thought you was." Her shoulders sagged hopelessly.

"Oh, I see." He'd wanted to be kind but he'd wanted to laugh so very badly, as well. The girl had spilled out her speech anyway, ending with, "I do what I can, sir. But my mistress, she's married him, and I can't look out for her all the time, if you see what I mean."

He'd said that he did see, and that he understood her to be a very loyal kind of person.

"I always thought it were funny peculiar, what happened just before Miss Gwen went away. He's always made it seem like she was afflicted. But I've known them girls longer 'n anybody. There's nothing mad about her. It's all just to hide what's happened, see. Because of her not being able to say now."

Scales' words then had come back to him, that Gwen would

know what to do. And he had no doubt that she would, if he were to tell her. But, whatever they were, he knew she would keep her conclusions to herself, as would he. A servant's ravings were hardly a sound basis for such a serious accusation. Scales, for all his faults, was after all, a scientist, and scientists were in the habit of collecting macabre objects of interest.

He put his forefinger to the map and traced the lines of the mountains, the contours of the coast. He paused, the servant girl's words trammelling his head: "I can't look out for her all the time, if you see what I mean."

"God's sake, I'm an ass. An eejit of the first order," he said out loud. He rang for the maid.

"Tell Cook hot porridge for Mrs Pemberton. I want you to take it up to her as soon as you can—tell Mrs Pemberton." He tapped the map on his desk as he thought it through.

"Would you please convey my apologies to my wife. I have to go out for a couple of hours; no more than that, I am sure."

The sun moved more fully into the room. Gwen sipped her water slowly. She thought, And still the birds are able to sing. She remembered the sharp clarity of everything her eye had rested on that next day in a life which had seemed so distant from this one. She held her empty glass, waiting for Gus to come back, as he always did, with her breakfast tray.

Effie, she thought, but nothing more than that.

The sun glanced off the mirrors, and a fabulous light ricocheted into the room.

Chapter LVIII

London. October 5, 1866.

Gus Pemberton felt empty as he watched the Jury stand up and
file out of the courtroom to consider their verdict. He knew that
had the Defence been conducted by his first choice of man, the
case would have been thrown out of court by the Judge, or that
the Judge, at least, would have made his direction to the Jury in
Gwen's favour. As it was, he couldn't imagine that anyone present
would be confident in guessing the verdict. All week, his fingernails
had dug into his palms as each witness had been called up by the
Prosecution. With each new name, Gus had wondered whether
this would be the person to give the most damning evidence of
all. When they did, for he was sure that such a person would have
been found by now, he knew that he would not be able to stand
it. Bettlesham and Bettlesham had kept their distance from the
whole proceedings. Henry Bettlesham Senior had said to Gus, with
a tone of regret the night before the first day of the trial, that he
thought it best if he kept the lowest profile in England.

Gus now wondered if his approach had been all wrong; if there
had been, perhaps, some other way of persuading Henry B. that
either himself or his son could act for his wife. There was a low
hum in the courtroom, shuffling, and much fidgeting as the spectators wondered how long they would have to wait or if there was
time to go and empty their bladders. Gus stared up at the ceiling,
as he dared not catch anyone's eye. He didn't trust himself not to
lose his composure. That first conversation with Henry B., after

he'd received Henry's astonishing letter, played out again in his mind. There had been no witness called with the secret information, but still Gus felt his body throbbing with worry that somehow, even at this late stage, this unknown person might still be produced.

Gus had paced about in Henry B.'s rooms, unable to contain his anxiety long enough to park his backside on the chair offered. He'd sucked and puffed on the cigars he'd taken up again since Gwen's arrest and waited for Henry's response.

Henry had said, "I'm sorry, Augustus. This is quite embarrassing as I am sure you will appreciate."

"Oh, come off it, Harry. I don't see how there can't be a way around this. If you won't do it then I won't have anyone but your son to represent my wife."

"It's not a question of won't, but can't; it's simply out of the question. Henry Bettlesham Junior is a fine lawyer, I will admit, but Shanks is his equal. I haven't yet released the details of the will and shan't, of course, until the whole business is concluded. There was no one besides myself at the interment, in any case; such a drab affair. And it is a maze of complications. But the implications for yourself and your wife could be—indeed, would be—very severe."

"You'll put it about that Scales was intestate?"

"I can't exactly do that, you know; not explicitly. But matters can be alluded to, should they crop up. I should hope they wouldn't. So should you."

"I know nothing about this Shanks fellow."

"He's first rate. You couldn't look for a better man."

"And he doesn't know about the will?"

"Good Lord, no. I must assure you; it hasn't gone beyond myself, Henry and now yourself. There were no copies which left these offices, either then or since."

"I can barely think why he came to you."

"You mustn't let it impinge. But Scales thought he was making provision for someone practically destitute. And, of course, he was under the impression that your wife was *not* married. As long as your wife was truly unaware of the change to Scales' will before his death, and as long as it remains undisclosed—suffice to say, we'll keep saying our prayers."

"But his widow came to see you yesterday. Surely—"

"I told her nothing. Of course, she was deeply distressed and presented some difficulties. She is very—"

"Accomplished. You'll remember I have met her."

"Quite so. Rest assured, she had nothing from me except my deepest condolences. She won't know the worst of it until it is all over, and she may attempt to contest the will, of course."

"I don't doubt it, though there may well be no need."

"Do not give in to the ogre of despair. The most important subject for now is your own wife and the ordeal she continues to face, and I do believe that Shanks is the best man to—"

"Save my wife from the noose and eternal infamy."

"Shanks is very competent."

"I don't want competent; I want extraordinary. I can't have some bastard come into court to reveal at the last minute that Gwen has inherited every last damn bit of Scales' estate."

"Dear man, do compose yourself. It will never come near to that."

Gus did not believe in tempting fate but he wished that Shanks had been a different kind of extraordinary. Perhaps he was being uncharitable but he felt he couldn't be held accountable for his feelings towards the man. When Shanks had failed to harangue Morrisson over his flaky evidence Gus had struggled to keep himself from getting up and doing it himself. The triumph he had felt at convincing Gwen's aunt to change her evidence at the last minute had been sweet but brief. The days had been relentless, and now the ticking of every bloody pocket watch in the courtroom seemed amplified in his brain as the minutes ticked on into eternity. As he brought his gaze down from the ceiling, two things happened. First, he made eye contact with Euphemia Scales, whose presence in the courtroom he had until that moment been entirely unaware of. Then, the Jury began to make their way back in.

Chapter LIX

Carrick House. October 5, 1866.

Susan had known that it had been awful of her not to have told her mistress about the murder at Hyde Park. She had tried to look for a sign, a solution. She had gone to the Reverend for advice, but it had been Mrs Brewin who had said that it wasn't really Susan's responsibility to make sure her mistress read every square inch of the daily paper, and that if it had been put on the pile in the scullery, well, that was it done with. Mrs Brewin also pointed out that there were other ways the widow would find out, sooner or later. So, Susan had made peace with her troubled conscience and cut and strung the lavatory paper as usual.

Susan had followed the trial meticulously while her mistress had stayed in London. Running the house and taking care of the boys wore Susan right out, and she'd had to enlist the help of Mrs Brewin, who had been very quick indeed to down pots and pans at the vicarage. In turn, the Reverend had realised at some point that unless he wanted to live off old beef dripping, runny jam, pickled beets and no bread to put it on, he had better walk the three-mile round trip to Carrick House every day and eat his meals there. He couldn't say it was a disagreeable arrangement, and he found that the rigorous, out-of-doors exercise helped him to think clearly and was more conducive to the composition of sermons than the pacing of carpet his study afforded.

He liked the little boys, who said amusing and mainly incomprehensible things, and who did not seem at all perturbed by the extended absence of their mother. He also noticed that there was a keener brightness to his surroundings at Carrick House. His preparations for his sermons, whilst rather different in tone and timbre to those he'd made for years at the vicarage were rather pleasing to his sensibilities. The surfaces of the furniture gleamed at him and seemed to cast God's light about the room in a rather fairylike manner. The windows seemed not to have been glazed at all until his head bumped up against the glass when he tried to peer at the view up the main drive further than the panes would permit. Over the first week or so, the Reverend gradually began to realise that the house was simply very clean. Mrs Brewin, firmly ensconced, took it upon herself to engage through an acquaintance in town an illiterate but excellent cook whose skills in preserving were exemplary.

The Reverend had followed the trial. Everyone he knew had been following the trial. He had tried to keep Mrs Pemberton's identity to himself, but the impossibility of that became clear as the trial had progressed. After all, Mr Scales had not taken a whole *harem* of lady watercolourists to Brazil.

Today, they were all waiting for the paper to arrive, each avoiding the other's eye. The Reverend peered again from the window at the view of the drive and stifled a release of digestive gas behind a clenched fist.

Waking to a dry mouth, bodies pressed against Euphemia as the shroud of an uncomforting sleep slipped away. The empty carriage she had chosen at the beginning of her journey had since quickly filled. The train gave out its final shudder of stopping at a station and the dent in her forehead from taking a sleep against the window frame began to make itself felt. The usual stink of such confinement—stale tobacco, boiled egg, old sweat, camphor, lavender,

naphthalene, rotten tooth, fart, wet wool—made her sit up straighter
and look about without looking at faces, to see who had travelled
with her, who had witnessed her sleep. The embarrassment of the
dream she'd been taken from was still fresh in her mind, and it was
possible that she had been calling out in her sleep. Euphemia turned
her face to the window. There was a wasp, late for its winter nest
or tardy in its dying. It butted against the window, and the screams
from the guard's whistle masked out its tiny noise.

Before boarding the train, Euphemia had bought herself a newspaper from one of the stands. There were many things, many
activities, according to some, which a female of certain rank should
not do, should not indulge in, should not permit herself to enjoy.
Buying a newspaper was one of them but Euphemia had given up
caring what other people would think of her. She had been there
to see her sister vilified all through those sweltering days and stuffy
hours of the trial. Euphemia had been incapable of restraining her
curiosity.

Euphemia had not opened the paper. She knew what the report
would say, so she kept the paper folded away in her travelling bag
as she reached in for her flask. There were hours yet of this journey
to endure, and Euphemia took a very tiny sip, just enough to wet
the sour taste on her tongue. Then, she brought out the tin of
sweets she had paid for along with the newspaper; she put one of
the sugared violets into her mouth and stared again out of the
window at the rushing by of the land and let her mind empty, of
everything, just for a few moments.

Chapter LX

THE TIMES, Friday, October 5, 1866.

MURDER TRIAL AT THE OLD BAILEY.

THE PRISONER has held herself well erect in the courtroom each day of the proceedings, and today was no time for the prisoner to deviate from her usual attitude. Her dress was quite impeccably attended and sombre. A thick veil half obscuring her face, the prisoner kept up a surreptitious knotting or sliding of her fingers against each other, slotting them together in a constant bid to make sure that her gloves were without wrinkles. When each person spoke, she attended to what that person had to say with silent acuity; to the reaction of others in the room, the prisoner seemed alert to every nuance of tone. She has betrayed no emotion during the last session of the proceedings. There has been nothing in her manner which could have been interpreted as that of a guilty party or otherwise. Her attitude has not, apart from the constant adjustment to her gloves, demonstrated that all of this bother has been centred around herself or that her life has been in the balance. Mr Probart for the Prosecution examined witnesses, during which time the Defence made several objections; some were upheld, others were not. However, by the end of the Defence cross-examination it was clear to all assembled in court that Mr Probart's witnesses served only to strengthen the case for the Defence. From the gallery a veritable hum of consternation and excitement could be discerned after the summing up by the Judge, Mr Justice Linden. The Jury retired and deliberated for more than forty-five minutes before they returned the verdict: the prisoner was found Not Guilty, the Jury concluding that the death of Mr Edward Scales was accidental. At which declaration, a roar of appreciation emitted from the gallery and rose to the roof, after which a general hubbub of whistles, cheers and cries of "Bless you, Mrs Pemberton' were audible amidst the noise. Mrs Pemberton was helped away from the courtroom by her husband and others.

Chapter LXI

Carrick House. November 1, 1866.

The Book of Phobias
by
C.R. Jeffreye

"The exercise of combining two emotions, so as to bring out a third different from either, is not intrinsically arduous. Everything depends on the facility of assuming the elementary feelings."

Bain, 1855.

(i)   And so we come to the most singularly intriguing case which has been a subject of my exploratory studies of the mind and its peculiarities under inspection. We shall call the specimen, [censored], or X, hereafter.

   X first came to my notice some years ago. The spouse had called to my attention, in my capacity as a Gentleman of Medicine, the distress caused to both parties on the occasion of the pinnacle feat of the nuptial requirements. This would not in itself cause undue concern under normal circumstances. My advice to the unhappy spouse of X was that Time would Unravel the Mysteries, and that All Would Be As Expected. The dysfunction, dissatisfaction and, moreover, disappointment over the lack of potential progeny continued, however, for several months, and the spouse sought my counsel once more. On this occasion, I was privy to further details, thus: X was unable to consummate his marriage due to an aversion to the follicular protuberances of his wife's [cut].

I delicately suggested the obstacle of consternation might be solved by a simple act of removal. This, she informed me, after many floods of tears and blushes, had been attempted without success. The renewal of such follicular emergence, before the next attempt by X, was in all senses, quite apart from being wholly distasteful in practical terms, more disastrous than the original state of affairs.

My suggestion then, was to allow a certain amount of time between our meeting and the next attempt, to allow for Nature's Replenishment of that which had been depilated. I suggested that I might have an interview with X, to which, after Gentle Persuasion, the Lady agreed.

(ii)   In earnest conversation with X, his inhibitions loosened medicinally, he unfolded his version of the sorry affair.

X began by relating to me the fact of his ignorance of the way nature has endowed the anatomy of the female. X stated that the sight of his naked wife on his wedding night was an absolute shock, his having come to expect a perfectly smooth creature, as portrayed in any tasteful work of art. After jovial reproach, I asked him to expand upon his reaction to this "discovery" of his. Utter revulsion, was his reply. He did not, could not, desire his wife in any measure from the neck down; that he regarded her as a grotesque freak of Nature.

I earnestly implored him to take the not uncommon measure of approach from afar. That completion of desire, could be attained, I assured him, by stealth. If the marble-like surface was what he desired, and nought else, a route from a different angle entirely, might ease his desire to a more satisfactory conclusion, i.e., that he must [deleted] at all. That he must approach her in this manner every night for a month, and, rather than try to force the issue, remain apart from her and regard the beauty as though a work of art were before him.

X went away much lighter in attitude and I fully expected to hear no more about it.

(iii) Two months later I was again in earnest confidence with X. The solution had, to a degree, been successful in that he had managed, after a number of weeks, to stand to and not lie asleep in his wife's presence. However, at the merest touch of passion, all was lost, and unrecoverable. X was utterly despondent and, alas, allowing this most private part of his life to overshadow everything in his path. In short, he was a most frustrated mess. At this point, I was quite at a loss as to how to proceed, if indeed it was possible to proceed.

Then, a moment of inspiration struck. I brought into the room a small fur, concealed behind my back. I asked X to close his eyes and to put out his hand. I laid the fur into his hand. He seemed puzzled, but not at all vexed by the article. So, I surmised to X, that it was not a case of pelts *per se*. No, he concurred; in any case, he said, this sable was like silk. His wife's [removed] resembled his beard: wiry and manly and unladylike. I assured him that the [erased] he so desired could be found within, if only he could overcome his aversion to the fact that all women, not only his wife, were so endowed. That he must make himself familiar with his wife at all costs, as his health demanded it. The next suggestion I made was that in [section expurgated]. In this, I assured him, he might be so satisfied that he may climb to the next ridge of the mountain and thus from here admire the vista.

(iv) Unhappily, X was to confide some while later that the weather was not at all suitable or conducive to mountain scrambles. I then suggested to X that he should familiarise himself with the true meaning of Freak of Nature. He accompanied me on an excursion to witness the various exhibits at Saville House where I had heard one particular hirsute lady performed.

X became obsessed with this personage and would not leave the subject alone. I perceived an unhealthy attitude in his attention to the female, and advised X that his energy must be spent on the sole prize of [excised] his wife in her [eliminated].

After some deep consideration I altered my opinion; this phenomenon, I had come to realise, was hysteria induced by suggestion, which could, therefore, following Babinski's principle, be cured by persuasion. I divined that if X should so encounter a woman, covered in hair from top to toe, then the revulsion would be so complete that the cure would be instantaneous and a happy marriage might flower. Now here, one might be forgiven for supposing that my inclinations on this matter were correct. Not so.

X, upon meeting this hirsute female, did lose all feelings of revulsion when faced with this peculiar Nondescript. However, X did not go home at once and make up for time lost, so to speak. X became [withdrawn] fascinated with the Nondescript, and commenced an affair with same, and in so doing lost all interest, desire and what little passion he had so far achieved for his wife. It was some months before this fact became known to me, and, by that time, the obsession was intensely and irrevocably carved into his fevered brain.

Euphemia put the book and chinagraph pencil down on her desk to rub crumbs of sleep from the corners of her eyes. The cutting from the previous week's newspaper had been at her elbow, and now it fluttered noiselessly from her desk to the floor. She eyed it for some seconds where it had come to rest then stuck out her foot to retrieve it. She drew it close with her bare heel and kept it there, under her skirts.

A knock on the bedroom door made her start. Then she remembered that this was the day. "Come," she said, and the door swung wide. "Susan," she said, looking up.

"Ma'am, they are here."

"All right. Is everything made ready?"

"Ma'am."

"And the room is completely empty now?"

"Yes, ma'am. Just as you said. And Mr Pemberton says to give you this. I think it's a letter, ma'am. But I couldn't be sure."

Susan handed over the small portfolio she had been keeping behind her back.

"All right, Susan. You can see to the rest."

"Will you not be seeing them after all, ma'am?"

"No. There's no need. Just let me know when they have gone."

"Yes, ma'am," and the door swung shut behind her. From here, the house was utterly silent.

Euphemia untied the tapes at the sides and opened up the stiff covers. Inside, was a familiar document, slightly foxed, slightly dog-eared. With it were two letters which she tore open. The first was from Edward's solicitor, Mr Bettlesham. She did not read it properly; there was nothing there that she did not already know. The other was from her sister. Carrick House is yours . . . She did not read it further. Euphemia took both letters to the fire and threw them in; she turned away from the sudden flare as the letters began to curl and open up again in the heat. Euphemia closed the covers of the portfolio over the fragile deeds to Carrick House and tied up the tapes.

Chapter LXII

Backstage, Royal Opera House, London.
Friday, October 5, 1866.

"You may come with me now, Mrs Pemberton."

With tension rising in every part of her, Gwen followed the girl. Under her evening stole, she clasped her purse, which contained, as well as the programme for the evening's opera, her glasses and her fan, the incongruous inclusion of a certain very battered and hard-travelled book. Gwen passed sweaty people dressed in their costumes, and carrying parts of costumes, their greasy make-up running and smudged now after the efforts of their performances. They laughed under the yellow light and joked together, stepping aside to let her pass, not really noticing her. The girl stopped at the end of the long corridor and bowed her head outside the door, waiting for Gwen to catch up.

"Miss Jaspur will see you now, madam." She leaned forward and tapped lightly on the door before opening it and stepping back to let Gwen go inside. Gwen murmured her thanks to the girl who bobbed a curtsey and would not raise her head. The door shut quietly behind her.

She was sitting with her shrouded profile to the door.

"Miss Jaspur, good evening. Congratulations on a magnificent performance."

"Thank you. Please, come and sit down with me."

Gwen looked about the room, and saw that it was furnished very comfortably, if rather elaborately with a lot of lace and ruffles.

She sat down and felt a rush of heat flare through her body as a wave of nerves got the better of her.

"I don't mean to take up much of your time; thank you for agreeing to this interview."

The little woman laughed and leaned back in her seat. "Do you know, those were his exact words to me." She suddenly leaned forward to peer through the dark veil. She lifted it away from her face. "And he kept me awake all night. Though, of course, he did not come to see me any more once he had found you." Miss Jaspur looked firmly into Gwen's eyes. "You must have once loved him very much. Perhaps you loved him as much as I once did, to have found strength enough." She turned her face away. "Which performance did you mean, when you congratulated me?" She looked briefly into Gwen's eyes again before letting her gaze settle on Gwen's bare shoulder.

"This evening's, I'm sure."

"Well, congratulations are also due to yourself, Mrs Pemberton. I must say that I like your style. You emerge, free, saved from the gallows and what do you do? Go to the opera, of course! But what do you want here? Aren't we both free now, of him and of each other?"

Gwen's pulse thudded in her throat as she kept her gaze steady. She gripped her purse. "I have brought something with me —" Her voice broke. "I have brought something, which I wondered —" She fumbled with the clasp on the purse and managed to bring out the book wrapped in its handkerchief. "I wondered if you would be able to tell me anything about it." She held the book out and her hand shook violently. Miss Jaspur took the book from her hands. Gwen watched her turn it over.

"It is in a bad way, I think, Mrs Pemberton."

"That was all my fault."

"This little volume has a tale to tell, Mrs Pemberton, I can see."

Gwen's eyes pricked and welled. "There is no one left, whom I might ask. Did you not write a book, Miss Jaspur, and publish it?"

"This?" She ran her fingers over the tooling on the spine as Gwen had once done. "*Eternal Blazon*," she spelled out slowly. "You won't find another like it on any book stall, Mrs Pemberton. What few were bound are locked away, I think." Miss Jaspur sat back into her chair and held the stiff book in her lap. "Mrs Pemberton, I would like to know where you found this."

"It was sent to me an—"

"Anonymously." She rose from her seat and turned to face Gwen. "Mrs Pemberton, I can't tell you why she would have gone to the trouble of doing such a thing, when she might have just told you. Perhaps she was a little afraid."

"Who was afraid?"

"Isobel Scales. Isobel, his first wife. I did not have the money, then, for books. I did not have the stomach for dangerous games. I learned of it all too late, Mrs Pemberton; after you had gone. My attempts to contact you had come to nothing, but when I met your sister I knew I had failed to stop him." Miss Jaspur sat down again, and gave the book back to Gwen.

"Did you read it?" Gwen's question was a whisper.

"No." Miss Jaspur flapped her small hands in the air as if to push it away. "I had heard of it, of course, but I did not want to read it. The printer was imprisoned for it. And other books, not just that little thing."

For a long while neither woman said anything. Gwen felt the precision of Miss Jaspur's gaze; she knew Miss Jaspur was trying to fix in her mind the scene of Edward's death. The book slipped from her hands and Gwen knelt on the floor to retrieve it.

A Note on the Type

This book is set in Bembo, a humanist serif typeface commissioned by Aldus Manutius and cut by Francesco Griffo, a Venetian goldsmith, in the late fifteenth century.

This harmonious typeface has gone on to inspire generations of type founders, from Claude Garamond in the sixteenth century to Stanley Morison at the Monotype Corporation in the early twentieth century.